"You remembered," Arianna whispered, her voice husky with emotion.

It sounded like she was holding back tears. "How could I forget? It was the first time you cried in front of me," Connor said. "You had your heart set on a pink Christmas tree, and your mom refused to buy one."

"Glamma wanted one too. We thought it would be fun and would cheer everyone up." She gave a self-conscious laugh. "We expected a lot from a tree, didn't we?"

"I tried to buy you one back then. It was too late though. The hardware store special-ordered this one for me a few weeks ago."

She smiled and went up on her tiptoes to touch her mouth to his. "Thank you. Thank you for being the best boyfriend back then and for being the best secret admirer now," she murmured against his lips.

Praise for Debbie Mason's Harmony Harbor Series

Driftwood Cove

"Mason rolls out the excitement in the fifth book in the Harmony Harbor series."

—*RT Book Reviews*

"I love second-chance romances, and Debbie Mason has written another good one in her Harmony Harbor series with some pretty significant obstacles between our hero and heroine and their happy ending."

—TheRomanceDish.com

Sugarplum Way

"4 Stars! Harlequin Junkie Recommends! An amazing addition to this sweet and sassy series."

—HarlequinJunkie.com

"I really enjoyed this story... It had a lot of elements that, put together, made for a Christmas where dreams really do come true."

—RomancingTheBook.com

Primrose Lane

"4 Stars! This is a book worth savoring as it has all the elements of a fantastic read."

—*RT Book Reviews*

"Wow, do these books bring the feels. Deep emotion, heart-tugging romance, and a touch of suspense make them hard to put down, while the humor sprinkled throughout keeps the emotional intensity balanced with comic relief."

—TheRomanceDish.com

Starlight Bridge

"4 Stars! Mason gives Ava and Griffin a second chance at love. There's a mystery surrounding the sale of the estate...that adds a special appeal to the book."

—*RT Book Reviews*

"I loved this book. Debbie Mason writes romance like none other."

—FreshFiction.com

Mistletoe Cottage

"Top Pick! 4½ Stars! Mason has a knockout with the first book in her Harmony Harbor series."

—*RT Book Reviews*

"*Mistletoe Cottage* is anything but typical. It's a fast-paced story with colorful characters, lots of banter, and even more twists and turns."

—*Fort Worth Star-Telegram*

The Corner of Holly and Ivy

Also by Debbie Mason

The Harmony Harbor series

Mistletoe Cottage

"Christmas with an Angel" (short story)

Starlight Bridge

Primrose Lane

Sugarplum Way

Driftwood Cove

Sandpiper Shore

The Christmas, Colorado series

The Trouble with Christmas

Christmas in July

It Happened at Christmas

Wedding Bells in Christmas

Snowbound at Christmas

Kiss Me in Christmas

Happy Ever After in Christmas

"Marry Me at Christmas" (short story)

"Miracle at Christmas" (short story)

The Corner of Holly and Ivy

DEBBIE
MASON

FOREVER
New York Boston

This book is a work of fiction. Names, characters, places, and incidents are the product of the author's imagination or are used fictitiously. Any resemblance to actual events, locales, or persons, living or dead, is coincidental.

Forever
Hachette Book Group
1290 Avenue of the Americas, New York, NY 10104
forever-romance.com
twitter.com/foreverromance

First Edition: October 2018

Forever is an imprint of Grand Central Publishing. The Forever name and logo are trademarks of Hachette Book Group, Inc.

The publisher is not responsible for websites (or their content) that are not owned by the publisher.

The Hachette Speakers Bureau provides a wide range of authors for speaking events. To find out more, go to www.hachettespeakersbureau.com or call (866) 376-6591.

ISBNs: 978-1-5387-4424-6 (mass market); 978-1-5387-4423-9 (ebook)

Printed in the United States of America

OPM

10 9 8 7 6 5 4 3 2 1

This book is dedicated to the memory of Bella, our beloved Yorkie, who gave us seventeen years of love, laughter, and kisses.

Acknowledgments

Many thanks to my editor, Alex Logan, who goes above and beyond for me and my books and never fails to make them better. To Beth deGuzman, Amy Pierpont, Leah Hultenschmidt, Lexi Smail, Gabrielle Kelly, Jodi Rosoff, Estelle Hallick, Monisha Lakhotia, Tareth Mitch, Penina Lopez, Elizabeth Turner Stokes, and the sales department at Grand Central/Forever, thanks so very much for all your hard work on behalf of my books.

My heartfelt thanks to Pamela Harty for always being there for me. Thanks also to the members of Pamela's team at The Knight Agency, Deirdre Knight, Eileen Spencer, and Jamie Pritchett.

To my husband, children, and grandchildren for always supporting and encouraging me to follow my dreams, *thank you*. I love you all more than you'll ever know. Additional thanks to my daughter Jess for not only reading my first drafts and letting me talk endlessly about my stories, but also for agreeing to head up Team Mason. Thanks, honey.

And last but not least, I'm so very grateful for all the readers, reviewers, and bloggers who spend time with me in Harmony Harbor (and Christmas, Colorado) and on social media. Thank you for your kindness in sharing my stories with your friends and family and followers and for your continued support.

An extra special thanks to these awesome readers who named Comet, Cathy Burke, Missy Johnston Townes, Tiffany King Hall, and her daughter Keiley Hall. Additional thanks to Mary Mannella for not being mad at me for misspelling her name in *Sandpiper Shore's* dedication. Thanks again, Mary!

The Corner of Holly and Ivy

Chapter One

♥

At the sound of a drawer slamming outside her closed bedroom door, Arianna Bell awoke with a start. She blinked, trying to get her bearings. Was it morning or night? The blackout curtains in her bedroom made it difficult to tell. Down the hall, someone continued their frenetic opening and closing of drawers, and she sat up in bed.

Burglar or her grandmother? she wondered, not in the least alarmed either way. After barely surviving the fire that destroyed her business and three others, Arianna wasn't fazed by much these days. Besides, it wasn't like they had anything of real value in the small Cape Cod home where she now lived with her grandmother, Helen Fairchild.

Another drawer slammed. "Where did you put the damn car keys? I have to hit the campaign trail."

Arianna's stomach muscles bunched in response to her grandmother's angry question, making a lie of her claim that nothing fazed her anymore. At that moment she moved beyond slightly fazed to really worried.

And not because her grandmother was hitting the campaign trail. At eighty, Helen was the oldest woman to run for mayor of Harmony Harbor, a small town less than an hour from Boston. Her grandmother's habit of misplacing things was nothing new either. But over the past few weeks, Helen's forgetfulness hadn't been so easily explained away.

As much as Arianna would like to blame moments such as this on the stress of the mayoral race or the typical forgetfulness of old age, she couldn't. Her grandmother had given up driving a decade before and had sold her BMW around the same time. Arianna had lost her car in the fire. It had been parked in the alley between Tie the Knot and the beauty salon that had burned down.

Cradling her injured arm to her chest, Arianna scooted off the bed. She could count on one hand the number of times she'd gotten out of bed of her own volition in the past seven weeks. Which the piles of books, water glasses, and teacups on the floor by her bed attested to. One benefit of spending so much time in the dark was that she seemed to have developed bat-like sonar and safely made it through the obstacle course and to the other side of her bedroom without knocking something over or falling on her face. She reached for the doorknob with her good hand.

"Arianna, where"—the door flew open, shoving Arianna and her elbow into the wall at her back—"the hell are the keys to my Beemer?"

So much for my bat-like sonar, she thought, trying to breathe through the pain. It felt like someone had whacked the elbow of her damaged arm with a tuning fork, the ache vibrating up and down her forearm and hand. Which might have been a good thing—not the pain in her arm obviously, but her inability to speak. She had no idea how to deal with this. She didn't know whether she should tell her grandmother the truth or protect her with a lie.

"Where is that child?" her grandmother muttered, her voice raspy from years of smoking.

"Standing behind the door, Glamma," Arianna said through clenched teeth.

Her grandmother had coined the moniker *Glamma* years before it had become popular. Not a surprise since Helen had been forty for as long as Arianna could remember. She was all about fashion and glamour. Once a highly-sought-after runway model in Paris, she'd returned to Harmony Harbor to raise her daughter (Arianna's mother, Beverly) and open Tie the Knot, a bridal shop on Main Street. The shop she'd passed down to Arianna a decade before. The same shop the madman had burned to the ground in July.

"Don't go there," Arianna told herself firmly. She relived that night over and over again in her dreams and refused to relive it when she was wide-awake.

"Don't go where?" her grandmother asked, clapping her hands.

Arianna came out from behind the door. "Nowhere. You can stop clapping, Glamma. The lightbulbs are burned out. I have to replace them."

Arianna had a thing for Clap On! Clap Off! lights. Her baby sister, Jenna, knew about her secret addiction and had replaced the lights in Arianna's bedroom with Clappers the day she'd come to live with her grandmother. Jenna was the sweet, thoughtful sister. Much sweeter than Arianna deserved after the way she'd treated her growing up.

Glamma's lips thinned. Her silver-blond hair was pulled back from her face, giving her an instant face-lift and showcasing her pale-blue eyes and exquisite bone structure. "You mean I will. You haven't been out of the house since the day you got home from the hospital," she said as she walked to the window on the other side of the bedroom.

Arianna was so relieved her grandmother remembered exactly when she'd last ventured outside that her sarcastic tone didn't get under her skin. Besides, half of what came out of her grandmother's mouth had bite. She'd always had a dry sense of humor, something she'd passed on to Arianna. Although Arianna's sense of humor had been missing for quite some time.

The blackout curtains rattled along the rod as her grandmother whipped them open with strength and purpose. Just like her walk, Arianna thought with a smile. She must have been imagining things. There was nothing wrong with her grandmother, nothing wrong at all. Arianna felt like sinking to the area rug in relief. She might have if the bright autumn sunshine pouring through the window weren't half-blinding her.

Squinting, she turned away from the sun's rays. Big mistake. The position put her in direct view of the mirror on her dresser. There was a time not so long ago when catching a glimpse of her shoulder-length blond hair, blue eyes, and thin frame in the mirror wouldn't have bothered her. It did now.

"All right, I'm off to..." Helen frowned and then rubbed her forehead as though she'd forgotten what she'd been about to say, or maybe where she'd been about to go.

That wasn't unusual though. People complained about forgetting why they walked into a room all the time. You couldn't go a day on social media without a meme about it popping up. Women in their menopausal and post-menopausal years posted them all the time. No doubt if Glamma were on social media, she would too.

Helen lowered her fingers from her forehead and bent to pick up a copy of the town's local newspaper, the *Harmony Harbor Gazette*, from the floor.

Arianna was impressed and checked off another box in the "Glamma's fine" column. She wasn't nearly as flexible as her grandmother.

Helen's face cleared. "Campaigning, that's it. I have to get out there and pound the pavement. I'll see you later, darling. I won't be back until late. Don't forget to eat."

Arianna took in her grandmother's attire as she passed her on the way out the door. Just as she suspected, they were pajamas. Pink satin pajamas. "Wait. You don't mean you're leaving right this very minute, do you?"

"That's exactly what I mean. I have to get a leg up on the Gallagher boy."

This wasn't good. Not good at all. Arianna's heart began to gallop. She could barely look after herself.

How was she supposed to look after her grandmother? "Why don't we both get dressed and go together? It's about time I got out there on the campaign trail with you, don't you think?" Arianna said, working to keep the panic from her voice.

Her grandmother blinked at Arianna's suggestion and then blinked again like a sleepy owl. Arianna wasn't sure whether it was because Helen didn't recognize her or because she was stunned by her offer to accompany her.

"You want to come on the stump with me?"

Thank goodness it was the latter. Wait a minute. What had she been thinking? She'd just agreed to leave the house! "Yes. Unless you think it's going to rain and we both should stay home." She looked out the window, hoping to see water-logged black clouds darkening the cerulean sky.

Her grandmother's lips flattened. "I knew you'd back out."

"I'm not backing out. I'll bring an umbrella just in case."

"We don't need an umbrella. We'll take my car."

Arianna bowed her head and then lifted it to look at her grandmother. "Glamma, you—"

Helen interrupted her with a snap of her fingers. "I don't know what came over me. I haven't had that car in years."

She didn't know whether her grandmother truly remembered or had picked up on Arianna's distress. Memory issues aside, Helen Fairchild was one sharp cookie.

Arianna gave her grandmother a reassuring smile. “We all forget things now and again. No big deal, right?”

“Right. Right,” she said in a voice that didn’t sound nearly as confident as Arianna’s.

An hour later, her heart pounding like she’d run a one-minute mile, Arianna stepped out of the house on the corner of Holly and Ivy. Positive she was about to faint, she turned back to the door, fumbling for the knob with her good hand.

Obviously, she hadn’t learned from her past mistakes. She knew better than to allow strong emotions to influence her decisions. That was the one benefit that had come out of the fire on Main Street. Arianna no longer had feelings or acted upon them. She’d been an apathetic shell holed up in her room for the past seven weeks. Now look at her, venturing outside when she’d be perfectly content never to set foot out of the house again. A fact she couldn’t share with her closest friends and family because they had no problem sharing with her that they thought she needed professional help.

In the middle of the night when she woke up beneath sweat-soaked sheets and gasping for air, she agreed with them. But then morning would arrive and push back the shadows that haunted her, and she’d come to her senses. Nothing a therapist could say or do would help her recover from the Nightmare on Main Street.

Her grandmother called out to her from where she stood smoking, leaning against a white picket fence draped in ruby-red vines. “Come on, now. The primary is next week, and the *Gazette* says the Gallagher boy is in the lead. We don’t have a moment to lose.”

If her grandmother had been running a strong second, it would have been okay. Next Tuesday's primary election narrowed the field to two candidates from the seven currently in the race. However, according to the *Gazette's* latest poll, that was not the case. Helen Fairchild was running dead last in the mayoral race.

Arianna reluctantly released the doorknob. Her eighty-year-old grandmother had a dream. She wanted to be mayor to protect her beloved hometown from the vision Daniel Gallagher had for Harmony Harbor's future.

Arianna knew a little something about dreams herself. Before the Nightmare on Main Street, she'd lived and breathed her dream of becoming the next Vera Wang and of Tie the Knot becoming the next Kleinfeld Bridal. As a thirty-six-year-old (admittedly bitter) divorcée, it seemed her entire grown-up life had revolved around ensuring every bride had the wedding dress of her dream.

She'd spent twelve hours a day, seven days a week, working with customers who could turn into a bridezilla or a weepy mess in the blink of an eye. But the most difficult for her to deal with had been the sweet, wide-eyed innocents who thought their lives would be perfect the moment they said *I do*.

She'd survived the daily drama and stress without sarcastic rejoinders and eyes rolls because of what awaited her at the end of her day. The moment she retired to the room above her shop on Main Street, everything else faded away. It was the place where the magic happened.

Sometimes she'd be holed up there from dusk to dawn hand sewing lace, crystals, and pearls onto the tulle and organza gowns, turning them into one-of-a-kind works of art. And while the hours were long and the work sometimes tedious and backbreaking, she'd never once complained. After all, she'd been following her passion, living her dream.

Her dreams were over now. Everything had gone up in smoke. But it was more than guilt at the loss of her grandmother's legacy and worry about her that forced Arianna out of the house today. It was her deep and abiding love for the woman who was at that moment regarding her through narrowed eyes and a cloud of cigarette smoke.

"What on earth are you wearing?" asked the woman who only an hour before had planned to knock on doors in pink satin pajamas.

Arianna looked down at the mocha-colored lounge pants and top she wore beneath a calf-length blush velour cardigan. In deference to her damaged arm, the right sleeve was empty and the top two buttons fastened to conceal the sling she still wore. In deference to Helen, Arianna had swapped the pink sneakers her sister Jenna had paired with the outfit for brown suede ankle boots.

"It's the new trend. Loungewear chic," Arianna informed Helen, who'd obviously recovered from her momentary fashion lapse and looked effortlessly elegant in wide-legged cream pants and a blouse with a bronze-colored sweater draped casually around her shoulders and bronze ballerina slippers on her feet.

Arianna, who'd once been as style conscious as her grandmother, didn't care about that sort of thing anymore. Comfortable and cozy pajamas were her wardrobe of choice these days, which her sister knew. Not that Arianna would mention Jenna to Helen. She didn't blame the Nightmare on Main Street on her sister, but her grandmother did.

Helen's brow furrowed, the expression on her face turning from distaste to concern. She approached the step where Arianna stood poised to take flight. She could handle the distaste. The concern...not so much. But she didn't have time to run back inside. Helen was surprisingly fast for an eighty-year-old. She lifted her walking stick—most people would refer to it as a cane, but not her grandmother—and moved Arianna's cardigan aside. "You're too thin."

The statement took her aback. In Helen Fairchild's book, you could never be too rich or too thin.

Arianna was saved from responding by their neighbor from across the road. Mrs. Ranger looked up from raking the autumn leaves into a pile and smiled. "Arianna, it's so good see you, dear. How are you doing?"

She didn't expect the truth, did she? What if Arianna said *fine* like she always did and Mrs. Ranger wanted specifics—like how was her arm? It would open up a conversation about the Nightmare on Main Street, wouldn't it? Of course it would.

Obviously, Glamma had caught her at a weak moment. Arianna had been out of her flipping mind to agree to accompany her today. Because no matter how much she loved her grandmother and didn't want to see her hurt or embarrassed or her dreams dashed, Arianna wasn't up to interacting with people who weren't family or her closest friends. She had a difficult enough time interacting with them. And it'd be a cold day in hell before she'd talk to anyone about what happened on that warm summer night. Her sister Serena had been smart. She'd left town two days after Arianna was released from the hospital.

"I'm fine, Mrs. Ranger. Thanks for ask—"

Her grandmother interrupted her with a horrified gasp, which was immediately followed by choking from inhaling a stream of cigarette smoke.

"How could you, Irene?" Helen said once she got her coughing under control. "We've known each other for more than sixty years." Before Mrs. Ranger had a chance to respond, Helen strode down the leaf-littered flagstone walkway and flung open the front gate.

Arianna frowned, confused by her grandmother's angry outburst until she spotted Daniel Gallagher's campaign sign on the far side of Mrs. Ranger's front yard. And there it was, the main reason Arianna should have convinced her grandmother not to put her name in the race. Helen wouldn't take defeat well, and she had a temper. A temper that sometimes made her act without thinking.

Arianna protectively cradled her right arm to her chest to keep it from bouncing against her body as she hurried after her grandmother, who was already halfway across the road by then. "Glamma, you get back here."

Now in a face-off with Irene on her front lawn, Helen

ignored Arianna. She wished Mrs. Ranger would do the same to her grandmother. Instead, she'd apparently decided to add fuel to the fire. "Yes, we have, and you're the same age as me, Helen. Far too old for this sort of thing. It's time to give the younger generation a chance."

"Speak for yourself. I don't look a day over sixty, and I don't feel it either. And why should I give a man like him a chance?" She slapped the lawn sign with her cane. "He's going to ruin this town with his modern ideas. He hasn't lived in Harmony Harbor for decades. He's an outsider now."

Stuck on the other side of the street, thanks to slow-moving traffic, Arianna waved the rubberneckers on. "Nothing to see, folks. Move it along before you cause a pileup."

"Helen, he's a Gallagher. Without his family, Harmony Harbor wouldn't exist."

Arianna groaned. Her grandmother blamed Daniel Gallagher's nephew Connor for ruining Arianna's life and took it out on the rest of the family. Connor had represented her ex in their divorce, and Arianna had walked away without anything to show for the years she'd given to her marriage.

But she and Connor had had a history long before Gary and their divorce. Connor Gallagher had been her first love. And, at one time, she'd thought he'd be her only love. She considered herself lucky that her grandmother had no idea the price Arianna had paid for her teenage love affair with Connor. It was a price she'd continue to pay until the day she died.

"Don't talk about them as if they're something special. William Gallagher was a pirate who made his money on the high seas, burning and pillaging. The rest of them are no better. Especially him." She whacked the sign again, taking out one of Daniel Gallagher's blue eyes.

At Mrs. Ranger's outraged gasp, Arianna held up a hand and darted between the two idling cars on the street. She reached her grandmother just as she put her cane through Daniel's toothy grin.

"It's time we were on our way, Glamma. Sorry about that, Mrs. Ranger. The heat of the campaign and all that. I'll, ah, I guess I could call and ask for a replacement sign. I'm sure the Gallaghers have plenty on hand."

Tugging on her cane, her grandmother glared at her. Arianna glared back. It's not like she wanted to call the Gallagher campaign headquarters, but what did Helen expect her to do? She'd defaced the sign. It was a punishable offense. One of them had to be the responsible adult.

"I don't know, dear. There's been a run on the signs since Daniel's nephew Connor was put in charge of delivery and setup. He's a high-powered attorney, you know. Such a handsome boy. Charming too, just like his uncle."

Okay, so she wasn't going to be calling for a replacement sign after all. The last person she wanted to talk to was Connor.

She glanced at the cars idling on the street. Their audience had grown. Instead of four cars, there were now six. Seven, she corrected when a black Porsche slowed to a crawl. She sagged with relief when the Porsche pulled around the idling vehicles. Maybe now the others would get the idea they were blocking traffic and move on. Except the Porsche didn't keep driving. It pulled alongside the curb, and the others followed suit.

"You think Connor Gallagher is charming, do you, Irene? Well, have I got news for you," her grandmother said with another vicious tug of her cane, which remained firmly attached to Daniel Gallagher's mouth.

"Don't even," Arianna muttered near her grandmother's ear, closing the fingers of her good hand around the cane. "Let me do it."

While Arianna tried to wrestle the walking stick from the sign, her grandmother trash-talked the Gallagher men and Irene Ranger defended the handsome, blue-eyed devils. Frustrated with both women and her inability to unstick the cane, Arianna lifted her booted foot and kicked Daniel Gallagher in the head.

It felt so good to release some of her pent-up anger and emotion that she did it again and then again. A loud grunt escaped from her mouth each time she hit the sign with a solid *thwack*. It took a moment for her to realize that the only sound she heard was *thwack*, *grunt*, *thwack*, *grunt*. Helen and Irene were no longer arguing. Except for the god-awful noises Arianna was making, it was uncomfortably quiet.

She glanced over her shoulder to see her grandmother and Mrs. Ranger staring at her openmouthed, and just beyond them, a handsome blue-eyed devil watched her from where he leaned against the black Porsche.

Chapter Two

♥

The last time Connor Gallagher had seen Arianna Bell, she was dead. He'd been standing beside her hospital bed when the alarm screamed and the line on the monitor's screen went flat. It had been one of the most terrifying experiences of his life.

He'd felt helpless, gutted that he'd never again get the chance to look into her beautiful blue eyes or see her incredible smile. He'd had so much he wanted to tell her, to make up for. He hadn't wanted to lose her without her knowing he'd forgiven her for breaking his heart.

She was the only woman he'd ever wanted to share forever with. He'd loved her beyond reason, without fear or restraint. He'd been completely and madly devoted to her. Which was why, when she'd ended their two-year teenage love affair the summer she was seventeen and he was eighteen, he'd been wrecked.

A week after she'd walked away from him without any explanation, he'd made a vow that he'd kept for nineteen years. He never let another woman get that close to him again. But as he'd stood over Arianna's bed that night with the alarm screaming and her heart not beating, he'd realized the reason he hadn't let another woman into his heart had nothing to do with the vow he'd made. It was because Arianna still occupied a large part of it and there was barely room for anyone else.

He didn't know how he'd kept it together that night, but he had. His voice had remained calm and steady as he'd pleaded with her, begged her to stay, even as the doctors and nurses had shoved him out of the way. Even as they'd pressed the paddles to her chest. Even as they'd pushed him out the door and closed it in his face. He'd stood with his hand pressed to the glass, watching as they'd worked to save her, silently praying and pleading with her not to let go. And then her family had arrived and taken his place at her bedside. They'd had a right to be there; he hadn't.

So, to see her now, alive and well, brought a smile to his face. Even if she was beating the hell out of his uncle's campaign sign. Her grandmother's rival. Her grandmother who didn't like Connor all that much, which was evident when she fixed him with an icy-blue stare. As he knew from previous encounters with Arianna, her welcome would be as cold as her grandmother's.

The last time he'd tried to talk to Arianna had been outside the courtroom after her and her ex's divorce hearing. She'd told him to drop dead and had walked away before he'd even had a chance to open his mouth. He'd seen no signs over the past five years that she'd changed her mind about him. To the contrary, she avoided him like he was one of the Four Horsemen of the Apocalypse.

She glanced over her shoulder and met his gaze. Oh yeah, she definitely still wanted him dead. The animosity practically vibrated off her as her perfectly sculpted lips twisted and her beautiful blue eyes narrowed.

But instead of getting back in his car and driving off, as she no doubt wanted him to, he walked across Mrs. Ranger's front lawn. He needed to see for himself that Arianna was all right. He might live, work, and play in Boston, but he knew what was going on in Harmony Harbor. Most of his family lived in town, and his oldest brother, Logan, was engaged to Arianna's half sister, Jenna.

"Connor, dear, don't get upset with Arianna for destroying the sign. I think she had a"—Mrs. Ranger leaned toward him and whispered—"mental break."

Arianna's eyes went wide. "Mrs. Ranger, what are you talking about? I didn't have a mental . . . a meltdown. Glamma's cane was stuck in the sign. I was just trying—"

"How many times do I have to tell you it's a walking stick, not a cane, Arianna?" her grandmother said before turning on Mrs. Ranger. "If my granddaughter has a relapse, it's on you, Irene."

"Relapse? Relapse from what? Don't listen to her, Mrs. Ranger. I'm perfectly fine." Arianna glanced at Connor. "Sorry about the sign. I'll pay for another one. Just send me the bill."

"You will not. Look at my walking stick. It'll never be the same. Besides, you're penniless, and without me putting a roof over your head, you'd be homeless," Helen said.

Mrs. Ranger gasped, appearing stricken at the news, while Arianna stood frozen, staring at her grandmother.

"Yes, you heard me right, Irene. My granddaughter lost everything that night, including the ability to do the job she loved. She's crippled and barely able to get out of bed. I'm the only one she has to take care of her. The only one to put food on the table and keep a roof over our heads."

A dull red flush spread up Arianna's elegant neck. "That's enough, Glamma. Let's go," she said, and began walking away.

Connor stared after her, shocked silent. Wondering why no one had told him how dire the situation had become.

Helen's gaze followed her granddaughter, and then she gave a slow, sorrowful shake of her head. However, Connor, who up until a few weeks before had been one of the highest-paid attorneys in Boston (and for good reason), had a knack for reading people, for hearing the truth beneath a lie, for seeing it in a person's eyes, and Helen's expression said, that while the emotion was real and for the most part the words were true, she had an agenda.

"So think about that when you cast your vote for Daniel Gallagher next week, Irene. If I don't become mayor, not only will the town go to pot, but my granddaughter and I will be out on the street by Christmas. Is that what you want? Don't you think our family has suffered enough?"

"Oh, Helen. I'm so sorry. Why didn't you tell us how bad it was?"

Connor went after Arianna. The last thing she'd want is help from him, but given what he'd just heard… "Arianna, wait," he called out as she opened the gate in front of the white Cape Cod house.

With her back to him, she bowed her head, holding up her left hand as though warning him away. "We're fine, Connor. I'm fine."

"It didn't sound that way to me, Arianna," he said as he jogged across the road.

"Well, we are. It doesn't have anything to do with you anyway," she said as she turned to look at him, shutting the gate between them.

She might not be his anymore, but ever since the night he'd almost lost her for good, he hadn't been able to stop thinking about her. She mattered to him. A lot. It didn't make sense, and it sure as hell would tick Arianna off if she knew, but he couldn't seem to help himself where she was concerned. "You're wrong. It does. Your sister is marrying my brother, so that makes you family."

She rolled her eyes, and the familiar action made him smile. Only his smile slowly faded when he noticed the smudged circles under her eyes. This close and with nothing or no one to distract him, he noted other changes too, disturbing changes. Changes that bore witness to what her grandmother said. Arianna was far from all right.

"Not you too? I'm so sick of people looking at me like I'll break. There's nothing wrong with me."

He lifted his chin at her empty sleeve. "Why are you still wearing a sling? You should be trying to use your hand. If you don't—"

She raised a sarcastic eyebrow, but he didn't miss the way she cradled her arm protectively to her chest. "So, you're a doctor now too?"

No, but several of his golfing buddies were, and he questioned them extensively about Arianna every chance he got, asking about the best course of treatment for a woman with third-degree burns to her hand and just above her wrist that were deep enough to damage the nerves, along with extensive burns to the rest of her arm that caused her excruciating pain. At least in the beginning she'd been in pain. He'd assumed it was under control now, manageable at least. Obviously, it wasn't.

"Look, Arianna, I know—"

"Connor," a woman called from across the street.

He glanced over his shoulder and winced. He'd forgotten about his girlfriend, Brooklyn Rogers, who was waiting for him in the car.

When he'd discovered his mother and the Widows Club, of which his grandmother Kitty was a member, had set their matchmaking sights on him, he'd decided to go on the offense and brought Brooklyn for Sunday brunch at the manor. Built by the family's patriarch, William Gallagher, in the late eighteenth century, Greystone Manor resembled a medieval castle and sat on five thousand acres of land that was bordered by the ocean on one side and the forest on the other.

Brooklyn was everything his mother, Maura, wanted for Connor in a wife—stunning, rich, and well connected. His mother had been over the moon when he'd arrived at the manor with his girlfriend in tow. Except now he was afraid his offensive move might end up coming back to bite him. His mother wasn't the only one who had read something into him bringing a woman to the manor. So had his brothers and his grandmother.

Brooklyn still had no idea she was the only woman he'd ever introduced to his family. Something he'd prefer to keep from her until he knew exactly where their relationship was headed. A month after he'd started dating her, he'd begun to think she might be the one to make him break his long-ago vow. He ignored the voice in his head that said he'd known exactly where things were headed with Brooklyn until Arianna had been hurt in the fire at Tie the Knot.

"Sorry, babe. Just give me a minute."

"We're meeting Lyndsey and Tiff for drinks at four, Connor," she said, aiming a suspicious glance in Arianna's direction before powering up the window.

Connor would like nothing better than to miss their drinks and dinner date with Lyndsey and Tiff. And not just because he didn't want to leave until he knew exactly what was going on with Arianna. He wasn't a fan of Brooklyn's best friend and her partner, who spent their weekly dinner dates reminiscing about Brooklyn's ex, whom they apparently loved. Connor, they barely tolerated. Besides that, they were foodies and insisted on ordering Connor and Brooklyn's meals whenever they went out together. Last week Connor had discovered he'd eaten bull's balls.

He turned back to Arianna. “Look, I get—”

“Can we not do this, please? I’m tired. I’m sorry about the sign. Like I said, I’ll replace it.”

“Forget the sign. Forget our past. I just want to help, Arianna.” He held up a hand when it looked like she might argue. “Your grandmother says you’re penniless. What’s going on with your insurance? You should have received your claim by now.”

She chewed on her bottom lip and cast an anxious glance behind him before admitting, “I don’t know. I haven’t received anything from them.”

He had an uneasy feeling there was more at play here. He just didn’t know if it was on her end or with the insurance company. “Who’s your provider? I’ll give them a call and see what’s the holdup. I can at least get you an advance against the settlement to tide you over.”

“Move aside, boy,” a throaty voice said from behind him seconds before he was jabbed in the back of his knee with a cane.

He swallowed a pained grunt, stepping aside to let Helen Fairchild by. She opened the gate and waved over Arianna, who’d moved toward the front porch. “Thanks to you, the tide is turning in my favor, darling. You have to get out there and press the flesh,” Helen said to her granddaughter before turning a smug smile on Connor. “Your uncle doesn’t stand a chance now that I’ve found my secret weapon. Irene and her bridge club have thrown their support behind me.”

“No. No way are you using me to get the sympathy vote, Glamma. What you said to Mrs. Ranger—”

“Was the truth. I need this job, and you know it.”

"No, I don't. I had no idea things were that bad." She glanced at Connor before asking her grandmother, "When did you and Serena file the insurance claim?"

"I... What day is it now?" Arianna's grandmother asked as she rubbed her furrowed brow. "I don't... Why are you asking me anyway?" Helen's tone had gone from confused to defensive. "You should be talking to your sister. I have no time for this."

"Don't worry about it, Mrs. Fairchild," Connor said. "I'll take care of it. I deal with this sort of thing all the time. I'll have it straightened out for you in no time." He rarely dealt with insurance settlements, but he had no doubt he could handle this. Though it would definitely take some time, which, lucky for them, he had a lot of these days.

Helen studied him for a moment and then slowly nodded. "We'd be happy to accept your help, wouldn't we, Arianna? I may have misjudged you, young man." Helen smiled while tapping his leg with the end of her cane. More gently this time than the last.

"That's kind of you, Connor, but we don't need your help. I'm sure Serena took care of the claim," Arianna said.

But he could tell by the uneasy look in her eyes that she wasn't sure. She had reason to be wary. Lorenzo Romano, their sister Jenna's ex-fiancé, had shot Serena before setting fire to Tie the Knot. From all accounts, like Arianna, Serena had been having difficulty dealing with the trauma. After what they'd been through that night, it would be more surprising if that weren't the case. Unlike her sister though, Serena had left town to deal with her issues.

"Okay. Just give me the name of your insurance company then, and I'll put some pressure on them," he said.

"I don't remember it offhand. I'll get Serena to call—" The horn blasted from his Porsche, cutting off Arianna, who looked more than a little relieved at the interruption. "You'd better go, or you'll miss your drinks date," Arianna said with smile that didn't reach her eyes. She was obviously worried, and like her grandmother, overwhelmed.

He took out his phone, texted Jenna for Serena's cell phone number, and then texted Brooklyn to tell her he needed five more minutes, promising to make it up to her later.

He got an *Oh yeah, you will* from Brooklyn, and Serena's cell phone number from Jenna, as well as a question as to why he wanted it. He planned to stop by the manor to talk to Jenna, who was Greystone's wedding planner, before he left town. He'd answer her question then.

Helen once again tapped him on the shin. "Get off your device. It's rude. Young people these days…"

"Sorry about that. I just need one more minute to take care of something," he said as he added Serena's contact information and then quickly texted her his question.

Arianna looked from his phone to his face. "I don't believe you. You texted Serena, didn't you?"

He smiled, looking down at his phone when it

pinged. His smile turned into a grimace at Serena's response. He raised his gaze to Arianna. "You mind if I grab a glass of water before I hit the road?"

As though she could tell from his expression that the news wasn't good, she briefly closed her eyes before nodding. "Glamma, I'll meet up with you on Ivy Road."

"All right. Bring a bottle of hand sanitizer and some breath mints with you." She gave Connor another tap on the shin before jauntily walking away, swinging her cane. "Don't worry. I won't knock down any more of your uncle's signs," she called over her shoulder. "No need to now that we've got the primary in the bag."

"You might want to lose her cane. She doesn't look like she needs it," Connor said when he joined Arianna on the porch.

Arianna glanced at him as she opened the front door. "Serena didn't file the claim, did she?"

"I'm sorry. I wish I had better news, but no, she didn't. Your grandmother told her she'd taken care of it." Arianna looked demoralized at the news, and he went to give her shoulder a reassuring squeeze but thought better of it and lowered his hand.

As he followed her inside, he took in the open space. The living room was decorated in shades of cream and blue, with bookshelves on either side of doors that opened into a glass-enclosed, three-season room filled with plants and comfortable-looking furniture. He wasn't surprised to find the home beautifully furnished and decorated. Helen Fairchild had great taste. She'd passed down both her elegant style and talent for design to her granddaughter.

He'd visited the house as a teenager, when Arianna had stayed with her grandmother, and knew there were two bedrooms to his right, one on either end of the short hall. To his left was the French country-style kitchen with stainless-steel appliances and cream-colored cabinets that matched the bookshelves.

Arianna walked through to the kitchen and went to open one of the cupboards with her injured hand. He was close enough to hear her sharp inhalation, see her eyes squeeze shut.

"Let me," he said, gently cupping her shoulders to move her out of the way. He opened the cupboard. "Do you want a glass?"

"Please."

He wouldn't have heard her if she hadn't been standing beside him, so close her shoulder and hip brushed against him. So close he could smell her scent of orange blossoms and jasmine. It was a classic, timeless fragrance that spoke more of the woman she used to be than the one she'd become.

She seemed broken, defeated, and fragile now. When she'd been married to Summers, she'd been seductive, sophisticated, and outspoken. A woman who liked the finer things in life, who traveled to Provence and Positano, who'd once thrown lavish dinner parties that were the talk of Boston and designed wedding gowns that cost a small fortune.

He'd admired the woman she'd been, stood in awe of her talent, sophistication, and beauty. But this woman got under his skin and burrowed her way into his heart. He wanted to vanquish the demons that haunted her and take away her pain. But already he could feel her regaining control, breaking contact, putting up her walls.

With her head bowed and the fingers of her left hand curved around the marble countertop, she moved a few inches away.

"Can I get you anything for the pain?"

She shook her head, her buttermilk-blond hair falling forward to hide her face. "No. I'm fine."

"Don't, okay? It's me. The guy you dated for two years. The guy you told your secrets and dreams to." *The guy who loved you to distraction. The guy you said you'd love forever.*

Connor blew out a noisy breath, wondering what had gotten into him. Being this close to Arianna and actually having the woman talk to him after years of avoiding and ignoring him was messing with his head. Not to mention the part about her being alive and well. Even if she wasn't completely okay.

"Neither of us have been that guy or that girl for a very long time," she said, taking the glass from him and turning to walk to the sink in the turquoise island with its butcher-block countertop.

"No, we haven't. We've grown up. And evolved grown-ups let people help them. You don't have to deal with this alone, Arianna. I want to help. Think of it as my way of making amends for having to represent your ex in your divorce."

She snorted and turned on the tap. "Evolved grown-ups are also honest. You didn't just represent Gary. You used the divorce to get back at me. You never forgave me for breaking up with you."

"You don't seriously believe that, do you?" he said, instead of asking her why she'd broken up with him. It was something he'd always wanted to know. Because she had gutted him that long-ago summer night, and it had taken him months to get over her, even if it hadn't felt like he was over her at all that night in her hospital room.

"Oh, so you're telling me our breakup had nothing whatsoever to do with you representing Gary in our divorce?"

"That's exactly what I'm telling you," he said, leaning past her to fill his glass with water, getting another whiff of her perfume as he did. He needed to focus on something other than how amazing she smelled or he might do something stupid like bury his face in her neck. Instead he concentrated on putting the glass on the counter and taking the other glass from her to fill.

"I'm kinda shocked you think I'd do something like that." Maybe even a little hurt. "I'm a corporate attorney, Arianna. I don't handle divorces for our clients unless I have no choice, which, back then, I didn't. It was either represent Summers or forget about ever being made partner. His family is the firm's biggest and longest-standing account. Gary's godfather is one of the founding partners."

"I didn't know," she said, refusing to meet his eyes when he placed the glass in her hand.

"You should have known I wasn't that kind of man."

She lifted a shoulder. "For seven years I lived with a man who was. I guess that colored my perception."

For as long as he could remember, Connor had been

ambitious and laser-focused. As the middle son, he'd always felt like he had something to prove. And he liked the lifestyle his career afforded him. He would have laughed if someone suggested he'd put his job on the line by refusing to take on a case. But that had been before the night in the hospital with Arianna.

Her ex had come to him ten days after Arianna had nearly died. He'd wanted Connor to represent him in his divorce from wife number two. All Connor could see was Arianna's face on the day of her divorce hearing. He'd wanted to punch Summers in the face for putting him in that position. So he'd taken great pleasure in turning him down. But Summers was used to getting his way. His godfather begged and then tried to bribe Connor to take the case. Connor refused. He'd gambled and lost.

He pushed the thought aside, took a drink of water to wash away the bitter taste in his mouth, and then looked at Arianna. "Now that you know I had no choice but to represent Summers, can you forgive me?"

"I walked away without anything to show for those seven years. I lost clients because of him. I nearly lost Tie the Knot..." She gave her head a small shake. "It doesn't matter anymore."

"Yeah, it does. I can't apologize for doing my job back then, but I can help you now if you'd let me. You can start over, Arianna. The money from the insurance—"

"Start over? I can barely get dressed on my own, Connor. I can't legibly write my name or get a glass out of a cupboard or go one day without pain." She bowed her head and whispered, "Sometimes I wish they had let me die."

He reacted without thinking, grabbing her by the shoulders. "Don't. Don't say that, Arianna. Don't ever let me hear you say that again." Unlike that night at her hospital bedside, he was far from calm. He knew her, and he knew her well. Tie the Knot had been her life, her passion, her baby. And now it was gone, and he heard the abject despair in her voice. He shook her a little to get her to look at him, desperate to get through to her. "You've been home from the hospital just over a month. You need time to heal. It'll get better. I promise."

She lifted ocean-blue eyes filled with desperation and tears. "It won't get better, Connor. The scarring, the nerves in my . . ." She shook her head as if she could no longer go on.

He drew her carefully into his arms, surprised when, instead of pushing him away, she leaned heavily against him. It just about killed him. She'd always seemed so strong and self-sufficient. "It will. One step at a time. And the first step is getting your insurance claim settled."

"I don't even know where to start. I have nothing. No paperwork, no laptop or desktop. Everything was either in my apartment or in the shop." She hadn't lifted her head. Her lips moved against his chest, her warm breath heating the skin beneath his shirt.

The feel of her in his arms, her mouth against his skin, and the smell of her perfume brought back memories of the past, dreams he'd once had for their future.

He stroked her hair, getting lost in those memories and dreams for a minute. Something, he wasn't sure what, brought him back to the present. "Leave it with me. I'll figure it out."

He sensed they were no longer alone and glanced over his shoulder. No one was there. But as he returned his attention to Arianna, the cream wooden blinds on the window across from them clacked and flapped. He looked over his shoulder again, only this time he leaned back. The front door was open, ushering in a warm breeze that carried with it the smell of crushed autumn leaves. He'd just decided he hadn't closed the door properly when he heard the roar of a V10 engine. He knew then who'd opened the door. Brooklyn had gotten tired of waiting.

Arianna lifted her head from his chest. "Is that your car?"

"Yeah, and I have a feeling she isn't stopping"—he grimaced at the sound of squealing tires—"to pick me up."

"I'm sorry. It's my fault. I've kept you too long. If you hurry, maybe you can catch her," Arianna said, backing away.

He was sorry too. Sorry that she'd stepped away from him. He missed the feel of her in his arms, knowing at least for those few minutes she was safe and he didn't have to worry about her. He didn't want to leave her on her own, but it was obvious she now felt more uncomfortable than comforted.

"Unless Brooklyn gets pulled over, there's not much chance I'll catch up to her." Or make it up to her, for that matter. Which he felt bad about. But maybe, in the end, it was for the best. At least until he got Arianna out of his heart and his head for good. And that wasn't going to happen until he knew she was well on the road to recovery.

Chapter Three

♥

Colleen Gallagher stood in the manor's dining room beside the open French doors with Simon, her black cat, at her feet, watching as her grandson Daniel and her granddaughter-in-law, Maura, shared a leisurely cup of coffee on the patio now that Maura's sons and their significant others had taken their leave after Sunday brunch.

As it always did, seeing her great-grandsons happy and in love warmed Colleen's heart. Although she wasn't completely enamored with Connor's choice. Most likely because she knew down to her very soul that the only woman for Connor was Arianna Bell.

Colleen wondered if that's why it felt like a dark cloud had been following her about the manor today. She'd had similar feelings before, and it usually boded ill for Greystone Manor and the Gallaghers. She glanced at Maura and Daniel whispering at the table. If she had to point a finger at where the trouble might be coming from this time, she'd aim it directly at her grandson. His campaign promise to build an office tower on Main Street was sowing discord in town as much as his attempts to seduce Maura, his brother Sean's wife, were sowing discord in the family.

And while they'd seen their fair share of trouble at the manor since Colleen's heart had given out on All Saints Day two years past, this thing between Daniel and Sean had the makings of an all-out family war. Colleen knew without a doubt, if she didn't up her ghostly game, there wouldn't be much she could do to keep her family together.

They were all that mattered to her, them and the manor, and Simon, of course. From where she stood, she could see where she'd died despite her family's best efforts to save her. At a hundred and four, it had been a good day to die and a good way to go. Except she was still here. More or less. A ghost of her former self.

"I'm not any better at this ghost gig than I was the day I missed my ride to heaven, now, am I, Simon?"

He was too busy tracking a blue jay flitting from cedar to oak tree to confirm or refute her observation. Whether he did or not, she knew it to be true.

She'd been a little worried she might be headed for hell instead of heaven that afternoon in November, so she appreciated the extra time the Lord had granted her to make things right. For the most part, she'd made good use of her time, righting wrongs from the past, matching her great-grandchildren with the loves of their lives. But she could no longer be satisfied with the status quo as far as her ghostly abilities went.

As it stood, she couldn't stick a toe out of the manor. Oh, she'd tried, all right, and had been bounced back by an electric force field. There were a few things she could do though. Like if she yelled loud enough in the ear of someone staying in her old suite, they sometimes heard her. Typically scared the living bejaysus out of them too.

She could also walk through walls and such, and people, which was almost as discombobulating as sticking a toe outside the manor. If she concentrated really hard, she could even lift and push things about. It didn't always work, and when it did, it depleted her energy, leaving her as weak as a baby.

And it wasn't like she could easily call on someone to lend a hand. Other than Simon (who didn't have opposable thumbs), no one could see or hear her when she needed them to. Sometimes the wee ones were able to see her, which caused its own set of problems. Jasper knew when she was about. He'd sensed her presence almost from the beginning. He used Simon as her tell. If he saw the cat, Jasper knew Colleen was somewhere close by. Though Simon seemed to have an agenda of his own these days.

Almost from the beginning she'd known he was not your average cat. He'd arrived at the manor days before Colleen passed. Over the last few months she'd seen signs that Simon, who at times acted like lord of the manor, might actually be William Gallagher. The family's patriarch and once privateer. Or pirate, some said.

William had claimed most of the property in the area known as Harmony Harbor in the early seventeenth century and had gone on to build what would eventually become Greystone Manor. Over the centuries the sandstone-colored mansion had been added to and improved upon until it had become what it was today, their home and a hotel.

Just before she'd passed, Colleen had been fighting to keep a developer's hands off her beloved Greystone. He was the canny sort, trying every dirty trick in the book. He'd been quiet these past months, but she was certain he was out there somewhere, plotting his next move.

She'd done what she could to thwart him by locking the estate up tight in her will. She'd left it to her great-grandchildren. The only way it could be sold was if they all agreed. You could bet she'd haunt every last one of them if they decided to sell.

So far, six of her great-grandsons were on board to keep the estate in the family, along with the loves of their lives. The women were the key. More often than not, it was that way in life. A woman steering her man in the right direction with but a whisper in his ear. Some of them needed a shout—not her great-grandsons, mind. The younger generation was smarter than the last. And at that moment, she'd like to give Daniel more than a shout in his ear; she'd like to give him a kick in the behind.

The grandson in question pushed back from the table and then went to Maura's side, holding out the chair for her. "You know, Maura my love, it might be time for you to set my brother free, ask him for a divorce. It's clear he has no interest in being around you and the boys anymore. When was the last time he visited you here? Better for you to move on, if you ask me."

"Did you hear that, Simon? Did you hear what he just said to Maura? Imagine him telling her it was time for her to move on, time for her to ask Sean for a divorce." Colleen was fit to be tied. Maura wasn't helping matters with her silence. Colleen didn't know what was wrong with the lot of them.

Her daughter-in-law Kitty, Daniel's mother, should have intervened long before now. Even Jasper, Kitty's beau and Colleen's long-time confidante and right-hand man, should have made his thoughts known, especially since they coincided with hers. She understood his reluctance to do so though. He wouldn't feel it was his place.

But Kitty was a different story entirely. The only reason Colleen could see for her daughter-in-law to turn a blind eye to the whole affair was Daniel had once been an attentive, loving son, whom they'd rarely seen before he arrived at Greystone this past June. Colleen could count on two hands the number of times he'd been home in the past forty years.

He was a busy man; she'd grant him that. He'd had his archaeological digs, papers to write, lectures to give, and families to raise. But Colleen didn't think it was a coincidence that Daniel had left days before Maura and Sean's wedding all those years before, only to return when it appeared the couple's marriage was over. If Daniel had his way, it looked like there'd be no chance for the reconciliation Sean and Maura's sons hoped for. And Colleen could only imagine what Sean's reaction would be if Maura did indeed ask him for a divorce.

"Best we batten down the hatches, Simon. I think we're in for quite the storm."

* * *

It would have been faster for Connor to walk from Arianna's to Greystone Manor than to accept Mrs. Ranger's offer of a ride. Except then he wouldn't have discovered exactly what was going on at the house on the corner of Holly and Ivy.

After what he'd witnessed this morning, it didn't surprise him that today was the first time Arianna had set foot outside. It worried him though. The entire situation did. It was why he'd come directly to Greystone Manor to talk to Jenna rather than call an Uber and head to Raw, the Boston restaurant Lyndsey and Tiff had chosen for drinks and dinner, where he had every expectation of finding Brooklyn and his car. And that had been before Mrs. Ranger shared how truly bad things were.

"Are you sure it's not just everyday forgetfulness? Helen's eighty. It not uncommon for someone to be forgetful at her age." Before she'd died, his great-grandmother Colleen (or GG as they called her) often forgot appointments and people's names. She also misplaced things and repeated herself. Granted, it hadn't become noticeable up until a few years before she died.

In six weeks, it would be the second anniversary of her death. Sometimes it felt like she'd been gone much longer. He missed her a lot. They all did.

"Trust me, as an eighty-year-old whose been known to mix up her grandchildren and children's names and frequently repeats herself, I'm well aware what's normal and what's not. Helen doesn't have the garden-variety kind of senior moments, I'm afraid. Why, just the other night, I spied her in her front flower bed, digging up the tulip bulbs she'd planted a week before."

Mrs. Ranger gave a sorrowful shake of her head as she drove under the stone arch into Greystone Manor's parking lot. "I think she mixed up the months. She probably thought it was July and put the bulbs back in their paper bags, tucking them away in the cellar. I hope she doesn't remember what she's done. She'd be devastated. She's a master gardener, you know. She's the one who organized the Harmony Harbor in Bloom event. If she becomes mayor, she plans to hold an annual garden festival on Mother's Day weekend. A few years ago, when she had her wits about her, she would have been the best mayor Harmony Harbor could have asked for. Far better than your uncle, if you don't mind me saying."

"Not at all. But why did you have his sign on your lawn?" He wasn't exactly a fan of his uncle's plans for the town, but family was family. And Connor's mother was Daniel's campaign manager.

Mrs. Ranger pulled into a parking spot at the side of the sprawling mansion. The local sand-colored granite sparkled in the midday sun.

Shifting in the driver's seat, Mrs. Ranger faced him. "I might not be enamored of his plan to revitalize Main Street, but I trust your family to do what's best for the town. And it's not like I can vote for Helen knowing what I do. Except after hearing the sorry situation they're in, I told her I'd not only vote for her, I'd get my bridge club to do the same. I feel sick about it. Sick at the thought of all the ways she might embarrass herself.

What if she's being interviewed and forgets her words? And heaven help you if you try to correct her or point out there's a problem. She'll turn on you faster than a pit bull. She always had a temper, but not like this. Look at what she did to your uncle's sign."

He didn't point out that Arianna had actually done the most damage.

"She's frustrated and afraid. That's why she's acting out." Mrs. Ranger sniffed and reached into the pocket of her red plaid jacket, pulling out a tissue.

Given what he'd witnessed this morning, Helen Fairchild wasn't the only one who was frustrated and afraid. So was her granddaughter. Connor kept the observation to himself. Sometimes the best way to learn what you needed to know was to sit back and listen. The tactic had served him well in court and in negotiations. Except he wasn't sure how much more he could learn about Arianna's current situation without losing it on his brother's fiancée. He didn't understand why Jenna hadn't intervened before now.

Dabbing at her eyes with the tissue, Mrs. Ranger said, "Heaven help us if Helen wins. She forgets to pay her bills, you know. A few weeks back a man from the power company came around to talk to her, all set to cut her off if Helen didn't pay up." She gave her head a sad shake. "I just can't. I can't vote for her knowing what I do. For Helen's sake, as much as the town's. There has to be another way to help them. You used to date Arianna, didn't you, dear? Surely you want to help her."

"Of course I do. And I will. They can't continue living like this."

"I agree. Arianna is all but skin and bones. I was shocked when I saw her. I shouldn't have been surprised, I suppose. I ran into Helen at the grocery store a few weeks back. She had next to nothing in her cart. Just a few frozen dinners and two tubs of maple-walnut ice cream. It's Arianna's favorite, you know."

He did. Back in the day, he'd made it his mission to find out everything about Arianna Bell. It was good to know some things had stayed the same. Other things he wished hadn't, like Arianna's mother. "Does Beverly have any idea what's going on with her daughter and mother?"

"That girl, honestly. Helen says she's taken up with her pool boy. I don't know what a thirty-year-old man sees in a sixty-year-old woman, but who am I to judge? Helen had been visiting Beverly in California when they got the call about Arianna, you know. They caught the first flight home, and then two days later Beverly high-tailed it back to her pool boy. If you ask me, she's not happy her mother chose to remain with Arianna instead of returning to California with her. She's always been jealous of their relationship. Helen and Arianna have a special bond. It'll kill that child to lose her grandma."

The more the older woman talked, the worse it got. He couldn't think about how Arianna would deal with finding out that while she might not physically be losing her grandmother, she was, for all intents and purposes, losing her. After what Arianna had said earlier, he knew she couldn't handle another emotional hit. He put his hand on the door, about to get out of the car, but Mrs. Ranger wasn't finished torturing him.

"She's lost so much. It wasn't right, Serena leaving her like she did. Those two were joined at the hip."

He should have ended the conversation five minutes ago. "I'm sure Arianna understood why Serena needed to get out of town. It's not forever. And she has Jenna." Mrs. Ranger opened her mouth, and he practically leaped out of the car. "Thanks again for the ride."

She leaned across the console. "You should stay in town. Arianna needs a friend close by, and you used to be a good one. Your brother Michael commuted to Boston when he was with the FBI. You could do the same."

Only he wouldn't need to commute to work because he no longer had a job. He'd gambled that his years as the top earner and the best closer at his firm would outweigh the founding partners' loyalty to the Summers family. He'd been wrong.

"I'll think about it," he said as he reached into the back pocket of his jeans for his wallet. Leaning into the car, he handed Mrs. Ranger his card. "Do me a favor. Keep an eye on Arianna and Helen. Call my cell phone if you're concerned. Doesn't matter what time, day or night."

"Don't you worry. I'll keep an eye on them. I'll make a casserole when I get home and drop it by for their dinner tonight. I'll talk to the ladies in my bridge club and the garden club too. We'll come up with a schedule to cover their meals for the next month at least. I should have done it sooner, but I didn't want to seem nosy or interfering. Helen can be a little prickly, if you know what I mean."

He did. Her granddaughter could be the same. At least before the fire. It used to drive him nuts. Now he'd give anything to see a hint of the hardheaded woman he remembered. "Don't let her intimidate you."

No doubt he'd end up taking his own advice before this was over. As dysfunctional and potentially dangerous as their current situation was, he had a feeling neither Arianna nor Helen would be particularly pleased when he and their neighbors intervened.

Connor returned Mrs. Ranger's wave as she pulled away and then headed for the walkway in hopes of finding his family still hanging out on the patio. Sunday brunch had become something of a tradition for them since the weekend back in June when his baby brother had organized an intervention.

Back then Connor had been as concerned about his mother's health as his siblings but hadn't been thrilled at the idea of confronting her. Unless it was in the courtroom or at the negotiating table, he didn't do conflict well. Maybe because he'd always been on the losing end of every family debate or argument, his opinion never carrying quite the same weight as those of his overachieving brothers—his baby brother, Michael, with the photographic memory and his older brother, Logan, who could do no wrong in their parents' eyes.

In the end, despite their mother being upset at the time, things had turned out pretty well. She'd agreed to the consultation he'd set up with a renowned oncologist, learned the ovarian tumor was benign, and had recovered swiftly from her surgery.

The reason he and his brothers didn't judge the intervention a complete success was at that moment walking down the manor's front steps. Caught up in her conversation with his uncle Daniel, Connor's mother was oblivious to his presence. The pair shared a smile that caused his jaw to clench. Like his brothers, he didn't understand why his mother was still hanging out in Harmony Harbor instead of back home in Boston with her husband of forty years. Although more and more it was looking like his uncle might be the reason, and not just because of his political campaign.

For the most part, Connor liked his uncle, whereas Mike could barely stand to be in the same room with the man. He didn't trust him. Connor had a feeling Mike was right, at least to a point. There was definitely more to their father's older brother than the happy-go-lucky charmer he allowed the world to see. But Connor found the well-respected archaeologist interesting to talk to and enjoyed hanging out with him. That didn't mean he wanted him with his mother though.

Daniel said something to Maura that made her laugh, duck her head, and then tuck her brown hair behind her ear. Connor's eyes narrowed at the blush pinking her cheeks, and he cleared his throat. He didn't care that his parents were technically separated or that his father had supposedly stolen his mother away from Daniel decades before. The last thing Connor needed was evidence the two had picked up where they'd left off.

With a twinkle in his Gallagher-blue eyes and a roguish grin on his ruggedly handsome face, Connor's uncle looked like he'd just been caught with his hand in the cookie jar. Connor gave him a look that said to keep his hands out of that particular jar because those cookies were spoken for.

The older man chuckled as if he'd read Connor's mind, then said in a thick brogue that guaranteed the ladies of Harmony Harbor would be lining up to give him their vote, "There's my favorite nephew. Did you find out who's been defacing my signs, boyo?"

Today wasn't the first time a member of his uncle's fan club had sent up the alarm that a campaign sign had been damaged, although it was the first time Connor had been asked to look into it.

"No red spray paint involved this time around; just an accident. Arianna Bell was at her neighbor's place and tripped over the sign." *Then kicked you in the face a couple of times.* Connor fought back a smile at the thought. He would have preferred to leave Arianna's name out of it, but there'd been too many witnesses. Hopefully, like him, they were feeling protective of her and wouldn't share the real story with half the town.

"She's not going to sue, is she?" his mother asked, smoothing back her hair with a subtle glance at Daniel before refocusing on Connor. "Is that why you're here? I thought you and Brooklyn would be in Boston by now."

Okay, so clearly he hadn't thought this through. "Arianna's not going to sue, Mom. She, ah, walked into the sign. It didn't walk into—"

He was relieved when his uncle interrupted him, because his mother's eyes had narrowed as though she'd just remembered he'd dated Arianna. And if she discovered Brooklyn had taken off without him, she might figure out the reason he was still in Harmony Harbor and his girlfriend was not had something to do with Arianna.

"Where did you park, lad?" his uncle asked with a frown, leaning around him to scan the lot.

Connor stared at his uncle, wondering why he'd even thought to ask. Unless the news had already hit the Harmony Harbor gossip grapevine and people in town weren't feeling as protective of Arianna as he was. He'd seen signs his uncle was as tapped into the town's gossip as GG used to be. A scary thought if it was true.

"Brooklyn headed back to Boston without me," Connor said, doing his best to avoid his mother's probing gaze. "I wanted to talk to J—Logan about something and didn't want Brooklyn to be late for drinks with her friends."

"Arianna Bell. Why does that name sound familiar?" his mother asked, tapping a manicured finger against her chin.

"Maybe because Logan is marrying her sister and she was injured in a fire that destroyed several shops on Main Street, including hers," Connor said.

"Don't be silly. Of course I know *who* she is. Besides being Jenna's sister, she's a well-known and talented wedding dress designer. But that's not what I was talking about." She lifted her hands as though she couldn't believe she'd forgotten. "Now I remember. Either Michael or Logan dated her. Whichever one it was, I seem to remember he was quite taken with her."

"Really, Mom? It was me. I was in love with Arianna, not Michael or Logan. Me. We dated for two years."

"Little touchy, aren't you, boyo? Must have been a first love." Daniel raised his index finger in a *gotcha* gesture. "It was, wasn't it? Oh yes, there it is, written all over your face. Don't bother denying it. I can commiserate," he said, putting an arm around Connor's mother's shoulders and smiling tenderly down at her. "Your mother was mine, and I never got over her."

Connor wanted to yank his mother away from Daniel, which might have been why he said dryly, "I doubt that. You were married three times."

"And that says it all, doesn't it, now? No one measured up to your mother. If I hadn't called your father to help—"

"We shouldn't keep Connor, Daniel," his mother said, looking uncomfortable. Which Connor was relieved to see. She should bloody well be uncomfortable. "I'm sure he wants to speak to his brother so he can get back to Boston and Brooklyn." She frowned. "Darling, why didn't you just call Logan?"

"He asked me to take care of a legal matter for him, and I forgot to have him sign off on the paperwork." He lied so smoothly that you'd think he made a habit of it. He didn't. He was just really good at thinking on his feet.

His mother and his uncle looked at his empty hands.

Blowing out an irritated breath, he took his phone from his back pocket and held it up. "It's all here. I just e-mail the file to his printer. Now, if we're all good, I'll go and do that."

"You'll need to replace the sign the Bell girl knocked over before you head back to Boston," his uncle reminded him.

Yeah, right. "I'll do that," he said, leaning in to kiss his mother's cheek. He then rounded the pair and continued up the walkway to the front door. Out of the corner of his eye, he spied something hurtling through the sky toward him and turned in time to catch the football.

"You still got it, bro," his brother Logan called out. "Come on. We're having a game of pickup. The summer Gallaghers versus the Harmony Harbor Gallaghers." His cousins had been born and raised in Harmony Harbor, while Connor and his brothers were born and raised in Boston. Growing up, they'd spent the summers and holidays here. When he was dating Arianna, Connor spent as many weekends as he could in the town by the sea.

He tossed the football in the air and then caught it as he walked across the lawn toward the bridge. His brothers and cousins and their significant others—kids and pets too—were gathered in the wide-open space on the other side of the pond. No windows or guests to take out with an errant football. Watching his cousins and brothers joking around, Connor was tempted to stay for the day. They'd had good times growing up together, and it wasn't like he had anything waiting for him in Boston.

There was a telling thought. Feeling guilty about it, he tucked the football under his arm and pulled out his phone. Brooklyn picked up on the second ring. Only it wasn't Brooklyn's voice on the other end; it was Lyndsey. "You finally managed to pull yourself out of the blonde's arms, did you?"

He really didn't want to deal with this now. "Not that

I owe you an explanation, but she's an old friend and she's going through a difficult time."

"Thanks to you, so is my old friend. Make this right or else, Gallagher." Before Brooklyn came on the line, he heard Lyndsey mutter, "I don't know why you waste your time with this guy. He's not into you, not like Ben was."

Lyndsey's observation brought him up short. Halfway across the bridge, he leaned against the rail, remembering the emotions that had swamped him as he'd stood by Arianna's hospital bed back in July. How he'd felt watching her today and holding her in his arms. As hard as it was to admit, as much as he didn't want to, Lyndsey was right. He'd never felt those same pulse-pounding, breath-stealing emotions with Brooklyn. Except up until that night in the hospital, he'd thought his feelings for Brooklyn had been just as deep as they'd been for Arianna.

He looked over to where Logan was laughing with Jenna and his brother Michael stood watching Shay love on his dog, which was the size of a pony. Connor wished his feelings for Brooklyn were as deep and true as he'd once believed. He wanted what his brothers and his cousins had. And Brooklyn had seemed like his chance to have it.

It wasn't fair to lead her on. Not that he planned to tell her over the phone. There was a part of him that wanted to act like a jerk for the next few weeks so she'd break up with him instead, but he didn't want to be that guy.

There was a gasp on the other end of the line, and he

was afraid he'd said the words out loud until he caught part of a whispered conversation. "I can't believe you invited Ben for drinks, Tiff. Jeez." After a ticked-off sigh, Brooklyn said, "Hey, sorry I left you stranded."

They invited Ben for drinks? Connor opened his mouth to ask but cleared his throat instead. In the end, he wanted Brooklyn to be happy. Not immediately, of course. He did have a healthy ego, after all. But maybe her friends were right and Ben was the better man.

"No. I'm the one who should apologize. I shouldn't have kept you waiting. But it wasn't what it looked like, Brooklyn. Arianna's an old friend. She's practically family. You met her sister Jenna at brunch."

"Hang on a sec."

Connor heard her muffled voice as she spoke to someone, the sound of a chair scraping across a wooden floor, people laughing and talking loudly, and he figured she was stepping outside for some privacy. He took the opportunity to throw the football to one of his cousins, earning a scowl from his brother.

He heard horns honking and then Brooklyn's voice came back over the line. "I know who she is, Connor. I was at your place the night you came back from the hospital, remember? I've never seen you that torn up before."

"Swear to God, there's nothing going on between us."

"Maybe not, but I saw the way you looked at her. You've never looked at me that way. Not once. Lyndsey's right. I wish she wasn't, but she is."

"We're not doing this now, Brooklyn. Not over the phone. Logan's leaving for DC in a few hours. He can drop me off on his way to the airport. We'll order in. We'll talk. Okay?"

"Not tonight. I need a couple days."

He heard the dejection in her voice and wished he could say *Love you, babe*, but he couldn't. He'd never said it before, so it wouldn't be fair if he said it now. They made a date for early in the week and arranged a time for him to pick up his car.

"You look like you just lost your best friend."

Connor turned at the sound of Logan's voice, disconnected the phone, and shoved it in his pocket. "It's been one of those days," he admitted.

"You wanna talk about it?" Logan asked, looking toward the parking lot. "Where's Brooklyn?"

"In Boston, with my car. I'm going to catch a ride in with you."

"What's going on? Everything seemed okay with you guys at brunch."

"It was. Until I ended up on Holly Road at Mrs. Ranger's place." He saw his brother Michael glance their way, frown, say something to Shay, and then saunter over. "What's up?"

"I think we're about to find out," Logan said. "Arianna lives on the corner of Holly and Ivy, across from Mrs. Ranger. This wouldn't happen to have anything to do with her, would it?"

"Everything. You know how fond I am of Jenna, Logan, but it's bad. She should have intervened long before now. Arianna needs her."

His brother crossed his arms, eyes narrowed. The three of them looked a lot alike. They had dark hair and blue eyes, but whereas Connor and Michael were six two, Logan was closer to six four and more blatantly muscular than they were. And at that moment he was wearing his intimidating Secret Service face. He was an agent with the president's security detail.

Michael raised his eyebrows at Connor as if to say, *You've done it now*. He kinda already got that from Logan's expression, but he didn't care. They hadn't been there.

"You have no idea what you're talking about," Logan said, his voice almost a growl.

"Then I guess I'll find out." Connor went to walk past his brother.

Logan's arm shot out and grabbed his. "You're not talking to her about this. It'll just upset her. You know Jenna, Connor. Do you really think she wouldn't be there for Arianna when she needs her? But you weren't there when Arianna's mother and grandmother kicked Jenna out of the hospital room. As bad off as she was, Arianna stood up to her mother. Told her Jenna was her family too, and if she couldn't deal, to go back to California, and that's what Beverly did. Helen is tougher and smarter than her daughter. Arianna probably has no idea how often Jenna has stopped by or called only to be turned away. She's lucky if she's managed to see Arianna a handful of times."

"And...?" Connor said, because he could tell his brother was holding something back.

"Jenna says Arianna has given up. She rarely leaves her room. The nerves in her hand are damaged to the point she can't use it. And if she can't use her hand—"

"She can't design wedding dresses, so she has no reason to live," Connor finished for him.

"Really? I had no idea it was this bad. I doubt anyone in town does," Michael said.

"It's worse than even Jenna probably knows," Connor said, and filled his brothers in on the insurance claim and Helen.

"Okay. I'll help Jenna deal with the insurance claim. I'm sure Serena will help with it too. It doesn't sound like she knows how bad things have gotten either," Logan said.

"All right, you guys handle the insurance, and I'll talk to Finn about Helen." Their cousin Finn was a doctor at the family clinic in town. "See what options are available," Michael said. "And you know Grams. As soon as she finds out Helen and Arianna are in trouble, she and the Widows Club will get involved."

"Hey, wait a minute. Who put you two in charge? I've got this, thanks. I'll take care of the insurance claim with Jenna and Serena. And I'll talk to Finn. As far as Grams and the Widows Club, are you out of your mind? Arianna is as proud as her grandmother. She'd rather be out on the street than know people are talking about her." His brothers shared a glance. "What? Why are you looking at me like that?"

"You do realize you sound like a man looking out for his woman, don't you?" Michael said.

"And you do know you sound like you're eighty and not thirty-six, don't you?" Connor said to Michael.

"Well, that explains why Brooklyn is in Boston with your car and not you," Logan said.

Michael frowned. “Wait a sec. Mom was all but planning your wedding at the brunch, and you didn’t look like you were going to lose your ever-loving mind like you usually do when someone starts talking about weddings featuring you in the starring role. What happened between then and now?”

“Arianna,” Logan said, fighting a grin. He patted Connor on the back. “It’s for the best. Brooklyn wasn’t that into you.”

“You can’t be serious. Of course she was into—”

Michael cut off Connor. “I don’t know. She was pretty into him. At least into his fancy wheels, million-dollar condo, and his high-powered job. But once she finds out you’re now an unemployed lawyer who will probably have to get rid of his wheels and condo to make ends meet, she’ll move on to someone else anyway.”

He didn’t want to admit it, but there could be some truth to his brother’s observation. It might be the reason Connor had put off telling Brooklyn about losing his job. One way to find out—he’d come clean before they had their *talk*. “Just FYI, I won’t have to sell my Porsche or condo. I’m fine financially.” At least for a while.

Chapter Four

♥

Arianna stared at the piles of Tupperware containers and plastic-wrap-covered dishes and platters on the kitchen counters. The cupboards, refrigerator, and freezer were jam-packed, thanks to the man knocking on their front door. She knew it was Connor not only by the confident knock but because he'd called earlier and talked to her grandmother to arrange a time to come over today.

Glamma loved him now that he'd promised to take care of the insurance claim. Arianna didn't. And if Glamma knew half of what people in town were saying about the two of them, thanks to Connor sharing their private business, she wouldn't have the warm fuzzies for the man. He certainly wouldn't be standing on their front porch knocking on the door. He might very well be six feet under.

The knocking continued. A part of her wanted to throw open the door and tell Connor exactly what she thought of him, while the other part of her wanted to crawl back into bed and go to sleep. Except he was so annoyingly persistent he'd probably stand there all night, drawing the attention of their nosy and interfering neighbors. The thought made up her mind. She strode to the front door, slowing as she caught a glimpse of herself in the mirror over the entry table.

It was three o'clock in the afternoon, and she was wearing pajamas. She tilted her head to the side, looking at herself through his eyes. The gray fleece top and bottoms could pass for sweats. Even her hair could pass for workout hair instead of bedhead. She considered slipping on a pair of sneakers to complete the subterfuge but didn't have the energy to hunt them down.

She walked to the door, taking a moment before opening it. She had to prepare herself before she saw his face. It didn't seem to matter that she'd spent years nurturing her anger toward him. One full-on, close-up look at his gorgeous face was all it took to turn back time.

As she'd noticed the other day, the years had been kind to him. If possible, he was even more attractive. Time had etched faint lines at the corners of his vibrant blue eyes and bracketed his mouth, adding more character to his too-handsome face. His hair was as thick and as dark as she remembered, only now it was obvious a talented—and no doubt expensive—stylist cut his raven-black locks. Lucky stylist, she thought, remembering how his hair had felt sliding between her fingers and over her body when he...

"Are you insane, you ridiculous woman?" she whispered to her reflection, rolling her eyes when the knocking turned to pounding.

"Arianna, if you don't open up, I'm calling the police."

She stormed to the door, fighting to get it open with her left hand. Finally, the knob turned, and she wrenched it open. "Have you not embarrassed us enough? Or is this just some ridiculous ploy by your uncle to get my grandmother out of the race?"

He rubbed his fingers across his mouth. He had beautiful hands, strong, talented fingers and... Wait. Was he holding back a laugh? She curled her good hand into a fist, tempted to punch him. There was nothing remotely funny about the situation. He'd made her and her grandmother the object of everyone's pity.

"Helen's dead last, honey. I don't think she even shows up on my uncle's radar."

"Don't you *honey* me." She'd like to tell him not to look at her either, because his eyes were her downfall. They always had been. "And you might want to tell your uncle not to underestimate my grandmother. Polls have been known to be wrong." She narrowed her eyes at him. He was smiling now, a sexy smile with an annoying display of perfectly white and even teeth. "Why are you smiling at me?"

"Because you're mad."

She was afraid she knew what he meant. "Your powers of observation are as sharply honed as ever, I see."

He laughed. She wasn't going to ask why. She didn't have to. She could see something other than just amusement in his eyes. He used to like nothing better than to tease her into a temper. "What do you want, Connor?"

He held her gaze for a moment too long. She must be misreading his intent. He couldn't possibly be intimating he wanted her, a scarred cripple who had nothing left to offer. He had a girlfriend, a woman of stunning, glossy perfection.

The thought caused an odd mixture of desire, envy, and despair to flare to life inside her. “You might as well come in. You’ve already given the neighbors enough to talk about.”

“What do you mean?” he asked as he closed the door behind him.

“Oh please. Don’t pretend you don’t know what I’m talking about.” She strode into the kitchen and gestured at the island and counters. “We could feed a small country. The fridge and freezer are full too.”

“I don’t understand,” he said, doing a slow turn, his eyes narrowing on the table before shooting back to her. “Is that—”

“Envelopes of money? Yes. Bills, coins, checks, even some IOUs.” Heat rose to her cheeks, and she turned away. She’d cried in front of him yesterday; she wasn’t about to cry in front of him today. Even if they were angry and embarrassed tears. Even if it meant he might take her in his arms again. It had been so long since she’d been held by a man, especially a man she’d once loved with all her heart and soul.

She’d been such a romantic back then, positive they’d be together forever. Then her life had begun to unravel, and she’d made choices based on emotions and pain that had nothing to do with Connor. She’d regretted the decision to end their relationship almost from the moment she’d made it, but her father’s affair with another woman had cut deep and Arianna couldn’t think straight or see past the pain to know how big a mistake she'd made. And then, just when she'd decided she'd been foolish to allow her father's betrayal to mess with her head and her relationship with Connor, life had thrown her a curveball. Everything had changed, and her decision and choices were no longer just about her or hers to make.

"It wasn't me, Arianna," he said from behind her. She heard him put down the messenger bag he'd been carrying, and then his hands were on her shoulders, drawing her back against his chest. He smelled like fall, fresh air and autumn leaves. He felt solid and strong, and she let herself relax against him in hopes of absorbing some of his confidence and strength. She didn't know this woman she'd become. She didn't like her very much.

He wrapped his arms around her chest and dipped his head, his warm breath tickling her ear. "I know you. I wouldn't do that to you."

She should move away from him. Show him she wasn't as weak or as pitiful as he and everyone else seemed to think. But she was weak and pitiful, and he felt like a warm, heavy blanket wrapped around her.

If her body wouldn't do as it should, she'd use her mind and mouth to push him away. "I don't believe you."

There wasn't an ounce of the sarcasm she had intended in her voice. He wouldn't step away to defend himself now, not with her sounding all swoony and breathless. But before she could berate herself, Connor released her, gently turning her to face him. So, it had worked after all. She should be happy, not disappointed at the loss of his comfort and warmth. Or maybe terrified that he was making her feel anything at all. She preferred the numbness, the dark well of nothingness of the past several weeks.

"Arianna, look at me."

There was something about the tone of his voice, deep and soothing, yet demanding, that reminded her of the one she'd been hearing in her nightmares and dreams ever since leaving the hospital. The voice that had begged her to stay, pleaded with her to fight, and reminded her of those she'd leave behind. "You told me you loved me," she said without meaning to, though certain now that it had been Connor's seductive baritone that had crept into her head and heart that night and demanded she live.

He stepped back, his hands falling to his sides. He wore a black leather jacket, jeans, and a blue V-neck sweater that deepened the color of his eyes. Wary eyes that stared back at her. "I'm not sure I know what you mean. I used to tell you I loved you all the time. But that was a long time ago."

She should let it go, but instead she shook her head. "No. It was mere weeks ago actually. At the hospital. I heard you. You told me you loved me. You told me not to give up." Anger tinged the edges of her speech.

It was him. Connor was the one who'd dragged her back into the nightmare that was her life. She'd spent hours in the hospital listening to the voices of doctors, nurses, techs, and porters, hours thinking of what she'd say to the man once she found him. And here he stood, right in front of her, and all she could do was stare.

He stood silent, a muscle pulsing in his stubbled jaw, as though debating whether to tell her the truth or not.

"What did you want me to do? I watched you take what could have been your last breath. You died right before my eyes, Arianna. I couldn't save you. Do you know what that feels like, to stand beside someone you care about and know there's not anything you can do? All I could do was try to reach the woman I remembered. You used to be a fighter. You needed to be that woman then. You need to be her now."

"I didn't want to fight. I was ready to die." And none of them knew why. It was just one more secret she'd take to her grave. A silent shame she'd locked away years before. If Connor knew, he wouldn't have been there that night begging her to live.

"You didn't die. Stop acting like you did. You have people who care about you and need you, so instead of hiding away in your bedroom, maybe you should start living again."

"How dare you judge me! You have no idea what it's like to lose absolutely everything and be left with this." She raised her injured arm in the sling, just the tips of her fingers visible in the black compression glove.

He glanced at her hand and then lifted his gaze to hers. "Why did you go back to your office that night? You had to know it was dangerous, that there was a chance you might not make it out alive."

Everyone asked the same question, and she told them the same lie she told Connor now. "I don't know why. Maybe I was overcome by the smoke and got disoriented."

"No. You tied a tourniquet around Serena's leg and

ensured that Jenna would get her out. When she asked where you were going, you told her your office. What was so important that you risked your life?"

"You have no idea what it was like that night. I wasn't thinking straight, Connor. I was traumatized. Lorenzo kidnapped us, tied us up, then shot Serena and my stepmother. I thought we were going to die."

In some ways she had been traumatized, but she'd also known exactly what she was doing. Only on another level, she'd told the truth. She hadn't been thinking straight. She'd let emotions rule her actions and had suffered the consequences, losing even more than she'd thought she would.

"And you would have died if you hadn't shot him. You and your sisters are alive because of you, Arianna. You were incredibly brave."

"I wasn't. Jenna was. If it weren't for her, none of us would have gotten out alive."

"Your grandmother might say if it weren't for Jenna bringing Lorenzo into your lives, none of this would have happened."

"She didn't say that to Jenna, did she?"

"I don't know, though I imagine she does hold Jenna partially to blame. Makes sense, right? She blames her for ruining your parents' marriage."

"I know. So does my mother. Did you talk to Jenna about this? Is that why she's only dropped by a few times?"

"Logan told me. But that's why I mentioned it. I didn't want you to think she doesn't care. She does. It's just that Helen makes it difficult for her to see you."

"I don't know why you'd think it would bother me. Jenna's busy. I understand... Wait a minute. You were talking about me to Logan? Why? When?"

"Sunday. After I left here. I was worried about you. Can you blame me?"

"Yes. Yes, I can. Because this"—she waved her good hand around the room—"is your fault."

"How do you figure that? It's not like I put an announcement in the *Gazette*. The only people I talked to were my brothers. They wouldn't say anything to anyone else." He rubbed the back of his neck. "I talked to Mrs. Ranger about you and Helen on the way to the manor. She actually did most of the talking. It's possible she's behind this." He gestured to the containers. "She was going to get in touch with her bridge club and make a schedule. They must have messed up. It was supposed to be one meal a day or something like that."

"Oh no, we got that schedule too. See, right there on the fridge. That's the list of meals that will be arriving every day at four p.m. for the next month. The rest of this is courtesy of the Widows Club and the ladies of Immaculate Conception."

"Swear to God, I never mentioned anything to my grandmother. I'm telling the absolute truth, Arianna. I know how private you are. I wouldn't do that."

She sighed. He'd always been open and honest with her in the past. She didn't see any reason for him to lie to her now. "It was probably Mrs. Ranger. Word must have gotten out when she organized our nightly meals. What on earth were you two talking about that made her think we needed to be fed?"

"Your grandmother telling her you were penniless and would soon be homeless may be partially to blame," he said, moving to pick up his messenger bag.

"Is there something else you're not telling me?"

"Why do you ask?"

"Because you're avoiding looking at me. And now I'm sure of it because you just answered a question with a question."

The smile he gave her faded. "You don't look like you're eating. And Mrs.—"

"The pills I had to take made me sick to my stomach. I couldn't eat. But I'm starting to feel better now." That was true, to a point. In the beginning, the pills had made her sick, but she no longer had to take them. She wasn't not eating on purpose. It's just that she slept through most meals, and they hadn't had a lot of food on hand. "Honestly, don't people around here have enough to occupy their time?"

"You didn't let me finish. Mrs. Ranger has some concerns about Helen's mental health. Have you noticed anything lately? Has your grandmother been confused, repeating herself, behaving erratically?"

"I don't believe this. They think I'm anorexic and my grandmother has Alzheimer's." She tried to keep the panic from her voice. So it wasn't just her. Other people had noticed her grandmother was losing it too.

"Are you okay? You got pale all of a sudden. Sit down." He guided her to the table and pulled out a chair. "You want a cup of tea, a glass of juice?"

"Juice, please," she said as she sat down, noticing a slight tremor in the fingers of her good hand as she carefully pushed the envelopes away. "I can't believe people are sending us money. Maybe now Glamma will think twice about trying to get the sympathy vote."

Connor didn't say anything. He'd taken off his leather jacket and draped it on a chair at the table, placing his messenger bag beside it. His back was to her as he rummaged around in the fridge. Maybe the hum of the refrigerator had drowned out her voice, or perhaps he was just stupefied by his choices of juice. People had dropped off several containers of juice, along with eggs, bacon, and bread. Obviously they'd been put in charge of breakfast.

"I'm not fussy. Any kind is fine," she said, noting Connor rubbing the back of his neck.

"It's not that. I know you like grape juice. I'm just trying to decide if you meant this to be in here or not." He turned with a black lace La Perla bra dangling from his finger. It was hers.

It was only because she knew he was seeing it as evidence that either she or her grandmother had lost their marbles that she told him the truth. "I, ah, haven't been able to put on a bra since the fire. I thought I'd try to this morning. It didn't go well. I was frustrated and attempted to throw it in the garbage can and missed by a mile, just as Glamma ushered in several firefighters, including your cousin Liam and Marco DiRossi, who were dropping off more containers of food. I scooped up the bra and shoved it in the closet thing to me—the refrigerator."

"Okay. I didn't really need to know all the details, but—"

"Yes, you did. You seem to think Glamma and I are losing it."

"No, I don't think you are. You've—"

"Ah, I see, so I'm fine. It's just Glamma who you think is crazy. Did you ever stop to think that she might be a little stressed? She's eighty years old, and she's taking care of me and running for mayor."

He poured her a glass of grape juice as she talked and then walked to the table and placed it in front of her, setting her bra by her arm. "I'm sure she is stressed," he said as he took a seat.

She grabbed the bra and stuffed it under her bottom. "Stress can make you forgetful."

"You're right; it can."

"Stop being so agreeable. I know what you're doing. You think if you stay quiet, I'll just keep talking until I admit Glamma's been repeating herself and forgetting to pay bills and missing appointments. She's eighty, Connor. It only stands to reason she would have some minor memory problems."

"If you think Helen's fine, then great. There's nothing to be concerned about. But if you are concerned, you don't have to deal with it alone. For now, why don't we take care of the insurance claim? That should help alleviate at least some of yours and Helen's stress."

She slumped in the chair. "Can we do it tomorrow? It's been a long day."

"I'm afraid we can't. There's honestly not a lot left to do. I've been working on it with Serena and Jenna for the last couple of days. But something Helen said was bothering me, and I talked about it to Jenna. She said you took out a loan a few weeks before the fire."

"Yes, I did. I planned to expand. But Glamma had nothing to do with that. I did it on my own."

"That's the thing, you didn't. I called the bank after I talked to Jenna, leaned on the manager a bit, and he admitted that, because Helen held the initial loan on Tie the Knot, he'd asked her to cosign."

"No. That's not right. When Glamma gave me the shop, I took over her loan. She's had nothing to do with Tie the Knot for years."

"I know, and so did the manager. We'll get back to that, but right now I need to talk to your grandmother, and I need you to hire me as your attorney."

"Why? What's going on?"

"Helen cosigned the loan using this house as collateral. You're almost two months behind on your loan payments."

"That's why Glamma said we'll be out on the street by Christmas. They're going to foreclose." She pressed her hand to her mouth and closed her eyes.

"Hey, look at me. It's going to be okay. Once you've hired me as your attorney, I'll go in and demand to see the notifications they say they've sent."

"You don't think they've sent them?"

"No, I'm pretty sure they have and Helen ignored them. The thing is, the manager never should have asked your grandmother to cosign and put up her house as collateral. But because her name is on the loan, my hands are tied. There is a way to get you a couple of extra months' grace. You're not going to like it though."

"You're going to say Glamma is mentally incompetent."

"Look, I know this is the last thing you want to do. If it makes it easier, just think of it as a legal strategy to save your home."

"But you think it's the truth."

"I'm sorry. I do."

"If you've been working on the claim, which, I really appreciate, by the way, can't you get them to give us an advance against the settlement that we can put toward what's owed on the house?"

"I tried. But they're pushing back because the claim is being filed almost two months after the fact. There is another option."

"What?"

"You can let me loan you the money, or you can use the money—"

"No. Thank you, but no. We're not a charity case. This isn't our fault. I have insurance for this very reason. And what the bank did is wrong."

"It is. So hire me. I'll make them both pay."

"Where do I sign?" she said, suddenly feeling like she could breathe again.

"For now we'll just shake on it."

She went to give him her injured hand, then self-consciously lifted her left. He took it, smiled, and then brought it to his lips, pressing a gentle kiss to her palm. "Does this mean I'm forgiven for representing Summers in your divorce?"

She tried to come back with a sharp rejoinder to make him laugh, but feeling his warm lips on her skin and seeing his dark head bent over her hand had turned her brain to mush. All she could manage was a small smile and a nod.

An hour later she couldn't manage a smile or a nod if she tried. They'd made it through fifteen pages of the itemized lists he'd put together with her sisters' help and had barely put a dent in the pile of papers, so it surprised Arianna when Connor reached behind him for his leather jacket.

He smiled as he stood up and shrugged into his jacket. "If you can get through a good chunk of it tonight, we should be able to put in the claim by Thursday at the latest."

"You're leaving?" she asked, wondering if he heard the hint of panic in her voice.

"Yeah. I have to get going, but you're doing great."

She wasn't doing great. She wasn't doing anywhere close to great. She'd just gotten really good at hiding her feelings. "Why don't you stay for dinner? There's lasagna in the fridge. Rosa DiRossi made it," she quickly added when it looked like he might refuse. Rosa DiRossi made the best Italian food in all of Massachusetts.

"I'm sorry. I wish I could. But Brooklyn's coming to my place for dinner, and it's too late to cancel."

"Oh, I see," she said, working to keep the disappointment from her voice, maybe a touch of jealousy too. Until she thought about what he said. He was having dinner with Brooklyn. His girlfriend. The girlfriend she'd assumed he'd broken up with. And she'd assumed this because of how he'd been acting with her.

"I really would love to stay. It's just that—"

"It's fine." Arianna grimaced as the words came out of her mouth cold and clipped. She didn't mean for her anger to be so clearly evident. She pushed back her chair and got to her feet, not looking at him as she led the way to the front door. "Thank you for your help today."

Chapter Five

♥

Curled up in a chair in the dark living room, Arianna startled awake. She must have fallen asleep not long after Connor left. The movement caused the papers to fall from her lap onto the hardwood floor.

It wasn't a nightmare that awakened her. She'd been dreaming about Connor, a hazy montage from their past. Images of them lying in the sand at Kismet Cove, holding hands, dancing in the rain, kissing under the stars, making love at Starlight Pointe. They'd been as young and perfect as their love. Nothing between them, no secrets, no hurtful words.

She straightened in the chair, grateful for whatever had pulled her from the dream. They'd had their chance; she'd ruined it.

As she leaned over to scoop up the papers from the floor, the copy of the loan agreement caught her eye. She hadn't been sure she would get the loan to expand Tie the Knot and had been thrilled when the manager had called to say he'd *found a way* to approve it. She'd been so relieved that she hadn't thought to question what strings he'd had to pull to make it happen. He'd been called away on the day she'd gone to the bank to sign. She couldn't recall seeing the cosignature line; his assistant certainly hadn't pointed it out. There definitely hadn't been a signature at the time—that she would have noticed. Now there was, right below her name.

Once again anger welled up inside her at the manager for taking advantage of her grandmother even if he'd done so to help Arianna. Her anger was quickly followed by gratitude that Connor had taken it upon himself to insert himself into her problems and her life. Not that she'd tell him. If she gave Mr. Fixer an inch, she had no doubt he'd take a mile.

She sat back in the chair, thinking about earlier. He'd had no idea how big a deal it was that she'd asked him to stay for dinner tonight. These days, she didn't eat in front of anyone, including her grandmother. Eating with her left hand was an art Arianna had yet to master. She still couldn't believe that she'd asked him. Clearly, embarrassment over her ability to handle a fork and spoon with all the finesse of a toddler was preferable to facing the inventory of what she'd lost alone.

It was probably for the best his girlfriend was going to his place for dinner. Although that's not how Arianna had felt upon learning the news. Even as he'd kissed her palm, held her in his arms, looked at her in that special way he used to, he had a girlfriend waiting in the wings. As the daughter of an unfaithful man and the wife of an unfaithful husband, she found that unforgivable.

No doubt Connor had left her place wondering what

was wrong with her. One minute she'd been warm and friendly, and the next, a snippy woman who'd shown him the door. Maybe he wasn't wondering at all. She'd done it to him before, after all. The day she'd ended their two-year teenage love affair.

Arianna gave her head a small shake. The past was in the past. She and Connor had no future. He was her lawyer now. Nothing more, nothing less. She returned the thick sheaf of papers to the side table, calculating the hours that he must have spent on the insurance claim. He hadn't done all this work because he thought of her as a client. He'd done it because he cared. She owed him an apology.

Maybe she could do him a favor and show him the error of his ways. He may not know how easily a kiss on the hand or holding someone in your arms could be misconstrued, especially by a woman who hadn't known a man's tender touch in years. Connor had been a charming teenager. Now he was a lethally charming man.

She thought about how awkward the conversation would be and decided she'd pretend nothing had happened. She'd make it up to him in other ways. All he'd asked when he'd left was for her to look over a few more pages by tomorrow. She'd finish them tonight, as much for him as for herself.

It wouldn't be the first time she'd pulled an all-nighter. She used to do it on a weekly basis at Tie the Knot. Her stomach took a perilous dip at the thought, threatening to pull her into the quicksand of depressing emotions. She'd barely pulled herself out. She couldn't afford to get swallowed up by her anger and grief. At least not until the insurance claim was settled and Glamma's house saved.

As Arianna got up to make her first pot of coffee in months, there was a flash of yellow light in the back windows that was immediately followed by a clap of thunder. She wondered if that was what had woken her or if it was the sound of teeming rain. Whatever it had been, she was glad of it when she noted the time on the stove. It was ten o'clock.

She looked around the kitchen with a frown. Glamma usually had a cup of tea before bed. She'd had two political events today. A late-afternoon tea at the seniors residence and a potluck dinner with the bridge club, which would be followed by a game of cards. Maybe they were running late.

Arianna decided to make tea instead of coffee. That way it would be ready when her grandmother came home. Waiting for the water to boil, she leaned against the counter, listening to the rain slash against the windowpane. She shivered, glad to be inside where it was warm. Though the house wasn't as warm as she liked. If she had her way, it would stay at seventy-five. Glamma preferred sixty-nine. Since her grandmother was up and about more than Arianna, she always won.

Not tonight though. She could warm up the house a bit before Glamma came home. Arianna walked to the thermostat on the wall beside the entryway table, noting her grandmother's umbrella leaning against the front hall closet door. Once she'd adjusted the temperature a few degrees, she peeked out the glass panel beside the door. Surely Mrs. Ranger would drop Glamma off at the front gate.

That's odd, Arianna thought as she pressed her face against the windowpane, squinting through the gloom and rain. It looked like Mrs. Ranger's car was parked in her driveway. Maybe they'd decided to have a cup of tea together before calling it a night.

At the whistling of the kettle, Arianna walked back to the kitchen. Her stomach dipped a little as she carefully removed the kettle from the gas stove and saw the open flame. She gave herself a mental pat on the back when her breathing remained even and her hand didn't shake. It was a small victory. Being around a flame of any kind or even extreme heat or smoke had the power to send her into a full-blown panic attack. The same kind her sister Serena had.

Arianna found it difficult to think of her sister without tearing up. She missed her, sometimes desperately. Serena had been more than just a sister. She'd been her best friend, and she'd left Arianna without a backward glance. She should be used to it by now. People always left her. The only one who'd stuck around was her grandmother.

Arianna glanced at the clock on the stove, wondering if Mrs. Ranger would think her rude for calling this late. Probably not. They all apparently believed she was not only penniless and starving, she was also helpless. Admittedly, she hadn't done much to prove them wrong. Truth be told, she considered herself helpless and penniless too. But at that moment, she didn't really care what anyone said about her, because the more she thought about Glamma being out this late, the more she didn't like it.

She probably had Connor to thank for the anxious knot in her chest. He hadn't done a very good job hiding the fact that he believed her grandmother's memory lapses were more serious than Arianna wanted to see. He'd let it go for one reason and one reason only: He didn't think she could handle the thought of Glamma losing her mind without losing hers. He was right.

Arianna looked up Mrs. Ranger's number on the piece of paper tacked on the wall beside the phone, relieved to find their neighbor had been programmed in with a number. Everything was a struggle with only one hand. She put the receiver between her shoulder and ear and pressed six.

With every unanswered ring, the knot in Arianna's chest tightened. "I'm so sorry to bother you, Mrs. Ranger," she said as soon as the phone picked up.

"Arianna dear, is that you?" the older woman asked, sounding as if she'd just woken up.

Arianna felt like she might hyperventilate. "Yes, it's me. I was wondering if Glamma was with you." *Please, please let her be there.*

"No. I dropped her off an hour ago." She could hear a creak and a faint rustling as if Mrs. Ranger had just sat up in bed. "Have you checked her bedroom, dear?"

"I'll go check right now," she said, her heart racing.

"You do that. I'll stay on the line."

"Thank you." She dropped the phone and ran to her grandmother's bedroom, praying as she flipped on the light. At the sight of the neatly made bed, a panicked sound built in Arianna's throat. She didn't know how her legs carried her back to the kitchen.

"She's not here, Mrs. Ranger," she said, her voice barely a whisper.

"All right. Don't panic. It hasn't been all that long. Check the backyard and the shed, dear. The neighbors on either side too. While you're doing that, I'll call everyone we know."

"Okay. I'll do that. I'll do that right now." She hung up the phone. The receiver fell off, and she returned it to the cradle. It fell off again. She picked it up, slamming it into the cradle again and again. "Stop it!" she yelled at herself. "Just stop it and find her."

But she didn't find her in the backyard or in the shed or in the backyards or sheds of the neighbors on either side of them. A porch light flipped on as she got down on her knees to search beneath Mr. Simpson's hedges.

"Hey there. What are you about?"

She pulled her head from under the bush. "It's Glamma, Mr. Simpson. I can't find her. She's missing." Her voice caught on a sob as the panic settled deep.

"Give us a minute. Me and the missus will be out to help you look."

She was about to force a thank-you from between her trembling lips when she heard her name being called from the sidewalk.

"Did you find her?" she yelled back, scrambling to her feet, her sneakers sliding on the muddy grass. She knew the answer as soon as she reached the sidewalk. Several of their neighbors were congregated around Mrs. Ranger, all of them looking concerned.

"I'm sorry, dear. Not yet. But we're organizing a search party. Here." She handed her a cell phone. "I called Connor."

"Irene, go in and get the child a rain jacket and boots. Her lips are blue, and she's shivering," Mr. Simpson said, holding an umbrella over Arianna's head.

"I'm okay, thanks," she said, taking the phone from Mrs. Ranger. "Connor."

"You're not okay. And you won't do your grandmother any good if you come down with pneumonia. Now, go get dry and get some rain gear on. I should be there in forty-five minutes."

"You're coming?" She clenched her teeth to hold back a sob.

"Do you really even have to ask?"

"It's my fault. I fell asleep. If I had—"

"Don't, okay? Jenna should be at your place in a few minutes with Michael and Shay. My cousins and Uncle Colin are also on their way." His uncle was the fire chief. "We'll find her, honey."

But half an hour later, they still hadn't found her. Their kitchen had been transformed into command central. Typically search and rescue and the police wouldn't be involved until a person had been missing twenty-four hours. But the Gallaghers were well connected and pulled in favors. Even if they hadn't, Arianna had a feeling search and rescue and the police wouldn't have waited the obligatory twenty-fours, not when the senior missing was believed to have dementia.

Every time she heard the words *dementia* or *Alzheimer's*, she cringed. It seemed like she was the only one in town who hadn't realized how bad her grandmother was. She'd been oblivious, so caught up in her grief and anger she hadn't noticed what was happening right before her very eyes. But that wasn't really true. A part of her had seen it; she just didn't want to believe it. She couldn't. If she did, that meant she'd lose her grandmother, too.

"I have to go look for her, Jenna. I can't stand around doing nothing."

It wasn't like she'd been standing around for long, really. It had taken her a half hour to get changed, remove the wet compression bandage, and carefully dry her arm before replacing it with another bandage. Her knees went weak every time she looked at her ruined arm and hand. At least the black compression garment she wore for twenty-three hours a day covered everything from her underarm to her fingertips. She had to wear it for the next year, maybe longer. It was meant to keep the scars from becoming thick and ropy, even uglier than they already were.

Her sister Jenna stroked her good arm, regaining her attention. She was seven years younger than Arianna, with big, earnest green eyes and shoulder-length auburn hair caught up in a messy ponytail. She hadn't taken the time to get dressed. She wore a yellow raincoat over her pajamas.

"I know you want to help, but there's at least a hundred people searching, with more arriving every minute," Jenna said, continuing to stroke Arianna's arm as though recognizing the panic she struggled to contain. "Please stay here. I'm worried about you. You're not completely recovered. You've already gotten soaked once. Your hair's still wet."

Blow-drying her hair was exhausting, not to mention a waste of time when she was just going to get it wet again. "Glamma's eighty. She's been out there in the dark, in the rain, for close to two hours." Feeling like curling in upon herself as the *what ifs* crowded her brain, Arianna wrapped her arm around her waist. It didn't help. "What if she went down to the docks? What if—"

"Stop torturing yourself. Mrs. Ranger said it wasn't raining when she dropped off Helen. Maybe she went for a walk and got caught in the rain. She probably found somewhere dry to wait out the storm. Even if your grandmother is having some memory problems, she's a smart, resourceful woman."

"She is, and she does like to walk at night. Maybe you're right. Maybe that's what happened." Looking around the packed kitchen, she had to cling to hope. Conversation hummed as members from the police and the fire department coordinated the search. People were on phones checking in with friends and family, asking them to be on the lookout for her grandmother, while others looked at a map that covered the kitchen table. "It's too warm in here. I can't take the noise. Would you mind bringing me a sandwich and a cup of tea in the solarium?"

"No. Of course not. Go sit. I'll be right there."

"Thank you." She placed her hand over her sister's and gave it a gentle squeeze, feeling guilty for what she planned to do. She didn't have a choice. If she didn't do something, the fear she could barely keep at bay would overtake her. "I'm glad you're here. I needed you tonight." It was the truth, and something she wanted her sister to know, especially after learning from Connor that Glamma had been keeping Jenna away. All her baby sister had ever wanted from Arianna and Serena was their love. For far too long, for silly reasons, they'd withheld it. Especially her. "I'm going to miss you when you move to DC." Jenna was leaving in the beginning of November to be with Logan.

Her sister gave her a small smile that didn't reach her eyes. "I don't know if I'm going. We'll talk about it another day."

Selfishly, she wanted her to stay. But Jenna was right. This wasn't the time to talk about it. Arianna nodded, attempted a smile, and then slipped out of the kitchen. With a glance over her shoulder, she made sure Jenna was heading for the older women doling out sandwiches at the island. Confident her sister would be occupied for at least five minutes, Arianna hurried to the front hall.

She opened the closet door, reached inside for two rain jackets, one for her and one for her grandmother, and then slipped on a pair of Glamma's gardening boots. To avoid getting caught, she planned to dress outside, so she tossed the rain jackets over her shoulder. Spotting an abandoned flashlight on the entryway table, she picked it up and stuck it between her teeth before opening the front door.

Doing her best to stay under the overhang and out of the rain, she placed the jackets and flashlight on the porch. Jenna was right; she couldn't afford to catch a chill. She had to stay as dry as possible, which meant she had to get rid of her sling. Other than to shower, she never took it off. Intellectually, she knew she didn't need the sling. It had become something of a security blanket, protecting her as much as her damaged arm.

Without her grandmother's help, she'd never get it untied, so she bowed her head, reaching back to curl her fingers around the knot. She tugged, but it didn't fit over her head. She tried to loosen the knot. With only one hand and her teeth, it was useless, and she didn't have time to waste. Bending her head once again, she tugged and pulled on the fabric, ripping out strands of hair as she did. Her neck hurt, and her arm cramped. She was sweating from the exertion, angry, frustrated tears welling in her eyes. She cursed Lorenzo and the sentimentality that had sent her back to her office that night. Then, with one last vicious yank, she pulled the fabric over her head. She dropped the sling on the porch, physically exhausted.

She stared down at the raincoats, not sure she had the energy to put them on, raising her gaze when lightning crackled and thunder boomed in the distance. Fog rolled up the road, ominous and eerie. She thought of her grandmother out there alone and reached for the jacket. Gritting her teeth, she pulled on one raincoat and then the other. She mostly used her good arm; her damaged arm hung lifeless at her side. Still, she'd moved it.

From within the house, someone called her name.

Grabbing the flashlight, she ran down the path and opened the front gate. She'd made it to the end of the street before Jenna called for her through the open door. Arianna was about to yell that she was fine when the flashlight she'd been sweeping over a front yard illuminated one of Daniel Gallagher's campaign signs. A sign that had been defaced with red spray paint.

The handsome older man now sported devil horns, a handlebar mustache, and a goatee in a vibrant shade of blood-red. Her grandmother often referred to the Gallagher men as blue-eyed devils, Arianna thought, feeling a surge of hope at what she prayed was her first clue to Helen's whereabouts. The house was only around the block from theirs, so she knew the yard had been searched, but she checked again. Deflated when she didn't find any sign of her grandmother, she continued along the sidewalk.

Four houses down, her spirits lifted. There was another defaced sign. Positive she was onto something, Arianna hunted for Daniel's campaign signs, thinking of them as bread crumbs that would eventually lead to her grandmother. Whenever she found a vandalized sign, she carefully checked the front and backyard, and when she didn't find her, she moved on to the next sign.

For every fifty of Daniel's signs, her grandmother was lucky to have one. Arianna felt sad on her behalf, guilty too. She'd played no part in her grandmother's campaign. In the beginning, she supposed she had an excuse. But she didn't for the past few weeks. Her flashlight swept over another front yard and another sign. There was a difference with this one—horns but no mustache or goatee. A white can with splotches of red gleamed at the base of the sign. Arianna's heart thudded with hope. She called to her grandmother as she raced to the back of the house, searching behind and under bushes, in a playhouse, in and around a shed.

She wasn't there, and there would be no more clues to follow. In desperation, Arianna ran around the house to the front door and knocked. She didn't know where else to look, what else to do. She was terrified that her worst fears, the ones she didn't dare acknowledge, would come true.

A man opened the door, clearly unhappy that a soaking-wet woman was pounding on his door in the middle of the night. "I'm sorry to wake you. My eighty-year-old grandmother has been missing for hours, and I think she might have been in your yard. Did you see her? Maybe bring her inside to get dry?" She said the last on a hopeful note.

"I saw her all right. She was spray-painting my sign. Told her I'd call the cops if she didn't stop."

"Thank God. Where is she?" She went on her tiptoes to look past him.

"Ya think I'd let some old lady who was defacing signs into my house? What do you take me for, lady? A moron?"

"No. You're not a moron. You're a sorry excuse for a human being. Don't you have any decency? She's eighty, and she has . . . She has dementia, and she's out there all alone in the rain because you couldn't show her some compassion."

"If the old lady has dementia, you shoulda put her in a home. Don't come around here blaming me because you lost your grandma. Now get out of here before I call the cops." He slammed the door in her face.

Arianna briefly closed her eyes. She'd been so caught up in her own pity party that she hadn't taken care of the only person who'd loved her enough to stick around.

"Where are you, Glamma? I know you're out here somewhere," she said, her throat raw from yelling Helen's name earlier. She shivered, and her teeth began to chatter. Now that she'd reached a dead end in her search, the adrenaline rush that had kept her from feeling the cold had faded.

Wrapping an arm around her waist in an effort to contain the body-racking shivers, she crossed the man's yard. She might not have found her grandmother, but she had been on the right track. No one knew Helen Fairchild better than she did. In many ways, she was more like her grandmother than she was like her mother. Beverly often said the same.

Arianna didn't want to think about her mother now. After finding out what she'd done, Arianna couldn't be in the same room with her. Still, as much as she wanted nothing to do with her mother, she would call her if she thought she could help find Glamma. But if Arianna couldn't think where her grandmother would have gone, her mother wouldn't have a clue. Arianna had barely finished the thought when it came to her: Tie the Knot.

If her grandmother had gotten herself turned around and her mind was turned around too, she'd head for the shop on Main Street. In her place, Arianna would do the same. Tie the Knot had been their passion, their joy. It was one of the reasons her grandmother was running for mayor.

Daniel Gallagher planned to bulldoze the remains of Tie the Knot and the other shops and allow a modern, eight-story-high office building to be built in place of the businesses they'd lost. Her grandmother wanted to rebuild the bridal shop. So it stood to reason that while spray-painting Daniel Gallagher's signs, she would have been thinking about Tie the Knot. And if dementia had stolen her present memories but had left the past intact, she'd remember the shop on Main Street. It had been her home as well as her business for decades.

From behind her came the smooth rumble of a powerful engine, its halogen lights cutting through the fog ahead of her. "Arianna," a deep voice called out to her.

She turned to see a black Porsche pull up along the sidewalk. The door opened, and Connor got out.

She sagged in relief. "I think I know—"

He grabbed her by the shoulders and shook her. "What were you thinking? Do you have any idea—" He swore and then crushed her against him, holding her so tight she could barely breathe.

She tipped her head back. "Connor, why are you—"

His mouth came down on hers in a punishing kiss, stealing her words and what was left of her breath. It had been years since he'd kissed her, but she still remembered the feel of his mouth on hers. His full, beautiful lips ravaged her, devoured her. He was bigger, stronger, more experienced than when they were together, yet there was something familiar about this kiss.

It reminded her of the last one they'd shared. A kiss of desperation and pain.

She squeezed her eyes shut. She'd been hurting so badly that night that his pain had barely registered. It did now. She didn't know why he was hurting or desperate or both right now, but she kissed him back. As though her response broke through to him, she felt his tension ease. He raised his hands, cupping the back of her head. His lips softened, gentled, lingered. Then, after one last touch of his mouth to hers, he slowly lifted his head, searching her eyes before stepping back. He took the flashlight from her and then took her hand, leading her to the other side of his car. He opened the passenger door.

She stared at him, dazed. "What was that about?"

Chapter Six

♥

Connor had thought he'd lost her. He'd been driving the streets of Harmony Harbor for more than an hour, searching for her. Other than the night at her hospital bedside, he'd never felt as helpless or as desperate as he had only moments ago.

His gaze moved from her hair plastered to her pale, wet face to her lips swollen from his kiss. They'd been pink seconds ago; now they were turning blue. He went to raise his fingers to gently rub his thumb over her mouth. Instead, he curled them around the doorframe.

He owed her an apology. He never should have grabbed her or kissed her like he had. There was no excuse. He didn't know how to explain what had come over him. Seeing her walking down the sidewalk, alive when he'd been picturing her dead…

There was a part of him that was furious at her for making him feel so deeply, so completely, while the other part of him was just so damn glad she was okay he'd wanted to pick her up and spin her around and shout it to the world. Instead he'd kissed the hell out of her.

Jaw clenched, he looked away. "The other day you told me you wished they would have let you die. I know how you feel about your grandmother. She's missing. I thought—" He returned his gaze to her. "Jenna said you were in bad shape. That you were blaming yourself. You said the same to me."

Her eyes widened. She knew what he'd been about to say. He didn't need to say the words out loud. She touched his arm. "I'm sorry I worried you. I should have waited until you got there. I wasn't thinking straight."

"Yeah, you should have waited," he said, anger winning out over relief. "Your lips are blue, and your teeth are chattering. Get in the car."

"I think Glamma might be at Tie the Knot," she said as she got inside, letting out a small moan of pleasure.

She'd made the same sound when he'd kissed her. She probably didn't remember. No doubt in shock. He still needed to apologize.

"Will you take me?" she asked.

If she only knew how much he wanted to. When he finally got past the innuendo, the context in which she asked the question managed to penetrate his desire and his anger. He silently cursed himself, nodded, and then closed the door.

He pulled out his phone from the pocket of his leather jacket as he rounded the car. Jenna picked up on the first ring. "I've got her. She's cold and wet but otherwise okay. She thinks Helen is at Tie the Knot. Can you pass me to my uncle? Thanks."

Within seconds, his uncle was on the line. "Hey,

Uncle Colin, has anyone searched the area around Tie the Knot? Arianna thinks Helen might be there. Yeah, I thought you would have. I think it'd be a good idea if they searched it again though." He opened the driver's door. "Okay. Good. Thanks. We'll be there within ten minutes," he said as he slid behind the wheel.

He took one look at Arianna and turned up the heat. "They've searched Main Street, but they're going back to take another look. There's a search party one block over, so they're sending them there now." He leaned over to adjust the vent so the hot air would blow directly on her.

"Thank you," she said, her teeth chattering uncontrollably now.

Anger whipped through him, and it was all he could do not to pull her into his arms. "Ten minutes. I got there ten minutes after you left," he gritted out.

She leaned her head back against the seat. "I'm sorry. I just couldn't stand around there doing nothing. I was going crazy."

"Ten. Minutes," he repeated, unable to help himself. He'd broken every posted speed limit to get to her only to find her gone and her sister as worried as he was. He pushed away the memory, wishing he could erase it, then reached for the bag on the back seat. "You're soaked through. I've got a thermal blanket and another jacket. Hot tea too."

Her chin went up. "Stop saying 'ten minutes' like it was seconds. Every minute feels like an hour right now. You have no idea what it felt like—"

"Yeah, I do." He placed the bag on his lap and pulled

out the thermos of tea first. He handed it to her. "Drink some. Then we'll get you out of the raincoat."

"The tea's fine. I'll be okay. Let's just go now."

"If you let me help you, it'll take less than a minute to get you out of your raincoat and into a warm jacket."

"I can do it by myself." She nodded at the steering wheel. "Drive."

"Fine." He put the car into gear and pulled away from the sidewalk. He felt her eyes on him. "I'm sorry I kissed you."

"Why did you?"

"I don't know, Arianna. Maybe because I thought we'd be pulling your dead body out of the ocean and was so damn glad to find you alive I kissed you to make sure you were real."

"I really am sorry, Connor."

Now she was just making him feel pathetic. "I wasn't the only one who was worried about you. So were Jenna and your friends. There are a lot of people in town who care about you, Arianna."

"Do you think you could maybe stop with the guilt trip? My grandmother is the one who is missing, not me. And whether you agree with what I did or not, I did something."

Now that his worry and anger had begun to subside, he could see her point. After weeks of hiding away in her room, it was actually a big deal that she'd gotten out there to search for her grandmother. He didn't realize how big a deal until he noticed she'd removed her sling. Head bent, she tugged on the snaps of her raincoat, muttering her frustration when they failed to open.

"You sure you don't want my help?"

"I'm not an invalid. I'm perfectly capable of undoing a couple of snaps, Connor," she said, sounding a little like the stubborn woman he remembered.

"No one would ever mistake you for anything other than capable, babe," he said, unable to keep the smile from his voice.

"Now you're just being condescending. And annoying." She made a ticked-off sound in her throat when she once again failed to open the snap.

He glanced at her with a grin. "Who's annoying, me or the snaps?" Then, keeping an eye on the road, he reached over and curled his fingers around the wet vinyl. "Hold the other side," he said, and then gave a firm pull. There was a satisfying *click, click, click* as the row of snaps opened…to reveal another raincoat underneath.

"Creative thinking," he said. "Too bad it didn't do a better job keeping you warm."

"It was for Glamma when I found her. All she has on is a silk blouse and a blazer. She'll be—"

He cut her off with a firm "okay," though he was beginning to worry that might not be the case. A couple hundred people had been searching for more than three hours with no sign of the woman. It was like she had vanished. "We're going to find her, Arianna."

"I thought I had," she said, holding up her good arm to him. "Can you pull, please?"

"What do you mean, you thought you'd found her?" he asked as he helped her out of the raincoat.

"You're my lawyer now, so anything I say falls under attorney-client privilege, doesn't it?"

"Seriously? You ask me not to say something, I keep it to myself. Whether I'm your lawyer or not." There might have been an edge to his voice. He didn't like that she didn't trust him not to say anything. There was also a possibility that he didn't want her thinking of him as only her lawyer. A really faint possibility, he told himself.

"I know, but you are a representative of the court. Doesn't that mean you have to report it if you hear about something illegal? Unless it somehow involves your client."

"We're all required to say something if we hear or see illegal activity. I'm not held to a higher standard just because I have a law degree."

"Oh, okay," she said, and then almost immediately shook her head. "It's probably best I don't tell you given your involvement in your uncle's campaign."

"My mother is my uncle's campaign manager, not me. She just uses me to do stuff that no one else wants to, like putting up the signs." He grinned at her. "Or replacing them when someone beats them up."

She made a face. "Or gets creative with red spray paint?"

"Yeah, how did you…?" He glanced at her. "Helen's the one who's been turning my uncle into the devil?"

She nodded. "I had a feeling it was her handiwork. Glamma always refers to your uncle as a blue-eyed devil, so I followed the signs. At the house just down from where you picked me up, the mustache and goatee were missing, and I found a can of red spray paint." She told him what happened when she knocked on the door. Connor planned to pay the guy a visit tomorrow.

"What made you think she'd go from there to Tie the Knot?" he asked as he turned onto Main Street. He felt Arianna stiffen beside him. "I'm not saying you're wrong. I just—" He caught a glimpse of her profile and immediately pulled into an empty parking spot alongside the curb. "I'm sorry. I should have warned you we were close. You haven't been on Main Street since the fire, have you?" Stupid question. Up until a couple days ago the woman hadn't been out of her house since she got home from the hospital.

"No. It's okay. I'll be okay. I just need a minute." She swallowed and then forced a tight smile that looked more like a grimace.

He lifted the blanket from his lap. "Lean forward." She did as he asked, and he wrapped it around her. "Drink the tea too. The sugar should help with the shakes."

Taking her in his arms and sharing his body heat would work better, but he didn't dare do so or even suggest it. He'd bulldozed through her boundaries when he'd pulled her into his arms and kissed her earlier. He wouldn't make the same mistake twice. For her sake and for his own.

Over the years he'd found himself thinking about their time together, especially when he'd see Arianna here in town or at an event in Boston. They'd traveled in the same social circle when she was married to Summers. She'd always been the most beautiful woman in the room, and he'd find himself remembering she'd once been his and how she'd felt in his arms and how her lips had felt under his. His memories hadn't done her justice. Her kiss had ignited a fiery flame, one that still burned bright inside him and showed no sign of dying down.

"Connor, I need to know if they found her," she whispered, focused on the thermos in her hand instead of the burned-out shells of the four businesses that had been caught up in Lorenzo Romano's madness. If it weren't for Connor's uncle and the men and women of the Harmony Harbor Fire Department, they might have lost an entire block. His cousin Liam, a firefighter with HHFD, had been the one to carry Arianna from the burning building.

"Stay here. No sense in you getting wet. I'll go talk to them," he said, even though he was fairly certain his uncle would have called by now if they'd found Helen.

Her bottom lip caught between her teeth, Arianna nodded. It was obvious her first sight of the blackened remains of Tie the Knot was doing a number on her.

"Hey"—he smoothed her damp hair from her face—"I can move the car to the side street if it would be easier for you."

"No. I need to do this. It's j-j-just—" She was shaking so hard her teeth were chattering.

"Okay, honey, I've got you." He drew her into his arms. "Nobody says you have to do this now. You've got enough going on without dealing with this too."

With her forehead pressed to his chest and her good hand clutching his shoulder, she shook her head. "I have to. I know she's here. I have to be here when they find her."

"I know you think she is, but she might not be. It doesn't mean anything if she isn't. It just means we keep looking."

"I do know. This is where I'd come. I need to do this now before I lose my nerve." She raised her gaze to his. "Don't let me go though. I don't think I can do it alone." She made a face. "I feel so weak asking you that."

"Join the club. How do you think I feel? What I went through was nothing compared to you, and look how I—"

"What do you mean?"

"About five minutes ago, when I grabbed you on the sidewalk and ravaged you with a kiss."

The corner of her mouth ticked up. "Ravaged?"

"Devoured you. Practically kissed your face off."

"Did it help?"

"God, yeah," he said without thinking, then looked down at her. "I still feel bad about it though. Weak, too."

"Maybe I should ravage you."

"If you think it will help, feel free to ravage me anytime."

All of a sudden her expression shuttered. "I'm sorry. I forgot you had a girlfriend." She drew away from him. "Apparently you forgot too."

"It's okay. You didn't do anything wrong. Brooklyn and I aren't seeing each other anymore."

"But I thought you were having dinner with her this evening."

"We did. We officially ended it tonight." It made it easier that his brothers had correctly guessed Brooklyn's reaction to him being unemployed. It had kind of surprised him, but he supposed it shouldn't have. She'd always liked the social perks and the status that came with his job, even more than he did. Still, it wasn't easy saying goodbye. For the most part, he'd really enjoyed being with her. Though he wouldn't miss their weekly dinner dates with Lyndsey and Tiff.

"So, do you think you can let me hold you without feeling guilty now?" He didn't add "kiss you." But the moment had passed, tension once more filling the Porsche as she glanced to where people milled around a police car.

"She's here. I know she is."

The scene told a different story. But he wasn't going to correct her. Even though it would be better if she saw the charred remains of what had been to her, her life, when she was better able to cope. Not on a night when someone she loved was missing.

"Why don't you let me go and check things out first?" He handed her the red plaid jacket she was struggling to grab from the backseat and then dug his phone from his pocket, handing it to her. "Call Jenna. She can fill you in on what's happening with the search while you wait. Hit last call," he said, knowing she'd have a hard time pressing the keys with one hand. "I won't be long."

She nodded without looking at him and brought the phone to her ear. He waited until she had Jenna on the other end before he closed the door. At least Arianna wouldn't feel like she was sitting in the car alone. She'd be able to avoid looking at the burned-out building for only so long.

He jogged across the rain-slicked street, spotting his cousin Aidan, a detective with the Harmony Harbor Police Department, in the middle of an angry mob. "There's nothing I can do about it, folks. It's for your own safety," his cousin told the crowd.

Now that he stood a few yards away from the burned-out buildings, Connor understood their frustration. The area was cordoned off with portable fencing to keep people out.

"Excuse me," Connor said as he made his way through the frustrated and muttering crowd to his cousin.

"Okay, don't you start yelling at me too," Aidan said when he reached him. "We can't let anyone in to search, Con. It wasn't safe before the rain, and it's less so now."

"What about search and rescue and the dogs? They're trained to work in less-than-ideal conditions."

His cousin looked around and then lowered his voice. "They're at the marina."

"That's not the news I wanted to hear," Connor said, glancing toward his car.

"They don't have anything definitive. An eyewitness thought they saw Helen trying to get in one of the boats docked at the marina."

"How long ago?"

"Within two hours of her going missing, I think."

"Doesn't fit." He told Aidan about the signs and the idiot who'd threatened to call the police.

"You're right. Timeline doesn't work, unless—"

"The older woman defacing the signs wasn't Helen after all," Connor said.

"I'll send an officer to the address with a photo of Helen to get a positive ID. Until then I don't feel comfortable pulling the team off the marina." His cousin lifted a flashlight and moved it over the charred remains of Tie the Knot. Several members of the disgruntled search party were doing the same. "We've seen nothing to indicate she's been here."

"What about radar that picks up heartbeats and breathing?" Connor asked, looking at the piles of debris.

"County applied for a FINDER device about six months ago. As far as I know, they haven't received either approval or a unit."

"Then we need the dogs." He saw the frustration on his cousin's face. "I get it, okay. There's not a chance in hell we're going to find her here. But for Arianna's sake, she has to see us actively search the area, including the fenced-off area. She believes her grandmother's—"

"I know you're behind this, and I'm not letting you get away with it," a man said, his angry voice loud enough that it drew Connor's attention. He was also intimately familiar with that voice. It belonged to his father, who was waving a piece of paper in his uncle Daniel's face, with Connor's mother looking on.

"What now?" Connor muttered.

"You don't know?"

"Know that our uncle is apparently dating my mother and my father is not only jealous but furious? Oh yeah, I got that."

"It's a little more than that now, Con. Uncle Sean got served with divorce papers an hour ago."

"She didn't?" He narrowed his eyes at his mother, who had a guilty look on her face. "She did. Dammit. Do me a favor and keep an eye on my car. If Arianna so much as opens the passenger door, call me," he said to his cousin, and then headed over to where his father, mother, and uncle stood before they drew everyone's attention, including the press. Across the road, a van with a local TV news station's logo emblazoned on the side pulled alongside the curb. Byron Harte, owner of the *Harmony Harbor Gazette*, was already standing by the fence a few yards away, speaking to one of the volunteers.

"Dad, quiet down or you'll find yourself the lead story on the morning news," Connor said as he came up behind his father. As soon as the words were out of his mouth, he wondered if that was exactly what his uncle Daniel had intended. Then again, no one could have predicted what had happened tonight.

"Listen to the lad. You're making a bloody fool of yourself holding on to a woman who no longer wants you," Daniel said.

His father responded with a low growl before lunging at his brother. Connor grabbed his dad around his waist, straining to hold him back. "You're playing into his hand, Dad. Calm the hell down." Where were his brothers when he freaking needed them?

As though Aidan had read his mind, he jogged over. "You two start something now, and I'm hauling you both to the station."

"Me? It's him who's acting the lunatic," Daniel said.

"Mom," Connor gritted out, straining to contain his

growling father. His mother blinked, looking like she was shocked by her husband's reaction.

"He's gone mad, he has. Put me down for one of those restraining—"

"All right, Uncle Daniel. Let's go," Aidan began, reaching for his uncle's arm, when a cry went up from near the fence.

"I saw someone!" a woman yelled.

Beams of light swept over the fenced-in area. "It's a woman," several people cried out.

Connor strained to see through the gloom to where they were pointing. They were right. It was a woman. A woman wearing the same jacket he'd handed to Arianna not five minutes ago.

"I told you to keep an eye on my car," he said to his cousin as he released his father to run to the fence.

"That's Arianna?" Aidan asked at the same time a beam of light shone on her face. "Damn. How did she get in there?"

Connor wasn't worried about that now. "Get the light out of her eyes! She can't see where she's stepping." He scanned the area to see how she'd gotten past them and located a gap in the fence. She must have squeezed through. He couldn't. "Arianna, get out of there now. It's dangerous. We're waiting for them to bring the dogs."

"She's here, Connor. I'm sure..." She cocked her head. "Glamma, is that you? Quiet. Everyone, quiet!" she shouted, and silence descended as the crowd strained to hear what she'd heard. Connor worried that maybe the stress of the night had gotten to her and this was nothing more than a woman's desperate attempt to deal with an untenable situation. "Glamma, call out to me so I know where you are." Arianna tried again, holding up a finger to silence the voices in the crowd.

Connor heard it then, a faint cry. "Aidan, call your dad and get everyone here five minutes ago."

"On their way."

"Arianna, did you hear that? Help is on the way. You need to get out of there—"

"No. I'm not leaving her under the—" She moved toward a pile of blackened debris.

"Lass, stop right where you are. Listen to me. I know what I'm talking about," his uncle said, coming to stand beside Connor. "The building, your business, it had a basement, did it?"

She nodded and then looked around as if just remembering she was standing on what had once been Tie the Knot. Connor's hands balled into fists as he silently prayed she held it together. For her own sake.

"Your granny must have fallen through the debris into the basement. You're a step away from doing the same, lass. Don't move." He turned. "Aidan, you got wire cutters in that cruiser of yours?" His cousin nodded. "Bring them to me, then. The lass isn't going to stay put for long, I can see it in her eyes."

Connor could feel it in her stance. He held his breath, releasing it slowly when she sank to the ground.

"Glamma, help is coming. Hang on a little longer, okay? Glamma, talk to me."

Aidan cut the padlock and pulled open the fence. "Everyone else, stay back."

"I'm going in," Connor said.

"I figured that. So am I."

"If you are, you'll both follow my lead." His uncle moved the beam of light over the ground. Connor still hadn't forgiven Daniel for what he'd pulled with his father, but he would be forever grateful that his expertise had saved Arianna from a fall. Within a couple yards of Arianna, Daniel stopped. "Okay, pay attention. Connor, stay to the right of the beam and make your way to the lass. Aidan, you move to the left of Connor." Once they moved to follow his direction, Daniel said, "Arianna, call to your granny. Get your granny to call to you."

"Glamma, we need to get a better idea of where you are. Call my name and keep calling."

Arianna smiled as Connor knelt by her side. Helen's voice was muffled, but she sounded strong. "I told you she was here."

"You always did have an annoying habit of being right. In this instance, I'm really, really glad you were." He drew her to his side and kissed her temple. "You did good, you stubborn woman." Then he let her go to start removing the charred wood, chunks of bricks, and what looked like paneling. She reached out to help, and he gave her a look. "I think you've done enough for one night."

His uncle crouched across from them, pointing out which piece to pull next. "Granny, can you hear me?"

"Granny," they heard Helen clearly mutter. "I'm no granny."

Daniel chuckled. "Helen, me love, it's your favorite opponent, Danny Boy. Can you tuck yourself away?

Pull something over your wee head so you don't get a knock on the noggin when we pull the last of the bits away."

"How in God's name you managed to get all those people to support you, I'll never know. You can't even speak proper English."

A wide smile lit up Arianna's face as she leaned into Connor. "I told you there was nothing wrong with her."

Chapter Seven

♥

Arianna woke to whispering in her grandmother's hospital room. Assuming the nurses were checking on Glamma, she pretended to be asleep. It was easy to do. She felt like she could sleep for a week after the drama and trauma of last night. She imagined Glamma felt the same.

They'd treated her for exposure and minor scrapes and bruises. She'd been lucky not to land on concrete or metal when she fell into the storage area, landing instead on scraps of wood. But while physically she was all right, Arianna worried about her mental state. It wasn't something they'd talked about yet. She'd wait until Glamma was released and in the comfort of her own home.

"Hi, Mrs. Fairchild. We didn't wake you, did we?"

"Who are you? What are you doing in my room?" her grandmother asked, sounding confused.

Behind her still-closed eyes, Arianna imagined the look the nurses must be exchanging. They'd been in and out of the room all night, so Glamma should recognize them or, at the very least, realize they were nurses by their uniform. The talk couldn't wait until they got home.

Arianna opened her eyes and then blinked in surprise before jumping out of the chair at the sight of a reporter and cameraman hovering over her grandmother. "Get out. Get out of here now!" she ordered, rushing to her grandmother's side to tug the curtain around the bed. There's nothing Glamma would hate more than people seeing her at less than her best.

"The primary is only three days away. Voters have a right to know if Mrs. Fairchild is bowing out of the race or not, don't you think?"

Arianna moved between the curtain and the reporter. "What I think is my grandmother has a right to her privacy. I won't tell you again. Get out. Both of you."

"But if you could just give us—"

"When my grandmother is ready to release a statement or give an interview, it will be to the *Harmony Harbor Gazette*." Arianna walked to the door and motioned for them to leave, pointedly ignoring the reporter when she said, "What do you think, Ms. Bell? Do you think your grandmother should remain in the race?"

Once they'd left the room, Arianna closed the door and then opened the privacy curtain. "I'm sorry, Glamma. I thought it was the nurses. Are you okay?"

"It doesn't matter. It's over. No one will vote for an old lady who gets lost in the rain and has to be rescued by her opponent. He's sure to win now. He'll paint himself a hero, and everyone will forget what's really at stake."

Arianna's eyes filled with tears. Her grandmother's dream had been as unfairly stolen from her as Arianna's had been from her. "It's okay, Glamma. We'll—"

Her grandmother raised a hand to her cheek, and then her eyes shot to Arianna. "Do you think the cameraman got any footage of me without my makeup on?"

"No. They weren't here long enough—"

"They were so. I woke up to them standing over my bed. Go. Track them down and take his tape. Have them sign something." She frantically waved Arianna off.

"I'll go. Just promise me you'll relax."

"I won't relax until I know I won't end up on the news looking like an eighty-year-old corpse."

Due to the crowded elevator stopping on every floor, dawdling visitors, and several people wanting to know about Glamma, all Arianna saw of the cameraman and reporter was the back end of their van leaving the parking lot. When she finally returned to Glamma's floor twenty minutes later, she stopped by the nurse's station to find out when her grandmother would be released.

"She's ready whenever you are. Mr. Gallagher took care of everything."

Of course he did, Arianna thought as she smiled her thanks at the nurse and walked to her grandmother's room. Instead of cursing Connor for interfering in their lives as she normally did, this time she welcomed it, relieved she wouldn't have to talk to her grandmother about her memory issues on her own. She smiled as she approached the open door and heard him talking to her grandmother, his voice soothing. He really was a sweet…Her eyes went wide as what he said, instead of how he said it, reached her ears.

"You don't have to give up on your dreams, Helen. Just like Tie the Knot, Arianna can fulfill them for you. All you have to do is tell your voters to write Arianna's name in place of yours on the ballot."

* * *

Arianna smelled doughnuts as soon as she left her bedroom. She followed the mouth-watering scent down the hall to the entryway, where Connor had just closed the front door while juggling a box and a lush floral arrangement of autumn orchids, orange berries, salmon, and cream-colored roses framed by ferns. No matter how pleasing to the eye and nose both the bouquet and the doughnuts were, neither compared to the decadently handsome man holding them.

A man she wasn't speaking to.

She lifted her chin and walked past him as if he didn't exist. He laughed. She clenched her teeth. He had some nerve finding her snit amusing after what he'd pulled. She wanted to kick him out, but it would be a waste of energy. Her grandmother had decided she loved him like a long-lost grandson. A sure sign the woman was losing her marbles like everyone said.

"Come on. It's been two days. You can't still be mad at me." He followed her into the kitchen. "I brought you your favorites—crullers and chocolate dip with sprinkles."

Her traitorous stomach growled. She walked to the

coffeepot and poured herself a cup with her good hand, pleased when she didn't spill a single drop. Pressing her lips together, she turned. Only to discover he was right behind her.

She looked up. He smiled down at her and took her cup. "Thanks."

He smelled as incredible as he looked, which may be why it took her a moment to react. When speech seemed beyond her, she drew a deep breath through her nose to illustrate to him just how ticked she was and belatedly realized what an idiotic idea that had been. Now his expensive cologne filled her senses. She was certain the perfumer must have overdosed that particular bottle with sex pheromones. It was the only explanation for why she had an almost uncontrollable desire to climb the man like he was a tree.

She managed an annoyed sound in her throat and turned back to the pot, pouring herself another cup. This time she spilled more than a drop. Frustrated, she slammed the pot back on the machine. A big hand appeared in her line of sight, offering her a cup.

"You drank out of it already," she said grumpily.

"So. My lips were on yours the other day and yours were on mine. What's the difference?"

"You are so annoying," she said, sighing when seconds later his hand reappeared with sheets of paper towel.

As she cleaned up the spill, he reached around her to pour himself another cup. "If I knew all it took to get you to talk to me was to give you my cup of coffee, I would have done it two days ago."

"It was *my* cup of coffee, not yours. And you're in my space." She edged around him and walked to the island where he'd left the doughnuts and flowers. No matter how mad she was at him, she couldn't leave the bouquet to wither and die. It was exquisite and obviously expensive. "There's a vase in the right-hand cupboard beside the stove."

Eyeing the box of doughnuts, she turned on the tap. She'd already blown her vow never to speak to Connor again, so she didn't see the point in denying herself some fried sugary goodness.

Connor nudged her aside with his hip, placing the vase under the running water. "Just so you know, the doughnuts are for you, but the flowers are for Glamma."

"She's not your grandmother," Arianna said through clenched teeth as she hip-checked him because she couldn't elbow him with her damaged arm. "Stop invading my space."

"First, your grandmother insisted I call her Glamma, and second"—he gave her a light hip-check back—"you're technically invading my space because I'm the one filling the vase." He held it up like it was evidence, turned off the tap, and then placed the glass container on the counter. "You mind getting me a pair of scissors?" He looked at her. "On second thought, I'm not sure I trust you around me with anything sharp, so just point me in the right direction."

"Proof you're as smart as everyone says you are." She pointed at the row of drawers to the right of the sink. "Second from the top."

He sighed. "Come on, give me a break. I was just trying to help. Helen was having a tough time facing the reality of the situation. She was depressed. All I did was make a suggestion that allowed her to hang on to her dream for a bit longer."

"It was her dream to be mayor, not mine."

"Honey, you're not going to win, so stop worrying about it. My uncle is twenty points ahead of Delaney Davis, the current mayor's communications officer, and she's his closest opponent. Helen only started her write-in campaign two days ago."

"Don't *honey* me. And she may only have started her write-in campaign two days ago, two minutes after you suggested it, but thanks to you and your father, we have had more momentum than any of the other candidates, including your uncle."

He winced. "Dad *has* gone a little overboard."

"You think? He took out full-page ads in the *Gazette*."

"Don't forget the billboard. But you know why he's—"

"Billboard?"

"You didn't know about that, did you?"

"Do I look like I did?"

"Nope. You don't sound like it either." He grimaced. "Sorry. I shouldn't tease you. But you're getting yourself worked up over nothing. Two days isn't enough time to change people's minds. People like and admire you, and they feel bad for what happened to you and to Helen, but admiration and sympathy will take you only so far. It's obvious to everyone that you don't want the job."

"That's not true. I pounded the pavement, knocked on doors, and said exactly what Glamma told me to."

Because as much as she hated to admit it, Connor had been right. Helen had perked up at his suggestion to put Arianna's name forward. Sometimes she seemed more excited and energized about Arianna running for mayor than she had been for herself. Arianna had a sneaking suspicion it was because, deep down, Helen had been worried about her ability to do the job with her memory blips.

Her grandmother no longer hid the fact she was having problems and talked about them openly. Arianna wished she wouldn't. It would be easier to pretend they'd be okay. Especially now that they didn't have to worry about the bank foreclosing on their home. Glamma's incident, as she liked to call it, had given Connor grounds to prove mental incompetency and build a solid case against the bank. He'd also filed the insurance claim yesterday. There wouldn't be much left once everything was paid off, but it would be enough to keep the creditors away, a roof over their heads, and food on the table.

"Okay, let me rephrase that—anyone who knows you." He stepped toward her and placed his hands on her shoulders. "Trust me, you have nothing to worry about. It'll all be over at ten tonight, and things will go back to normal."

He was right. The primary was today.

"It better," she said, ignoring the depressing weight that settled in her chest. As much as she didn't want to be in the mayoral race, she didn't know if she could take things going back to normal. The normal where she stayed in her pajamas and in her bedroom reading and streaming series TV and movies. A normal where Connor didn't stop by with doughnuts and flowers and to tease and hold her and make her believe life might one day be worth living again.

She didn't like the way his eyes narrowed as they searched her face. He saw too much, knew her too well. She stepped away from him, forcing a smile. "You'd better get those flowers in the vase before they wilt. Glamma will love them, by the way."

He opened the drawer. "Where is she?"

"Getting ready. She started an hour ago. We should make it to the polling station by eleven."

He laughed. "Babe, it's nine thirty. Dad's picking us up at ten."

"Don't tell me—he ordered a limo, didn't he?" When he began cutting the stem of an orchid without answering her, she said, "Connor."

"Make up your mind. Do you want to know or don't you?"

She sighed. "Glamma will be thrilled, but I can't imagine your uncle and mother will be." She inched the doughnut box toward her, hoping he wouldn't notice.

"No doubt Dad will get exactly the reaction from them that he's hoping for." He glanced at her with a grin. "Do you really think I can't see the box moving across the island? You can take one without admitting defeat, you know. We already made up. You forgave me."

"I wouldn't go that far," she said, pulling the box the rest of the way. She opened the lid, practically drooling as she lifted out a honey cruller. Raising it to her mouth, she closed her eyes in anticipation of her first bite. The doughnut disappeared from her fingers. Her eyes snapped open. "Connor!"

"What? It was a peace offering, and you just said you don't forgive me." He took a bite of the cruller. She couldn't look away. It shouldn't be sexy, but it was. She was jealous of the doughnut. Connor's lips curved as he finished the cruller, put a finger in his mouth and then slowly withdrew it only to do the same to the next. She lifted her gaze to his, saw a glint of amusement and something more, desire and heat.

Did he see the same emotions reflected in her eyes? The feelings were so strong she didn't know how he'd not notice.

"Arianna," he said, the need she saw in his eyes evident in the deep, seductive rumble of his voice.

No matter how much she wanted to be seduced by him in that moment, she couldn't allow him to get close to her. If she did, she wouldn't have the strength to push him away. She'd fall for him. She was halfway there. But her heart was stitched together with the finest of threads. She'd never survive another loss.

If Connor managed to do the impossible and convince her to give them a chance, she'd have no choice but to tell him why she'd gone back to her office the night of the fire. He'd never be able to forgive her once he knew. She couldn't bear to see hate and condemnation in his eyes when he looked at her.

"I can't," she blurted, and stepped back.

She saw a touch of hurt in his expression before he smoothed it away. "Sure you can. Say, 'Connor, I forgive you. I know you were just trying to help,'" he said, pretending he didn't know she'd been responding to the want and need in his eyes or her own desire. He reached into the box and held up a chocolate-dipped doughnut with sprinkles.

"I forgive you. Despite your annoying habit of thinking you know what's best for everyone, your heart is in the right place." She smiled and reached for the doughnut.

He held it away from her. "Other hand."

"That's exactly what I'm talking about!"

"Yeah, but like you said, my heart's in the right place. The only way you're going to regain the use of your hand is if you use it." He waved the doughnut at her. "Come on, you can do it. I know you can."

With her lips pressed tightly together, she held his gaze, and while doing so, she reached into the doughnut box and pulled out another cruller. "You have no idea what I can and can't do," she said, taking a ginormous bite of the doughnut.

"You're as stubborn as you always were. Sneaky too." He scowled and took a bite of the chocolate-dipped doughnut. "Umm, so good. You have no idea what you're missing." His reflexes were quicker, and he snagged the last two chocolate-dipped doughnuts from the box. "You might have had a chance if you'd used both hands." He waggled his eyebrows.

"You're as obnoxious as you always were. Controlling and bossy too."

"The two of you sound like children," her grandmother said as she strolled into the kitchen in her bathrobe. "Have you seen my cigarettes?"

"No, I haven't, Glamma."

Connor raised an eyebrow as if to say Arianna was a hypocrite. No longer able to pretend Helen didn't have issues with her memory, Arianna had decided to take her grandmother's health in hand. Last night, just as Arianna had been throwing out Helen's cigarettes, Connor had walked into the kitchen. Arianna didn't care. Cigarettes depleted oxygen to the brain, and Glamma's brain needed all the oxygen it could get. After doing a little research online, Arianna discovered that video games, exercise, and a Mediterranean diet had proven beneficial. The next step was to get Glamma to a doctor to see if medication would help. So far she'd refused to go.

Connor would no doubt say she and her grandmother were two of a kind. He'd be right, with one small and significant difference. Her grandmother was losing her mind; Arianna wasn't.

She ignored him and returned her attention to her grandmother, who had her face in the flowers. "Connor brought you the flowers, Glamma. Would you like to take them to your room? That way you can enjoy them while you put on your Primary-Day suit. You know, the one we picked out last night? It should be lying on your chair, with your shoes and accessories."

"I'm not deaf or slow, Arianna." Glamma rolled her eyes and said to Connor, "She thinks I've forgotten it's the primary. She lays out my clothes like I'm a toddler now. Next she'll be mashing my food. I wouldn't be surprised if she threw out my cigarettes." She stretched up on her toes to kiss Connor's cheek. "They're beautiful, my boy. Thank you."

"Beautiful flowers for a beautiful lady. And don't be upset with Arianna. She's just trying to help. She has a good heart."

Arianna rolled her eyes at his attempt to make his point.

"You two have the eye roll down to a science." He laughed before saying to her grandmother, "I don't want to rush you, Helen, but—"

"Glamma," her grandmother corrected.

With an *I told you so* look at Arianna, Connor said, "The limo will be here to pick us up in twenty minutes, Glamma."

"Why in heaven's name didn't you tell me earlier? Arianna, wipe the sugar off your face and get dressed. Put some makeup on while you're at it. You look like death."

"She looks beautiful."

"You don't have to defend me," Arianna said, embarrassment putting a bite in her voice. "What's wrong with what I'm wearing, Glamma? This is a perfectly lovely black suit."

"For an eighty-year-old going to a funeral. And don't bother denying it. I wore that suit to the last funeral, and you pilfered it from my closet."

"I borrowed it."

"Because all you've got is pajamas and loungewear. I have a Chanel and a Carolina Herrera that would be beautiful on you. They just need to be taken in. There's a sewing machine in the back of my closet. It'll take you no time at all."

Arianna turned on Connor. "You're behind this,

aren't you? You've gotten Glamma on board with your plan to force me to use my hand. Well, I have news for both of you. It won't work!" She reached for the coffee mug, and it slipped from her useless grip to smash on the floor. She didn't look at either of them as she strode from the room. "I'm not up to going out today."

She hadn't been in her room more than five minutes when there was a knock on the door. "Arianna, can I talk to you for a minute?"

"Go ahead." She lay curled on her right side. He could talk all he wanted. It didn't mean she'd listen.

The door opened.

"I didn't say to come in." She closed her eyes.

"I asked if I could talk to you. You clearly said go ahead."

"I meant through the door." The mattress dipped. She smelled doughnuts and fresh coffee. "Say what you came to say, Connor."

"Can you look at me, please?"

No. It was bad enough she could smell him, hear him, feel him. It didn't seem to matter how mad she was at him; his presence had the power to make her ignore the voice of reason in her head. The voice that said no one was as dangerous to her broken heart as the man who'd just wrapped his big hand gently around her smaller one. "Helen told me why she wants you to get better, Arianna. It has nothing to do with me. I never said anything to her about getting you to use your hand."

"She never mentioned it before now. You were at Mrs. Ranger's last week. You heard her say I was a crip—"

He placed a finger on her lips. "Don't. Don't ever let me hear you refer to yourself as that."

Whether she said it or not didn't make it any less true. She murmured "fine" against his finger, knowing he wouldn't remove it otherwise or he'd just argue with her. As she well knew, the man was very good at arguing and making his case. Her ex used to say Connor was the best fixer in the business. He'd certainly fixed her, legally speaking.

Connor removed his finger from her lips when she opened her eyes. Two chocolate-dipped doughnuts with sprinkles and a coffee mug sat on her bedside table. She kept her gaze there instead of on him when she asked, "So if it wasn't you, why does she all of a sudden want me to get better?"

His fingers found hers again. She looked down at their joined hands and then lifted her gaze to his face.

"Never mind. I don't want to know." She didn't want him to say the words out loud. She knew the answer by the sympathy in his eyes. It was only a matter of time before Arianna would be all alone.

"You should come. Wear what you have on. There's nothing wrong with it."

"She's right. I look like an eighty-year-old going to a funeral." She slid her hand from his and awkwardly maneuvered herself into an upright position.

"I wouldn't say that. More like a sixty-year-old going to a funeral. An extremely beautiful sixty-year-old."

"You Gallaghers should bottle your charm and sell it. You'd make a fortune."

"Somehow, I don't think you meant that as a compliment," he said as he pulled his phone from the pocket of his black suit coat. "I called the new shop in town, Merci Beaucoup. They've sent me photos of everything they have in a size four. Do you want to look at them?"

Trust Connor to know she wouldn't miss accompanying her grandmother to the polling station. "Whatever you choose will be fine," Arianna said, picking up a doughnut.

She wasn't overly concerned about letting him choose her outfit. He had great taste—he always had. He liked clothes, and he wore them extremely well, as evidenced by his black suit, dove-gray shirt, and steel-gray tie.

Connor turned the phone to her. It was a photo of a mauve dress with leather piping. There was just one problem. The sleeves were three-quarter length. As though Connor knew what she was about to say, he said, "It's cool enough you can wear one of those." He pointed to the wall to the right of the dress, where several styles of shawls and scarves were displayed. "Do you need shoes or boots?"

"Boots," she said, then thought to ask, "Will they put it on account?"

He ignored her as his fingers worked the phone. He went back and forth with whoever was on the other end and then stopped typing, shoving the phone in his pocket. "They're having everything sent over. Shouldn't take more than twenty minutes."

It was closer to forty, and Arianna knew why as soon as she opened the door. It looked like they were delivering the entire store, or at least everything they had in her size. "I'm sorry. There's been a mistake. I only needed—"

Connor nudged Arianna out of the way. "Thanks. I appreciate you taking care of everything." He grabbed six bags from one of the women, put them down in the entryway, and retrieved the rest from a cheerful redhead, who waved off the generous tip Connor tried to hand her.

"No, no. It was our pleasure to deliver everything. Call us anytime you need anything. We really appreciated the business." She smiled at Arianna. "Good luck today. We're all voting for you."

Despite feeling like she was going to throw up, Arianna managed a smile. "Thank you. That's very kind of you." As soon as the door closed, she pushed Connor's shoulder. "You said no one was going to vote for me!"

"No. I said—"

"*Don't worry, honey. You're not going to win,*" she mimicked. "*Sympathy and admiration will only get you so far. They know you don't really want the job.*" She pointed at the door. "She seems to think I do."

He laughed as he started toward her room, loaded down with bags. "Wow. You were actually listening to me. And they're only voting for you because you bought a crapload of clothes."

"No. You bought a crapload of clothes. I was just buying a dress and boots. What were you thinking, Connor? I can't afford all of this."

"You lost everything you owned in the fire. I've already forwarded the receipt to the insurance company. It's handled. Don't worry about it."

"But that's a lot of inventory to wait for the insurance company to pay." She looked at his face. "You paid for it, didn't you?"

He glanced at his watch. "Dad will be pulling up to the house any minute. Get moving, babe."

"Don't think you've heard the end of this, *babe*," she said before he practically shoved her into her bedroom and shut the door in her face.

Chapter Eight

♥

Arianna decided the one good thing about losing two dress sizes was that she didn't have to worry about wearing a bra. Still, she adjusted the shawl to cover her chest before opening the door to her bedroom.

"Hey, I was just... Wow. You look amazing," Connor said as she stepped into the hall. The appreciative gleam in his eyes made her believe she looked okay. Admittedly, it was hard to tell with him. He always seemed to look at her that way. Even the other night when she must have looked like a drowned cat.

"Thank you. Sorry to keep everyone waiting."

"No problem. They left for the polling station already." He gestured for her to go ahead of him. "Actually, I should rephrase that. They've gone ahead to not only one polling station, but all six. Dad plans to do some polling of his own, get a feel for how it's going. Just in case you need to start thinking of an acceptance speech."

"That's not the least bit funny."

"Sorry. If you want, I'll vote for my uncle."

She turned as she reached the entryway. "You can't vote. You don't live here."

"Actually, I do. It's been almost a week since I moved into the cottage beside my brother's place. I registered to vote a few days ago."

Her heart beat a little too fast. "Why did you move here?" *Please, please don't let it be because of me.* She couldn't take the pressure. It didn't matter how much she liked having him around—for the most part at least. She wasn't particularly pleased with him for suggesting the write-in campaign or trying to get her to use her hand. But there were as many positives as there were negatives to him living in town. Although the negatives outweighed the doughnuts, the support for her and her grandmother, and the feeling of safety and comfort from knowing he was a phone call away.

Once again she saw something that resembled hurt cross his face. It was like he could read her mind. Thinking of everything that had been going on in her brain lately, she really hoped that wasn't the case.

He held open the door. "We should get going."

"Please don't be upset. It's not that I don't like having you around. I do. I really do. But if you've moved back to Harmony Harbor for me, you should know that's not going to happen. It can't. I won't let it, Connor. I'm not ready for a relationship. I don't think I ever will be. So if that's what you're hoping for, you're wasting your time."

"You may not have noticed, but my parents are in the middle of getting a divorce, instigated, my brothers and I believe, by my uncle. We're trying to stop that from happening or, at the very least, make sure the entire Gallagher family doesn't get drawn into the fight."

"You could have interrupted me, you know."

He lifted a shoulder, closing the door behind them. He fit the key in the lock. "Seemed like something you needed to get off your chest."

"Yes, but...I'm sorry about your family. I'm sure it's a difficult time for all of you. You and your dad helping with my grandmother's campaign can only be making it worse. Come tomorrow, you'll at least have that off your plate. Things can go back to normal."

But twenty minutes later, after casting their votes at the polling station—Arianna voted for her grandmother; Conner wouldn't say who he voted for—they stepped out of Harmony Harbor Elementary and into the bright autumn sunshine. A black stretch limo pulled up. Her grandmother was out of the car before the driver got around to her side. Connor's father followed behind Glamma. At the sight of their wide smiles, Arianna felt faint.

"You've got the primary in the bag, darling."

"You're grandmother's right, Arianna. Every person we talked to said they were writing you in on the ballot."

Connor leaned down to whisper in her ear, "Breathe, honey. Let them have their moment in the sun. No one ever tells anyone who they're really voting for. Besides, they've been out there for less than an hour. No way is that a big enough sample for them to make a prediction."

Ten hours later, Arianna discovered Sean and Helen were right, while Connor was very, very wrong.

* * *

Colleen sat with Simon tucked in beside her on the brown leather wingback chair by the fire in what she referred to as the manor's great room. The rest of the family (guests too) referred to it as the lobby. It's where they had gathered tonight to watch the results come in for the primary election and to celebrate Daniel's win. His face had been a picture when they'd learned Arianna was less than forty-three votes behind him. The results had been so close that Sean had asked for a recount in one of the districts. Still, it seemed likely they would be pitted against each other in the race for mayor. The new numbers were promised at eleven.

Daniel looked calm as you please sitting beside Maura, watching himself talking to the reporter on the TV, chuckling a little at a quip he'd made. Colleen could see through him though. All you had to do was look in his eyes to know that he wasn't happy about the turn of events.

As far as she knew, he didn't have anything against Arianna. His problem was with her self-appointed campaign manager—his brother, Sean. Which meant it would soon become a problem for all of them. Already the fault lines were appearing in the family; the younger generation sneaking over to the Salty Dog for Arianna's after-party was a prime example.

Daniel had insisted they hold his party here so he could count the hotel guests as attendees. Although his plan probably hadn't gone as well as he expected. Tuesdays weren't busy at the manor. Jasper was working the bar, as they were short staffed, and a handful of guests were seated on barstools, uninterested in the evening news or the family gathered around the stone fireplace and TV. All except one, who appeared riveted by the whole affair.

The lass appeared to be in her thirties, a beauty with short dark hair and luminous blue eyes. She'd arrived at the manor this morning. There was something about the girl that seemed familiar. She wasn't sure why. The staff said she wasn't from around here. She had her own plane and flew private charters. Supposedly Sophie, the manager of the manor and Colleen's great-grandson Liam's wife, was meeting with the woman on the morrow. Colleen thought that a grand idea. It would provide a way for them to ferry the moneyed crowd to and from the manor, a new tour for the guests.

"You hear that? Even the reporter thinks it's bollocks that my brother is supporting someone other than me," Daniel blustered.

"Watch your language, darling," Kitty said to her son, patting his hand. "Don't take it personally. Your brother has always championed the underdog."

"Don't take it personally? Are you daft? Daniel's sitting here bold as brass with his arm around his brother's wife," Colleen said with feeling.

"There he is, the turncoat. Grinning like a fool with his arm around the lass." Daniel gestured at the screen.

Sean was indeed grinning on the television, but he looked far from a fool. He looked happier than Colleen had seen him in months. As handsome as Daniel, Sean wore his distinguished mane of silver hair brushed back from his face, his blue eyes bright and teeth ultrawhite. He had a smooth and polished look about him, whereas Daniel was more rough-and-tumble. And while Daniel was a neophyte in the game of politics, Sean was a dab hand.

He'd spent the majority of his married life in the political arena, his last years spent as governor before he returned to practicing law. Looking at him now, smiling on the big screen with his arm around Arianna's shoulders, Colleen wondered if he missed it. His wife certainly had. Maura had jumped at the chance to head up Daniel's campaign. Then again, maybe it was love for the man and not politics that was behind her decision to remain in Harmony Harbor.

Daniel leaned forward, elbows on his knees, eyeing the scene unfolding on the screen.

"Oh, ho, there may be more to this than meets the eye. My brother appears quite taken with the lass. She is a beauty. I'll give him that."

"Don't be ridiculous, Daniel. Arianna is young enough to be his daughter. Besides, Connor clearly has feelings for her," Maura said, obviously perturbed at Daniel's assertion.

Colleen smiled, pleased with her granddaughter-in-law's jealous display. Maybe Maura's decision to remain at the manor had to do with politics after all. But that wasn't all that made Colleen happy. It was seeing Arianna and Connor on the screen. She'd known almost from the first moment she'd seen Arianna and Connor together that the young couple were meant to be. And for almost two decades, Colleen had lived with the regret that her meddling in Arianna's father and Jenna's mother's affair had most likely played a role in Arianna breaking Connor's heart. By the time Colleen had learned the reason for her great-grandson's hangdog expression, it had been too late for her to get involved. Arianna had left Harmony Harbor to study design in California.

"Another turncoat, just like his father," Daniel grumbled.

"Do not speak about my son that way, Daniel. He was aboveboard with you from the very start. He told you exactly what he planned to do and why. He's a good boy."

"Well done, Maura. You stick up for your son." He'd be glad to hear it, Colleen thought. Growing up, Connor had been overshadowed by his brothers and his parents' political aspirations. She'd never understood why Sean and Maura had pinned their hopes on Logan and then Michael following in their father's footsteps. It had always been clear to her that Connor was more suited to the life than both his brothers combined.

"Maura's right, Daniel. And I for one am very proud of both my son and my grandson. I think it's marvelous what they've done for Helen and Arianna. After all they've been through, it's about time they have something to celebrate," Kitty said, smiling at the television when a cheer went up from the crowd gathered at the Salty Dog.

Colleen chuckled. Kitty never failed to surprise her.

"Well, going by the look of the lass"—Daniel pointed at Arianna, who was having a difficult time keeping a smile on her pale face—"she'll be bowing out of the race before the week is out."

Sadly, Colleen thought he might be right. Especially when Arianna pulled away from Sean and disappeared from view.

"It looks like they've received the final results," Maura said, pointing at the TV.

On the screen, Sean held up his phone and said to the reporter and the crowd at the Salty Dog, "We just got word that, after the recount, Delaney Davis finished four hundred and seventy-three votes behind Daniel Gallagher, with Arianna pulling ahead of Daniel by five votes." A cheer went up in the pub at the news. Sean waited for the crowd to quiet down before saying, "You all know what a difficult time Arianna has had of late, so I'm sure you understand she's overwhelmed—"

Helen leaned in and grabbed the microphone. "Arianna's overwhelmed with gratitude and asked me to thank you all from the bottom of her heart. Over the next few weeks, she plans to stop at every business and residence in town to personally thank you and share with you her vision for Harmony Harbor's future. You've all been there for us. Now we'll be there for all of you. Fighting—"

"Thank you." The reporter smiled tightly and wrestled the microphone from Helen. "Your Excellency—"

"Please, just call me Sean. I haven't been governor for years."

Daniel snorted as he brought his phone to his ear. No doubt to find out if the recount really had pushed the vote in Arianna's favor.

The reporter fluffed her hair and gave Colleen's grandson a winning smile. "All right, Sean. I'm sure our viewers would like to know why it is you're not supporting your brother in the mayoral race and your wife is."

Connor intervened, drawing the mic his way. "It's pretty simple and not nearly as controversial as people might think. My father's soon-to-be-daughter-in-law is Arianna's sister. In our eyes, that makes Arianna family too, and her vision for Harmony Harbor's waterfront and Main Street aligns with my father's. Besides that, after forty years of marriage, my parents like to spice things up every now and again with a little competition." He winked at the reporter. "I guess I was wrong. There might be something a bit salacious to it after all. What do you say, Dad? Do you want to share what the winner gets?"

"You know me, son. I'll never tell." Sean chuckled. "But, folks, the results tonight proved one thing. Every vote counts, and Arianna and Helen will be counting on you on November sixth. Drinks are on me, Shay darlin'!"

"Well played, Connor my boy. Well played." Colleen nudged Simon. "If anyone can beat Daniel at his own game, it's Connor. This may not turn out to be the disaster I had imagined. Maybe this election is just what's needed to get Connor and Arianna back together and to do the same for Sean and Maura."

Daniel, who was still on the phone, picked up the remote and turned off the television. Kitty and Maura said their good nights and then headed for their rooms.

Looking dejected, Daniel put his phone in his pocket.

The young pilot who'd captured Colleen's attention earlier walked over. "You look like you could use this," she said, handing Daniel a beer.

He straightened on the couch, flashing the girl a weak version of his usual roguish grin as he accepted the bottle. He was feeling left out and alone, and Colleen felt a twinge of sympathy for him. She wasn't happy with how he was behaving, neither him nor Maura, but she at least had an idea about what motivated her granddaughter-in-law.

Maura had arrived at the manor back in February a changed woman. Looking your own mortality in the face could do that to a person. All she'd cared about at the time was ensuring her sons were happily married and settled before she died. But Colleen had also seen signs that Sean had become complacent about his marriage and that Maura missed the life they used to have. As for Daniel, she had no idea what had set him on this course or what had happened to his own marriage and his life in Ireland.

The girl took a seat on the ledge of the fireplace. She wore a cream cable-knit sweater with jeans and short black boots. She had an interesting way about her. She seemed confident and aware of her surroundings. "Theia Lawson," she said in a low, smoky voice, offering Daniel her hand.

"Theia, Goddess of Light. Your parents named you well. Daniel Gallagher." He gave her hand a brief shake. "And as lovely as you are and as much as I hate to admit it, you're too young for me, lass."

Her laugh was as husky as her voice and caused several male heads to turn their way. "I'm glad to hear that, Daniel. I'm sure Mr. Elliot will be too."

Daniel stiffened and straightened on the couch, casting a nervous look around. He lowered his voice. "Is it *Caine* Elliot you'd be referring to?"

"Aye," she said, laying on the Irish, "it is indeed."

"You tell him I'll have no problem beating the Bell lass."

"Mr. Elliot has sent me to ensure that you don't."

"You work for the Wicklow Group, then?"

If Colleen's heart had been beating, it would have stopped. She'd thought Daniel slick as a snake-oil salesman with the gift of gab, a man of questionable moral character because he'd go after his own brother's wife, but never in her wildest dreams would she peg him as a traitor. Yet that's exactly what he was. The Wicklow Group was the corporation trying to buy the estate out from under them.

Chapter Nine

♥

The morning after the primary, Connor sat in his Porsche just down from Arianna's house having an imaginary conversation with her in his head. Of course he was winning his argument as to why she should stop giving him the silent treatment because arguing was what he did for a living, a lucrative living. But she blamed him that she'd ended up in the race for mayor, for promising her she didn't stand a chance in the primary when she obviously did. And no matter how good he was at presenting a compelling argument in the courtroom, Arianna was an expert at the silent treatment, the cold shoulder, and the glacial stare. She should be. She'd been practicing on him for years.

Which meant he should be used to it by now and should just go with the flow. Play it cool and give her some space. Obviously parking two doors down from her place at nine in the morning didn't equate to giving her space and playing it cool. He was disappointed in himself. Since when did he crowd a woman? Never, that's when. He wasn't that guy.

"Just a purr, baby, not a roar," he told the Porsche's engine as he pressed the button, fighting the urge to floor it and get rid of some of the pent-up tension he'd been carrying around from the moment it became clear Arianna was going to be a contender for mayor. The last thing he wanted was her to look out the window and see him sitting there. Stalker much?

He slowly drove up the road, unable to resist looking at her house in the rearview mirror, wondering what she was doing. The word *loser* popped into his head, and he crushed it, even though yeah, he might be feeling a little like the teenager she'd dumped almost two decades before.

"You need to get a life," he muttered increasing the volume on the radio. He felt better at the reminder. The only reason he was obsessing about Arianna was because he didn't have enough to occupy his mind. He was bored.

He called Mike. "Hey, bro, you wanna hit the links? It's going to be a beauty of a day." Connor loved to golf any time of year, but fall was his favorite.

"Some of us have to work for a living, Con."

"How about this? I'll handle a couple client meetings for you, and then we can get in a round before the end of the day."

"You need to get back to work. Call a meeting with the partners."

No matter how much he wanted to, Connor couldn't cave. It was the principle of the matter. He'd been unfairly treated. He'd worked his ass off for the firm, and yes, indirectly it was for himself, but when push came to shove, they hadn't stood by him. They'd sold him out for Summers.

"No. If they want me back, they'll call." They should have called by now. "I'll set up a meet with Steve." He was a big-deal headhunter who'd reached out as soon as word had hit the street that Connor had been fired. It wasn't the first time they'd talked. Steve had tried to bring Connor over to their major competitor years before. If they were still interested and the compensation package was where it should be, Connor would take the meet.

"Good. Just don't be surprised if the interest has cooled a bit, okay?" Mike said.

"What are you talking about?"

His brother's voice was muffled as he talked to someone, someone who sounded like Mike's soon-to-be-wife, Shay. Shay was a private investigator who'd done work for Connor in the past. There was no one better. Which made Connor nervous, because obviously Shay had been the one to convey the reason to his brother. Information they weren't sure they should share with him, as evidenced by the muffled conversation.

"Hello?"

"Sorry. I just wanted to make sure Shay was good with me telling you. Your firm called her on Monday to do some investigative work for them. While she was there, several people came to talk to her. People who care about you. They're upset about the way you've been treated. She's got a bunch of business cards for you from paralegals and admin assistants who intimated they'd hand in their notice that day if you'd take them on."

"That's nice to hear." Was he surprised? No. He knew how the majority of the employees at the firm felt about him. He might be a driven workaholic with a healthy ego, but he made sure everyone was treated with respect and their work acknowledged and appreciated, from the support staff to the cleaning crew. "But obviously there's more."

There was a *click*. "I've got you on speaker."

Shay's voice came over the line. "Hey, Connor, sorry to be the bearer of bad news. I would have told you as soon as I heard, but I wanted to check out the rumors first."

He pulled to the side of the road. "And…?"

"They weren't exaggerating. Because you didn't fold and the partners were unable to deliver on their promise to Summers, which was you, he and his family are actively in talks with other firms. Their one caveat is that you don't work there."

They were blackballing him. Now it made sense why he hadn't heard from any of the partners. They blamed him. Come to think of it, he hadn't heard from Steve for a couple of weeks either. A little less than a month ago, he'd been calling Connor practically every day.

"Looks like I might be coming to work with you after all, Mike. Unless you don't want me anymore. Which, bro, I'd totally understand," he said, keeping his voice light and jokey. He didn't want them to guess how he was feeling right now.

"Don't joke about this. It's serious. You, me, and Dad will sit down and talk it through tonight. Figure out how you want to move forward and what your options are. Give Steve a call and get the lay of the land."

"Look, don't worry about me. Up until now I hadn't realized I had a problem." Because for the past eight weeks he'd been preoccupied with thoughts of Arianna. Ever since the night he'd stood by her bed at the hospital, he hadn't been able to get her out of his head. "Now that I know I do, I'll take care of it."

"What are you going to do?" Mike asked.

"You sound nervous, baby brother."

"Only because I know you so well. You're going after him where it hurts, aren't you?"

"Oh yeah. Shay, if you've got some time, I've got a job for you."

"I figured you might. I've already opened a file on Summers and his wife. It seems lawyers keep quitting on her and someone is spreading pretty nasty rumors about her."

"Summers is a real piece of work." And Connor had represented him against Arianna. The thought made him sick. "I'll reach out to the wife today."

"We have an appointment with her tomorrow at eleven," Shay informed him.

Connor shook his head with a smile. "Lady, you are good. If you weren't marrying my brother, I'd propose to you right now." He waited for a reaction from Mike, but all he heard were muffled noises, something falling on the floor, and then some breathless laughter. "Oh, come on, are you two making out?"

"No. I just dropped my phone," Shay said, then under her breath, "Michael."

"Can you keep your hands off her for five minutes, baby brother? We were having a serious conversation."

"You were before—"

Shay cut off his brother. "I'm sure Summers has a tail on Danica, so I've arranged to pick her up at ten. I'll lose the tail and meet you here by eleven. That way Summers will have no idea what's coming his way."

"Sounds great. Send me what you've got so far, and I'll reach out to her attorneys."

"Will do. And just some food for thought: I think the three of us would make a pretty good team."

"I don't know, Shay. Watching my brother moon over you, when he isn't making out with you, might be hard to take."

"You're just jealous. If Arianna gave you the green light, you'd be—" his brother began before Connor cut him off.

"Hanging up now," he said, resting his head against the seat. And to think he'd called his brother for a simple game of golf. Connor needed this though. Already he felt more energized than he had in the past several weeks. This would solve his Arianna problem. He knew himself. If he wasn't busy, he'd have a hard time giving her space.

Even though he thought space was the last thing she needed. Somehow, he had to convince her that winning a spot in the mayoral race was the best thing that could have happened to her. They weren't much different really. Both of them had always been driven and ambitious. They were traits they'd admired in each other. He couldn't stand the thought of her retreating to her bedroom like she had before.

He shoved his fingers through his hair. Obviously, he'd need a lot more than one client to keep his mind off Arianna. It was irritating, maybe even a little scary, how quickly she'd become a part of his life again. She probably had no idea how often he thought about her in a day.

And as much as he'd been pretending it was worry that kept him checking up on her, hanging out with her, it wasn't. He liked being with her, looking at her, touching her, just listening to her talk. He liked the vulnerability she was able to show him, even though he hated that the fire had stripped away that veneer of toughness she'd worn like a protective skin. When they'd dated, she'd been strong, single-minded, stubborn, but there'd also been a softness, a sweetness. It didn't matter. Nothing would come of it. She'd made it perfectly clear where she stood on the idea of a relationship with him.

As he pulled away from the sidewalk, his cell phone buzzed. He looked at the screen and took a second before answering. He was pretty sure Helen didn't know his number and Arianna was on the other end. If she was, he didn't want her to pick up on how relieved he was that she was calling. He bowed his head and gave it a shake. If he wasn't careful, he'd end up a lovesick moron like his brother Mike.

Connor cleared his throat and then said, "Helen, is everything—"

"It's not Glamma. It's me."

He couldn't help himself. He grinned at the irritation in her voice. "Arianna? Is that you?"

"You know it's me, Connor. I'm calling from my grandmother's landline. It shows up on your screen."

"I wasn't sure. Last night you told me you were never speaking to me again, and I know how good you are at holding a grudge, so I thought it might be Jenna."

"Well, it's not. It's me. And I wouldn't be speaking to you unless I needed you."

"You need me?"

She huffed. "I don't need you the way your voice is implying I do."

"How is my voice implying I need you?" He winced, wondering if she'd pick up on the pronoun slip.

"You know exactly how. It's all deep and gravelly."

"I have a deep voice. It's the same voice I use every day."

"Don't try to wind me up. I'm already wound up enough as it is, thanks to your father." Her voice dropped to a whisper. "You have to come get him. He's planning all these events and speeches for me, and Glamma promised the entire town I would come to their homes and personally thank them. Do you know how many homes there are in Harmony Harbor, Connor? Do you?"

His amusement of seconds ago faded in response to the panic in her voice. "Calm down," he said, taking a sharp turn without slowing down. His tires squealed, the smell of burning rubber coming through the vents. "I'm on my way."

Less than three minutes later, he was knocking on the door.

Arianna opened it with a frown. "How did you get here so fast?"

"You said you needed me. So here I am." In no way at all did he want that to sound like a come-on, but sexual innuendo would have been better than how it sounded to his ears. Needy. Desperate. The woman would be the death of his alpha-male card. He thought of his brother Mike and shuddered.

Stepping inside, Connor reached back to close the door. Instead of backing up to usher him into the kitchen, Arianna moved into him and rested a hand on his chest. She smelled good. Her hair was piled on her head in a messy knot. She wore mascara and coral lipstick with a touch of color on her cheeks. He thought it was also a good sign she had on a sweater and leggings instead of pajamas or sweats. There was only one problem: She'd put her sling back on. Still, she looked twenty times better than the day he'd seen her on Mrs. Ranger's front lawn. There were no longer dark smudges under her eyes, her skin glowed, and the hollows under her cheeks were less pronounced.

Rising up on her toes, she whispered in his ear, "Don't tell your dad I called you. Just pretend you stopped by to see me and then figure out a way to get him to leave without hurting his feelings."

Connor slid an arm around her waist and brought his mouth to her ear. "He was there when you told me you never wanted to see or speak to me again. I can't see him believing I'd drop by after that, can you?"

She drew in a long, aggravated breath, which caused her breasts to rub against his chest. She tried to conceal a small gasp and failed. It sounded like a gasp of want and need to him, but that was probably wishful thinking on his part. And since his mind went to a place of wishful thinking, it took a detour to their conversation the day he'd pulled her bra out of the refrigerator—a black lace number that she'd confessed she could no longer put on by herself. And yes, right then a totally inappropriate and inconvenient question popped into his head. Had she or hadn't she managed to put on a bra today?

"I, um, yes, yes, he would. If you tell him you just stopped by, he'll believe you," Arianna said, and the way she said it made him think they'd better agree on how they were going to handle this sooner rather than later or he'd have a hard time concealing his desire. Perfect. He'd just taken care of that problem with the thought of walking stiff-legged into the kitchen with his father and Arianna's grandmother looking on.

"We need a better excuse. How about you asked me over to apologize to me?" he suggested. The idea worked for him, and he straightened, removing his arm from her waist.

"Why would I apologize to you?" She dropped down on her feet, but her hand remained on his chest, her head tipped back. Her cheeks were flushed, her lips slightly parted.

He slid his arm back around her waist, but this time he didn't whisper in her ear. Drawing her snug against him, he leaned over her to get a look into the kitchen. "Because nothing I did or said was meant to hurt you. I was just trying to help." He glanced in the direction of the kitchen table and then returned his gaze to hers. Her eyes darkened and her breathing quickened. "Maybe we should kiss and make up?"

"Maybe," she said, adding a small, encouraging nod.

He smiled and then kissed her, keeping an eye on the kitchen as he did. This kiss was nothing like the one they'd shared on the sidewalk in the pouring rain. That kiss had been fueled by fear and frustration and relief. This one was a soft exploration of lips and a mouth that he could trace and taste from memory. There were only a few things he'd liked more in life than kissing Arianna Bell. He thought of those things now when she touched her tongue to his and the kiss became about much more than memories and making up. If he hadn't heard the scrape of a chair on hardwood, he might have given in to the temptation to further explore the woman in his arms.

He drew back, kissing the tip of her nose when she groaned. "If I get rid of my father and your grandmother, will you apologize to me some more?"

He wanted to groan his own frustration when her expression closed off. He knew what was coming next. She'd shut down any idea that they could have more than whatever this was.

"I don't know what I was thinking. I shouldn't have kiss..." She trailed off as though just realizing she was no longer whispering, glancing toward the kitchen before saying, "Apologized to you. I won't be apologizing to you again."

"Don't be so sure about that."

She harrumphed and tossed her head. Her attitude made him laugh, but there was something that didn't. As she turned to walk away, he hooked his arm around her waist. "Hold up a minute."

She looked over her shoulder. "Why? What are—"

"You know how you don't like people getting a read on you?" he asked as he brushed aside strands of hair that had fallen loose to get at the fabric knot at her neck.

"Connor, don't—" She reached back to pull his hand away.

"Stop," he said as he untied the sling. He held it up. "This right here is your tell, Arianna. You're using the sling like a security blanket. When you're being pushed out of your comfort zone, back on it goes."

"You have no idea what you're talking about." She went to move away, but he still had his arm around her. "Let me go."

"Just give me a minute." He brought his free hand to her neck and gently kneaded the red mark left by the fabric. She bowed her head, and he drew his arm from around her waist to massage her neck and shoulders with both hands. He felt her relax under his fingers and didn't want to stop, but Helen and his father were craning their necks to see what was going on. "Better?" he asked, lowering his hands.

"No. There was nothing wrong with my neck."

He couldn't resist and pressed his lips to her nape. "Liar," he said, nipping the spot he'd just kissed.

"Connor, I told you—"

"Yeah, yeah, I know. You're not interested in a relationship." He could say he wasn't either, but it wouldn't be the truth. He sauntered past her into the kitchen, smiling when she blew out an irritated breath behind him. "Hey, Dad, Glamma. Wow, you guys have been busy," he said, doing a lousy job of keeping his amusement under wraps.

They'd hung two whiteboards on the kitchen wall and had a gigantic easel in the corner. At the top of one whiteboard there was a drawing of a devil beside his uncle's name, along with a list of Daniel's campaign promises and initiatives. On the other there was an angel beside Arianna's name. So far there was nothing written under her name. Flyer and sign designs littered the kitchen table. He reached for a flyer mock-up to hide his smile and got a light punch in his kidney from Arianna, who stood behind him. He faked a cough to cover his laugh. "I need a coffee. Anyone else want one?"

"No time for a coffee break, son. Your uncle has months on us. We're going to have to pull some all-nighters to catch up. We're up for it though, aren't we, Helen?"

"We sure are, Sean. And so are my friends and Arianna's. They'll hit the ground running once we have the flyers and signs ready."

"You two are quite the team. Uncle Daniel and Mom won't know what hit them when you debut Arianna's campaign."

"Neither will you," Arianna muttered, following close on his heels. "You're supposed to be discouraging them, not encouraging them."

Ignoring her, he lifted the coffeepot from the machine and poured himself a cup. "You'll both be happy to know that Arianna apologized and she's no longer mad at me, so you can put me back on the team."

"We figured it out when we heard you playing kissy face in the entryway. Now get over here and help us come up with a campaign slogan. I was thinking 'Rise from the Ashes' because Main Street is rising from the ashes and so is Arianna, but Sean thinks it's a bit... What was that word you used?"

His father winced when Arianna lost the color in her face and strode from the room.

"I think you'd better come up with something else, Glamma," Connor said. "I'll be right back."

He put his mug of coffee down to follow Arianna. She didn't go to her bedroom. Instead, she headed out the front door. He wondered if that was because she knew he was coming after her and didn't think it was a good idea to be shut up in her bedroom with him. She'd be wrong if that was the reason she'd chosen to go outside. The best place for her would be in his arms on a soft mattress with no one watching or interrupting them.

She ran down the front steps and ducked around the side of the house to the backyard.

He slowed his pace to give her a few minutes alone. Standing on the front lawn, he shoved his hands in the pockets of his leather jacket and admired the gardens, noting the upturned earth around the oak tree in the center of the yard. He wondered what Helen thought when she saw the holes. Did she know she'd dug up the tulips? He crouched beside the tree and used his hands to fill in the holes and hide the evidence of what she'd done.

"She came out here at midnight a few weeks ago and dug up her prized tulips. I told her the squirrels did it," Arianna said, coming to kneel beside him. She smoothed her hand over the hole he'd just filled.

"Mrs. Ranger told me about it. Good idea to blame the squirrels."

"I thought she'd be upset. She doesn't spend much time in her garden anymore. I wonder if it has anything to do with the...her memory." She glanced at him. "It's silly, isn't it? I'd rather say she has memory problems than dementia, and dementia rather than Alzheimer's."

"No. It's just starting to sink in. Give yourself time."

"Do you think she has time?"

"Yeah, for sure I do." He turned and sat under the tree so he could look at her. "Just hear me out, okay? I know you hate the idea of running for mayor. I get it. I do. You feel like you were pushed into—"

"Manipulated into it."

"Okay, point taken. But all that aside—and be honest—did you see how engaged Helen is?"

"Yes, and I know that staying active and socializing is important, but—"

"Just a sec. I'm not finished. It's not just Helen I'm thinking about; it's my dad. He needs this too. He and my mom, they belong together. And I think this race might be the ticket to getting them back together. My mom's been at Greystone since February, and this is the longest my dad's stuck around."

"That's not fair. You want me to stay in the race for my grandmother and your parents."

"Yeah, I do." He did, but he also wanted her to stay in the race for her, and maybe for him, too. Because as much as he saw it as a second chance for his parents, he thought it might also be a second chance for him and Arianna.

Chapter Ten

♥

Arianna sat on the stage at the Salty Dog, a pirate-themed pub, looking out at a sea of signs. She'd never seen so many images of herself in her entire life, and she didn't think she could stand the sight of one more. It had been weeks since Connor had emotionally blackmailed her into staying in the race, and by now she'd fully expected to have gracefully (albeit guiltily) withdrawn her name. But Connor had been right, damn him. Every time she'd hinted at pulling out, Glamma had looked like she was going to have a coronary or go into a deep depression.

Now Arianna felt like the one about to have a coronary. The signs, buttons, and flyers had arrived two weeks before, and with the help of an enthusiastic team of friends and family, the entire town had been papered with her face and slogan—*All in for Arianna*. She wasn't sure they meant it like she was all in. Which clearly wasn't the case. Or did it mean the entire town was all in with her? Not the case either, as proven by a recent poll in the *Gazette*, which indicated Daniel was ahead of her by five points. Arianna made sure no one was around when she did a happy dance upon learning the news.

If she had known the five-point lead would send her campaign managers into overdrive, she would have gone to bed and pulled the covers over her head instead. This week they'd made good on Helen's promise that Arianna would personally visit every residence in Harmony Harbor. Now they were taking care of the businesses in town with a rally at the Salty Dog. Pretzels and beer were flowing, and so were the buttons and signs.

Sean had asked her friends, many of whom were local business owners, to say a few words before she made her speech. So far, Mackenzie from Truly Scrumptious had spoken, as well as Lily from In Bloom and Olivia Gallagher, Greystone's event planner. Even Arianna's sister Jenna, the manor's wedding planner, who was less than two weeks from leaving town, had spoken.

Arianna couldn't think about that now, not while she was sitting onstage in clear view of what felt like half the town. She smiled at Mr. O'Malley, who winked at her before taking his place behind the podium. The older man operated the local hardware-slash-general store with his son. The senior Mr. O'Malley was a sweet, diminutive man with white tufts of hair over his ears and a mischievous grin. He reminded Arianna of an elf. His black pants were held up by orange suspenders that were decorated with Arianna's campaign buttons, and he wore a flashing orange bow tie in honor of Halloween being less than ten days away.

"My son John wanted to speak, my grandson too, but I told them Sean specifically requested the good-looking O'Malley with all the charm." He snapped his suspenders, rocking on his heels as he soaked up the crowd's laughter. "All right, now, that'll be the last joke you're getting from me. This is serious business, my friends. I'll not say anything negative about Arianna's opponent—that's not how we do things around here—but if he has his way, Main Street will never be the same. We're the heart of this town, and don't any of you ever forget it. That's why I'm voting for Arianna. I've known her since she was knee-high to a grasshopper. Always said she'd go places, didn't I, John?" He directed his question at a handsome man sitting on a barrel at one of the tables.

"Yes, you did, Dad. And when she got older, you used to say you wished you were forty years younger."

That got some laughter, hoots and hollers, and a round of applause.

"Listen to him, thinking he's as funny as his old man," Mr. O'Malley said, but anyone could see he was busting with pride. John O'Malley wasn't known for speaking up or out. "But I must confess, what he said is true. Arianna is as beautiful as her mother and her grandmother. Now that I think about it, I've been admiring the Fairchild women from afar for years. I should probably do something about that, shouldn't I?" He turned, waggling his bushy eyebrows at her grandmother. "Helen, I'm free after I'm done here."

Her grandmother waved her hand in a *go on with you* gesture. "Silly old man," she said with a smile.

"Did that sound like a *yes* to you, folks?" he asked. Everyone cheered. "Even if it wasn't, I'd still vote for Arianna, and you know why?"

"Why?" several people yelled.

"I'm glad you asked. Now pay attention. I'm voting for her because she's one of us. If she wins, we all win. Out of all of us, out of all of the businesses on Main Street, no one worked as hard as she did to make a success of Tie the Knot. I'd see her in the little room above her shop—" There were some guffaws. "Now, stop that. I'm no Peeping Tom. She did her sewing in that room, and she burned the midnight oil for as long as I can remember. You know what else she did?"

"What?"

"Thanks for asking." He hooked his fingers in his suspenders and rocked on his heels. "She made a name for herself. She was going to be big. We all knew it and were pleased as punch to see her name in the papers and in all those fancy bridal magazines. But as big as she was getting to be, she stayed true to her small-town values and to Harmony Harbor. She was given an opportunity to set up shop in Boston, and she refused. Made the trek out here almost every day when she was married. She's gone through her trials and tribulations, but did she let them beat her?"

"No!"

"And do you know why?" He cupped his hand behind his ear.

"She's a fighter!" the audience yelled.

It took everything Arianna had not to run off the stage. She wasn't a fighter. She was a fraud.

"That she is. And we're going to fight to help her win, aren't we?"

"Yes!"

"And we're going to save Main Street, aren't we?"

"Yes!"

"And when she's ready, we're going to help rebuild Tie the Knot!"

Everybody jumped to their feet and cheered, waving their placards.

"And here she is, the heart of Harmony Harbor, our own Arianna Bell!" Julia Gallagher, who'd volunteered to be MC for the event, shouted her introduction, clapping as wildly as the rest of the crowd. Dark-haired and adorable, Julia owned Books and Beans and was married to Connor's cousin Aidan. She must have come straight from children's story hour because she was dressed as a witch, her pointy black hat adorned with Arianna's campaign buttons.

"Heart of Harmony Harbor, why didn't we think of that?" Sean murmured as he rose from his seat on the stage to join in the clapping.

Because Arianna would have vetoed the slogan if they had. She had never been the heart of this town, not like Julia or Mr. O'Malley. And how was she supposed to follow Mr. O'Malley? Her emotions were bubbling inside her, and she was afraid they were going to bubble over.

She thanked Julia and Mr. O'Malley, kissing the older man's cheek before taking her place behind the podium. She decided the only way to get through this was to be honest. "Wow. You're a hard act to follow, Mr. O'Malley."

"My boys tell me that all the time."

Arianna smiled, waiting until the laughter died down. "I can't tell you how much your support and kind words mean to me. Without all of you, the business community of Harmony Harbor, I wouldn't be here. And I definitely wouldn't be here without my amazing campaign managers, my grandmother Helen, and His Excellency, Sean Gallagher."

"Oh now, none of that 'excellency' business, darlin'."

"You don't fool us. You love it, Gallagher," one of the older men yelled from the bar.

"You're right, I do." Sean grinned, his blue eyes twinkling.

He was a handsome man and as charming as his son. She'd grown fond of the older man. She wished he'd keep talking. He was so much better at this than her. For that matter, so were her grandmother and Connor.

Sean gave her a subtle, encouraging nod. It was all she could do to hold back her sigh. She didn't think any of them realized how hard this was for her. *Be honest*, she reminded herself. "My grandmother has passed the torch to me twice in my life, once with Tie the Knot." *Don't cry; don't cry*. She blinked her eyes and cleared the emotion from her voice. "And now as the representative of her vision for Harmony Harbor's future. I believe in what my grandmother believes in. I believe in Harmony Harbor. I believe in all of you. And I believe that if we work together we can find ways to create more jobs without compromising our small-town values and charm."

As though he sensed that was all she had—and he'd be right—Sean stood and walked to the podium, giving her shoulder a gentle squeeze. "Connor would be proud of you tonight," he said, and then to their audience, "Thanks so much for coming out. Don't forget, every vote counts, and we'd appreciate yours. Beer's on the house."

A chorus of *All in for Arianna* started through the bar, with signs waving.

"Now, isn't that a beautiful sight," her grandmother said, coming to join them. She patted Arianna's cheek. "You made me proud tonight."

"Thanks, Glamma," she said, her voice still husky with emotion, her stomach jittery with nerves.

"Your grandmother and I are going to call it a night," Sean said, acknowledging old friends with a smile and a wave. He turned back to them and held up his cell phone, as though he'd just heard from someone. "Connor's dinner meeting is wrapping up. He'll pick you up here or see you back at the house."

A warm glow of anticipation filled her. Which was ridiculous. She saw the man practically every day. Though things had changed over the past few weeks. Before he used to drop in at any time of the day. Now she mostly saw him after work and on the weekends.

Up until two weeks ago she'd had no idea he'd left his firm to work with Michael and Shay. She'd been surprised he'd left the Three Bs: Barnes, Brooks, and Baker. It was the most prestigious law firm in Boston. It would have to be since the Summers family was a client, and they didn't settle for anything less than the best, as Gary used to like to remind Arianna.

Connor had been a bit evasive as to why he'd left, but he seemed happy enough. No doubt his old firm wasn't. Over the past two weeks, he'd been actively wining and dining his former clients to bring them over to Gallagher and Gallagher. And Arianna knew better than anyone that when Connor set his mind to winning someone over, he went all out.

She smiled, remembering his reaction upon discovering the golf game and client dinner he'd scheduled for today overlapped with the rally at the Salty Dog. He'd wanted to cancel, but she'd insisted he keep his plans. She, out of anyone, understood the sacrifices you sometimes had to make to get a business off the ground. Besides, he'd rarely missed a single event and, with his father in charge, there had been many of them.

Arianna kissed her grandmother's cheek and gave Sean a one-armed hug. "Thanks for organizing this. It was fun. I think I'll stay a while longer."

Helen and Sean shared a shocked look and then beamed at her. She held back a wry laugh. She hadn't made things easy for them. Well, she wasn't going to burst their bubbles by sharing that she didn't plan to do any more campaigning or schmoozing, no matter how much she loved her friends and appreciated their support. As tonight had proven, time and the campaign were getting away from her. She needed to sort things out before it was too late. And she needed to do that alone.

It turned out it wasn't as easy to get away as she'd anticipated. Now that her friends and her sister had her out on the town, they didn't seem prepared to let her go. "Okay," she agreed. "I'll have one more drink with you."

"Great. I want you guys to try one of the cocktails we'll be serving at Shay and Michael's wedding reception," her sister said. "Six sweet poisons, Cherry. No, wait, make that seven. Eight if you can sit with us, nine if Shay can." Jenna waved to a woman on the other side of the bar while smiling up at Cherry, the manager of the pub and one of her sister's best friends. Shay was Jenna's childhood best friend and was working behind the bar tonight. She co-owned the pub with her uncle Charlie.

Neither of her sister's BFFs were Arianna's biggest fans, so she was a little surprised when Cherry leaned over and pulled her in for a hug, smothering her in her voluptuous chest and the scent of cotton candy. "It's really good to see you. We were all worried about you."

"Thank you. I appreciate it. I got your card." Helen had nearly fallen off the bed when she'd opened the envelope.

"Shay thought it was a little inappropriate, but nothing like a hot, naked man to make you feel better, I always say."

"Cherry, you didn't." Jenna groaned.

"Oh please, I basically gave you the same advice. If you hadn't followed it, you wouldn't be with your hot secret agent man, now, would you?"

"I think the sex on the beach had more to do with—"

They cut off her sister with a group groan. "TMI," Lily, the owner of In Bloom, said.

Jenna rolled her eyes. "The drink, ladies. Get your minds out of the gutter."

"I never did understand that expression. What do hot men and sweaty sex have to do with a gutter?" Cherry shrugged, her burgundy wench's costume sliding off her shoulder. She glanced at it, smiled, and tugged it a little lower. Jutting out her hip, she rested her serving tray on it as if she intended to stay awhile. "Now, listen, I know you've got your girls here, but once Jellybean is gone and you need another sister-friend, you just give me a call," she said.

"Cherry, stop talking and start serving," Shay called from the bar.

"Shaybae, you're sounding a little cranky. Do I need to talk to that man of yours?" Cherry chuckled when Shay flipped her off. "She's been so busy lately, she's probably not getting herself some somethin' somethin'. You know what I mean?"

Arianna was afraid she did, and even more afraid she knew where the conversation was headed when Cherry cocked her head to look at her more closely and said, "So, you and Connor—"

Arianna pretended not to hear her and responded to her *sister-friend* offer instead. "I'll definitely give you a call when Jenna's gone. Thanks. I really appreciate the offer." She did, even though it was slightly terrifying.

Her sister and her friends, who'd clearly picked up on Arianna's panic, were having a difficult time keeping straight faces.

"Okay. Great. And we're a hundred percent behind your bid for mayor, so just let me know what we can do to help. Hey, has anyone thought of T-shirts? We could wear them here."

"No, but that's a really good idea," Arianna said, a visual of her face spread across Cherry's boobs popping into her head. "I'll let Sean know."

"Cherry," Shay called again from behind the bar.

"I better get your drinks before she fires me again." Cherry huffed, walking off with her hips swaying.

Arianna looked at her sister. "I know I told you to go, but I really think you should stay." She said it as a joke, but deep down she meant it. The night Glamma had gone missing, it had sounded like Jenna might stay in town. Arianna had thought it had to do with her job, only to discover Jenna had been worried about her.

Her friends laughed as she had meant them to, but Jenna looked at her more closely. She leaned into her. "Are you okay?"

She nodded. "It's just been a busy few weeks." She looked up as the woman Jenna had been waving to earlier approached the table.

"Hey, Evie, come sit down. I ordered you a drink. Guys, Evangeline just took over Holiday House from her aunt." She introduced the woman around the table. Despite a warm smile that showed off dimples in her cheeks, there was something wary in the way the woman's dark gaze moved around the pub. Jenna patted the stool beside Arianna. "Here, sit beside my sister."

There was something about the way Jenna insisted the woman sit beside her that put Arianna on alert.

"I'm so glad you've taken over the store. We were

afraid it was closing for good, Ev…Do you prefer Evangeline or Evie?" Julia asked.

"Evie." She smiled. "I wouldn't have known the store was closed if Jenna hadn't gotten in touch with me."

"I needed stuff for Shay and Michael's wedding, and we always support local, so I'd ordered everything from Evie's aunt," Jenna explained. "When I couldn't reach her, I mentioned it to Kitty. You know the Widows Club. If you need to find out about someone's family, they're the ones to ask. They got Evie's number for me."

Here it comes now, Arianna thought when her sister glanced at her from under her eyelashes. "Evie's aunt had been taken to the hospital, and no one had tried to look for a family member."

"Oh, I'm so sorry. I had no idea she was sick," Mackenzie, the owner of Truly Scrumptious, said. "I feel so bad. My bakery is two doors up from Holiday House. I supply the seasonal cookies for the shop."

Holiday House was a year-round Christmas store that also carried other seasonal holiday lines.

"I know, and I hope you'll continue to do so. Don't feel bad though. None of us knew my aunt was having problems. She's just been diagnosed with Alzheimer's."

They all made sympathetic noises, including Arianna, who pinned her sister with an *I'm onto you* stare that had no effect on Jenna whatsoever because she continued to avoid Arianna's gaze.

"Are you going to run the store or try to sell it, Evie?" Lily asked.

"I'm keeping it. I've sold everything I own and

moved here. Fingers double crossed that I can make a go of it. The only retail experience I have is from when I stayed with my aunt during the summers."

Arianna breathed a little easier. Maybe that's all it was. Jenna wanted her to take the new girl on the block under her wing.

Or so she thought, until Mackenzie asked, "What did you do before?" And Jenna once again cast Arianna a nervous, sidelong glance.

"I was a therapist in New York," she said, and Arianna could have sworn Jenna and Evie shared a glance.

Arianna pushed back from the table and stood. "It was lovely to meet you, Evie. Good luck with Holiday House." She gave her sister and friends quick hugs, thanked them for the night and for all their help over the past few weeks, and then got the heck out of there before Jenna or Cherry could stop her.

Once outside, she inhaled deeply, allowing the crisp October air to calm her frazzled nerves. It helped until her eyes were automatically drawn to the burned-out remains of the four stores up the road. She bowed her head and walked quickly to the side street. Just a few months before, she'd been like nearly every one of the people crowded into the pub tonight, thinking of ways to increase sales and attract more customers.

Now with Daniel Gallagher's plan to modernize Main Street, razing half the block and putting up a modern office building which included storefronts, they had a very good chance of losing their dreams for their business's futures too. And they were looking to her to protect them, to save them. She didn't understand how they could put their faith in her: Didn't they see she was a fake, a fraud?

Of course they didn't see her for who she was, she thought, when she walked by house after house with her campaign sign on their front lawn. It wasn't even a recent photo of her. They'd used one a professional had done years before, when she'd been the type of woman who deserved their faith. A woman who could fight and win.

Arianna dug in the leather hobo bag she wore over her shoulder, searching for her lipstick. She pulled it out, using her teeth to take off the lid. Then, with her left hand, she awkwardly drew a mustache, thick eyebrows, and a goatee on the sign sitting almost hidden beneath a big oak tree. By the time she'd gone through the red tube of lipstick, half a tube of peach, and five signs, her artistic skills had improved.

"You do know it's a misdemeanor to deface campaign signs, don't you, lady?"

She briefly closed her eyes and sighed. She should have known he'd somehow catch her in the act. She turned. Connor leaned against his car, arms crossed, with her favorite smile on his handsome face.

"Are you going to make a citizen's arrest?"

"I should," he said as he pushed off the car to walk toward her. "I happen to be very fond of the candidate and her face."

Chapter Eleven

♥

As they got out of the cab on Primrose Lane, her grandmother made a face at the white Cape Cod that housed the clinic. "I don't know why we had to come today. It's not as if I'm sick, and we can't afford to take time off the campaign trail. There's less than twelve days to the election."

Arianna got queasy at the reminder. It felt like she was on the chopping block, the ax about to fall. She could see it hovering above her. Feel the blade—shiny and sharp—swinging closer and closer to her neck, and still she put off making a decision.

There was a very good reason why she did. Because while she didn't like being in the spotlight, giving speeches and handing out flyers and living in constant fear that someone was going to bring up the fire or ask about her arm or when she was going to reopen Tie the Knot, it beat how she'd been living before. She hadn't been living, really. She'd been slowly dying. Just the thought of going back to that place made her even more queasy than the thought of winning the mayoral race. Which was why she'd yet to make a decision.

Afraid Glamma was going to bolt, Arianna used the excuse Connor had come up with. "You promised Sean and Connor that you'd have a physical and get some bloodwork done. They're worried all the hours you're putting in on the campaign are too much for you. Unless you want them to start treating you like you're eighty, you have to suck it up."

"Easy for you to say," Helen muttered, swinging her cane as she walked up the stone path to the door. She stopped and held it open for Arianna. "But if it means you'll let them check your arm, I'll do it."

Arianna clenched her jaw, cursing Connor in her head. Of course Mr. Fixer had come up with the idea to use her to blackmail Glamma into getting checked out. He'd played on their weaknesses—each other.

And speaking of the handsome, blue-eyed devil, there he was. She turned at the sexy purr of the Porsche's engine, watching as Connor pulled into the spot the taxi had just vacated. He'd had client meetings in Boston all morning and hadn't been sure he'd make it back in time for their appointments, though he had promised to try.

While she'd been disappointed he wouldn't be there when they did a cognition test on her grandmother, she'd also been relieved. Arianna didn't want him anywhere near her when they removed the compression bandage from her arm.

A flurry of butterflies took flight in her stomach when he rounded the front of his car. She tried to convince herself any woman would get butterflies at the sight of him in his elegantly fitted black suit. He looked powerful, successful, and in complete and utter control of himself and everything around him.

But as his long, loose-limbed strides ate up the distance between them, she cracked under the pressure of her lie. She was days, hours, minutes, seconds away from falling in love with him.

Her heart hurt, and her thoughts were as chaotic as the butterflies that took flight in her stomach. She should drag him into the examination room with her. Have him stand by her side as they peeled back the bandage to reveal her ruined arm. He'd see her for how she really was, ugly and deformed.

That's what she wanted, wasn't it? For him to see who she'd become. See that she was no longer the blue-eyed blonde with smooth, silky skin, a limitless future, and an unblemished past whom he'd fallen in love with. That was the woman he wanted, the woman he loved. If he knew her secret, saw how ugly she'd become, he'd walk away like every other man in her life had done.

"Stop mooning over him. He's coming." Glamma motioned her inside with the cane.

She wasn't mooning. She was memorizing the perfection of his face, of his smile, the way his intent blue eyes moved over her. It wasn't enough. She needed more time. More time in his arms, more time with his mouth on hers, more time to regain her own confidence and strength. If she said goodbye too soon, if he was no longer in her life, no longer there for her to lean on, she was afraid she wouldn't have the strength to give her grandmother the care she needed. She wouldn't even let her mind go to the place where her grandmother was gone and she was alone.

"You need your glasses, Glamma. I wasn't mooning over him. I was smiling." She was proud of herself. Her voice didn't reveal even a hint of the fear and shame that were coursing through her body and brain. "I'm glad you came," she said to Connor, mentally pushing up the faltering edges of her lips.

"Me too," he said, a slight furrow appearing on his brow. He placed his big hand above her grandmother's head to hold open the entrance door.

As Arianna walked into the waiting room, she heard Glamma whisper, "Good thing you made it, my boy. I'm pretty sure she was about to bolt."

Focused on finding three unoccupied seats as far away from the other patients as possible without looking like that was what she was doing, Arianna didn't hear Connor's reply. She spotted three chairs tucked in a corner and fast walked to the other side of the waiting room before Connor or her grandmother could stop her. She took a seat, smiling and nodding at the other people in the room. Her grandmother and Connor would have to be satisfied. She didn't think it was fair that she had to play mayoral candidate every minute of every day, especially here.

Obviously, Glamma disagreed. She shot a scowl in Arianna's direction and then pasted a smile on her face and went to speak to a familiar-looking older woman. Connor said hello to a couple older men, returned several women's flirtatious smiles with one of his own, and responded to people asking after his family. Glamma was still glad-handing and gabbing when Connor went to speak to the receptionist, receiving another come-hither smile for his effort.

"Not a word," she said when he took the seat beside her, positive he was going to give her crap for not doing her candidate duties. No doubt Daniel would have had the patients in hysterics by now, which made Arianna feel a little hysterical.

Connor nudged her with his shoulder, and she looked up.

"How about a kiss, then?" he said.

She supposed she didn't blame him for asking. Of late, she'd been a bit too free with her kisses. Her gaze dropped to his mouth. He had the most beautiful lips, and his kisses were absolutely delicious and had her dreaming of more.

He lifted her hand and pressed his lips to her knuckles. "You didn't think I was going to kiss you on your lips in the middle of the doctor's office, did you?" he asked with a teasing grin.

"No. I didn't think you'd kiss me at all." She tugged her hand free and caught a glimpse of her grandmother beaming their way. "You've done it now. Just look at her. She's probably telling them we're romantically involved."

He smiled, looking completely relaxed and unaffected at the possibility.

"Doesn't it concern you that people are talking about us?" She nudged him with her elbow when he didn't immediately respond. "Connor?"

"Babe, you seem to be the only one who doesn't realize we're romantically involved. Now, if Glamma tells them we're getting married next week, I'll get concerned."

She stared at him.

He shrugged. "I've told you before, don't ask a question unless you can handle the answer."

"Helen Fairchild," an attractive white-haired woman called, scanning the waiting room. It was the clinic's nurse, Dorothy DiRossi.

Glamma kept her back to Dorothy, continuing her conversation with her friends.

"Sorry. I think she must be losing her hearing too," Arianna said loud enough for her grandmother to hear and smiled at the nurse. "I'll get her for you."

Connor laughed. "You're going to pay for that, babe."

Sure enough, Glamma lifted her chin and walked by Arianna, saying, "You go sit yourself down. I'm quite capable of seeing the doctor on my own."

"Of course you are," Dorothy said. "Come with me, Helen. My stepdaughter Ava will be doing your physical today. You're going to love her."

"Relax," Connor said as Arianna stared after the two older women, unsure what she should do.

And because she was anxious about her grandmother's appointment and her own, she snapped at him. "How am I supposed to relax? If it's one of the days she's decided she's perfectly fine—and I think it is one of those days—she won't tell them anything, and then she won't remember half of what I need to know."

Her aggrieved tone didn't seem to bother him. He just cocked his head to the side and said equably, "You do know Ava is married to my cousin Griffin and that they live a stone's throw from me, right?"

"Of course I do. Ava and I are good friends. But what does...? Oh." She sighed. "I should have known. Ava already has a complete and up-to-date history on my grandmother thanks to you, doesn't she?"

"She does, and on you too. So don't think *I'm fine* is going to cut it with her."

She looked away. "She's removing the compression bandage, Connor. I think she'll realize I'm far from fine."

"I know. And that's why you're here and why I'm here, honey." He tugged gently on her hand to get her attention. "Will you let me come in the room with you?"

Despite thinking that she should only seconds before while walking through the clinic's front door, she couldn't do it. The thought of him seeing her arm made her feel sick. She jerked her hand away. "Of course I won't. I'm quite capable of dealing with this on my own." She shot to her feet. "I need to check on Glamma."

It wasn't until she was halfway down the hall that she realized she'd said to him almost exactly what her grandmother had said to her. If Glamma felt anything close to what she did at the thought of Connor being in the room, the last thing Arianna should do is invade her privacy. Her grandmother deserved to keep her dignity and pride intact. There was just one problem with that. Now Arianna had to go back to the waiting room and ruin her dramatic exit. She snorted at the thought. Witchy exit more like. She owed Connor an apology.

He looked up from his phone when she walked back to her seat. "Glamma kick you out?"

"No. I realized it wasn't fair to do to her what I didn't want done to me." She sat and linked her fingers through his. "Sorry I snapped at you. You didn't deserve it."

He gave her hand a light squeeze. "It's okay. It's just...Look, I know you have issues with your burns, and I think it's important for us to talk about them."

"There's nothing to talk about. It won't change anything. I—"

"Arianna." Dorothy smiled from where she stood beside the reception desk. "You can come with me, dear. Connor can join you if you'd—"

"No." Realizing she'd almost shouted the word, Arianna calmed herself and her voice. "No, that's fine. Thank you." She glanced at Connor, forcing her lips to curve. "I won't be long."

She followed Dorothy to an examination room, wondering if she should offer an explanation as to why she didn't want Connor with her. But it seemed like a lot of effort, and right then she didn't have the energy. Nerves had taken over her body. Other than her grandmother, this would be the first time someone she knew saw her arm.

"Here, dear, let's get you up on the table." Dorothy gently guided her to the table and helped her up. "Would you like a glass of water?"

"I'm fine, thank you. I'm just a little overheated, I

think." Embarrassed that her nerves were obvious, Arianna focused on tugging the sleeve of her black leather jacket off her damaged arm and shaking it off her good arm.

"May I?" Dorothy asked.

Arianna nodded. "Thank you."

"What a gorgeous top," Dorothy said, admiring the hot pink ruffled shell Arianna wore with a pair of skinny-leg black pants. "Oh, and look at those adorable shoes." They were black kitten heels adorned with hot pink bows.

"Thank you. Everything's from Merci Beaucoup."

"I've been saying to Ava that I have to get in there and check it out. Now I definitely have to. If my husband gives me trouble, I'll tell him you're to blame." She patted Arianna's thigh with a smile. "Ava is going to be a little bit so, if you don't mind, I'll remove your bandage, check you over, and then all that'll be left is a quick chat with Ava. That way you'll be ready to leave about the same time as your grandmother."

"I'd like that, thank you," Arianna said, relieved.

Dorothy smiled. "Ava thought you might."

She was mortified they'd obviously talked about this, about her. "It's just . . ." She tried to think of an excuse that didn't make her sound weak or damaged but couldn't come up with one. "I have a difficult time looking at my arm myself. I know it doesn't make sense, but I feel like if my friends and family see it, they can't unsee it. Every time they look at me, that's all they'll see."

"Because that's all you see."

"Yes." She nodded, then drew in a long breath through her nose and released it. "And I know exactly how that sounds. There are so many people, children even, who have to deal with far worse than me without half the support. I just…I'm trying. I really am. And it is getting better." The campaign helped. Being busy helped. Having a purpose helped.

"It sounds to me like you're being too hard on yourself. It's been a little more than three months since you were released from the hospital. What you're experiencing—the anger, frustration, grief—it's all normal, lovey. But I can tell you, and Ava can tell you from personal experience, that the thing you least want to do is what will help you the most. You need to talk about how you're feeling."

Arianna shuddered at the idea of opening up to anyone. As though she sensed that wasn't going to happen anytime soon, Dorothy looked at her chart. "We'll get your weight, blood pressure, and temperature out of the way first. Then we'll check how your arm and tummy are healing." Because they were third-degree burns and the area involved was large, the doctors had done a full thickness autograft, using epidermis and dermis from her abdomen.

Quickly and efficiently, Dorothy checked her weight (she could stand to gain a few pounds), temperature (normal), blood pressure (a little high) and updated her file in a matter of minutes, bringing them to the part Arianna dreaded most.

"Lie back and we'll check your tummy first."

Arianna did as Dorothy asked, turning her head to

look at the wall when Dorothy lifted her blouse to bare her stomach and then gently palpated her abdomen. "No pain?"

She shook her head, wondering if Dorothy noticed her other scar. Ava would have. She would have been surprised, curious. It was another reason why Arianna preferred someone who didn't know her to perform the exam. Other than her mother and grandmother, no one knew about the baby. She needed to keep it that way.

Dorothy smiled. "Everything looks good. You've healed well. Now let's have a look at your arm and hand," she said matter-of-factly as she began removing the compression bandage.

Arianna once again turned her eyes to the wall instead of looking at Dorothy's face when she saw her arm.

"How are your pain levels?"

"Better. I just take something at bed now."

Dorothy moved her fingers. "I notice you don't use your hand at all. Have you been seeing your occupational and physical therapists?"

She ignored the first comment. Though she wished she could ignore the question too. "I did. In the hospital."

"You haven't kept your appointments since, have you?"

She shook her head. "At first I wasn't feeling well enough, and then it was difficult to get there. Now it doesn't seem worth it. My hand and arm are useless."

"Of course they are. They've been severely injured, and there's nerve damage in your hand. But that doesn't mean you can't eventually regain some—if not all—of your strength and fine-motor control. I understand it might have been difficult for you to get into Boston every couple of days, but we have excellent occupational and physical therapists right here at North Shore General. I'll have your appointments scheduled before you and your grandmother leave."

She chuckled at what must have been Arianna's peeved expression. "You really didn't think we were going to let you out of here without doing everything we can to get our future mayor one hundred percent, did you?"

* * *

Connor sat in the clinic's waiting room, working on his phone. It wasn't how he'd seen himself spending his afternoon. He wasn't completely surprised by Arianna's reaction, but he'd held out hope for a different one. Her burns were an issue they needed to deal with before they moved to the next level of their relationship, and he was more than ready to do that. Most of the time she gave every indication she was on the same page. Unless she overthought it.

He looked up at the sound of her voice. She thanked Dorothy DiRossi and then walked into the waiting room with Helen "So, how did it go? You both good?"

"Perfect. The picture of health, my boy. I got the all clear," Helen said.

"Great." He looked at Arianna, who wouldn't meet his eyes. "And you?"

"Fine, thank you," she said, tugging her black leather sleeve over her bandage.

He really hated that word. "Good news all around, then," he said, coming to his feet. "We should go out and celebrate. My treat." He knew as soon as the words were out of his mouth that Arianna would veto the idea. She still didn't like to eat in front of anyone. Even though she ate perfectly well, she needed help cutting her food.

"It's been a busy few days. I'd rather eat in, if that's okay."

At least she wasn't giving him the brush-off. "Sure. I'll call you a cab." There was only room for two in his Porsche. "I need to talk to Ava about one of my mom's prescriptions, so I'll be a few minutes. Decide what you want to eat and text me. Sound good?"

Arianna's eyes narrowed. "Connor—"

"Fish and chips from Jolly Rogers," Helen said, interrupting Arianna. She tucked her arm through her granddaughter's. "We'll get in a little campaigning before our ride arrives."

Once they were occupied talking to an older man and his wife, Connor headed past the receptionist, who was on the phone, and down the hall past the examination rooms. He came to a door with Ava's name on it and knocked.

"Come in, Connor."

He frowned and opened the door. "How did you know it was me?"

Ava leaned back in the chair behind the desk. She was a beautiful woman with olive skin and long, curly black hair. "You're a Gallagher man in love with a woman who's going through a difficult time." She smiled gently. "You're also a smart man and a lawyer, and you know I can't tell you anything."

"Right." He took the chair across from her. "Okay, instead of speaking as a medical professional, how about you speak to me as her friend. Are you worried about your friend, who might or might not be Arianna?"

"Yes."

"On a scale of one to ten?"

"Seven." He had hoped she was doing much better than that. His disappointment must have shown on his face because Ava said, "I know that's not what you wanted to hear. But I saw her two weeks after she came home from the hospital, and trust me when I say I wasn't sure she'd be at seven a year from today."

"Do you think the campaign is helping or hurting her?"

"To a degree I think it has been good for her, but I do have concerns. Just like the concerns I have about Helen's involvement."

"This is damn frustrating, you know. I should have had them give me medical power of attorney."

"You might have had some luck with Helen, but not Arianna," she said, fighting a smile. "All I can tell you from my own personal experience is don't give up on her." She pulled a pad of paper toward her and wrote something down. She handed it to him. "You might find these websites helpful. They'll explain what Arianna's dealing with. There's also one for Helen. I think they're a package deal."

"Thanks." He tucked the paper in his pocket.

"Don't pressure her too much, but try to get her to talk about what we discussed today."

"Her arm—"

"Is healing well."

He nodded, pulling out his phone as soon as he closed the office door behind him. "Hey, Dad, it's Connor. You'd said you were going to ask the *Gazette* for a look at their latest poll numbers before they published the results. Any chance you have those now? Oh, yeah. That good, huh. Absolutely. I wouldn't expect anything less with you heading up her campaign. Thanks, Dad."

There were twelve days left to go in the race and anything could happen, but right now Arianna had a five-point lead. And he had a strong feeling that wouldn't make her happy. He just wasn't sure what to do about it.

Chapter Twelve

♥

Halloween had been one of Colleen's favorite holidays. She'd always done it up big, with Jasper and Kitty's help, of course. For two weeks leading up to the night, they had haunted hayrides through the woods. Back at the manor, tables groaned with Halloween treats for the little ghosts and goblins after the ride. She chuckled, thinking in her new ghostly state she was perfectly suited to the holiday. If only people could see her.

But they were too busy with the evening's special event. Her great-grandson had married the love of his life in a quiet ceremony. It had been a private affair in the backyard of their cottage, but now they'd returned for the reception. In honor of the holiday and because Shay wasn't big on traditional weddings, she wore a tulle wedding gown embroidered with black lace, and Michael wore a black tuxedo and tails. His Irish wolfhound, Atticus, wearing a bow tie and top hat, loped ahead of them.

As the newlyweds walked across the great room toward the ballroom, Colleen smiled and cheered with the rest of the guests and the manor's staff, who were all in costume. But she admitted to feeling a touch downhearted that the couple didn't know she was with them on their special day. As though he sensed her mood, Simon padded her way and came to sit at her feet. He lifted his chin and meowed.

"I'm all right. It's just hard to be here, yet not be here, if you know what I mean."

He meowed in a manner that suggested he knew exactly what she meant. And if he was who she thought him to be, he most definitely did.

A voice on her other side murmured, "They know you're with them in spirit, madam. I told Master Michael that myself this morning. And Kitty gave Shay your locket, the one that holds pictures of you and your mother. She's wearing it now."

"Thank you, my boy. That does my heart good," she said, patting Jasper's arm, her hand going through it as it was wont to do.

Simon moved to sit in front of Jasper and lifted his paw. Now, that was a sight Colleen had never expected to see. Simon and Jasper were not overly fond of each other.

Jasper bent and shook Simon's paw. "Thank you, and thank you for taking care of Madam when I cannot." Simon gave him a regal nod, and then Jasper turned Colleen's way. "In case you're wondering, madam, I am Fred to Kitty's Ginger. I've been told we're to perform this evening. So you won't want to miss the night's entertainment. Your great-grandsons have also agreed to play a special number in your honor."

She smiled, knowing that while she might not be physically with them, they kept her alive in their hearts.

"Come along, madam, Simon," Jasper murmured in such a way that no one would notice.

Simon blinked up at Colleen.

"I know. It's amazing what a simple show of appreciation and respect will do, isn't it? Well done, my lord." She could have sworn she heard Simon chuckle. Until Charlie Angel, dressed as a pirate with a parrot on his shoulder, walked by and he hissed. "Be nice. Shay's now a member of this family, and that means her uncle is too."

Simon gave her a grudging *meow*.

"Oh my. Olivia and Jenna did a wonderful job," Colleen said as they followed the other guests into the ballroom.

The tables were covered in purple fabric, the chairs were black with red cushions, and the centerpieces were tall candelabras draped in cobwebs. Waiters dressed as Count Dracula served canapes and drinks with dry ice. A black tree stood at the rear of the stage with a full moon serving as its backdrop. Michael took the stage with Shay at his side. He leaned in to the microphone. "Shay and I want to thank you all for coming tonight." He thanked everyone who'd had a hand in making their day special, and then he named the family members that were no longer with them. So many of them gone now. "And last but not least, let's raise our glasses to the Gallagher family matriarch, Colleen. No one loved Halloween as much as she did or could have loved her family and Greystone more. To GG. I know you're up there smiling down on us today."

A chorus of "To GG" echoed throughout the cavernous room.

"Oh my, if I could cry, I'd be standing in a puddle of tears by now. There's nothing more important than family, family and love. And we were blessed with so much of it, even now," she said, looking out into the smiling, happy faces.

"My brother Connor has agreed to play the song for our first dance, and then my cousins, brothers, and I are going to perform a song in GG's memory. It was one of her favorites. Con." Michael waved his brother onto the stage to much cheering from family and friends.

As one of the groomsmen, Connor wore a black tux instead of a costume. He gave his audience a wave and a charming smile before turning to open a case on one of the tables, removing his saxophone. Before he walked to the stage, he curved a hand around Arianna's neck and whispered something into her ear. She looked beautiful in a sheer maxi-length coat dotted with crystal snowflakes over a long, ice-blue sparkling gown with a provocative slit from her ankle to her thigh and ice-blue satin gloves and slippers.

Colleen smiled at the way Arianna watched Connor take to the stage. "Now, that's a woman in love if ever I saw one. Oh ho," she said, spotting Jenna, who was dressed as Cinderella, lean in to her sister with a huge grin on her face. "She saw it too, Simon." Jenna had a special gift. If a couple stood close to each other in her presence, she could tell if they were meant to be or not. Colleen moved to stand beside the girls.

"I saw it plain as day, Arianna. He's your one, and you're his," Jenna said.

For one brief moment, Colleen was certain she saw a flicker of joy in Arianna's eyes before the hopeful light was blinked away. "We had our chance."

"So, this is your second chance. And don't say there's no such thing. All you have to do is look at Michael and Shay to know that's not true." Jenna nodded at the couple wrapped in each other's arms on the dance floor.

"There's more than her injuries holding her back, Simon. I'm sure of it. And just as sure as Jenna that Connor and Arianna are meant to be." If Colleen had any doubts, they would have disappeared at the look that came over Arianna's face the moment Connor started playing Sarah McLachlan's "Angel" for the bride and groom's first dance.

The boy had a talent. He felt the music deep down in his soul and poured it into the plaintive notes coming from the horn. You saw it in the way he moved on the stage, his fingers dancing over the keys. The Gallaghers' musical gifts and love of song had been passed down through the ages. Some said it was why William Gallagher had named the town Harmony Harbor. Wherever he went, he heard music, from the whistling winds in the forest trees to the ocean waves on the rocky shores.

Deep baritones joined the dulcet notes of the horn as Connor's brother Logan and his cousins joined him onstage. Around her, Colleen heard the rapturous sighs and smiled. Her great-grandsons were indeed a swoon-worthy bunch. Though they were blessed with good looks, talent, and smarts, their biggest blessings were their hearts. And all but one had been granted his heart's desire.

"I'll do what I can, Connor my boy." She would, even if her great-grandson's happiness were not at stake. If she wanted to ensure she was going to heaven and not hell, Colleen had to make amends for indirectly hurting Arianna with her meddling into the Bell family's affairs. She'd done right by Jenna. Now it was Arianna's turn.

"I'll make you a promise, right here and right now, Arianna Bell. Before this year is out, you and that man who is looking at you with his heart in his eyes will stand where Shay and Michael are now, with friends and family around you, celebrating your love for all of Harmony Harbor to see." Out of the corner of her eye, Colleen spotted Daniel, who was dressed as Indiana Jones, in the crowd ringing the dance floor. "And for the sake of us all, you better be mayor when you do."

Michael kissed Shay and then joined his brothers and cousins onstage. He took a seat at the piano, nodded at Connor, who raised the mouthpiece to his lips, and to his cousins and Logan, who joined him around the piano. "Our great-grandmother believed that at Halloween the veil between here and the other side thins." Michael looked up and smiled. "GG, this is for you."

Colleen moved toward the stage, oblivious to the

guests she walked through, to the feelings that usually sent a shiver down her spine. Her entire focus was on her great-grandsons singing and playing a song she had loved and sang a hundred times before, Josh Groban's "To Where You Are."

She wasn't blessed with their abilities. She was a Gallagher by marriage, not blood. But still she'd sung that song for the ones who'd gone on before her: husband, son, family, and friends. She'd loved large and lost many. Only now she had proof they were but a breath away, whether she could see them or not.

"I'm here, my boys. I'll be with you forevermore." Without thinking, she once again lifted a hand to her cheek, expecting tears where there were none and could never be. If she were able to cry, she would have cried even harder at the sight that now greeted her. Her grandsons Colin and Sean walked onstage to sing for her, to sing with their sons. But where was Daniel? she wondered. It wasn't like him to miss out on the spotlight. He had a good—maybe better—voice than his brothers and nephews.

She looked around the ballroom, but the crowd gathered at the stage blocked her view. From behind her came a persistent meowing and then from the parrot on Charlie Angel's shoulder, "Whatcha doin', big boy? Can you fly?"

"Stop eyeing the sword and pestering the parrot," Colleen told Simon as she continued her visual search for Daniel. She had a strong feeling something wasn't right. A feeling that intensified when she spotted wisps of fog slithering through the ballroom doors. Her grandson Colin would have a right fit. He'd banned Colleen and Kitty from using the fog machines years before on account because he he deemed them a fire hazard.

Colleen was torn. She didn't want to leave before her song was done. But it seemed that Simon wasn't pestering the parrot; he was after her attention. As she moved to the outer edges of the crowd, he looked at her, looked at the entrance to the ballroom, and then did it a few times more with dizzying speed, all the while meowing.

"All right, all right, I'm coming," she said, and he scampered off. She raced after him, her feet not touching the floor. She followed Simon's meows as he disappeared from view behind the grand staircase. She didn't have to wonder where he was headed as fog rolled from the other side of the stairs and crept across the floor. Behind the grand staircase was the door to the storage area where the fog machines were kept as well as the tunnels.

When Colleen rounded the corner, she heard a woman shooing off Simon. "Away with you, now."

It was Theia Lawson, the pilot who worked for Colleen's nemesis, Caine Elliot. The man behind Wicklow Developments. The man using her grandson to steal Greystone Manor out from under them. Theia wore a heavily ruffled white negligee and had a red flower in her hair and a drink in her hand. She was acting like a wedding guest, but it was obvious by her stance and the way she scanned the surrounding area that she was the lookout.

"He's here, Simon. I feel it in my bones. That's why the lass wasn't about today. She'd gone to fetch him."

Colleen walked through the door and the fog, following the barely audible sound of two male voices down the stairs. One she recognized as Daniel; the other she had heard once before, when he'd first approached her about buying the estate. There'd been a touch of Ireland in his deep, cultured voice. She heard it again now as she moved past the storage area to the maze of tunnels with their rough, damp walls, the sound of the sea permeating the stone. Up ahead, she saw a glow of light to her right and turned that way. She could make out what they were saying now.

"I'm telling you I can win. Don't give up on me yet. I'll get dirt on the lass. It shouldn't be hard. My grandmother kept a book of everyone in Harmony Harbor's secrets. From what I heard, there was a panic when she died. Folks in town were terrified her book would be found."

"Is that right?" Caine Elliot said, sounding intrigued, which would have sent Colleen into spasms of alarm if she weren't alarmed already.

"It is. My granny was known as the Secret Keeper of Harmony Harbor. She had a way about her. People told her their secrets, and if they didn't, she had her ear to the ground and found out what they were hiding. For weeks after she died, people snuck into the manor to search for her memoir. It hasn't been found, as far as I know. I'll find it though. It has to be here. Once I have it in hand, I'll expose Arianna's secrets. No doubt her family has them, just like the rest of us," Daniel murmured.

Colleen racked her brain, trying to recall what he'd

find to use against Arianna in her memoir, *The Secret Keeper of Harmony Harbor*. Off the top of her head, she couldn't think of anything. The truth about the affair between Arianna's father and Jenna's mother had come out months before and wouldn't change voters' minds. Admittedly, there was a small chance there was something Daniel could use. Colleen's memory wasn't as reliable as it used to be.

"She's seven points ahead of you in the most recent polls and appears to be gaining momentum. She's a beautiful woman with a tragic story and a history in this town."

"You canna believe the polls." Her grandson's brogue thickened with nerves.

"Very true. Which is why Theia is here. From her observations and interactions with the people in Harmony Harbor, she believes Ms. Bell will win. I trust her opinion."

"She's wrong. I've held back because of my nephew, but no more. The gloves come off. My family founded this town. Our name carries weight. In the end, it will win the day."

Colleen edged into the cell-like space and stopped short at the sight of her nemesis. Tall and powerfully built, he was dressed as the Phantom of the Opera. Theia's costume now made sense. She was Christine Daaé.

The man regarded Daniel, his blue eyes piercing, mocking, even the one through the white mask. He had hair as black as night and wore it slicked back from a face as beautiful as a dark angel.

"You're right. Your name does carry weight, and it's carrying it for Arianna. She has your brother, the former governor, your nephews, and as the town seems to know but you don't, the unspoken support of the majority of your family."

"You can't renege on our deal. We made a bargain."

"A devil's bargain, you traitor," Colleen said.

"The deal was you would win the mayoral race and then repeal any bylaws on the books, any objections by the historical society, or any environmental issues that might prevent my development on Main Street and my eventual plans for the manor and the surrounding grounds."

"You canny devil," Colleen muttered as his plan was revealed.

"If you don't win, you're of no use to me, Daniel. I'll have to write off your campaign and personal expenses as it is. I run a business, not a charity."

"I'm desperate. I need the money you promised me. If I don't get it, I'm going to lose everything. I tell you, I'm onto something there, but unless I meet the farmer's demands, he's threatening to shut down my dig and kick us off his property."

"Why don't you just ask your family for the money?" The devil asked her grandson the exact question that was on the tip of Colleen's tongue.

"Because I'd have to tell them I've lost everything. My wife, my home, and my professional reputation."

"Pride goeth before a fall." Caine Elliot's movements were contained as he went to take his leave, yet she sensed his barely leashed power beneath the polished facade. He'd own any situation, any room he entered. She didn't know what had possessed her grandson to make…Ah, but she did know, didn't she? Desperation, guilt, shame, that's why he'd made a bargain with the devil. It was as clear as day. As clear as his play for Maura. He envied his brother. Sean had everything Daniel wanted: success, wealth, respect, and the love of his children.

It was nothing new. Daniel had always wanted what Sean had. They were born eleven months apart and had waged a continuous battle for their parents' attention almost from the womb. Colin, the youngest son and the peacemaker, had escaped their jealousy and fights.

"Wait, please. Give me another chance."

"I'll cover your expenses until the end of the campaign, Daniel. Nothing more." Caine went to duck beneath the low opening, then stopped and glanced back. "You let your emotions, your jealousy, get the better of you. If you hadn't alienated your brother and his sons by making a move on his wife, they would have supported you. You would have presented a united front to the town. And because you're right and your family's name does carry weight in this town, you would have won."

Daniel stared after him. Colleen could practically hear the wheels turning in her grandson's head. And if his mind went where hers had, they were in bigger trouble than before.

"That's it," Daniel whispered, and then went to chase the devil down.

Colleen followed close behind, praying she was wrong.

"Hold up." He grabbed Caine's cape, taking a step back and holding up both hands when the bigger man whipped around. "Sorry. It's just that I have a plan. I promise, it'll work."

"I'm listening."

Colleen wondered at the younger man's self-possession. He had to be almost half Daniel's age, yet no one would know it from his demeanor.

"You know how Old Lady Fairchild started the write-in campaign for her granddaughter? I'll do the same."

"It won't work. People identified with Helen. They were sympathetic to her plight. And just a thought—you might want to stop calling her *Old Lady* Fairchild."

"Right, but you didn't let me finish. I'll fake a heart attack, and I'll beg my nephew Connor to take my place. I have an in on the town council. Actually, two for sure, with a possible third. I'm sure we can find a way around the election rules. They'll let him take my place. If they don't, my brother will make it happen. There's nothing he wants more than to have one of his sons fill his shoes. Maura even more so than him."

"You're grasping, Daniel. Your nephew will never take your place. As I understand it, he's in a relationship with Arianna Bell."

Colleen wished the devil were right, but he wasn't. Daniel knew it. Just like he knew he'd twigged Caine's interest.

"Yes, he will. My nephew is the middle son, and for whatever reason, my brother and sister-in-law overlooked him in their bid for Sean's successor. They shouldn't have. He wants it. His brothers don't. As far as Arianna goes, he knows she's in the race only for her grandmother's sake, but it's too late to get her out of it now. Unless he runs. Then she has an excuse to bow out gracefully, and he can give her grandmother some work at the town hall to keep her busy. Everybody's happy."

"I'm still not sure that it's enough."

"Don't you worry. It will be. I've told Maura I'll hire her as my personal assistant if I become mayor. I'll tell Connor he's the only one I trust to take my place. If he won't do it, I'll just have to run. That alone will be incentive enough. Those boys want their parents back together. They'll see this as a way to do that." He shifted in his boots. "So, are we good? Agreement's back on?"

"If your nephew wins and you ensure he clears the way for my developments, then yes, I'll honor our deal."

"Great. That's great, Caine. Thank you." They shook hands.

"I suggest you move ahead with your plan sooner rather than later, Daniel. The election is six days away."

"Funny you should mention it. I'm not feeling so well."

"You'd be feeling a lot worse if you could see me, boyo," Colleen said, and strode through him, wondering what she could do to stop this. At that moment, all she could think was to get Connor and Arianna away from the manor and hopefully buy herself some time.

Daniel shuddered. "Whoa, that was weird. It felt like someone walked over my grave."

Chapter Thirteen

♥

"You should have let me call a cab like I wanted to, Connor. It's your brother's wedding," Arianna said from the passenger side of the Porsche. She was sitting on towels so as not to ruin the leather upholstery. "It was bad enough I made a fool of myself overturning a tray of drinks. Now your family will be upset with me for dragging you from the party."

He took his eyes off the road to glance her way. "Are you done feeling sorry for yourself?"

"I'm not feeling sorry for myself. I feel like an idiot. I still can't believe I did it. I can't even remember bumping the tray." She looked down at the grape-colored splotch that marred the front of the beautiful costume Jenna had rented for her. "I don't know if I can get the stain out."

"If you can't, you can't. I'll cover the cost of the costume," he said as he turned slowly onto her street, keeping an eye out for older trick-or-treaters.

Carved pumpkins glowed from the neighbors' front porches. Their house was the only one on the street not decorated for the holiday. The campaign had taken its toll on both of them. Glamma had been too tired to come to the manor tonight, for which Arianna was secretly glad. She'd been worried about what she'd say to Daniel. Arianna had been a little leery about going herself. Only she'd thought it would be her interaction with Daniel that would be the problem, not her clumsiness.

She drew her gaze from the skeleton hanging on the neighbor's tree to look at Connor. "Of course it's easy for you to be blasé about it. You're not the one who made a fool of himself. And I don't need you to cover the cost of the costume, thanks. I have money." The insurance settlement hadn't come in yet, but Connor had managed to get them a decent advance.

He pulled alongside the curb in front of their house and turned off the engine before shifting in the seat. He reached out and gently twisted a strand of her hair around his finger. "You're beautiful. When you walked into the ballroom tonight, I'm pretty sure my heart stopped. And just when it started beating again and I'd recovered enough to trust my legs to go get you, Olaf beat me to it. Old Man O'Malley is lucky he's cute and about half my size or I might have kicked his snowman's ass."

She snorted a laugh, which didn't sound nearly as cynical as she'd intended. Probably because he'd called her beautiful and meant it. She could tell by the warmth in his eyes that he did. It also didn't hurt that he'd looked seriously gorgeous and sexy tonight playing his sax onstage, and she was still feeling a little like a girl who'd left the concert with the lead in a boy band. If she hadn't ruined the evening, she had a sneaking suspicion their date wouldn't have ended with just a kiss at the door. She took a page from his blasé book. "I'm sure. And I know what you're doing, and it won't work."

"You need to channel Elsa and let it go, babe." He grinned and got out of the car, humming the song as he came around to her side. He opened the door and reached across her to undo her seat belt, turning his head to lightly touch his mouth to hers before backing out. "People barely noticed when the tray fell. They were too busy listening to me kill 'I Will Always Love You.'"

She laughed, a real laugh this time. The man was ridiculously self-confident, and it was just one of the many things she loved about...Her laughter got stuck in her throat, and she stared up at the familiar and gorgeous face of the man she apparently *loved*. Not just a man she liked, felt comfortable with, leaned on, desired, but a man she *Loved* with a capital *L*. She didn't know why she was surprised. Less than an hour before, her sister had told her they were meant to be. Arianna had tried to play it cool, but inside she'd been ridiculously happy and hopeful.

Two emotions she hadn't felt in a very long time, well before the Nightmare on Main Street. But within seconds she tucked the feelings away, afraid to let herself hope, afraid to let herself feel, afraid to open herself up to more pain. It felt like by acknowledging her feelings for him, if only to herself, she'd crossed an invisible line and couldn't go back.

"Where did you just go?" he asked quietly, a note of concern in his voice.

Someplace scary. Really scary. She smiled and moved to get out of the car. “Back to the manor and Cinderella and Prince Charming’s dance. They looked happy, didn’t they?” she said, referring to her sister and Logan.

“They did. They are.” Connor slid an arm around her waist. “I don’t want to put a damper on the night, but how are you feeling about Jenna moving to DC?”

“I think I already put a damper on the night,” Arianna said wryly, pulling the sopping fabric from her stomach.

He opened the gate. “Honey, I promise, once we get you out of that dress, we can heat things right back up.”

Her brain and body both seemed on board with that plan, warming up at just the thought of him helping her out of the dress. “I, ah, thought you were going back to the manor,” she said. Her tongue felt thick and the words slightly garbled.

He stopped to take her purse. In the shadow of the dark house, she couldn’t see his eyes or read the expression on his face. “Do you want me to go back to the manor?”

He probably had no idea how difficult his question was for her to answer. How much he was asking of her. It was a huge risk, one she wasn’t sure she was willing to take. She’d no longer be able to pretend this wasn’t real, a romantic, intimate relationship and all the feelings and possibilities for hurt that came with it if they made love. “It’s your brother’s wedding. I didn’t think you had a choice.”

“Everyone always has a choice. Me. You.” He dug

her key from her purse. "I can kiss you good night at the door, undo your zipper if you need me to, or I can come inside. If I come inside, I won't be leaving until morning. Your choice."

She leaned into him as he put the key in the lock. "Decide for me."

"Not a good idea," he said. "I made up my mind about us weeks ago. I've just been waiting for you to get on board."

"It's not that easy. Maybe it is for you, but it isn't for me. I don't have a good track record. If we don't—"

He pressed his finger to her lips and then replaced it with his mouth. His kiss was soft and tender at first, as if he knew her heart was in fight-or-flight mode. He pulled her closer, and she went to warn him she'd ruin his tux but didn't get a chance because his tongue slipped past her parted lips and the thinking part of her brain immediately shut down. All she could do now was feel. His hand at her waist holding her in place, his body heat, his desire, hers. The kiss deepened, and she clutched at his shoulder, straining against him, wanting more, needing more. She broke the kiss. "Come…come inside," she said breathlessly.

He groaned and then lifted his head, his eyes heavy-lidded as he stared at her for a couple of beats. "We're going to my place. We'll grab—"

"I can't leave Glamma alone all night. If you're thinking we'll…she'll…She takes her hearing aid out to sleep."

She'd barely stepped across the threshold when he had her back in his arms. The house was dark and quiet. He tossed her purse and keys on the entryway table, closed the door with his foot, then reached back to lock it.

Reluctantly, she stepped away from him. "I need to check on Glamma."

He seemed just as reluctant to let her go, leaning in to kiss her again before doing so. "Do you want anything to eat, drink?"

She was tempted to say yes to stall. So much could go wrong; so much could go right. A bundle of nerves, she shook her head and went directly to her grandmother's door. She leaned against it in an attempt to regain her composure.

"Are you okay?" he whispered, barely a foot away.

She pressed a finger to her lips, losing any chance of keeping her feelings from her grandmother when she turned to face him. The light they'd left on in the hall at night shone down on Connor, his white shirt damp from where she'd pressed against him, his desire clearly evident in his black pants.

He followed her gaze. "I'll, ah, wait for you in your room."

She touched her cheek. It was hot, and she imagined flushed. Fanning herself, she fought to keep her gaze off Connor opening her bedroom door. He glanced at her before he closed it behind him, mouthing, *Hurry up. I'm dying.*

It wasn't a surprise he wanted her. He hadn't tried to rush her, but he'd made it known in the way he touched her and looked at her. She wanted him too. She just had so much more to lose. She pressed her good hand to her stomach, wondering if he'd recognize the scar from the caesarean, wondering if she owed him the truth.

It wouldn't make any difference. Their son was lost to them both. Like her, Connor would be tortured by the *what ifs*. They'd broken her in the beginning. Her heart hadn't fully recovered. It never would. It would be better for Connor if he never knew what he'd lost. She wouldn't unburden herself at his expense. Afraid Connor would come looking for her and read the guilt and turmoil on her face, she carefully opened her grandmother's door.

Propped up on two pillows, Helen snored softly. Her bedside lamp was on, a book resting on top of the duvet. Arianna carefully picked it up so as not to disturb her. She smiled at the title, *The Campaign Manager* by Catherine Shaw, and placed it on the bedside table before turning off the light. Bending down, she kissed her grandmother's cheek.

In many ways, the campaign had been good for Glamma, but it would soon be over. In six days, they'd either be winners or losers. Arianna still didn't know which she'd prefer. Although, as her grandmother had recently pointed out, a steady income would be a blessing. At eighty-five thousand dollars a year, the mayor's salary was nothing to sniff at. Even better, people would stop asking when she planned to rebuild Tie the Knot. But after today and the episode with the tray, the idea of losing held more appeal. She wasn't prepared to deal with the attention or the demands of the job. Not yet.

She tiptoed out of the room, quietly closing the door behind her. Looking down the hall at her closed bedroom door, she wondered if she should have been a little louder and woken up her grandmother. Nerves and doubts threatened to overwhelm her. As though Connor sensed something was wrong, the door to her room creaked open. Down the length of the hall, his eyes met hers. He leaned against the doorframe, crossing his arms over his broad chest. He hadn't taken off his shirt. Part of her wished he had; part of her was glad he hadn't.

"Change of heart?" he asked, his voice deep and sexy.

No. She didn't think her heart would ever be swayed. It had loved him before, and it loved him now. Her mind was something else entirely. It listened to the voices her heart ignored, like the voice of experience, the voice of reason.

He pushed off the doorjamb and walked toward her. "It's okay if you have. I'm not mad. But let's get you out of that wet dress, okay? Your lips are turning blue." His voice was low, calm, and steady. He wasn't angry. Concerned, maybe.

She took the hand he held out to her. "My lips aren't blue from the cold. They're blue from the drink."

"You sure? Maybe I should check," he said as they reached her bedroom.

She dropped her gaze to his mouth and nodded. "I think you should."

He pressed his lips to her mouth, a chaste kiss with no tongue or heat. She curved her arm around his neck. "You need to really kiss me to be able to tell," she murmured against his lips, reaching out to push the bedroom door closed. He needed no more encouragement than that; nor did she. She arched her back, dragging him with her. He lifted his mouth from hers and then dipped his head to feather kisses along her collarbone, along the neckline of her dress.

Mesmerized at the feel of his warm mouth on her skin, she barely noticed that he'd removed her costume's sheer overcoat and his fingers were now on the zipper at her back. Above their heavy breathing, she heard the sound of it sliding open. Slowly, inch by inch. Soon his hands would be on her. She ached with need, the desire to rip off her clothing and his building. Somehow the thought penetrated the erotic thoughts. Within seconds she'd be naked, exposed, vulnerable. She stretched out her arm, her fingers reaching the light switch. The room went dark. Connor's head came up.

"I want to see you. I need to see you." His voice rasped against her skin.

It was as much a sacrifice for her as it was for him. She was desperate to see him. "Not yet. Not tonight."

"Okay," he agreed, but she could tell it was a struggle for him not to argue. As good as he was, this was one argument he wouldn't win. "Is there anything I need to know? Do I have to be careful?"

"Just of my arm."

He didn't ask if she wanted to remove the glove, and she was grateful. In the dark, she could pretend she was whole. His fingers caressed her skin as he lowered the dress from her shoulders, his mouth following the path lower and lower while his lips danced over her skin. She gasped and squirmed. He smiled against her thigh, then said, “Step out,” before kissing his way back up her body and starting all over again with her bra and then her panties.

Much later, boneless and sated, they lay entwined on her bed, breathing heavily. Her room was dark, but her eyes had adjusted enough to make out the angles and contours of his body. He was big and beautiful, and…She felt him stiffen and swear under his breath. “What’s wrong?”

He practically leaped off the bed. “I’ll be back in a minute. I just have to check…” Grabbing her comforter off the floor, he wrapped it around himself and headed out the door. She waited for five very tense minutes before he came back into the room. He rejoined her on the bed, draping the cover over her.

“Connor, what is it? What’s wrong?”

“There was a tear in the condom. But you don’t have to worry. I’m clean.” He blew out a breath and then carefully drew her into his arms. “I freaked out a little until I remembered you can’t have kids. Jesus, sorry. I shouldn’t have blurted it out like that. I know it’s something you struggled with.”

She stared at him, wondering what he was talking about until she remembered her divorce. She’d found out about her son while she was married to Gary. At the time, after learning the truth, she couldn’t contemplate having another baby. She should have told Gary everything, but they’d been having problems for a while, and she didn’t trust him with her secret. He’d held her unwillingness to have a baby over her head for years. She didn’t know why—maybe it was some kind of ego thing—but he'd told friends and family, and obviously his lawyer, that she was barren.

Connor's hand moved over her stomach, a soft, tender caress, as though soothing her for what could never be. There wasn't an inch of her his fingers and mouth hadn't touched or stroked. He must have attributed the scars on her stomach to the skin graft. The scar from the C-section went deeper than all of the rest; it cut through to her heart and her soul. It made her who she was, made it even harder for her to trust.

Yet she knew for this to work with Connor, she had to tell him the truth. Even if she was scared to death of what it meant for them. With Gary, she'd been one of those sweet, wide-eyed brides who thought everything would be perfect as soon their vows were said. But her secret had come between them, widening the fault line that had developed in their marriage within a year of saying *I do*.

Connor rose onto his elbow to look down at her, brushing the hair out of her eyes. "Please tell me I didn't just blow our night together."

"You didn't. You couldn't. But we need to talk—"

"Hold that thought," he said when his cell phone rang. He reached across her to retrieve it from the nightstand. Checking the screen, he frowned. "Sorry, honey. I have to take it." He kissed her forehead as he brought the phone to his ear. "Hey, what's up? You know it's after midnight... What? When? Okay, yeah. I'm on my way."

"Connor, what's wrong?" she asked when he disconnected.

"They think Uncle Daniel had a mild heart attack. I wouldn't be surprised if it was indigestion. You wouldn't believe what the guy eats. Anyway, they can't get him to go to the hospital. I don't know why, but they seem to think he'll listen to me. Which would be a first in my family." He leaned across her and turned on the light.

"Connor!"

"Relax. You're covered. I can't see anything but your beautiful face." He smiled down at her. "I wanted to see if you looked the same as you used to after we made love."

Self-consciously she lifted a hand to her face. "I was seventeen."

"Yeah, and you look exactly the same. All soft and glowy, your eyes sleepy." He framed her face with his big hands. "And the last thing I want to do is leave." The kiss he gave her conveyed how badly he wanted to stay, as did the frustrated sound he made when he stood up.

Oh. My. He definitely didn't look exactly the same as before. In a good way, a very good way. Her hand, fingers, and lips hadn't done him justice. And by his cocky grin, he knew what she was thinking. It wasn't until she'd said goodbye to him at the door that her lust-filled haze dissipated, and she realized the consequences of the phone call he'd taken. If Connor was wrong and Daniel really did have a heart attack, he'd drop out of the race, and she'd win by default.

Chapter Fourteen

♥

As the elevator doors opened on the top floor of the manor's tower where the family's residences were housed, Connor stepped out. His brothers were waiting for him outside the closed door of the room where his uncle had been staying since he'd first arrived. Connor had fond memories of the suite. It had been his great-grandmother's.

There were three places you were guaranteed to find GG when she was alive. Her study, the library, and her suite. The tower room was his favorite place to visit. She'd always have a plate of cookies and a glass of chocolate milk waiting just for him and another adventure story ready to tell. She'd probably done the same for each of her great-grandchildren, but she had a way of making you feel like you were her most-loved. And for a kid who'd never felt like anyone's favorite, that was pretty special.

His baby brother scowled at Connor as he walked their way. "You look like I'm supposed to. It's my wedding night and you're the one who obviously got lucky."

"Seriously? You've been living with Shay for months. You get lucky all the time. I don't." Despite what his brothers seemed to think, it was true.

What he'd experienced with Arianna transcended luck. It had been one of the best nights of his life. And not because the sex had been off-the-charts amazing. There'd been some awkward moments. She'd been overly cautious of her arm, self-conscious of the scars on her stomach, and a little uptight.

But none of that mattered; he'd gotten a second chance with his first love. A woman who, although he hadn't been willing to admit it until now, had been his only love. Now he fully intended for her to be his last. He just had to convince her.

"No need to ask who with; the evidence is on your tux," his older brother said, lifting his chin at the dark stain. Logan looked about as pleased with him as Mike did. "Jenna ordered Arianna's costume, which means she's on the hook for repair and replacement."

"Relax. I'll take care of it. But I didn't leave—" He cleared his throat. He wasn't a kiss-and-tell kind of guy. "I didn't come out in the middle of the night to take crap from the two of you. And if you're out here giving me crap instead of in there with Uncle Daniel, I'm assuming everything's good and I can leave."

Mike grabbed his arm. "No. Don't. We're sorry. We shouldn't have jumped all over you. It's just that Mom had no problem calling me and telling me to get my ass here right away, and Dad did the same to Logan. And you, you get off scot-free like always."

And there it was, more evidence of his place in his

family. They didn't need him. They had Mike, the brilliant one, and Logan, the dependable one. But what Connor didn't understand was how his brilliant brother, who was also in touch with his feelings, didn't seem to get how what he'd just said felt like a slap in Connor's face.

"What can I say? It's good to be me." He went with his default defense mechanism, the one that never failed to tick off his baby brother.

"Do you always have to be so cocky?" Mike said.

"Do you always have to be such a sanctimonious pain in my ass?" Connor said, sticking to his usual script.

"Jesus, you're not teenagers anymore. This is serious. And Mike's right, Con. You've skated through life with no real demands put on you by the family. I'm not blaming you, so don't get defensive. It is what it is. But right now you're being given an opportunity to step up to the plate, and I for one would appreciate it if you did."

"So would I," Mike said.

He didn't know what they were talking about. He always showed up when any of his family called. "I'm here. What more do you want from me?"

"It's not what we want. It's what Uncle Daniel wants."

"Since when do you care what Uncle Daniel wants, Mike? You can barely stand to be in the same room with the guy."

"I know, but here's the thing. If you do what he wants, you have the best chance to get Mom away from him and back with Dad," his baby brother said, looking almost feverish with excitement.

"You wanna maybe relax there, Mike. You're starting to worry me," Connor said.

"Always the smart-ass," his baby brother muttered.

Logan sighed. "You guys realize you're just like Dad and Uncle Daniel, right? Why you're partnering up together, I'll never know."

"Yeah, and that's the only problem I see with Uncle Daniel's plan. How's Con going to work with me and be mayor?" Mike asked Logan.

"What are you talking about? I'm not running for..." He gaped at his brothers. "Come on, you can't be serious. He's bowing out of the race and wants me to run in his place?" No way. They had to be pulling his leg. "Okay, I guess I deserved that for leaving your wedding early. But you took it a little far, don't you think? You had me going though. I didn't think you two had it in you." He lifted his arms to give them both a fist bump. At the expressions on their faces, he lowered his hands to his sides. "You have got to be kidding me. You are serious."

"Yeah, and from the look on your face, you're going to refuse. Can't say I'm surprised," Mike said, shoving his hands in the pockets of his pants.

"I would damn well hope you wouldn't be surprised, genius. The woman I'm in love with is running against our uncle. She's also the woman our father has been doing his damnedest to get elected. So if you think I'm going—"

Logan put a hand on his shoulder. "Settle down.

You know us better than that. Even if it was our best shot to get Mom and Dad back together, we wouldn't have suggested it if we thought Arianna wanted to be mayor. But not more than ten days ago, you told me you were worried about her. You had serious doubts she even wanted the job. And just so you know, Jenna feels the same. She thinks the only reason Arianna has stayed in the race is because of Dad and Helen."

Mike nodded. "And don't bite my head off—I'm only the messenger—but Dad is all in. So is Mom. You should hear them, Con. It's just like old times. Only now they're pinning all their hopes on you to follow in Dad's footsteps instead of me and Logan. Seriously, I never understood why they didn't pin them on you in the first place. Uncle Daniel said the same thing."

Connor wondered if this was a new tactic to get him to go along with the plan. It would be just like Mike to figure out Connor's Achilles' heel and use it against him. This was the day he'd been dreaming of for as long as he could remember.

Only the cost was too high. Or was it? Because he was worried about Arianna and her ability to take on the job as mayor. Today was a prime example that she wasn't ready. Like Jenna, he believed Arianna was going along with it to keep everyone happy. And that was on him. He'd been the one to put her in that position in the first place. And now he might just have been handed the perfect way to get her out.

The door opened, and his dad stuck his head into the hall. His face lit up when he saw Connor. "There you are. I was getting worried. Get in here. Your uncle wants to talk to you."

"I'll be right there," he said, motioning for his dad to join them in the hall.

His father frowned and then nodded, stepping back into the room. "I'll just be a minute, Danny."

Connor gave his brothers an *are you kidding me* look.

"And that's why the family needs you to do this, Con. This feud between Dad and Uncle Daniel has been tough on everyone, especially Grams," Logan murmured.

Out of all of them, their grandmother had been having the hardest time with the battle being waged between her sons. Lately, she'd been caught in the crossfire, and it was taking a toll. Several people had commented at the wedding on how tired she looked. His father and uncle were lucky Jasper hadn't overheard the remarks. No doubt Kitty had been doing her best to hide from Jasper how she really felt.

His dad closed the door behind him and stepped into the hall. "Your brothers told you Danny wants you to run in his stead?"

"Ah, yeah, Dad. And they also told me you were all for it. So what, you just drop Arianna now? How do you think she'll feel? How do you think Helen will feel?" Connor shoved his fingers through his hair. What had he been thinking to even consider this?

"You know your old man. Does that sound like me? I've come to love that girl like a daughter, and Helen has become like a second mother to me. The last thing

I'd ever want to do is hurt them. Tell the truth, son. It's just the four of us here. It'll go no further. Do you truly believe Arianna wants to be mayor? If you do, I'll convince my brother to concede. You have my word."

Connor bowed his head and closed his eyes, thinking back over the past several weeks. The image that stuck most clearly in his head was of Arianna defacing her own campaign signs. "No, I don't believe she does. But I also know she'd do anything to make her grandmother happy. She thinks Helen is doing better because she's engaged in the campaign." He grimaced. "I might have had something to do with that."

"You can't take all the blame, son. I'm as guilty as you. At least you were motivated by love. I'm not proud of it, but I used Arianna's campaign to get back at my brother." He glanced at the closed door. "And now I have to live with nearly putting him in an early grave. It would have been my fault if we lost him tonight. My mother never would have forgiven me."

"I understand you're feeling guilty, Dad. But let's keep things in perspective," Connor said. "Uncle Daniel is hardly a saint."

His father glanced at the door again. "When it looked like he might go to meet his Maker, he grabbed my hand. Begged for my forgiveness." His father self-consciously wiped at his eyes. "I gave it to him. Promised we'd do this for him, for the family. You'll do it, won't you, son?"

"I have to talk to Arianna first. I won't do this unless she gives me her blessing. And we need to figure out something for Helen, and then there's Mike and the clients I've just brought on board." It was all happening too fast.

"You'll be able to run this town blindfolded with a hand tied behind your back. You have more energy and smarts than four men put together. You can easily put a few hours in at the firm at night, and I can put in a few days a week. Retirement isn't all that it's cracked up to be anyway," his father said just as Connor's mother stepped out of the room.

"Did I hear you right, Sean? You're coming out of retirement?"

"I am. My sons need me, and you know I've always been there for my boys, Maura." He got his arms around all three of them, dragging them closer.

"Yes, you always have," Connor's mother murmured, and then looked up at him. "Are you going to do it, darling? Are you going to run in Daniel's place?"

"We'll see. I need to—"

"Of course he is." His father rocked Connor against him. "It's happening, Maura. Just like we always dreamed it would. Once Connor's settled into office, we'll get started on his campaign for governor."

"Okay, you're getting a little ahead of yourself, Dad."

His mother and father completely ignored him. His mother was smiling like she'd just been handed a couple million, and his dad let go of Connor to join her.

"Why wait? We'll get started right away. I don't think I could sleep anyway. Connor can sit with Daniel and Kitty until Finn comes back with the results from the bloodwork. Do you want to go down to the bar and get a drink?" his mother asked his father.

"Nothing I'd like better. Boys, we'll be at the bar if you need us," his father said, smiling down at their mother, who smiled up at him.

"I'm pretty sure the bar is closed, and there are things we need to talk about—"

Holding the elevator door open for Maura, his father cut off Connor. "You forget, I'm one of the owners, son. I can get a drink anytime I want."

"Actually, Dad, you aren't one of the owners; we are. And I think you both should stay here." They were either ignoring him or didn't hear him because they were deep in conversation and getting onto the elevator. He turned to see both of his brothers grinning at him.

"Told you; it's just like old times," Mike said. "Isn't it great?"

Connor flipped them off. But the thing was, he understood why they were happy. After the stress of dealing with their warring parents and their mother's health scare these past nine months, it was a huge relief to see their parents talking and smiling again. And it wasn't like Connor hadn't toyed with the idea of running for office in the somewhat distant future. He just didn't think he'd have to throw the woman he loved under the bus to make it happen.

"I'm serious, you guys. No one breathes a word that I'm even considering taking Uncle Daniel's place until I've had a chance to talk to Arianna."

* * *

Arianna stretched in her bed, smiling when muscles she hadn't used in a very long time twinged, letting her know they were alive and well and very happy. She snorted at herself. Happy muscles, really? Connor was turning her into a...She smiled. He was turning her into a happy woman. "You're a miracle worker, Connor Gallagher," she murmured, and then yawned, glancing at the alarm clock on the nightstand.

Eight o'clock. With only five full days until the election, she imagined Sean and her grandmother were already in the kitchen having an early-morning strategy session. She didn't know how many times she'd rolled out of bed to find they'd already put in three hours at the kitchen table. It was a little depressing that they had so much more energy than she did. No doubt they'd planned an early start to her day. She never bothered checking the schedule of the day's events. She just followed their lead, did what she was told, and said what they told her to. In some ways it was like they were in the race and not her.

Except if Connor was wrong and Daniel wasn't suffering from just a bad case of indigestion...No, Connor was right. He had to be, she thought, tamping down a sudden rush of panic. She got out of bed and grabbed a robe. She'd get a cup of coffee, calm her sudden, totally out-of-proportion case of nerves, and call Connor. He had a way of calming her down. She smiled at the thought and then laughed at herself.

Three smiles in less than three minutes—she was acting like a lovestruck teenager. She took a minute before opening her bedroom door to put on her professional-candidate face. The last thing she needed was for Glamma to figure out she and Connor had had a sleepover. Only it wasn't really a sleepover because he'd left in the middle of the night, which was probably for the best, now that she thought about it. She didn't need Glamma getting any ideas.

Arianna opened her bedroom door, half-expecting to hear Sean's and Helen's voices, like she did most mornings. She inhaled deeply. Odd. The coffee hadn't been put on. As she walked toward the kitchen, she heard a sniffle from the living room. She turned to see her grandmother sitting on the chair, crying.

"Glamma, what is it?" She rushed to her side, kneeling at her feet.

Helen pressed her blue-veined hand to Arianna's cheek. "My darling girl, I should have known. I should have seen it coming. Blue-eyed devils, the whole lot of them."

She was about to ask if Daniel Gallagher had died, but nothing her grandmother was saying made sense. Oh God. Had the campaign become too much for her? Ava had been worried it might. They hadn't been to the specialist yet, but there were indications that Glamma was in the early stages of dementia. Ava hadn't said it in so many words, and she certainly hadn't meant to put the blame on Arianna, but she believed the stress of losing Tie the Knot and Arianna's injuries had taken as much of a toll on her grandmother as it had on her. Then there was the night Glamma had gotten lost. The stress of the campaign had become too much for her then. And now here they were again. All because Arianna hadn't looked beyond her grandmother's newfound zest for life and her vibrant energy to see that they might be doing her more harm than good.

She covered her grandmother's hand with her own. "Why don't I make you something to eat, and we'll have a cup of tea together? Take the morning off and relax."

"Relax? We can't relax. We have to beat those devils at their own game. They've messed with the wrong women. They think you're weak and crippled and that I'm old and deranged. Ha! We'll show them."

"Glamma, stop it! You're worrying me. I have no idea what you're talking about it."

Her grandmother slumped in the chair, looking every one of her eighty years. "I'm sorry, darling. You're just like me. We weren't meant to have a man in our lives."

"This is about Connor?" She couldn't think what else it could be.

"Don't mention that name in this house. He's even more handsome and slick than his uncle and his father combined. Pretending they cared about us when all along they were leading us on. The writing was on the wall. You were going to beat his uncle and the Gallaghers can't stand losing, so they've pulled strings and replaced him with his nephew. But we'll show them, won't we? You'll beat him, darling. Beat him and his horrible family at their own game."

Connor had changed sides. He was running against her. Last night they'd made love, and this morning he'd left her. Her chest and throat were so tight she couldn't speak. Arianna dropped to her bottom on the hardwood.

She lifted her eyes to her grandmother, staring at her through a wet film. "Are you sure?" she finally managed to whisper.

She reached for Arianna's good hand and gave it a comforting squeeze. "Byron Harte from the *Harmony Harbor Gazette* called to say that there'd been an emergency meeting of the town council after midnight, and they'd agreed, on compassionate grounds, to allow Connor to run in his uncle's stead. The Harte boy asked for a comment."

"Did you…? Did you give him one?"

Her grandmother smiled. "I gave him one the town of Harmony Harbor will never forget."

Chapter Fifteen

♥

After he read the piece in the online version of the *Harmony Harbor Gazette*, it took everything Connor had not to throw his iPhone across his grandmother's suite. "Who. Talked. To. The. Press?"

"It wasn't me, boyo. I've been here all night long. You should know. You were with me. Staying with me in my time of need. I won't soon forget it." His uncle sat propped up in the dark wood canopied bed with a breakfast tray on his lap. He looked pretty perky for a man who'd asked for his last rites at three this morning. Connor had nodded off around five and had been woken up by his father fifteen minutes ago to the news he'd been outed in the *Harmony Harbor Gazette* with a response from his opponent.

As of yet Arianna hadn't withdrawn from the race or wished him luck. She'd wished him straight to hell along with the rest of the blue-eyed devils in his family. And that was the nicest thing she had to say about him, and his father.

He understood she was hurt. She had every right to

be, and if she'd pick up the damn phone, he'd explain what had happened, but she wouldn't. Well, she'd pick up, but then she'd slam the receiver in his ear as soon as he got half a word out of his mouth.

His father grabbed Daniel's iPad and sat on the edge of the bed.

"Do yourself a favor and don't read it," Connor told his dad. He wished he hadn't read it. No matter how mad Arianna was at him, he couldn't believe she'd gone that far.

"Now, come on. Buck up. You know this business isn't for the faint of heart. You can't overreact to everything you read about yourself in the press," his father said with a patronizing smile.

If the accusations and aspersions cast against their characters hadn't been made by the woman Connor loved, he'd be handling it a lot better than he was. He glanced at his dad, whose eyes got bigger the further along he read. His uncle put his tray aside and crawled across the bed to lean over Sean's shoulder and read the article.

"I didn't know the lass had it in her. If it weren't my brother and nephew she was eviscerating in the press, I'd admire her fighting spirit." He made a face at Connor. "Sorry, boyo. It looks like you might have lost your girl. You can always go back to the other one. Brooklyn, wasn't it? Now, she was a real looker, and not nearly as vengeful as this one. Or as canny about the voters. If you want to win the mayoral race, I suggest you get out there and show your pretty face." His uncle went back to reading the article with a half smile on his face, apparently oblivious to the fact that he was ultimately responsible for Connor losing his girl.

That wasn't completely true though. In the end it had been Connor's decision to run. Sure, taking one for the Gallagher family team had played a role. But it wasn't only for the backslaps and the pride on his parents' faces or that he'd be the one to make their dreams come true. It was because he'd one day dreamed of following in his father's footsteps. He just hadn't gotten up the nerve to share his ambitions with his parents, afraid of being shut down or simply ignored.

His uncle's half smile abruptly disappeared. "What does she mean we're sexual deviants? You, Maura, and I have never had a threesome. And why is she comparing me to King Henry VIII? I've only had three wives, and they're all alive. Sue the shrew. Sue her for defamation of character."

"We're not suing anyone. Think of how Arianna feels right now. She thinks I used her, betrayed her. And think how it would look if we sued her, a woman who only months ago lost everything she owned and almost lost her life. Now settle down and lie back in bed. You're supposed to be resting." His uncle's blood work had been inconclusive. Because he'd gotten so worked up at the mere suggestion of going to the hospital, Finn had agreed to treat him at home.

Connor's father tapped the iPad while glaring at him. "Think how *she* feels? Did you read the entire thing? Did you read what she said about our family? About you? She makes it sound like you ripped her to shreds during her divorce hearing, made up vicious lies about her, left her destitute. And this"—he stabbed the screen—"she claims you were cheating on her with four women while dating her in your teens."

Connor rubbed the bridge of his nose between his thumb and forefinger. "I know what she said, and you know her, Dad. For two seconds, put yourself in her shoes. Think how she felt when she got that call this morning. Less than eight hours after we'd..." Okay, he wasn't going there. "It'll be fine. I'll go talk to her and straighten everything out. I'll ask her to print a—" *Retraction* got drowned out by his mother storming into the room shrieking, "She's ruined us! She's ruined our chances to get back in the governor's mansion, Sean! Connor will never recover from this! People in Harmony Harbor won't vote for him now!"

He could reason with his uncle and his father, his mother, not so much. Surreptitiously, he pulled his phone from his pocket and texted his brothers on their group chat. *Uncle Daniel's room, stat. You talked me into this, and I can't deal with them by myself.*

Almost immediately Michael responded. *Sorry. You're on your own. The story must have been picked up in Boston, because I'm fielding calls from the clients you just brought on board, who are wondering how you'll have the time to look after them when you're also running for mayor. Since it's starting to look like you won't win, I shared that it was highly doubtful you'd be elected. Which seemed to appease them.*

Arianna's charges in the *Gazette* wouldn't matter to his clients. All they cared about was that he had enough time in the day to devote to their needs.

Oh, hell. Apparently dealing with irate clients is going to be the most pleasant part of my morning. Cherry just marched into the office with several of Arianna's campaign signs. It looks like she's staging a sit-in.

Logan chimed in. *At least Shay hasn't turned on you. Jenna packed a bag, and she's moving in with her sister.*

Good. I mean, not good that Jenna's left, but now that she has, you can come over and help me out here. Connor glanced at his parents and bowed his head. *Mom looks like she's going to cry.*

Are you crazy? I can't let this fester. I'm heading over to Arianna's to talk to the three of them, and then I'm bringing Jenna home.

Okay, good. Pick me up. And you can tell Arianna exactly who came up with this brilliant plan.

Logan typed, *What I'd like to know is who leaked this to the press.*

You and me both, Connor typed with feeling, noticing Logan hadn't said he'd tell Arianna the truth.

We just have to figure out who had the most to gain, his brother the former FBI agent responded.

And that was the question of the day. Connor had been racking his brain, trying to figure out that very thing. Other than close family members, no one else knew.

There was a knock on the door, and Byron Harte poked his head in the room. "Hi. I was told it was okay to—"

"You have a lot of nerve coming here after printing the Bell girl's lies, Harte," Daniel said, looking like he might throw the iPad at the man.

"That's why I'm here, actually. It was Arianna's grandmother Helen who issued the comments, supposedly relaying them verbatim from Arianna. Which, I've since learned, was not the case. Arianna called and cleared that up a few minutes ago. My sister's getting the retraction online as we speak, and we'll correct the print issue before it goes out tomorrow. I had my doubts about some of the story, but Helen can be persuasive. I wanted to personally offer my apologies."

"I bet you wanted to offer your apologies. You were that close"—Daniel pinched his forefinger and thumb together—"to being sued for everything you own. You don't mess with the Gallaghers and get away with it. Why you'd listen to Arianna's granny, I'll never know. The woman's loopers."

"Uncle Daniel." Connor gave his uncle a censorious look, then turned to Byron. "We appreciate you coming by and clearing things up, Byron. I'm glad to hear that Arianna had nothing to do with the comments in the paper. The news I was running in my uncle's place came as a shock to her, but I'm sure once we get a chance to talk we can clear everything up. After we do, I wouldn't be surprised if she had an announcement of her own to make."

"Uh, just so you know, the comments being removed are the ones along the line of the deviant behavior remarks. Threesome, that sort of thing. Arianna didn't retract the comments about either you or your father, unless they were in relation to the previously stated deviant... Well, you know. And she already made an announcement."

"Great. I'm happy to hear that. Campaigning has been tough on her, you know. She's not fully recovered."

"Son." His dad cleared his throat.

Connor nodded and picked up the container of water on the table beside the chair and poured his dad a glass while saying to Byron, "It's probably no surprise to anyone that the only reason Arianna was in the race was because we sort of coerced her into it. Helen's the one who really wanted to be mayor. It's too bad she's having issues with her mem—"

"Jaysus, son, he's a reporter, not your best friend," his father said, taking the glass from Connor's hand.

He couldn't believe it. Since when did he blab to reporters? He didn't blab to anyone. He always kept his own counsel; he was totally cool under pressure. Until now. He was just so relieved that he and Arianna wouldn't be opponents that he'd run off at the mouth. "That was off-the-record, Harte."

"I figured. But I think you may have misunderstood about Arianna's announcement. She's staying in the race."

"For mayor? She's staying in the race for mayor?" He said it twice because he didn't sound like enough of an idiot saying it once.

"That's the only race I know of. Unless you're thinking of the Turkey Run at Thanksgiving?" Byron said.

"Of course I'm not thinking of the Turkey Run. I just didn't think she'd want to stay in the race." Now, why did he keep blurting out stuff like that to Harte?

"I know; it's off-the-record." He gave Connor a sympathetic smile. "You're in a tough spot. I get it. Everyone knows you two were dating and you and your dad were her biggest supporters. But blood is blood. Your uncle got sick—"

"Ticker just about gave out," Daniel corrected. "I had the last rites. Almost met my Maker on the same day as my grandmother. Imagine that? All Saints Day. Must be something to that, don't you think?"

For a man who'd almost met his Maker, his uncle was looking surprisingly well, Connor thought for the second time that morning. Which made him wonder about something else. "Byron, how exactly did you get word that I was taking my uncle's place?"

"I got a phone call around one thirty this morning. Called and confirmed with one of the town councilors around six. Then I wrote up the story and added in the quotes from Helen once I reached her this morning."

"Do you know who called you?"

"A woman, but I didn't recognize the voice."

Connor rounded on his mother. "How could you, Mom? You had to know I wanted to break the news to Arianna myself."

"Why do you immediately blame me? Maybe it was—"

"It was you. I know it was. Just come clean, Mom."

"Yes. Yes, it was me." She lifted pleading eyes to him. "I'm sorry. I didn't mean to hurt your relationship with Arianna, darling. You all said she didn't want to be in the race, so I thought... I didn't want you to get cold feet. Don't you see? Your father and I..." She lowered her eyes to her lap. "I'll call Arianna and tell her it was my fault she had to read the news in the paper."

In the past his mother never would have apologized or tried to make things right, and he didn't think it was because things had gone very, very wrong. This had to do with her and his dad. He was sure of it. She'd see this as a way for them to have a second chance. And despite her possibly blowing his chance with Arianna, he couldn't stay angry at her. "I'd appreciate if you call her, Mom."

"You'll stay in the race?" she said, and then bit down on her bottom lip as though afraid he was going to take away all her hopes and dreams with a single word.

"I think so, yeah." He glanced at Harte. He'd forgotten the reporter was still in the room.

The owner of the *Gazette* sighed. "I know. It's off-the-record."

* * *

"I guess that's the one positive in all of this," Logan said when Connor told him their mother was the one who leaked the news to the press. "Thanks to you, Mom and Dad might finally get back together."

"Yeah, and I might lose Arianna forever," he said as his brother pulled his truck in front of the house on the corner of Holly and Ivy.

"Mom was calling her when we left the manor. So Arianna knows you told everyone you wanted to talk about it with her before you made your decision."

"And what if she asks me to bow out of the race?"

"The horse has kind of left the barn on that one, don't you think? Besides, Jenna's ticked at how everything went down and wants to make sure Arianna knows she has her back, but I could tell she was relieved at the thought that her sister would be out of the race. I think she was as surprised as all of us that she's staying in."

"I'm going to do my best to talk her out of it."

"Shouldn't be that tough. You're the one who talked her into it in the first place."

"Thanks. I really needed that reminder." He undid his seat belt. "Here goes nothing."

"Don't worry. I have your back." Logan got out of the truck. "Helen doesn't happen to have a gun, does she?"

"You're just a regular comedian today, aren't you?"

"I wasn't trying to be funny." Logan pointed at something poking out from the mail slot in the door. "Just hang on until I text Jenna and get the all clear."

A couple minutes later the metal flap on the slat closed, and the door opened a crack. Helen poked her face out, a lit cigarette hanging out of her mouth. "You have two minutes to get off my property before I call the—" She started to choke, and a hand shot out to remove the cigarette from her mouth.

He recognized that hand. "Arianna, please, just give me five minutes to explain." He cautiously opened the gate and walked up the path. "Please, babe, the last thing I meant to do was hurt you. Either of you."

"Oh, don't you use that voice on her, all low and sexy. We know what you Gallaghers are about. You got what you wanted and then tossed us aside. You made us think we were in this together, that we were on the same team. But as soon as a better offer came along—"

"Glamma, you have to trust me. It wasn't like that. I wanted to talk to you and Arianna first. My mother called, didn't she?" he said as he carefully made his way to the porch, desperate to get a glimpse of Arianna. He saw a shadow in the window and suspected it was her.

"She called, all right. She told us that on account of your being a lawyer you were more qualified for the job."

So much for his mother turning over a new leaf. "Did she tell you I wouldn't make a decision until I talked to you both? The announcement wasn't supposed to be made until later today."

Arianna appeared in the doorway. Her grandmother made a disgusted sound and walked away. Arianna was pale, her eyes red-rimmed. She still had on her robe. Her hair was messy, sexy, like she'd yet to brush it since last night.

Instinctively he reached for her.

She held up a hand. "But the announcement still would have been made, wouldn't it? You were going to do this whether I planned to stay in the race or not."

He couldn't deny it. "I'm not just doing it for me. My family—" She went to close the door. "Come on, just let me in. We can work this out." He couldn't help himself and reached for her hand. "Don't throw everything away because of this. How many times did you tell me that you didn't want to be in the race?"

"How many times did you tell me it was good for me, good for Glamma?"

"Is it good for you? Do you honestly want to run? Not just for Helen, not just because you're angry at me. Do you want to be mayor of Harmony Harbor?"

"Do you?"

"I think I do, but I don't want to lose you. Not when I've just gotten you back." Something in her face changed, and he thought he might be getting through to her. "Arianna, please—"

There was a shotgun blast, followed by the sound of something exploding. Connor grabbed Arianna and pulled her out of the house to safety. Logan ran past them into the line of fire, calling for Jenna.

Arianna stared up at him, her eyes wide and panicked. She clutched his arm. "She wouldn't. She wouldn't hurt Jenna."

"All clear," Logan called out through what sounded like clenched teeth.

Arianna sagged against Connor for all of a minute before quickly straightening and hurrying into the house. Connor followed, taking in the scene as he walked into the living room. His brother was scowling down at Helen as he removed the bullets from the rifle. Jenna was behind him, where his brother had no doubt shoved her, looking shaky but otherwise okay.

"Glamma, what did you do?" Arianna demanded.

"I shot the blue-eyed devil in the head."

Arianna cast Connor a fretful glance before saying in a solicitous voice, "There's no one here, Glamma. You shot the TV."

"Do you think I don't know that? He was on there, being interviewed by the woman from North Shore News."

"My uncle was on the news?" Connor asked.

"Don't act all innocent and concerned. You know darn well he was. They sent you here to distract us. You didn't think we'd hear what he was saying about us on the TV, did you? Telling voters I'm old and senile and that Arianna's not up for the job on the account she's a cripple. He says she never wanted to be mayor anyway. That she's only running on account of me. I wonder who he heard that from." She shooed them away. "You've overstayed your welcome. You've got two minutes before I call the cops."

"Arianna, you've got to believe me. I had no idea my uncle—" Connor began.

"My grandmother's right. You need to leave."

Chapter Sixteen

♥

Arianna was in it to win it. She didn't have a choice. She didn't just want to win; she needed to. Yesterday, listening to Connor plead his case, or at least trying to, she'd considered dropping out. But the more she thought about it, the more panicked she got. No matter how conflicted her feelings for Connor, she was positive of one thing: She couldn't go back to the life she'd been living all those weeks before. Which meant she not only had to stay in the race, she had to win.

And she didn't feel one iota of guilt for making that choice. For Connor, being mayor would just be the crown on top of his already perfect life. From what Jenna had told her of his plans for his political future, the mayorship was the first rung on the ladder to the top. As far as Arianna was concerned, he could find another ladder to climb, because this one was hers.

In the physical therapist's room at North Shore General, Arianna went back to straightening her fingers, slowly curling them into a hook, and then making a fist. The three movements combined took her several minutes to make. Since she hadn't intentionally moved her fingers in months, it was a small victory. But she found it a little hard to celebrate when, sitting in the chair beside her, her grandmother had done it at least twenty times to Arianna's one. Now Glamma was shadow boxing.

The physical therapist, Rachel, a thirtysomething woman with a headful of corkscrew curls and luminous brown eyes behind her stylish green-framed glasses, pressed her lips together in an effort, Arianna assumed, not to laugh. She clearly found Glamma hilarious.

"You're doing great," she said to Arianna, her voice warm and encouraging.

Arianna raised an eyebrow, glancing at her grandmother.

Rachel laughed. "She has arthritis. She's not recovering from third-degree burns." She reached over and gave Arianna's good arm a gentle squeeze. "Trust me, if you do your exercises and keep your appointments with me and Mark, you will regain the use of your hand and fingers. It's just going to take some time and a lot of work on your part." Mark was Arianna's occupational therapist.

"She doesn't have time. The election is four days away, and we need people to see she can do anything the blue-eyed devil can do. They're making her out to be weak and a cripple," Glamma said.

Rachel winced. "Let's not use that word, okay, Helen? Not only because it's offensive, it's also not true. And both you and Arianna need to realize that. Words have weight; they have power." She gently lifted Arianna's damaged hand. "Make a fist."

Slowly, but a little less so than the last time, Arianna folded her fingers into her palm.

"Awesome. Now raise your arm chest height and hold it there."

Not so awesome and a lot harder. Finally, after some struggles and breathing through the pain, she managed to do it.

Rachel smiled and raised her hand to give her a careful fist bump. "And that's who you are, Arianna Bell. A fighter. And don't let anyone make you feel otherwise."

Helen nodded. "She is. We both are, and we're going to show those Gallagher men exactly what the Fairchild women are made of. And let me tell you, it's not sugar and spice and everything nice."

Rachel grinned. "You have my vote. I'll see you Monday for your next appointment." She stood up and held out her hand.

Arianna looked down at it, caught her bottom lip between her teeth, and then slowly raised her right hand to clasp Rachel's. It was the very definition of a limp handshake, but she'd done it.

Rachel smiled. "Fighter."

"Winner," Helen declared.

And right then, for the first time in what felt like forever, Arianna believed them. She smiled. "Thank you. Now, Glamma, it's your turn."

"We're going up to neurology for my mental test," she confided to Rachel. "I have an appointment with a specialist in Boston, but it's after the election, and we want proof that I'm not a loon toon."

"Remember, Helen, words matter," Rachel said.

"I know. That's what tripped me up the last time I took the test with Ava over at the clinic. But Arianna and I have been practicing."

"Glamma, I think what Helen meant was for you to stop calling yourself a loon toon."

"I didn't realize I referred to myself like that, but I suppose I do. I'll put a stop to that right now. I'm a genius. I. Am. A. Genius."

An hour later, Helen proudly waved her test results in the air. "Rachel's right—words really do matter."

She'd scored thirty out of thirty on the Folstein test. Which didn't rule out that she may be in the beginning stages of dementia, especially since she'd shown signs of clinical and cognitive impairments over the past few months, but all Arianna cared about right now was that her grandmother was happy and feeling confident.

"We should go show Rachel," Helen said as they walked to the elevator.

"We'll bring it to my appointment on Monday. She's probably with a client. Besides, we're on a tight schedule." They had events booked straight through from noon to ten p.m. They'd gotten a late start because of their hair appointments first thing this morning and their appointments here.

Time well spent, Arianna thought, when they stepped off the elevator on the main floor of the hospital and she spotted a horde of people crowded near the front doors, several women holding up their phones to take pictures.

"There must be a celebrity visiting. I wonder who," Helen said, fussing with her hair.

"It's not a celebrity. It's Connor," Arianna said,

surreptitiously raising a hand to her own hair. It had nothing to do with him, she assured herself. She had to look her best. With the recent coverage in the press, it was more important than ever that she look put together.

She thought she did. The stylist had not only done her hair but also her makeup. Then Arianna had returned more than half of what Connor had bought her at Merci Beaucoup, picking up a couple new pieces her grandmother insisted she buy. Arianna wore one of the outfits now, a gorgeous black-and-white abstract print jacket over a black cami and slim-fit, ankle-length pants, a pair of black heels, and a fringed black wrap worn around her shoulders.

The crowd suddenly parted, and there he was. He wore a black Armani suit, the expensive dress shirt underneath open at the neck, the blue a perfect complement to his eyes. The man and the two women who walked with Connor appeared to be hanging on his every word. As Arianna knew, he was very good with words—and promises. And attracting the attention of every woman within a ten-mile radius.

Even in the middle of his conversation, he managed a smile for the staff, who were clearly thrilled to have him there. And, dammit, it wasn't just the women. She shouldn't have been surprised; the man could charm a monkey out of a tree filled with bananas…and a woman who'd been living in the dark and liking it, into the light.

"That's the head of the hospital, and the two women are in charge of fundraising and marketing," Helen said with a hint of both irritation and admiration in her voice.

"Well, then, we'd better introduce ourselves," Arianna said with way more confidence than she was feeling. The words "fake it till you make it" popped into her head. She should be just fine, then. She'd become a pro at faking it. Except as she and her grandmother approached the group of people and Connor looked over, she wasn't sure she could fake that she didn't still have feelings for him.

He didn't even bother hiding his, a slow smile curving his mouth, his very talented mouth, a mouth that had made her—

A voice, her grandmother's voice, immediately brought her mind back to where it belonged. "Arianna and I were just coming to see you, Bill." She winked at the man who stood beside Connor with one of those smiles on his face that said he was racking his brain for her name because he should undoubtedly know hers if she knew his. He had no idea who he was dealing with. "You don't know me personally, but I know all about you. Your grandmother's in my garden club." She held out her hand. "Helen Fairchild. You obviously know my granddaughter Arianna Bell, the next mayor of Harmony Harbor."

The crowd went quiet, people nervously casting Connor sidelong glances, visibly relaxing when he laughed. "I don't know about that, but she is a formidable opponent." Connor's eyes briefly met hers, dancing with amusement and a challenge before he said, "Liz, Jean, have you met Arianna?"

"Not personally, but I've heard all about her," Liz said. She glanced at Arianna's hand with the compression bandage visible and smiled instead of proffering hers. No doubt out of consideration for Arianna's injury. "You designed the dresses at an event I attended in Boston a few years back. They were divine."

"You designed my daughter's wedding gown," Jean said, and unlike Liz, she didn't look at Arianna's hand before offering hers. "She loved working with you and your sister. Her gown was stunning."

"Thank you. Thank you both," Arianna said, hoping no one noticed the perspiration gathering on her brow as she worked to clasp Jean's hand.

"I'm so sorry. I didn't realize," Jean said. "I hope I didn't hurt you."

"Not at all, and I know I don't have to worry about hurting you. I haven't got much of a grip yet," she quipped, to make light of the moment. "But I will. Your therapists Mark and Rachel are wonderful." She felt Connor staring at her and couldn't meet his eyes. She was afraid if she did, and he reacted like she thought he would, she might do something stupid like walk into his arms and never walk away.

"Don't forget Denise up in neurology," Glamma said, waving her paper in Connor's face. Arianna had wondered how long it would take. "She did the MMSE test on me. I don't like to call it a mini-mental state examination because of the negative connotations," Glamma confided, then smiled. "I aced it. Passed with flying colors. I'll make you a copy and you can give it to the adulterer—sorry, I mean your uncle," she said to Connor, whose eyes Arianna could still feel on her. "You know, the one on whose record you're running."

By the way her grandmother was tilting her head to the side, Arianna knew where she was going with this and took her by the arm. "Sorry. We have a luncheon we have to get to. It was nice meeting all of you. I have an appointment here Monday morning. If you have some time, I'd love to schedule a meeting with you, Bill, and you too, Liz and Jean. Connor"—she forced herself to look at him—"in case I don't see you before Tuesday, good luck."

He smiled and offered his hand. She inwardly groaned, wishing she'd just walked away. Instead she clasped his hand, and he gave it a gentle squeeze that contained a wealth of meaning and emotion. "I think I'm going to need it," he said.

He probably had no idea how much his words meant to her.

* * *

Later that evening Arianna glanced at her grandmother as she opened the front door. Glamma looked like she felt. "I'm going to make a few changes to this weekend's schedule. You obviously can go all day and night without a break, Glamma, but I can't."

"You should probably do that, then. We can't have you looking like a wilted flower." She made a face as she walked past Arianna into the house. "Your opponent obviously has more energy than the two of us combined."

They'd both been invited to the grand opening of a

new gym in town. Sadly for her, they'd arrived within five minutes of Connor and his entourage. "He did at least fifty of those one-armed push-ups before the man who challenged him gave up. I think you'd moved on to the yoga room by then."

She'd pretended she was going to check out the yoga studio but instead had been watching Connor like every other woman in the place. Unlike every other woman in the place, she had intimate knowledge of his strength and stamina. She never, ever should have slept with the man. And she definitely shouldn't be thinking of him before she went to bed.

She went to shut the door and noticed the envelope on the floor, smiling when she saw the return address. "Glamma, we can't go to bed," she called out as she shut and locked the door. "We have to celebrate."

"What are we celebrating?" Glamma said from the kitchen.

Arianna walked to the counter where her grandmother was plugging in the kettle for tea and waved the envelope in front of her face.

"It's here." Helen cheered and kissed the envelope. "What should we buy first?"

"A car. Taxi fares add up, and as much as walking is good for us, it's getting cold." They'd woken up to heavy frost two days in a row.

"Let's buy a Beemer. I loved that car. Remember her? She was a beauty."

"I'm not promising anything. We have to pay off everyone first. Once we know what we have left, maybe we can check out used Beemers."

"I thought Connor said the insurance pays off all the creditors."

"Huh. I think you're right. Your new mantra is paying off, Glamma."

"I. Am. A. Genius." She laughed and waved her hand. "Come on, open the envelope."

She might be able to make a fist and give a limp handshake, but envelope opening seemed to be beyond her. She handed it to her grandmother. "You'll have to do it."

"Don't get down on yourself. Look what you've already accomplished. You'll be opening an envelope in no time at all."

"Thanks, Glamma. Hurry up. Don't keep me in suspense." It wasn't as if they were going to be wealthy or as if they were destitute now. Arianna was just ready for that part of her life to be over. Now that the check had been delivered, it felt like they could close the door on that terrifying night in July.

She thought maybe Serena would feel the same and decided to call her as soon as Glamma went to bed. Her sister had basically dropped off the face of the planet, yet Arianna hadn't had the energy to chase her down. She knew she was okay. Arianna had finally bought a cell phone, and they texted every second day. But never more than a few lines. They hadn't talked on the phone for ages.

"What's wrong?" she asked when her grandmother simply stared at the check.

Glamma handed it to her. "This can't be right. I'm sure Connor said we'd be receiving a check for two hundred thousand."

The check was for half that. "I don't understand. Is there any paperwork in the envelope?"

Glamma turned it upside down. "Nothing." She met Arianna's gaze. "You have no choice. You have to call him."

"I know." Arianna hoped Glamma didn't hear the tiny note of excitement in her voice at the thought of talking to Connor. Given the circumstances, she didn't want to think about her reaction for too long. She walked over to the phone on the wall and picked it up. She pressed the number she'd assigned to him several weeks before, number one. It had made sense then. He was the first one she always called. The only one she ever really wanted to talk to. The one person who could calm her down with just the sound of his voice.

He didn't say hello or give her a chance to say it. As soon as he picked up, he said, "Are you okay? Is everything all right?"

"No to both," she admitted.

"I'll be there in five minutes," he said, raising his voice above the background noise.

It sounded like he was at a party or a bar. Which reminded her that they were no longer lovers or in a relationship; they were opponents in the race for mayor. "I appreciate the offer, but it's fine. I need to ask—"

"I want to."

"Everything's changed, Connor. We can't..." She closed her eyes, took a deep breath, and then said, "We got the check from the insurance company. It's for a hundred thousand."

"Yeah. They wrote two checks for a hundred thousand each. One for you, and one for Helen."

"Oh, I just assumed because I'd been the one making all the payments..."

"I know. It's not fair, but legally my hands were tied. I was able to get them to back off on foreclosing on the house, but that's all I could do. It's because Helen cosigned the loan and her name is still on the building that the payout was done that way. Sorry. I thought I'd explained that to you. Are you guys okay with it?"

"Of course. Only the other check isn't here."

"It wouldn't come to the house. Your mother is Helen's power of attorney. The settlement check would have been sent to her."

Chapter Seventeen

♥

Connor knew it was a setup as soon as he saw Helen, Arianna, and several of her business owner friends coming out of Holiday House on Main Street at the same time a local news van pulled into a parking space across the road.

He grabbed his parents by the arms, pulling them to a stop in the middle of the sidewalk five stores up from Holiday House. "Whatever you two have planned, forget about it."

"We don't have anything planned, son. Your mother just wanted to stop at the Christmas store before we head to Jolly Rogers for brunch."

"Sorry. I'm not buying it. And you know why I'm not? Because you won't look me in the eye, Dad. Come on. We're getting back in the car before the reporter and her cameraman cross the road."

Which might take them some time because the intersection was busy. Suspiciously busy, Connor decided as he took a better look around. Eleven on a Saturday morning on Main Street was no doubt a popular time to shop, but not this popular. He knew he was right when he spotted a bunch of his uncle's most ardent supporters piling out of a truck and a couple of cars.

"I have no idea what's gotten into you, Connor, but I suppose I can come back another time and pick up the ornaments," his mother said, glancing across the road. She put her hand behind her back, waving it in a *hurry up* gesture.

"I saw that, Mom. And I also see the signs in the back of that pickup." He glanced at Arianna and caught the exact moment she spotted the reporter and Daniel's supporters across the road. She looked up the street, saw him, and the *oh crap* look that had come over her face only seconds before changed to a *you're a piece of crap* look. He felt like it too. And if he stayed, it would only get worse. His hope of getting through the election without her hating him for the rest of his life was fading fast.

After his brief conversation with her last night, he had no idea why he still held out hope that they had a future together. It had been obvious that she wanted nothing more to do with him, other than information about the insurance settlement. At the hospital yesterday, it had been the same, only there'd been something about the way she'd looked at him that had made him believe they still had a chance.

She had no idea how hard it had been for him to keep his emotions in check when she'd shaken the hand of the head of the hospital's fundraising committee. Connor had wanted to pull Arianna into his arms and kiss her until everything and everyone disappeared. He'd wanted to shout to the world how amazing she was, how proud he was of her.

If nothing else came out of him entering the race, that moment right there had made it worthwhile. She'd shown him she wouldn't go down without a fight. He hadn't been joking or stroking her ego when he'd said he'd need some luck to beat her. It had been obvious she was determined to win, and he couldn't have been happier to catch a glimpse of the competitive and ambitious woman he knew and loved. She was just like him. Only he had more at stake than she did.

Helen would be disappointed for maybe a week if Arianna lost the mayoral race, but she'd love her the same as always. In his case, he'd disappoint his entire family and bring shame to the Gallagher name, or so his uncle had told him that morning. Connor imagined Daniel meant it to be a pep talk, but it had felt more like a threat.

Only for Connor it had never been about the entire family. It had been about his political parents. They needed a common goal to keep them together. If he lost, in their eyes that would mean he could kiss the future race for governor goodbye. And he was afraid that would be the kiss of death for their marriage.

Which meant he completely understood why his parents were doing everything in their power to help him win the race, and for the most part he appreciated their efforts. He just didn't want their game plan to interfere with his, and a direct confrontation over the future development of Main Street would deliver the killing blow to his relationship with Arianna.

"I'll catch up with you guys at Jolly Rogers," he said, turning to walk away.

"Mr. Gallagher. Connor!" a man yelled from across the road.

Connor groaned when several other voices hailed him. He turned with a forced smile, praying Arianna at least had the good sense to leave. She hadn't, probably because Helen was hanging on to her arm. Eight men and three women swarmed him. They were carrying his uncle's campaign signs.

"Me and my friends were big supporters of your uncle's and, as you know, he's asking us to throw our support behind you. From what we've heard, you're a good guy, but we were voting for your uncle because he believed that the rezoning of Main Street was the best way to ensure Harmony Harbor's future. So, what's it going to be, Connor? Are you for or against the office building development?"

Connor had been hoping to keep that part of his campaign under the radar. Since it had been his uncle's platform, avoiding talking about it had been a long shot. Still, a guy could hope. Especially a guy who was in love with his opponent. They had enough hurdles without adding another one.

He looked over to see his mom and dad watching him. Like him, they knew this was a do-or-die moment. He didn't let his gaze drift to where Arianna stood, instead focusing on the men and women who'd pinned their hopes on his uncle for one reason—the promise of a brighter future. "After some careful consideration, I've decided to back the rezoning of Main Street to allow for the construction of the office building. I believe it can be done in a way that won't impact the look or charm of Main Street."

A cheer went up from the growing crowd around him, as well as several shoppers across the road. From outside Holiday House, there were a chorus of *boo*s. And that's when a microphone was shoved in his face.

"Mr. Gallagher, you and your opponent share markedly different visions for the future of Main Street, and since we're here and you're here and so is Ms. Bell, it seems to me this is the perfect opportunity and the perfect place for a candidate's debate on the issue that's nearest and dearest to the hearts of the citizens of this lovely town."

As much as he wanted to, he couldn't back down. His parents looked anywhere else but at him. He inhaled deeply through his nose and then gave the reporter a clipped nod. His supporters cheered, then jeered when the woman called to Arianna.

"Either you keep it civil, or this isn't happening. Do we understand each other?" Connor said to the ringleader.

It turned out it wasn't the ringleader he had to worry about; it was Glamma.

They were standing in front of the security fencing that surrounded the blackened remains of Tie the Knot and the other three businesses. Connor didn't know whose brilliant idea it was to hold the debate there or why he'd agreed. Actually, he wasn't sure he had agreed.

He'd been too busy trying to have a private word

with Arianna for the last five minutes. He wanted to explain why he'd changed his mind on the development and to see if she and Helen were really okay with the insurance settlement. But he hadn't gotten a chance, mostly because she was doing her best to ignore him. He wished he could do as good a job ignoring her.

"So, Ms. Bell, you're saying that, up until a week ago, you were under the impression Mr. Gallagher shared your vision for the future of Main Street?" the reporter asked.

"Yes, but up until a week ago, I also thought he was supporting me. I had no idea he planned to run against me."

"Hold up a sec. I didn't know I'd be running against—" He tried to get his point in, but once again Arianna ignored him, talking over him.

"So yes, it came as a complete surprise to me—" she continued before her grandmother cut her off.

"Proves that you can't trust a Gallagher. Especially this Gallagher. When he's not playing divorce attorney for his wealthy clients and ruining young women's lives, he's a corporate lawyer. You know the type. He fixes his clients' problems by threatening small businesses and buying them up or putting them out of business. His talent lies in tearing things down, while my granddaughter's talent lies in making things more beautiful, building them up," Helen finished for Arianna. Ad-libbing, Connor hoped. But given his opponent's icy-blue stare, he wasn't so sure.

"That's right. You owned one of the businesses that burned down, didn't you, Ms. Bell? Wasn't it your sister's ex-fiancé who started the fire? You received the injuries to your hand and arm when you—"

Connor wasn't sure Arianna could handle this line of questioning, so he interrupted the reporter. "Aren't you supposed to be impartial, Donna?" She gave him a confused look. "Is that a *yes*? You are supposed to be impartial, aren't you?"

"Yes, of course, but I'm not sure I understand what you're getting at."

Both Arianna and Helen did, because they looked relieved. But if he thought that would play in his favor, he was sadly mistaken.

"I'm glad to hear you're not giving Ms. Bell more time than me because you want her to win," he continued. "Now we'll have to see if I believe it. And you better hope that I do, Donna, because Mrs. Fairchild is right; I am a lawyer. A very good lawyer, who has set up shop with my brother in the town my family founded."

He decided he might as well get that in there before they painted him as an outsider. Something he'd heard Helen was doing every chance she got on the campaign trail. And it ticked him off because it had always been a sore spot for him and his brothers. There'd been nothing they'd wanted more when they were growing up than to be the Harmony Harbor Gallaghers instead of the summer ones.

"If this were a real debate, I would have been given the opportunity to defend myself against Mrs. Fairchild's slanderous remarks." He'd probably gone a little overboard, but at least it had taken the reporter's focus off Arianna and the fire. Which, given the topic of conversation and location, wouldn't last long. The only way to protect Arianna was to end the debate before the reporter circled back.

"Despite what Mrs. Fairchild and her granddaughter have said, as a corporate attorney, my job is to protect my clients and their assets. I've helped several of them become Fortune 500 companies, and that's exactly what I plan to do for this town. I'll protect the best of Harmony Harbor while at the same time helping the town grow. Currently, we have people leaving because they can't find work. New development will provide the jobs they desperately need."

"If you had lived here for more than a month, Mr. Gallagher, you would have a better understanding of Harmony Harbor," Arianna said. "We don't need new development. We need to protect and grow the businesses we already have before they start closing their doors. The Wicklow Group plans to lease the lower half of the office building to discount chain stores that will compete with our locally owned shops."

He was pleased to note the color had returned to Arianna's cheeks, even if anger at him had put it there. "Studies have shown that not to be the case, Ms. Bell. The brand-name stores will draw more customers to town. The development will revitalize Main Street as well as give us the office space we need to attract companies to Harmony Harbor."

"The building they're proposing will destroy the look and feel of Main Street. Some of us prefer small-town charm to big-city flash, Mr. Gallagher."

Connor sensed the reporter getting antsy. She wanted to get back to the real story, the story that would provide the most drama and ratings. She wanted to know what he and everyone else did—why had Arianna gone back to her office that night? He had to end the interview now, and he had to do it in such a way that would undoubtedly cause Arianna to hate him even more. It was his way of taking a bullet for her, he supposed.

He gave Arianna a condescending smile. She really didn't like that, he thought when she stiffened and her eyes narrowed. "Ms. Bell, have you actually looked at the specs for the proposed building?"

"Well, no, but I was told that—"

"Hearsay is rarely admissible in court, so how about we deal in facts and only the facts, ma'am?" he interrupted her with a wink. She hated to be called *ma'am*, and his cocky delivery would bug her too. "I've had a chance to go over the artist's renderings as well as speak to the architect. Have you, Ms. Bell? No? I'm surprised," he said, when she gave her head a brief, negative shake.

"Why? Unlike you and your uncle, my granddaughter is not in bed with the developer. No one's offered her a private viewing of the architect's drawings. Knowing you and your uncle, the architect is probably a woman."

Connor groaned inwardly. "As a matter of fact, she is. Although I fail to see what her gender has to do with anything. Surely you're not suggesting she's not up for the job because she's a woman. That would be a little sexist, wouldn't it?"

Not only were Arianna and her grandmother now glaring at him, so were her friends.

"The point I'm trying to make is that I'm confident we can reach a deal with the developer that will address your concerns and those of the other business owners without risking at least one hundred and fifty jobs during the construction phase and upward to two hundred and fifty when the building is fully leased, instead of scuttling the entire deal for the reasons you're suggesting, Ms. Bell. As someone who has spent more than a decade negotiating with landowners and developers, I'm fully confident I can get the best deal for the citizens of Harmony Harbor, and that includes you and the other business owners, of which I'm one." He angled his arm to look at his watch. "Sorry. That's all the time I've got. I have a meeting with the town's planning committee in ten minutes. And I'm sure Ms. Bell and her friends would like to get back to their shopping."

* * *

A few days after Saturday's fiasco and one day before the election, Connor and his father were getting in some last-minute door-to-door campaigning.

"Change of plans, son," his father said from the passenger seat of the Porsche. "Harmony Harbor PD has asked that we avoid Main Street. Protesters on both sides are out in full force. Drive by the harbor and see if we can get a look without being spotted."

Connor knew exactly why his father wanted to have a look. "You won't be able to gauge how big the crowd is for either side from the harbor front. Arianna's supporters will be marching where the stores burned down, while mine will be across the street, annoying the hell out of the shopkeepers like they have for the past three days." No matter how often Connor had asked them not to.

He glanced at his father, who'd yet to respond because he was texting on his phone. Connor turned right at the stop sign.

"Any reason in particular we're less than a block from Arianna's?" his father asked casually, still focused on his phone.

"Are we? I didn't know. Probably as good a neighborhood to hit as any though. We can change a few of her supporters' minds." He pulled alongside the curb, wondering if his dad bought his lie. Not about bringing some of her supporters over to his side. Yesterday's poll in the *Gazette* indicated the race was tight. But as much as Connor wanted to win, he wanted to get a glimpse of Arianna.

He hadn't seen or heard from her since their Saturday-morning debate on Main Street. He'd tried to call her a couple times before checking in with Jenna to be sure she was all right. According to Jenna, she was; she just had no interest in speaking to him. Jenna didn't seem to have much of an interest in speaking to him either. Though she'd softened a bit when he explained why he'd acted like such a jerk during the interview.

His father looked up from his phone. "You don't have to pretend with me, son. I know you're in love with Arianna, and I'm pretty sure she's in love with you. Just give her a couple weeks to get over the loss—"

"As much as I appreciate your confidence in me, Dad, last time I checked we were neck and neck," he said not only to give himself the opportunity to study his father's reaction to the news but to talk about his own concerns about his standings in the polls. His father didn't appear the least bit concerned, which made Connor nervous, especially as his mother had been surprisingly absent from this morning's strategy session. She was the more devious of the two. "What's Mom up to?"

"Nothing. Nothing at all, son." Avoiding Connor's gaze, he glanced out the windshield. "Oh ho, would you look at that? There's Arianna and Helen coming around the corner. Come on, I want to congratulate them."

While Connor knew his dad cared about them and had been genuinely happy to learn Helen had scored well on the Folstein test and Arianna was attending physical therapy, he sensed there was something else going on here. But he didn't get a chance to question his father further because he was already out of the car.

Connor had almost caught up to him when his dad reached Arianna and Helen with his arms wide, the bottom of his black coat flapping in the cool November breeze. "Hello, my two favorite ladies. I wanted to congratulate you both on your good news."

"What, your son dropped out of the race? Or did your brother drop dead?"

"Glamma," Arianna said in an exasperated tone that reminded Connor of how many times he'd heard her use that voice before they were on opposite sides. He smiled, but her gaze flitted past him to his dad. "Thank you, Sean."

"Why are you thanking him? He's a..." Helen frowned and turned around. "I've felt like someone's been following us all morning...Do you...? There! I'd know that head of hair anywhere. Maura Gallagher, you get out from behind that bush this minute!"

Arianna gasped, turning on Connor. "You have your mother spying on me?"

Chapter Eighteen

♥

By the time election night rolled around and Arianna walked into the town hall, Connor and his family were still in her bad books. Due to how divisive their campaigns had become, the current mayor and the town council had decided that the announcement would be made in the town hall to avoid rioting in the streets when either Arianna or Connor was declared the winner. She thought they were being a tad dramatic.

But Hazel Winters, the current mayor, had overridden her objections on the conference call with Connor this morning. Connor had agreed easily to the woman's every request, of course.

"I can't wait until this is over," Arianna murmured to her grandmother, who merely grunted her agreement. She'd been acting strangely today. Actually, Arianna supposed it wasn't so strange really. Helen had been born to campaign. At least for someone else. And now the everyday excitement would be over.

A tightness built in Arianna's chest at the thought. She pressed her fingers against the ice-blue cape she wore over a winter-white cashmere sweater and wide-leg pants in an effort to rub away her panic.

"Just breathe," she whispered to herself through the clenched-teeth smile she offered her supporters in the right-hand rows of seats. Several of them held up signs, quickly hiding them before security took them away. The town council had banned campaign signs in hopes of starting the healing. Arianna thought they were being a little idealistic and overly optimistic.

And speaking of overly optimistic, supremely confident, and obnoxiously gorgeous, Connor stood as she approached the row of reserved seats at the front of the room.

Okay, so maybe supremely confident was pushing it. His smile seemed tentative, his "You look beautiful" quiet and a little gruff. He'd apologized to her before the conference call with Hazel ended. Even though her sister had explained why he'd made Arianna look like an idiot in front of nearly all of New England, she couldn't bring herself to forgive him.

"Of course she does, and you're not the only one who thinks so. Ask her where she got the cape. Come on, ask," her grandmother challenged him.

"Glamma, stop it and take a seat." Arianna looked around. "Do you know where I'm supposed to sit?" she asked him, even though she was afraid she already knew.

His mouth crooked at the corner, and just like she'd thought, he gestured to the empty seat beside him. "In an effort to promote unity instead of division," he said, repeating what Hazel had told them that morning.

Arianna sighed and took a seat. He sat beside her, then leaned in to her, his broad shoulder crowding her, his spicy, masculine scent enveloping her, his breath tickling her cheek and warming her ear. "So, where did you get the cape?"

"Turns out she has a secret admirer. He left it for her on the front porch this morning. It's a good-luck present. Not that she needs it."

Arianna pursed her lips at her grandmother. "It's amazing what you can hear when you put your mind to it."

Glamma shrugged. "Just a good guess."

"Whoever your secret admirer is, they have great taste. The cape matches your eyes."

She wished he hadn't mentioned her eyes because it brought her gaze to his. Her eyes were ordinary blue; Connor's weren't. His were a deep cobalt, framed by black lashes that were thick and long. It should be illegal for a man to have eyes as beautiful as his. But right then it wasn't the color that captured her attention. Some people wore their hearts on their sleeves, but Connor expressed his deepest emotions with his eyes.

"Do you remember exactly how friendly Hazel wanted us to be?" he asked, his gaze dropping to her mouth.

"Not that friendly," she said, forcing her lips into a straight line. It wasn't as easy as it should have been. She should be ticked he asked. Did he seriously expect her to forget that his mother had posted a highly inflammatory video of Arianna online yesterday?

There seemed to be an unwritten rule that politicians

were supposed to kiss every baby handed to them. No one seemed to care if said child had a snotty nose or a dirty face and grubby hands. Still, she had tried to do it a couple times, on the top of their heads, of course. If it weren't for Connor's mom, no one would have seen the face Arianna had made. She hadn't known she'd made one.

She found it easier not to be around children. It wasn't that she didn't like them per se. She just didn't like to be reminded of what she'd lost. What she'd never have. She didn't like to be around dogs either. Like children, they seemed to sense that. Unlike children, dogs could kill you or maim you with their sharp canine teeth. It wasn't her fault that when the dog jumped on her, she'd assumed he was going to attack and she pushed him away. Perhaps a little more forcefully than was necessary, which made the mother of the dog angry and her children cry.

She felt the weight of Connor's gaze and glanced at him. He smiled. Once again she had to remind herself she was mad at him and didn't want to kiss him. Apparently, her lips disagreed.

"You're right. We're supposed to wait until the announcement is made to kiss." His voice was low, sexy, his eyes back on her mouth.

"You obviously heard an entirely different conversation than I did. But in case I blocked it out, I'll agree to kiss your cheek when Hazel announces that I won." Until that moment, she hadn't realized how hard it was to hold a smug smile when you felt like you were going to throw up. Her reaction to both winning and losing the mayoral race was similar, though losing took the prize for almost sending her into a panic attack.

"No cheek kiss from me when I win. I'll kiss you on the mouth." He lifted his hand, holding her gaze as he gently rubbed her bottom lip with his thumb. "You have the most beautiful mouth."

She reached up with her good hand to remove his fingers from her chin. "Thank you, but a cheek kiss is fine."

"I'm sure Hazel said we're to do whatever we can to eliminate any doubt that we're really good friends. Close friends."

"That hardly constitutes making out in the middle of the town hall."

"I don't know. Making out works for me." Before she could disabuse him of the idea, he frowned and leaned in to her again. "Is there something wrong with Glamma? She's not reacting to me flirting with you."

So, he hadn't been flirting with her because he wanted to. He was doing it to get a rise out of her grandmother. Which should fill her with relief, not frustration and disappointment. At least relief on her own behalf. Glamma was a different story.

"She's been acting strange all day," she told him, glad to be able to unburden herself to someone who cared about her grandmother. Because despite everything, she knew both Connor and his father did. "I think she's worried that life will go back to the way it was before. She's always preferred to be busy and involved. And we've been that times ten these past several weeks. As soon as we wake up in the morning, we're off and running. You wouldn't believe the number of breakfasts, luncheons, and potlucks we've attended."

"I don't know. I got the impression she was pretty busy before she entered the mayoral race. Wasn't she involved in a bunch of clubs with Mrs. Ranger?"

Maybe he was right and Arianna was projecting. Still... "Yes, but this was different."

He linked his fingers through hers and gave her hand a gentle squeeze. "Because you were with her. She adores you. She was relieved, happy to see you putting yourself out there again."

Hazel took the stage. The sixtysomething woman wore her signature power suit in the same color as her brown hair and eyes. Around them, the low hum of conversation ended as everyone went quiet.

Except Connor, who whispered, "Whatever happens, we'll make it work. Glamma will have a job and so will you."

She wanted to groan her frustration. This time she leaned in to him, willing her brain not to think about how hard and muscular his arm felt or how good he smelled. "No more trying to fix my life. Look what happened the last time you did," she whispered back.

"From where I'm sitting, it's looking pretty damn good."

"Oh, be quiet," she muttered. "And stop acting like you've won."

Hazel bent toward the standing mic. "Ladies and gentlemen, I'll now read the election results. Please hold your applause until the end," the mayor said, and then began to read off the names of the winners for councilor at large, ward councilors, and the school board. She cleared her throat. "Arianna Bell and Connor Gallagher are tied for mayor."

Over the smattering of applause and *boo*s, people yelled that either Arianna or Connor had been robbed.

"All right, settle down," Hazel demanded as Glamma and Daniel Gallagher shouted for a recount, which spurred pretty much everyone in the hall to call for the same.

"We already have one under way," Hazel reassured the crowd. "That being said, we won't have the results until morning. In the event that we have another tie, the town council and I had a brief meeting before I shared this evening's results with you. If Arianna and Connor remain tied after the recount, they'll begin their tenure immediately and will serve jointly as mayor until December twenty-fourth. This will give the town council ample time to observe their abilities and conduct while in office and allow us to choose the perfect candidate for mayor in time for the inauguration on January first. We'll render our decision here on Monday, December twenty-fourth at three p.m." When people started to yell their dissatisfaction, Hazel raised a hand and her voice. "Arianna, Connor, do you have any objections to how we plan to proceed in the event of a tie?"

Almost positive the recount would yield a clear winner, even if by only a small margin, Arianna rose to her feet. "No. I agree with how you've chosen to declare a winner in the event of a tie."

"So do I," Connor said, standing beside her. He turned to give his muttering uncle Daniel a look.

"Excellent," Hazel said, clearly relieved at their support. "We'll announce the final results of the election tomorrow at ten a.m. If you can't make it to the town hall, the results will be published in a special online edition of the *Gazette* at noon. As well, I've been told that, thanks to one of our candidates' ties to the former governor of our fair state, several media outlets will be airing the results. Thank you all for coming and for your patience."

"That was somewhat anticlimactic, wasn't it?" Connor's father said before offering Arianna and her grandmother a smile. "We're having a small gathering at the manor, and we'd love for you both to join us."

"Thank you. We appreciate—" Arianna was about to politely refuse before her grandmother abruptly cut her off.

"We can't. We're taking my Beemer out for a cruise. They just delivered her today, and the only place we've driven her so far is here. I want to feel the wind on my face and blast some Buddy Holly and Elvis."

"It's a little cold to have the top down, Glamma." Arianna didn't add that she doubted they'd find Buddy Holly and Elvis on the radio.

Her grandmother didn't respond. She was already on her way out of the town hall.

"She bought a BMW?" Connor asked.

"Technically, I bought it. We needed a car, and I made the mistake of not saying an outright *no* when she started talking about getting a BMW. She loved her old car so much and was so excited about it, I didn't have the heart to say no. We got a pretty good deal on a used one." She would have liked a better deal, not that she'd share that with Connor, who looked concerned. "Glamma is paying half. She insisted." And she'd called Arianna's mother when they'd gotten back from the dealership late Saturday afternoon to tell her to send the check. Arianna wasn't entirely sure how the conversation had gone because Glamma hadn't been herself after the call. Like now.

Connor frowned. "What's going on? Are you okay?"

"I'm fine, thanks." Arianna forced a smile, having a difficult time shutting down the voice in her head that said everything might not be fine, especially if she wasn't reimbursed for half the cost of the car. There was no way she'd be able to convince her grandmother to get rid of her beloved Beemer. Arianna had a feeling she'd better start praying she ended up the winner after the recount, because it was looking like she'd need a job sooner rather than later.

* * *

Her grandmother was possessed. Arianna didn't know exactly what she was possessed by, but she was acting manic. And it was scaring Arianna to the point she was tempted to call Connor.

"Okay, Glamma, it's time to go home. You're turning blue, and my teeth are chattering," Arianna said from where she was huddled down on the passenger seat of the emerald-green Beemer. She'd agreed to cruise with the top down for five minutes, only now they couldn't get it up.

"Not yet. I want to cruise to my heart's content. I don't have much time left." Glamma grimaced like she'd said too much.

Arianna straightened in the seat to stare at her grandmother, barely noticing the bitter wind whipping her hair around her face. "What are you talking about? Ava said your heart and blood pressure were fine at your physical. Is that not true? Did you tell her to lie to me?" Arianna had to practically shout to be heard.

Her grandmother stared straight ahead. "I'm healthy as a horse, just like she said."

"Then what is it? You've been acting strange all night. Are you upset the campaign is over? Are you worried we won't win?"

Glamma shook her head. "I knew my time was up long before tonight. I just didn't want to say anything." She glanced at Arianna, her cheeks and nose red, her eyes glassy. Whether from the cold or unshed tears, Arianna couldn't be sure. "Just let me enjoy a few more minutes of freedom, will you, darling?"

"Of course, Glamma." Oh God, please don't let her be dying, Arianna prayed. She should text Connor. He'd tell her Glamma was fine. That it was the stress of having to wait until tomorrow for the results. But it was more than that, and Arianna knew it.

Ten minutes later Glamma turned off Ivy onto Holly Road. Arianna could tell she'd done so reluctantly. The cold had finally gotten to her.

Arianna shivered. "It feels like it might snow. I think there's a tarp we can cover Annabelle with tonight," she said, referring to the car. Glamma had named her. "Mrs.

Ranger is pretty handy with cars. We'll ask her to have a look in the morning."

"It won't matter," Glamma said, her voice a monotone as she got out of the car.

"Stop it. I can't take this anymore. I need to know what's going on," Arianna said as she joined Helen at the front gate.

Her grandmother reached up, placing her cold palm against Arianna's cheek. "Just remember, when the day comes that my brain forgets you, my heart never will. I love you, my darling. I don't want to go, but I made her a promise."

She covered Glamma's hand with hers, fighting back tears, forcing the words past her clogged throat. "It'll be okay. We have an appointment with the memory specialist next week. We'll—"

The front door swung open to reveal Arianna's mother standing there. She wore her blond hair in a messy topknot, her blue eyes bright in her tanned face. Outfitted in a long-sleeve white T-shirt and skinny jeans, she looked more like the daughter and Arianna the mother. "Where have you been? I was about to call the police."

"What's going on? Why are you here?" Arianna snapped, because she knew... She knew without really knowing that her mother was the reason Glamma was acting this way.

"It'll always be like this, won't it? You'll never forgive me. I'll always be the evil witch in your eyes." Beverly crossed her arms, moving aside to let them into the house. "Aren't you the lucky one, Mother? You got off scot-free. Then again, she always loved you more, didn't she?"

"What do you expect? You stole my son. You told me he'd died and had me sign the adoption papers when I was still groggy from anesthetic, when I believed what I was signing were papers to have him cremated. I wore a necklace with what I thought were his ashes up until the day I discovered they weren't."

"I've heard it all before, Arianna. It's been years, remember? Most daughters would have forgiven their mother by now. I did what I thought was best for you. You were seventeen. Seventeen, Arianna. You could barely look after yourself, let alone a child."

"Maybe, but I should have been given a choice."

"You were adamant you wanted to keep him."

"And you were adamant I wasn't going to. I could have, you know, if you would have helped. But you were too busy hating Daddy and trying to make him pay for leaving you for another woman. You had no time for me, sending me off to your best friend, who was even more self-involved than you."

Her mother raised her hand as though to slap Arianna's face. Arianna raised her own to stop her, but Glamma was faster. "You've hurt the child enough, and you won't do it again in my presence. Do you understand?"

"Fine, Mother. I hope you're packed and ready to go first thing in the morning."

"I'm not going anywhere until the results of the election are announced."

Arianna grabbed her grandmother's hand. "Glamma,

what are you talking about? You aren't leaving. You're staying here with me."

Her mother gave Glamma a raised-eyebrow look. "Really? You didn't tell her?" She shook her head and sauntered off to the kitchen. "I need a drink."

"Come on, we'll have a cup of tea and get warmed up." Glamma smiled at Arianna with watery eyes. "What were you thinking letting me drive us around with the top down? We'll be lucky if we don't get pneumonia," her grandmother teased.

"It's not funny. And I'm not sitting in the kitchen with her."

Glamma put her hands on Arianna's shoulders. "She's right, you know. I knew what she planned to do and didn't talk her out of it. I didn't tell you either. If I had, who knows...?" She shook her head. "It was a terribly sad business for everyone involved. But we didn't make the decision to hurt you. We made it because we loved you."

Arianna looked pointedly at her mother pouring herself a glass of wine at the island.

Glamma shrugged. "She's never been very good at showing it, but she did. She does. And it's time for you to let go of the anger and blame. For your own sake, not hers."

"I don't know if I can, Glamma. But what I do know is she's not taking you from me too."

"She's not. Not really. Just before we got the call about the fire, I'd agreed to move to California for good." She gave Arianna a sad smile. "It made her happy. She'd been lonely. It's probably why she ended up with the pool boy. Anyway, I promised to come back as soon as you were on your feet. When she found out you were running for mayor, she decided my time here was up."

"It doesn't have to be. You can stay with me." Her heart was racing; she felt hot when only moments ago her body had been an ice cube.

"I can't, darling. I gave her my word."

Her mother walked into the living room and took a seat. "She did. And in case you've forgotten, Arianna, I have power of attorney. Which means I can choose to give you half the money for the car or not. It also means I can choose whether or not to sell this house." She looked around. "It's quite lovely, isn't it? I wonder what it's worth."

Glamma blanched, and it was then Arianna felt certain she wasn't moving of her own free will. Her mother was blackmailing her into doing what she wanted. But there was no way Arianna could prove it.

"That's enough, Beverly. You'll write a check for half the car now, and don't hold the sale of this house over either of our heads. As you're well aware, I've left it to Arianna and Serena," her grandmother said, sounding strong and in command.

"Another member of my family you turned against me, Arianna. How is my other daughter?"

"You managed to do that on your own, Mother. And she's doing better." Arianna didn't know if that was the truth or a lie because lately Serena had been difficult to reach. Supposedly she was traveling somewhere in Europe. Arianna was hoping the settlement check would lure her home. She planned to share some of it with her sister. Although both their shares were dwindling by the minute. "I'll make the tea, Glamma."

She felt her mother's gaze following her into the kitchen. "So, is no one going to tell me what happened? I gather my darling daughter didn't win the election by a landslide like you predicted, Mother?" Beverly laughed as though the idea of Arianna becoming mayor of Harmony Harbor was the funniest thing she'd ever heard. And right then Arianna had never wanted to win so badly.

* * *

At six the next morning, her grandmother sat on the edge of Arianna's bed, already dressed. "She had our tickets booked, and it's too expensive to change. I called Hazel and told her I had to leave town unexpectedly and wanted to hear the news straight from the horse's mouth. She made some calls and just phoned me back. I'm sorry, darling, you and Connor are still tied. We'll have to wait until Christmas Eve to find out who will be mayor. My bet is on you, of course."

Arianna couldn't speak. She lay on her back blinking her tears away. She didn't care whether she won or lost. Her grandmother was the one person she'd depended on, the one person she'd known would never leave her. Yet she was going today, leaving Arianna on her own. Nothing she'd said had been enough to change her grandmother's or her mother's mind. "My bet is on Connor. I should just let him have it. It's not—"

"No granddaughter of mine is going to walk away without a fight. Do you hear me? You promise me right this very minute that you will do your best to win."

Arianna turned her head to stare at the blackout curtains.

Glamma gently shook her. "The only way I can leave here, leave you, is knowing that every day you're going to get out of this bed and go to work. That you're going to keep your appointments at the hospital. That you're going to take Annabelle out for a drive. That you're going to be here in this house that I love, living a life that will make me proud. Promise me." She choked on a sob. "Promise me right now."

"I promise, Glamma."

Chapter Nineteen

♥

Connor had been shocked, and yes, a little hurt, when he'd learned Helen had left Harmony Harbor with Arianna's mother. She'd been gone almost two weeks now, and his shock and hurt had morphed into anger. He was the one who had to stand by and watch Arianna sleepwalk through her days. Whenever he stopped by her office at the town hall with coffee and doughnuts, she'd say she was fine when she clearly wasn't, and then she'd send him on his way with a smile that didn't reach her eyes. He didn't understand how Helen could have left her on her own. Sure, she was an adult. But she was an adult who had only recently gotten back on her feet.

And if all that weren't bad enough, Helen had left without telling him goodbye. Sure, they'd been on opposing sides during the last week of the mayoral race—in a way, he supposed they still were—but dammit, he'd loved the crazy old lady. And he'd thought she'd come to love him too. All Arianna would tell him was that Helen was on a month-long vacation in the sun.

He didn't buy it. It didn't make sense. Days before she'd left, Helen had bought her precious emerald-green BMW. Who does that? He ignored the voice in his head that said someone with dementia did. Dementia or not, he didn't believe Helen would. And not only had she left town, but Jenna had left too.

Arianna had insisted she go, while Connor had insisted she stay. He'd thought he'd had her convinced, but apparently his older brother was more convincing than him. He and Logan weren't speaking at the moment. Connor supposed he didn't blame his brother for wanting his fiancee by his side. Still, Arianna was all alone.

Desperate times called for desperate measures.

Which was why Connor crouched on the frozen grass at the side of the house on the corner of Holly and Ivy at eight in the morning. From careful surveillance—his own—he knew that Arianna left for work at precisely eight forty-five every morning. "Okay, little guy, this is a tough assignment, but you're too cute to fail. It'll be love at first sight for both of you. All you have to do is keep her company," he said to the four-month-old cream-colored puppy he'd rescued from the shelter. An older man had brought the little guy in just as Connor had been leaving empty-handed.

The dogs they'd had that day at the shelter were older and bigger, and given the video that had gone viral, he knew dogs made Arianna nervous. So the pup was perfect. The old guy had been heartbroken he had to give him up, but it was either the pup left or his wife did. The older man said it hadn't been an easy decision.

Connor tucked a dog bone, a small teddy bear, a squeeze toy, and a leash beside the sheep's wool bed in the box. Then he placed a powder-blue blanket over the puppy. He patted its head. "Showtime, buddy. Don't be scared," he said as he fitted the lid on the box. He pressed his eye to one of the holes he'd made in the lid. "I'm still here, and in a couple minutes you'll meet your new mommy. She might not give you the warm-and-fuzzies right away, but trust me, she's a softy under that coat of armor."

Connor tucked the card from Arianna's secret admirer under the bow and then picked up the box. He hoped she liked the puppy as much as she'd seemed to like the cape he'd left for her the morning of the election.

His dress shoes slid across the frozen ground, and he jostled the box in his fight to stay upright. "It's okay, buddy," he whispered as he regained his footing. Crouched down so she wouldn't see him, Connor placed the box on the front porch, slid it closer to the door, and then reached up to ring the bell. He kept his finger on the bell for a few seconds too long and then whipped around, slipping and sliding his way to the big oak tree in the middle of the yard. He hid behind it, counting down the seconds in his head. No matter how warm he'd tried to make the puppy, he didn't want to leave him out there for more than a minute or two.

He peeked around the tree. "Come on, Arianna. Come on." If she didn't show in the next sixty seconds, he'd ring the bell one last time. His shoulders relaxed under his black wool coat when he heard the door opening. He pulled his head back behind the tree and then leaned against it, smiling at the thought of her face when she caught sight of the adorable pup. He wished he could risk taking another peek but was afraid she'd see him. He didn't want her to know he was her secret admirer.

He heard her whispered "What the heck?" and waited for her reaction to seeing the dog. "No, no way." She groaned and then cursed loud enough for him to hear her.

What the hell? He'd never heard her swear before. Seriously, who could look into the puppy's big brown eyes and not fall in love?

"You're a hard-ass, Arianna Bell," Connor said under his breath, and then rubbed the back of his neck when another thought came to him. Maybe she wasn't. Maybe she hadn't only been afraid of dogs who were big enough to gnaw on your head but adorable puppies too. Now what was he supposed to do? Definitely not let her discover he was her secret admirer, that's for sure.

"Mrs. Ranger, did you see who left this box on my front porch?"

Connor's gaze shot to the house across the road. Sure enough, Irene Ranger was out scraping the ice from her car with a clear view of him behind the tree. He could tell by her half smile that she saw him.

"I'm sorry, dear. I didn't. Is it from your secret admirer?" Mrs. Ranger asked.

Connor sagged against the tree in relief that she hadn't outed him.

"Yes, and I've decided I don't want one anymore."

"Why? What did he give you this time?"

"This." Connor pictured Arianna cuddling the dog to her chest and knew it was the exact moment she'd fall in love. He couldn't resist sneaking a peek and carefully poked his head from behind the tree.

What the hell? She was holding the puppy straight-armed in front of her. He pulled his head back around, trying to come up with one good reason why he shouldn't run across the lawn and rescue the dog. A reason that didn't involve him keeping his secret-admirer identity intact. And that's when he remembered why he'd wanted her to have a pet in the first place. Whether she'd admit it or not—and clearly, she was on the *not* side—she needed someone to love her unconditionally, someone for her to love in return. And since she wouldn't let that someone be him...

When he gave some more thought to what he'd just witnessed, he decided it could be viewed as a positive as much as a negative. After all, she'd actually picked up the dog. And apparently she'd continued to see both the occupational and physical therapists at North Shore General because she was able to hold the puppy in the air. Who knew, maybe she was re-creating the "Circle of Life" moment from *The Lion King*.

"My secret admirer doesn't know me as well as I thought. And he mustn't be on social media, or he would have seen the video that clearly shows I hate dogs. Which probably means Mr. O'Malley is my secret admirer."

Connor sighed. It looked like he'd be getting a new roommate in the not-so-distant future.

Mrs. Ranger laughed. It sounded like she was standing at the front gate. "Maybe he knows you better than you think. You used to love my Yorkie Bella."

"Until she nearly bit off Serena's finger."

Connor bowed his head.

"Right, I forgot about that. But Bella was getting old and wasn't used to having little girls around. You don't have to worry about that with this little guy. All you have to do is look in his eyes to know he's—"

"He peed on me!" Arianna shrieked, cutting off Mrs. Ranger, who sounded like she was choking on laughter.

Connor covered his face with his hands, swallowing a groan.

"Oh my, let me help," the older woman said, unable to keep the amusement from her voice. He heard the gate open and the sound of her footsteps running up the walkway. He poked his head from behind the tree. He wanted Mrs. Ranger to take the dog when she went home, and Connor would pick him up at her place. As though she sensed him watching her, Mrs. Ranger put her hand behind her back and waved him off before reaching for the box. Arianna disappeared through the open door.

Connor put his phone to his ear, letting his assistant know he'd be delayed. "Yes, Mom, I know you expected me to show up every morning at eight, but I had something important to do. Don't worry. I'll be there in plenty of time for my meeting with the planning commissioner at ten... Technically, Hazel is still the mayor, so it makes sense she gets to keep the office. I'm not too worried about looking like I'm in a position of power...No, my office isn't that small. Arianna's office is the same size." And just like that he came up with an alternate plan to bring the woman he loved back to life. Like he'd done by entering the mayoral race, he'd make her angry enough to encourage her competitive spirit and drive.

"You know what, Mom? You're right. I'll give Hazel a call and let her know that Arianna and I will be moving into her office first thing tomorrow." His mother had no idea that Hazel had offered them the office last week, and they'd both refused. "Are you kidding? I'll be taking Hazel's desk, not Arianna. No way am I giving up the view of the harbor. We'll find a nice, tiny desk for Arianna and stick it in a corner, a dark one."

* * *

The wind practically whipped the door to the community center out of Arianna's hand. Sadly, the turkey hat remained firmly on her head. She considered tossing it and blaming the wind, but she couldn't do that because Finn and Olivia Gallagher's six-year-old daughter, George, had made it especially for her to wear today, and the child was supposed to be here. Arianna was almost positive that Connor had put the little girl up to it yesterday when he'd given his entire family a tour of *his* office.

Just thinking about the man made her blood boil. Arianna's secret admirer and Maura weren't in her good book either. It felt like the world was conspiring against her. Over the past two days she'd somehow found herself sharing her grandmother's house with a dog that kept her awake half the night howling until she brought him into bed with her.

She'd called everyone she knew, but no one wanted a puppy. Even when she'd lied and said he was trained and really, really cute. Well, he was cute. He just wasn't trained. And every time she turned around, he was gnawing on something, and it was never his bone or his toys or food. Yet despite how bad it was to share the house with a mischievous puppy, it was far worse sharing an office with Connor.

He spent most of the day lording it over her from behind his massive mahogany desk surrounded by beautiful mullioned windows and a gorgeous view of the harbor front, while she sat in a dark corner at a desk she was positive had been requisitioned from a 1930s schoolroom. If that wasn't bad enough, Maura and Hazel seemed to forget she was just as much provisional mayor as he was and not his flipping secretary. She couldn't believe that almost a month before she'd imagined herself in love with the man.

Her boiling blood must be having a positive effect on her strength because she pulled the door shut relatively easily. Now that she was inside the building, she could hear the loud hum of voices mixed with laughter, and her nerves got the better of her.

The new owner of Holiday House, Evie, had come to Arianna the day after Glamma had left for California with the idea that they host a free Thanksgiving Dinner at the community center. At that point Arianna had barely managed a couple hours of sleep, and the idea of hosting a dinner for half the town had been beyond her. It hadn't been beyond Connor, who'd happened to overhear the conversation when he'd arrived at her then-office with coffee and doughnuts.

He'd glommed onto the idea immediately, believing it was the perfect way to mend the rifts of the campaign and bring a sense of belonging and togetherness to the town. He was right, of course. The churches and the town council had contributed as much as they could; Connor covered the shortfall.

So Arianna had no choice but to agree to cohost with him and help serve and clean up, even if she was terrified she was going to make a complete fool of herself in front of what sounded like a thousand people. She'd gained some strength in her upper arm, but she still didn't have much of a grip to speak of, and her fine-motor skills were still about the same as those of a toddler.

But she'd promised Glamma when they'd spoken this morning that she'd come. They couldn't talk for long. Supposedly her mother had become tightfisted, at least where long-distance phone calls were concerned. Arianna planned to send a cell phone to her grandmother and put her on her plan. At least they could talk without her mother monitoring their phone calls. Then Arianna would know for sure if Glamma really wanted to be there.

She took off her coat and glanced at the lone spare hanger on one of the many metal coatracks that lined the hall. She was glad no one was around because hanging a coat on a hanger wasn't as easy as everyone thought. Stretching up on her toes, she tossed her coat over the top of the rack. Self-consciously, she tugged the sleeve of her sweater over her compression bandage and then took a restorative breath before following the noise to the double doors.

The smile she'd pasted on her face faltered when she entered the packed and overheated room. And it wasn't only a case of nerves that caused the smile to fall from her face. It was the fact that everyone seated at the tables looked like they were almost finished with their meal. She looked around to see if it was just at this end of the room. It wasn't. Anger vanquished what was left of her nerves, and she marched to where the volunteers were now preparing to serve dessert.

"Hey, partner, nice hat. Where have you been? We were getting worried about you," Connor said, giving her one of his panty-melting grins. He wore a chef's hat and an apron over a white shirt and jeans, which should have ensured he looked like an idiot and all panties stayed firmly in place. Instead, he looked delicious. Clearly her anger was making her delirious. But if he thought the grin would work on her and she'd forgive him, he was oh so wrong.

"Sorry I'm late, Evie," she said to the dark-haired woman a few places down from Connor. "*Someone* put the wrong time on my calendar."

"Really? The time was right on mine. I actually got here an hour early. I helped with the setup, didn't I, Evie?" Connor said, holding Arianna's gaze.

"Yes, and you were a big help, Connor," Evie said, offering Arianna a smile. "Don't worry about it. Grab an apron and—"

"Get over here, partner. There's lots of room beside me. I'll show you how it's done." Connor winked, gesturing to the pumpkin pies in front of him.

"There's a reason why there's room beside him, Arianna. He's a little aggressive with the pie knife. You're probably safer down here with us," Sean called from the other end of the long line of tables.

"I should be okay, thanks. And I need a word with my *partner*."

"Maybe it's you who should be careful, son. Those sounded like fighting words to me." Sean chuckled.

"No worries. I'm armed and dangerously sweet and tasty." Connor held up a can of whipped cream and waggled his eyebrows at her as she came around the table, drawing laughter and groans from the other servers.

Arianna gave him a look and then moved in beside him. "I'm onto you, *partner*," she said out of the side of her mouth.

"Come on, you don't really think I'd put the wrong time on your calendar, do you?" he said as he put down the can and turned to get an apron off one of the carts behind him.

"It's more your mother's style, but I wouldn't put it past you." She shivered when his warm hand curved around the nape of her neck. "You would do anything to win, and don't bother denying it."

"As long as it was legal and didn't hurt anyone,

you're right. I would. Now put your hand here so I can tie your apron," he said, holding her hair against her head.

She did as he asked, a little startled when, after he knotted the ties at her neck, he reached around her waist. "It's okay. I can do it."

His head dipped, his lips grazing her ear. "You forget I share an office with you." He finished tying the bow at her waist and then straightened, smiling down at her. "I can't believe you wore that thing," he said, and flicked the paper turkey's head.

"I promised George."

"See. You proved my point. You don't hate kids. You love them. Just like you don't hate dogs. Here." He took out his phone, and before she could stop him, he took a picture. He looked down at the screen and laughed. "We need to take another one. You look like you're planning to murder someone."

"I am. You."

"You know what they say: Hate is just love in disguise."

She thought it was a good thing his phone pinged as the last word left his mouth, drawing his attention to the screen instead of her. Because she was afraid her expression might give too much away.

"George thinks you look great in the hat. She says if the *Gazette* takes a picture of you to let them know she made it. The kid's something else," he said with a grin, looking down when there was another ping. "What did you name your dog? She has a bet with her friends. And here's a hint—because, from the look on your face, I can tell you haven't named him yet—they think you'll go with a Christmassy name since he was obviously an early Christmas present."

Mrs. Ranger had been unable to babysit the puppy yesterday, so Arianna had taken him to work with her. He'd been a hit with the youngest generation of Gallaghers, every last one of them, and there were quite a few. Arianna was just happy he hadn't bitten anybody. Truth be told, she was quite proud of how he'd behaved. He did have some adorable moments.

"Of course he has a name." She lied because when she'd called the dog *dog* during the Gallagher-clan visit yesterday and they'd discovered the puppy didn't have a name, they had been horrified. "It's...Humbug," she said, drawing a pumpkin pie toward her. She glanced down the table to see what size slices everyone was cutting.

"So what, that makes you the Grinch?" Connor asked.

"It does." And without her grandmother here and with the year she'd had, Arianna thought it apropos.

"I don't believe you. Just like I don't believe you don't like kids and dogs." He leaned in to her. "Just like I don't believe you don't lo—like me."

She pretended she didn't hear him and picked up the knife with her left hand. After several months of it, using the wrong hand to cut was beginning to feel normal. Except she needed her other hand to hold the pie plate.

Connor took the knife and plate from her. "Sorry. I don't trust you with a knife," he said, surprising her by letting her lack of response to his *lo—like* comment go.

Lately he seemed to be all about pushing her buttons, and he'd just pushed the biggest button of all. No matter how much he drove her crazy, she couldn't deny she still had feelings for him. Given the way the majority of women in town responded to him, she should probably cut herself some slack. The man was easy to fall for; it was falling out of love with him that was hard.

"All right, if you had your heart set on being the pie cutter on our team, I'll be the plater and the whipped creamer."

He must have mistaken the expression on her face as disappointment that he'd taken the knife from her. Well, it wasn't like she planned to correct him, at least about that. "Those aren't even words, and we're not partners or a team. We're opponents, competitors."

"You're looking at it all wrong. Sure, we're both going after the same job. But right now our mandate is to repair the rift our campaigns created in town. By working together, working through our differences, we'll show the people of Harmony Harbor that they can too. Events like this one are perfect. They bring people together. There's proof." He pointed the can of whipped cream at the table across from them. "It took four people to pull those two off each other at the last protest march on Main Street, and now they're breaking bread together."

"Actually, I think they're fighting over the last bun."

He grinned. "Still, you have to admit it's a major improvement over beating each other senseless with our campaign signs."

"Well, Thanksgiving is pretty much over, so—"

"Babe, we have the biggest, bestest almost-month-long event of all time just around the corner—Christmas."

"Bah humbug."

Chapter Twenty

♥

Nine days later, on a snowy Saturday night, Arianna was having a hard time keeping up her Grinch persona.

"Was that an *ooh* or an *aah*?" Connor asked as he tucked the white furry blanket around her and her puppy (now known as Comet, thanks to George and her cousins) in the back of the horse-drawn carriage. They were the grand marshals of Harmony Harbor's holiday parade.

"You have to admit Julia's window display is pretty spectacular," Arianna said, waving to the crowd gathered along Main Street. The owner of Books and Beans had outdone herself this year. She'd re-created the ballroom scene from *Beauty and the Beast*. The loudspeaker piped "Tale as Old as Time" onto the street. Last year Julia had taken over the parade and added her own magical touch, ensuring the local businesses were more prominently featured than ever before. As the floats rolled up Main Street, each of the stores lit up with a wave of the grand marshal's wand.

Connor laughed. "Yeah, Aidan makes a great Beast."

He made a *give me* gesture with his fingers. "It's my turn to wave the wand."

"You've had twice as many turns as me."

"Fine. We'll wave it together." He wrapped his hand around hers and made an elaborate arc before pointing the wand at Holiday House. As if by magic, the shop lit up with pink, green, and yellow lights, and the crisp night air filled with the sounds of "We Wish You a Merry Christmas." The front door opened, and children dressed as elves flooded onto the sidewalk to hand out candy canes. "How about two for your mayors?" he called to the elves.

They were immediately showered with candy canes. Arianna ducked, covering her head. "Maybe you should have pointed to one elf."

"No way. This is awesome," Connor said, sticking a candy cane in his mouth and stuffing the others in his pockets—before Comet could eat one, she assumed. "Aren't you going to compliment me on saying 'mayors' instead of 'mayor'?"

"Uh, no. It's about time it sank in that you're not the only one—" She sighed as they passed the burned-out buildings. "You're trying to distract me, aren't you?"

He shrugged. "You were having fun. I didn't want the memories of that night to spoil this one."

"I appreciate the thought, but I'm honestly much better. I'm at Holiday House at least a couple times a week, working with Evie on our proposals for the community center. We're presenting them to the council next week." She nudged him with her shoulder. "Surprised you, didn't I? You're not the only one who wants to make a difference in Harmony Harbor, you know."

"That's great. Tell me—"

"Wave the wand!" people yelled from either side of the street. Connor looked around. "We're falling down on the job." He stood up and moved the wand like a conductor leading his orchestra. All around them the darkened storefronts lit up, and the carols rang out in discordant notes on the street.

"You're fired!" his brother Michael called from farther down the road.

Connor waved the wand like he was throwing a football in the pub's direction at the same time the carriage hit a rut in the road, throwing him off-balance. He lurched forward, and Arianna lunged, grabbing the back of his coat. She jostled Comet, who'd been buried under the blankets half-asleep, and he started barking. Which must have spooked the horses, because they took off.

"Hang on!" the driver yelled, trying to get the horses under control.

"I wanted to hold on to you all night, but this isn't exactly what I had in mind," Connor said, his arms wrapped tightly around both her and Comet, who was squashed between them. Comet didn't seem to mind; he'd stopped barking at least. "Thanks for saving me, by the way. I should probably kiss you in case we don't survive this wild ride."

"Connor, we haven't been on a wild ride since about half a minute after it started." She laughed at his genuine look of surprise.

"Seriously?" he said.

"Just kiss the girl," Charlie Angel yelled. He stood outside the Salty Dog wearing a pirate's costume.

Connor pointed the wand over his shoulder, and scenes from *The Little Mermaid* began playing across the front of the pub, with the song "Kiss the Girl" coming through the speakers.

"I don't know about you, but I think that's a sign," Connor said.

Arianna angled her head to the side. "Is that Cherry dressed as Ariel?" Connor glanced over his shoulder. "In the canoe in front of the pub," she told him.

"Yep, and if that big guy gets in with her, they're going to end up on the sidewalk." He leaned over to tap the driver on the shoulder. "Can you stop at the harbor front? Thanks," he said when the older man nodded. "We'll stand up and wave the wand together."

The boats in the harbor were also decorated with Christmas lights. Once Connor and Arianna waved the wand, the boats would light up and fireworks would illuminate the night sky, signaling the end of the parade.

Connor looked down at Comet. "We should probably put the blanket over him so he doesn't bark. We don't want to end up in the harbor. Grams will never forgive us if we don't get to the manor on time."

"I wasn't planning on going back to the manor, Connor. I have to work on the proposals tonight."

"You have to come to the manor. We're playing Mr. and Mrs. Claus."

"You can't be serious?"

* * *

Colleen sent a book sailing across Kitty's suite in the manor's tower, hitting her grandson on the behind.

"Bloody hell," Daniel yelped from where he knelt on the floor with his head under his mother's bed, searching for Colleen's memoir. He pulled his head out to look around the room. "Nothing but dust bunnies under there," he said, retrieving the book Colleen had thrown.

Rubbing his behind with his free hand, he stood and put the book on the bed and then walked to the desk he'd searched earlier to no avail. He didn't realize that Jasper had recently moved her memoir from the locked drawer in the desk to a safe behind the landscape on the wall. Jasper had moved it after Colleen's failed attempts to get in the drawer had resulted in her spilling a cup of tea on important papers.

"Oh no, you don't," Colleen murmured when her grandson reached for the painting hanging on the wall above the desk. She focused on the two books on the coffee table in the sitting area. Once they were hovering in midair, she sent a blast of mental energy at them. One after another, they smacked Daniel on the back of his head. He dropped to his knees, covering his head like he was under attack. He stayed that way for several minutes before slowly lowering his arms to look around, his face pale. Staggering to his feet, he hightailed it out of the room.

Following after him, Colleen chuckled when he closed the door behind him, muttering, "The room's bloody haunted. The damn book isn't worth getting myself killed for. There's probably nothing of value in it anyway." He walked off, casting a nervous glance back at the room while rubbing his head.

"My ghostercising paid off, Simon," Colleen told her sidekick when he joined her on her walk to the great room. "Now that I've taken care of Daniel, we can enjoy a stress-free Christmas party."

After the local Santa Claus parade, the doors to the manor would be opened wide to welcome the paradegoers with hot chocolate and cookies, a special appearance by the Widows Club carolers, and a visit with the jolly old elf himself.

"Do you realize, Simon, that this will be the first drama-free Christmas season we've had in two years? Last year was even worse than the year before, although it turned out well in the end. But it'll be a real treat to get into the spirit of the holidays without a looming disaster hanging over our heads."

Simon gave her the side-eye and a *you're tempting fate* meow.

"Oh, go on with you. Daniel might sulk a bit, but he's given up on the book and causing trouble for Arianna and Connor. And those two, from what I've heard, are one step closer to their happily-ever-after."

That got her another tempting-fate meow.

"I admit, it doesn't look good with them on opposing sides, but they're working hard to bring the town together. And they might not know it yet, but it's also bringing them closer together. It's just a matter of time before Arianna brings Connor around to her vision for Main Street."

Simon parked himself in front of Colleen and cocked

his head to the side. If he were a person, she'd no doubt be getting a pursed-lip look. "Why are you staring at me like that?"

He responded with one of his *you can't be serious* meows.

Colleen had no idea what he was going on about, but she was quite impressed with how well she'd come to read his... "Bejaysus, you're right. I was so wrapped up in their romance, I forgot what was at stake. If Arianna brings Connor over to her side, Daniel has too much to lose to sit on the sidelines. And if Connor brings her over to his, Caine Elliot is one step closer to razing the manor. Except I'm as canny as the lad and outmaneuvered him. All we have left of my great-grandchildren to get on to Save Team Greystone are...Daniel's daughters."

She sighed. She didn't need to overtax her brain to know which way they'd vote. They'd barely spent any time at the manor with Colleen and the family. Still, she'd added a codicil to her will that just might turn the tide in the manor's favor. "Don't bother with any more of your smarty-pants meows. I know very well the fix we might be in, but I refuse to let it ruin my day."

She floated from the top of the second floor down the grand staircase with a smile forming on her lips. Boughs of cedar were draped on the banisters and decorated with trailing gold bows and fruit. Gold pots of poinsettias graced either side of the red runner. In the great room with its soaring ceilings, there was a roaring fire in the stone fireplace, beside which stood an elegant eighteen-foot tree decorated in white lights with red and gold balls and ribbons. In front of the tree sat a red velvet wingback chair waiting for Santa.

"Perfect. It all looks perfect," she said, breathing in the scent of fresh cedar, hot chocolate, and sugar cookies. The doors to the manor opened, and children and adults poured inside, filling the great room with laughter and good cheer. Jasper, in his familiar black suit, and Kitty, wearing her caroling outfit of a red velvet dress, white fur shawl, and a brimmed red bonnet, greeted their guests, welcoming them to the manor.

"I don't think we've ever had a bigger crowd than this, Simon." At the sound of a familiar *ho ho ho*, Colleen began to laugh. "I wonder how they roped Connor into playing Santa," she said, searching for Arianna.

Colleen thought she may have been the one to convince him to take on the role until she remembered the conversation she'd overheard at Thanksgiving. George had been comically horrified to learn that Arianna had called her new pup Humbug, which seemed to indicate Arianna wasn't a fan of the holidays.

After what she'd been through these past few months, Colleen didn't blame her. Especially now that Beverly had spirited Helen away. Beverly wouldn't be happy until she had her mother's attention all to herself. She'd been an only child raised by a single mother. Helen had doted on her when she was young. It was no wonder Beverly grew up believing the world revolved around her.

The children swarmed Connor as he made his way to his chair in front of the Christmas tree. Sophie and Olivia rescued him, organizing the children into a long line.

"Hey, Santa, where's your little helper?" Michael called out from where he stood by the bar with his cousins, having a good laugh at Connor's expense.

"Ho, ho, ho. I didn't bring an elf this year. I brought my beautiful wife." Her great-grandson's deep voice was even deeper than usual. "Have any of you seen Mrs. Claus? She seems to have disappeared," he said to the children. "Maybe we should call her. What do you think?" They nodded, and Connor and the children called for Mrs. Claus.

Seconds later, Arianna appeared in the entryway wearing a Mrs. Claus costume with a put-upon expression on her face. As she came down the stairs into the great room, Colleen noticed the leash she held with a cream-colored dog attached to it. The pup wore a pair of reindeer antlers on his head.

"Comet!" George ran over to cuddle the pup and then convinced Arianna to let her take care of the dog while she performed her Mrs. Claus duties.

"There she is." Connor smiled when Arianna came to stand beside him. "How about a kiss for your husband?" He puckered up, drawing *ewws* and *grosses* from the children and laughter from his brother and cousins.

"How about a picture for the *Gazette*?" Byron Harte said, crouching a few feet away with a camera in his hand.

"Ho ho ho, anything for our favorite reporter," Connor said, patting his knee, a slash of white teeth showing through his beard. "Come here, wife."

Colleen chuckled. Poor Arianna. It was clear the lad intended to torture her today.

Arianna released a gusty sigh as she plunked down on his knee.

He grinned, patting her behind. "Now I know where all my cookies went."

Arianna leaned back, and whatever she whispered to Connor made him throw back his head and laugh, and then he faced her, pulled a sprig of mistletoe out of his pocket, and kissed her. At the same time, Byron took their picture.

"Admit it. It's the perfect shot for the paper," Connor whispered, trying to appease a clearly not pleased Arianna. "It's exactly the message we're trying to get out there."

"No, it's not. That picture says—" Arianna began before George cut her off.

"Santa, can you and Mrs. Claus stop fighting so we can tell you what we want for Christmas?"

Connor glared at Arianna, and she glared right back. Too bad Colleen couldn't share with her great-grandson that the best-laid plans had a way of going wrong. She wandered away, stopping at groups of people she knew, listening in on their conversations, catching up on the gossip. It was her favorite pastime.

Over in a corner, she caught sight of Rosa DiRossi, Kitty's childhood best friend. Rosa stood near the atrium, wearing her caroling outfit and eating Christmas cookies as she chatted to Daniel's partner in crime, Theia. Colleen knew exactly what Rosa was up to. For the past year, she'd been trying to find her grandson Marco, a firefighter at HHFD, the perfect match. "You'd best walk away from that one, Rosa. She's Trouble with a capital *T*."

But instead of walking away, Rosa dragged the girl over to the stairs to join the Widows Club. Colleen could see why. They appeared to be shy a few members. Theia, wearing black pants and a red and black sweater, tried to demur, but she was no match for Rosa.

"Don't be nervous, dear," Kitty said. "None of us had ever sung professionally before."

Colleen could see Theia trying to hide a smile, which seemed a kinder thing to do than laugh outright that Kitty thought this a professional event. "Thanks, but I'm used to singing for an audience. My mom began dragging me on to the stage at the age of four." She said it in such a way that indicated she had fond memories of her time with her mother. Another mark in her favor, Colleen thought, wondering if she'd misjudged the girl based on the company she kept.

"And where was it you used to sing with your mother?" Kitty asked, her eyes narrowing on the girl for some reason.

"Mostly in pubs in Dublin and Cork," she said, a little more of the Emerald Isles coming out in her voice.

"You're from Ireland? I never would have guessed," Kitty said, chewing on her lower lip while her gaze darted around the packed great room.

"What is going on with you?" Colleen murmured, frustrated that her daughter-in-law couldn't see or hear her.

"No. I'm from Boston originally, but my mom had family in Dublin. And every summer she'd drag me to Ireland to find my father. They'd met in a pub, singing for their supper, she used to say." She smiled at the older women hanging on to her every word. The Widows Club were a romantic bunch.

"You never found him, did you?" Kitty said.

"No, but I got a lot of practice singing in public. Should we start?" she asked, looking over the great room as though searching for someone.

"Yes, of course. Is there a song you and your mother liked to sing at Christmas?" Kitty asked.

Theia nodded with a wistful expression on her face. "'Mary, Did You Know?'"

Yes, Colleen thought, she'd misjudged the girl. And she had no idea how much until Theia opened her mouth and out came the voice of an angel. A hush fell over the crowd gathered in the great room as they turned to stare at the girl on the stairs. Daniel used to make heads turn when he sang, just like this... one. And like Kitty had done only moments before, Colleen narrowed her eyes to study Theia's features more closely. Holy Mother of God, she was one of theirs. Kitty had seen it too. She would have remembered the times Daniel had written home to tell them about his grand adventures, of singing in the pubs of Dublin and Cork.

She wondered if Daniel had noticed the resemblance and turned to survey the crowd. He was no longer where she'd last seen him on his phone. She spotted him scurrying up the stairs to the entryway, glancing over his shoulder in a furtive manner before veering sharply to his left and down the hall. And just as had happened at Halloween, Colleen found herself chasing after her grandson. She prayed whatever he was up to wasn't as bad as that night.

She followed Daniel into the library, surprised when he removed several books from the middle of one shelf and pressed a button. A hidden door clicked open. He replaced the books on the shelf and then walked into the dark, confined space. Colleen followed him. Once inside, he pulled a lever on the wall. The hidden library door swung closed, leaving them in the dark. But not for long. Daniel used the light on his cell phone to locate another hidden door. This one leading down to the tunnels below. Within minutes, they were back to where he'd held his clandestine meeting with Caine Elliot. Only it wasn't Caine who awaited him. It was Ryan Wilson.

Colleen hadn't believed Daniel could sink any lower, but he'd exceeded even her wildest imaginings. Given the circumstances of his earlier perfidy, she might have eventually forgiven him for making a pact with the devil, for offering up the family estate to protect his own.

This was worse. This was unforgivable.

A former officer with the Harmony Harbor Police Department, Ryan Wilson had a vendetta against the Gallaghers. Daniel had seen the man at his worst this past summer and knew him to be a snake of the Garden of Eden variety. But what her grandson might not know was that Ryan Wilson was a mere speck of evidence away from solving the case his grandfather had been working on at the HHPD before Colleen had had him thrown off the force. It appeared Daniel wouldn't be happy until he destroyed them all.

She held Caine Elliot to blame. He'd exploited her

grandson's weaknesses to get him on board with his plan.

"I'm curious to know what it is you want from me, Gallagher. Last time I was here, I wasn't made very welcome. In fact, if there hadn't been witnesses, I'm pretty sure your nephews would have beaten the hell out of me before trying to get me locked up."

"That's between you and them, not me. I want whatever dirt you can dig up on Arianna Bell, and I want it fast. No questions asked."

She could tell by the expression on Daniel's face that he didn't like the prospect of dragging Arianna's name through the mud, but he was desperate now. He'd pinned his hopes on Connor to win the election outright, and when that hadn't transpired, his almost daily powwows with Sean and Maura must have convinced him he had nothing to worry about. Except, ever since Thanksgiving, word around the manor was that Arianna had thrown herself into the job and her chances of being the council's pick had vastly improved.

Ryan Wilson cut off her thoughts with a low harrumph. If Colleen didn't know better, she'd assume he didn't want the job. She'd lay odds it was the exact opposite. He'd probably do it for free just to get back at Arianna. Not only did he bear a grudge toward the Gallaghers, he blamed the Bell sisters for ruining his life.

"You don't want the job, then?" Daniel frowned. "But I haven't even told you what the information is worth to me."

Colleen scowled at her grandson. "How are you going to pay? Pawn the family's silver?"

"No. I'm more than happy to get you dirt on Arianna, but it's not money I'm after. I want my job back at HHPD."

Daniel stuck out his hand. "You get me what I need before the town council and Hazel Winters cast their vote on Christmas Eve, and I'll use my influence with my nephew to ensure you're rehired."

Chapter Twenty-One

♥

Connor had to up his game. In a little more than a week, it would be December twenty-fourth, or D-day, as he'd come to think of it. His mother had been keeping her ear to the office walls at the town hall, of course, while his father had been out and about on the streets of Harmony Harbor, gauging how Connor was doing on the ground. Apparently very well, according to their latest report, which they gave him every night. It had become something of a routine. They'd either grab a late-night dinner at the manor or order in at his office at the town hall or at Gallagher and Gallagher.

And while he loved his parents and was thrilled to see them more or less back together, he would have preferred to spend his nights with Arianna. But the woman had put him firmly in the friend zone, which was the last place he wanted to be. Especially when all evidence pointed to him as the council's first choice. If that were the case, it was important that he and Arianna were in a good place before they rendered their decision on Christmas Eve.

Even more important to him was that Arianna was in a good place. She seemed to be. Sometimes it was hard to tell because he was in the friend zone. Although he'd begun to see cracks in her armor over the past week. Sadly, he thought Comet had more to do with her light-hearted smiles and relaxed demeanor than he did. Which brought him to where he was now—standing on her front porch bright and early on a snowy Saturday morning.

O'Malley's would be delivering her secret-admirer present to the front door in about half an hour. They'd ring the bell and then take off at a run. Connor would be there to help Arianna bring the box inside and, if the rest of the day went according to plan, he'd be out of the friend zone by tonight. Or at the very least, one step closer to where he wanted to be.

He checked his watch, waiting until it was exactly nine on the nose before ringing the bell. Just before the minute hand struck twelve, the door swung open. He smiled at Arianna, who looked like she'd rolled out of bed and into her boots and coat.

Her head was bent as she yawned through a warning to the dog at her feet. "Five minutes is all you have, Comet. And no barking. Some of the neighbors might still be sleeping. Lucky them," she muttered, yawning again as she picked up Comet and tucked him under her arm.

"Hey. How's it—" Connor didn't get to finish what he was about to say because Arianna walked out of the house and into him.

Comet yipped, and Arianna made an *oomph* sound. As Connor raised his hands to steady her, she looked up at him through bleary, accusing eyes. “Why did you walk into us?”

“Babe, you walked into—”

“Stop mumbling. I can’t hear a word you’re saying.” She made a face. “Sorry. I forgot I had earplugs in. I took Comet out at six, and he’s been howling at me ever since.” She put the dog down and then handed Connor the leash. Looking around him as she took out her earplugs and put them in the pocket of her coat, Arianna said, “Did you bring coffee?”

“Sorry, no, but it’s probably a good thing I didn’t, given how you walk—”

“I guess that means you didn’t bring doughnuts either,” she said, clearly disappointed in him.

Comet appeared to be too. He sat growling at Connor’s feet.

“I’m striking out this morning,” he murmured, praying this wasn’t a sign of things to come. He frowned when Comet’s growling intensified. “Why is he doing that?”

She shrugged. “Maybe he doesn’t like you.”

“Hey, where are you going?” he said when she turned to walk back into the house.

“To bed. I’m exhausted.”

He stared at the door she’d just shut in his face and then looked at Comet, who was no longer growling but was about to strangle himself by jumping off the porch. Scooping up the dog, Connor carried him to the middle of the lawn and placed him on the ground. Comet promptly lifted his leg.

Connor jumped out of the way. “I’m not a tree.

This is." He pointed at the big oak, lightly tugging on Comet's leash to get him to follow. His business done, the pup was more interested in catching snowflakes. Connor gave up and huddled in his jacket. "You've got ten minutes."

Ten minutes later Connor remained half-frozen in the middle of the lawn with Comet showing no signs of wanting to go inside. Comet looked like a snowball with a dog trapped in the middle as he rolled around and then gave a couple high-pitched yips. He'd caught himself in the leash.

"Stop rolling." Connor crouched beside him. "Just give me a second here, and I'll free your paw." He dropped the leash to untangle it from Comet's hind leg. "Okay, you're good to go, buddy." Patting the dog's head, he went to stand up, then remembered the leash.

Comet's eyes met his as Connor reached for the leash. In that brief eye lock, Connor knew the dog would take off if he didn't think fast. He needed a distraction. If Comet was anything like his doggy mommy… "Want a doughnut? I've got a doughnut right here," Connor said, slowly lowering himself back into a crouch.

He put his free hand in his pocket while inching his other hand toward the leash. Comet's eyes were glued to his pocket. The tips of Connor's fingers were less than a couple inches from the leash when a gust of wind rattled the branches of the oak, sending a flume of snow cascading toward them. Connor lunged for the leash at the same time Comet took off.

Connor ended up face-first in the snow. He wiped

the snow from his eyes and then pushed himself to his feet while visually searching for the dog. He spotted a lump of snow moving toward the backyard. Connor gave chase, which he quickly learned was a mistake with a playful pup.

"Comet, I'm not fooling around here," he said after he'd spent five minutes (which felt like twenty) running around in circles in Arianna's backyard. All he needed was to get close enough to grab the leash. Apparently, he wasn't the only one to figure that out. Comet made sure to leave at least a yard between them.

But the pup's biggest advantage was not his smarts; it was his boundless energy. Since Connor's energy was not boundless, he clearly needed a better strategy. He parked himself in the narrowest space he could find between the backyard and the front yard with his legs spread, his hands out, as though he planned to catch a football.

Comet sat at the other end of the backyard watching him with his head cocked. Great. He was taking a breather, Connor thought, praying his plan worked. Now that he was standing still, he noticed his jeans had gotten wet when he'd fallen face-first in the snow and were practically frozen to his thighs.

Connor turned his head and whistled over his shoulder. "What's that, Comet? Did you hear that?" He was about to do it again when a delivery truck rumbled down the street, the squeal of brakes loud as it parked just up from Arianna's. They were here to deliver his secret-admirer present to Arianna. Crap.

He whipped his head around. Sure enough, a white

blur was headed his way. The dog veered to his right. Connor bent down, twisted at his waist, hands out to catch either the dog or the leash as they tried to escape through…At the very last second, Comet zigged instead of zagged and ran between Connor's legs, the red leash dragging through the snow behind him.

Connor swung forward. With his head and hands between his legs, he reached for the leash and caught the end of it. Comet kept going, jerking the leash out of Connor's hand. The momentum pulled Connor's hands two inches too far. He did a somersault, landing on his back with a heavy *splat*, the wind knocked out of him, but not the thought that the deliverymen were moving toward the gate and Comet was loose.

Connor groaned as he raised his head. "Don't open the…" He trailed off when Comet raced back to him, licked him from his chin to his cheek, then turned to park himself by Connor's head, growling at the two laughing men who carried the tree box between them.

"Awesome somersault, dude. Too bad I couldn't get my phone out of my pocket. It would have gone viral for sure," the tall, skinny kid bringing up the rear said.

"You need a hand up?" the silver-haired man asked with a smile, the corner of his eyes crinkled. It was Mr. O'Malley's son John.

"Appreciate the offer, but I'm good, thanks." Connor's groan as he went to sit up belied his words.

They put the box on the front porch. John said something to the kid and then started across the lawn. The closer he got, the louder and more aggressively Comet growled.

"Cute protector you got there." John gave a nervous laugh when Comet snarled, showing his teeth. "Okay, maybe not so cute. You want to tell him I'm friend, not foe, before I stick my hand anywhere near his mouth? I've seen how high he can jump."

So that was one mystery solved. Comet hadn't been growling at Connor because he didn't like him; he'd been protecting his mommy. Connor smiled at the thought that must make him the daddy. He decided it might be best to keep that to himself.

"It's okay, buddy. I'm okay. Mr. O'Malley's a good guy." He rubbed Comet with one hand while raising his other one to John. Comet continued growling but didn't seem quite so threatening.

"You sure you're okay?" John asked when Connor got to his feet.

He pulled his phone from the back pocket of his jeans with one hand while rubbing his lower back with the other one. "I am. Phone isn't." He showed John the damaged screen, groaning when he bent to pick up Comet's leash. "Okay, so I guess I won't be practicing my golf swing for a while."

"Looks like. And I wouldn't worry about the dog. He's not going anywhere while we're here."

John was right. Comet stayed by Connor's side as the two men brought the artificial tree box into the house instead of leaving it on the front porch as planned. Connor would never get it inside on his own now. He leaned in to make sure Mr. O'Malley senior had attached Connor's secret-admirer note to the box and spotted it taped to the side.

"Right here's fine," Connor said, indicating the corner where the TV had once stood in the living room. Obviously, Arianna had yet to replace it. Ignoring the twinge in his back, he walked the two men to the door. "Go find Mommy," Connor said to Comet instead of bending down to pick up the pup. Comet cocked his head, and Connor pointed down the hall. "Go get her."

"Don't worry. I'll be fast when I shut the door," John said when Comet showed no signs of leaving. "Guess it's okay to give you this," John added, handing Connor the invoice to sign. "And a word from Arianna's other secret admirer. He says he might be old and short, but he could still kick your behind, so be sweet to his sweetheart."

Connor laughed and handed him back the pen. "He'd have no problem kicking it right now. But tell him he doesn't have to worry about me. I'm always sweet. It's Arianna who—"

John cleared his throat.

Connor glanced over his shoulder to find Arianna standing behind him. "How much of that did you hear?" he asked. She looked like she'd just rolled out of bed, only instead of flannel pajamas, this time she had on light-blue velour sweats and a matching top. The other difference from earlier—and the more important one—her eyes weren't sleepy and annoyed. They were sleepy and maybe a little amused.

"Sorry about that," John said, forcing Connor's gaze from Arianna and back to the door.

"Don't worry about it," he told the other man.

"Thank your dad for my cape and Comet, John. It was very sweet of him," Arianna said.

"I'm sure my dad would love to take the credit, but it wasn't him." He winked and nudged his head at Connor.

"At the very least, you can thank him for looking out for me. I appreciate it," she said, moving to pick up Comet's leash. Comet, who was once again growling low in his throat at Connor.

They said goodbye to John, and then Connor shut the door behind him, glancing at Arianna, who was now headed for the living room and the tree box.

"How come Old Man O'Malley gets a thank-you and I don't get anything?" he said. She didn't answer, and he walked to her side. She'd put down Comet to stroke the box leaning upright in the corner.

"You remembered," she murmured, her voice husky with emotion.

It sounded like she was holding back tears, and some of the tension, spiked by his worry she was mad, left him. "How could I forget? It was the first time you cried in front of me. You had your heart set on a pink tree and your mom refused to buy one."

"Glamma wanted one too. We thought it would be fun and would cheer everyone up." She gave a brittle laugh. "We expected a lot from a Christmas tree, didn't we?"

"I tried to buy you one back then. It was too late though. Mr. O'Malley special-ordered this one for me a few weeks ago."

She looked up at him then, the tears turning her eyes

ocean blue. She moved her hand from the box to stroke his face. "You were right when you told John you're sweet. You really are. As sweet as Mr. O'Malley."

He bowed his head and groaned. "Please tell me you did not just compare me to a ninety-year-old leprechaun?"

"I don't think he's ninety, more like ninety-three," she said, obviously trying not to laugh.

"You're messing with me, aren't you?" he said, framing her face with his hands.

"Maybe just a little." She smiled and went up on her tiptoes to press her lips to his. "Thank you. Thank you for being the best boyfriend back then and for being the best secret admirer now," she murmured against his lips.

It wasn't exactly what he wanted to hear, but at least she hadn't said best friend. Even better, now that she'd gone from talking to kissing, she could say whatever she wanted and he wouldn't care. All he wanted was her mouth on his, her hands...He broke the kiss to look down at Comet, who'd latched on to the bottom of Connor's jeans on his right leg, growling and shaking his head.

"He really doesn't like you, does he?"

"He loves me. He just loves you more. He thinks he needs to protect you from me. Just tell him he doesn't, and he'll be good. Won't you, buddy?" he said, grimacing at the twinge in his back when he bent to remove Comet's teeth from his pant leg.

"But I do need protection from you, Connor Gallagher. You're the one person who could completely break my heart, and I've vowed never to have it broken again. I don't think I could put it back together."

Holding her gaze, he slowly straightened. "I'm not asking for all of your heart. Just give me a piece of it. That's all I need. I love you enough for both of us."

"You already have all of my heart. Every time you did something sweet or kind or tried to help me, fix me, you stole a small piece of it until you'd stolen the whole thing."

"If I wasn't afraid my back would seize or Comet might attack me, I'd sweep you off your feet right now, carry you to your bed, and make mad, passionate love to you all day and night."

"What happed to your back?" she asked, looking concerned. He told her about his Olympic-worthy free fall and backflip, leaving out the part of him dropping the leash in case she proved to be an overprotective puppy mommy. She made a pained face. "I'm sorry you hurt your back."

"Not half as sorry as me, babe." He drew her carefully into his arms.

She looked up at him. "If you forgo the sweeping-me-off-my-feet-and-carrying-me-to-my-bed part, what are our chances of the mad, passionate lovemaking happening tonight?"

"Not great, but on the other hand, I think we're a go for kissing, cuddling, and decorating the Christmas tree. I'll go high; you go low." He grinned when her cheeks flushed. "Babe, I was talking about putting the balls on the tree."

Chapter Twenty-Two

♥

They didn't get to trimming the tree until much later in the day. "You need a fireplace going and a Christmas movie on TV to give us the right ambience to decorate," Connor said as he tested the white twinkle lights for the tree.

Arianna smiled. The man was clearly a fan of the holidays. He also looked extremely sexy in his jeans and a black thermal Henley with his hair a little messy, the beginnings of a shadow on his jaw. "I've got Christmas cookies and hot chocolate with marshmallows, chocolate sauce, and chocolate chips on top. Does that help?" she asked as she carried the platter of cookies into the living room. His expression said *not much.*

She put the cookies on the side table and moved to stand by the tree. "We do have music." At that moment Kenny G's *Miracle: The Holiday Album* played softly in the background. Connor didn't look any more impressed, but he looked even more gorgeous captured in the glow of the pink tree and white lights, which may have been the reason she said, "How about once we're finished decorating, you unwrap me and we make mad, passionate love under the Christmas tree?"

"Still not sure about the mad, passionate part, but unwrapping you under the tree would definitely—" He was interrupted by a *pop*, *pop*, and then the string of lights in his hands went out. He sighed. "Looks like we're heading to Holiday House today instead of tomorrow."

Comet had broken several Christmas decorations—which was why he'd been banished to Glamma's bedroom—and Arianna had planned to replace them tomorrow. "A visit to Holiday House will put you in the Christmas spirit. Since we're downtown anyway, why don't we grab a bite at Jolly Rogers or the Salty Dog?" she suggested.

"Sure, and, ah, maybe we could stop by Merci Beaucoup. Talk to the owner about designing your dress for the Christmas Ball."

For years, Mayor Hazel Winters had hosted an open house at her home the week before Christmas, inviting her staff, the heads of departments, and members of the town council. But with their mandate to bring the town together, Connor and Arianna had decided to open it up to everyone who worked at the town hall as well as the local business community. The only place big enough to hold such an affair was the ballroom at Greystone Manor.

Connor had offered to foot the bill for the entire evening, of course, but Arianna didn't think it fair to him and had decided they'd charge twenty dollars a head. Two-thirds of what they raised in ticket sales would go to cover the cost of the buffet—it was a cash bar, and the entertainment (aka the Gallagher Boy Band) and room rental were free. The other third would go to support programs at the community center.

Which would be getting another injection of cash, thanks to everyone who'd sent money to Arianna and her grandmother back in September. Last week, in an open letter in the *Gazette*, she'd thanked everyone for their generosity and told them of her plans to donate the money. If they didn't agree with her decision, she encouraged them to get in touch with her. The only people she'd heard from were those who offered their wholehearted support for her initiatives. Evie, the owner of Holiday House, would help Arianna with the dispersal of funds.

"Sound like a good idea?" he asked.

She frowned at his tentative expression. "Why are you looking at me as if I'll be angry?"

"I'm just not sure where you're at with your hand, so I thought you might be upset I suggested you design a dress for the ball."

"Me? I thought you said talk to the owner about designing the dress."

"I kinda did, but I was hoping once we got there and you talked about it with her—"

"What? You thought I'd miraculously be able to sketch again?" She shook her head, angry at him for ruining what had been a perfect day up until then and had looked to be heading for a perfect night. "I'll never be able to draw like I used to. In all likelihood, I won't be able to draw at all. I can't even sign my name yet."

He reached for her damaged hand. “Don’t, please,” she whispered.

He ignored her, and her stomach turned when he brushed his lips across her fingers. “You might not be able to draw like you used to, but that doesn’t mean you can’t design anymore, does it?”

She pulled her hand away. “I don’t see how. I can’t sketch out my vision on paper well enough that someone else could create what I had in mind. I won’t be able to personally add the special touches that made my gowns unique.”

“I’m not saying it would be the same, but if you found someone who shared a similar vision, had similar taste, don’t you think you could work together to create a dress you’d be proud to put your name on?”

“I don’t know. Maybe. I haven’t thought about it.”

“Maybe you should. It can’t hurt to think about it, can it?”

She narrowed her eyes on him. “What are you up to now? You’ve already talked about this with the owner of Merci Beaucoup, haven’t you?”

“I might have mentioned something about it.”

“I don’t know why. If the town council and Hazel choose me to...That’s it, isn’t it? You don’t think I have a chance of being the one they pick, so you’re going to make sure I have something to fall back on.” She pushed him away. “I don’t believe you! And I can’t believe I slept with you again! Every time I do, I discover that you’re trying to screw me over.”

“Now, honey, I think you might be overreacting just a—”

"Do not *honey* me, Connor Gallagher. You need to leave."

He rubbed his hand over his jaw. "Babe, be reasonable. Your heart isn't in this."

"And yours is?"

"Of course it is. I've been working my ass off, and you know it."

She did, but that didn't mean she'd been sitting at her tiny little desk twiddling her thumbs... thumb. "You may not think my initiatives are as important as the projects you're working on with the police and the fire department, but they're important to me and the families of Harmony Harbor. And let's not forget the business community. They still won't even speak to you. So there."

"So there?" He raised an eyebrow as he clearly struggled not to laugh.

"I'm done talking to you. You can leave now." She closed her eyes, and almost immediately she felt his face coming closer to hers. "Do not even think about—" He kissed her. "Connor!"

"Look at me." He clasped her chin with his fingers.

She huffed out a breath before doing as he said. "What?"

"I love you. I just got you back. I don't want to lose you again."

"I love you too, but I don't like you very much right now."

"No? I like you," he said, leaning in to kiss her just below her ear.

She shivered. "Of course you do. Because you want

to have sex with me, and I don't want to have sex with you." She was such a liar. But it didn't matter what her heart or body wanted. Whether Connor believed her or not, this job was important to her.

"Ever?"

"We'll talk about it after Hazel and the town council make their decision on Christmas Eve. Until then I think it's best if we're friends, not lovers."

* * *

Along with the director of the senior residence, Arianna took Hazel and several members of the town council on a tour of the facilities, explaining the benefits of having a child and elderly care center combined.

Arianna had initially come up with the idea of opening an affordable day care on-site, but the more time she spent at the senior residence, the more she thought about Glamma and how, if her memory problems progressed, an elderly care center would be the perfect solution for not only Glamma and Arianna, but for other overwhelmed caregivers who wanted to keep their parents or grandparents at home but needed a break.

Although Arianna was getting ahead of herself. There was still no sign Glamma was coming home for good.

"Arianna's right. We have plenty of seniors in Harmony Harbor who don't require full-time care. Both they and their caregivers would benefit greatly from the center Arianna is proposing, as would the preschoolers. In my opinion, it would be a win for the entire community," the director said while Arianna handed out the information packets.

"You'll find studies that support our belief in the project as well as a cost analysis in your packet, but we wanted to give you a better idea by showing you the concept in action. If you'll follow me, we have a group of children and seniors busy at work together in the dining room. They've broken up into teams to participate in a gingerbread house competition." Arianna smiled as they rounded the corner and laughter, along with the smell of gingerbread, greeted them.

The director gave her a furtive thumbs-up.

Arianna's positive feelings vanished the moment she walked into the room and saw Connor sitting at one of the tables, helping two preschoolers and an older man.

Of course the members of the council and Hazel spotted him right away and hurried over to admire him and the gingerbread house.

She should have known he'd show up. Over the past few days, he'd been her shadow. Every meeting she took, he'd arrive five minutes before her or five minutes after. And he had an annoying habit of charming everyone in the room, just like he was doing now.

"Do you mind?" he asked Hazel, gesturing to the information packet in her hand. "Arianna is very closemouthed about her projects." He winked at her.

If people hadn't turned to look at her, she would have flipped him off. Instead, she said, "Connor, I need a word, if you don't mind."

"Anything you need, partner. I'm your man," he said, fueling the flames of her annoyance higher.

As soon as he reached her side, she spoke through her teeth while smiling for their audience. "If you keep this up, you're going to end up my frenemy instead of my friend."

"Because I like making gingerbread with the old folks and the kids, you're going to frenemy me?"

"Do not pretend you don't know what I'm talking about. You're trying to undermine me, Connor. Get a leg up on me."

He pressed a hand to his chest, which was lovingly encased in an indigo V-neck sweater that did wonderful things to his eyes. "I'm wounded."

"You are not. And stop calling me 'partner.' We're not partners."

"We could be if you weren't so competitive."

"Pot, meet kettle."

He grinned. "Yeah? Okay, here's the deal. You get yourself on a gingerbread house team, and if yours wins, I'll stay out of your way until the twenty-fourth. If I win, you can't complain when I show up at your events or meetings. You have to be…nice to me. Very nice to me."

"We've already had this conversation," she said, glancing at the older gentleman and two preschoolers at Connor's table, her gaze passing over their semi-completed house. "All right, you have a bet." She thrust out her hand when he leaned in to kiss her.

An hour later, as the judges, who were residents of the senior home, stopped by each table to view the entries, Arianna knew she was in trouble, and it had nothing to do with who had the more beautiful gingerbread house because, clearly, she did. It had to do with who was the best schmoozer, and Connor took the prize.

When they pinned the blue ribbon on his table, he looked over at Arianna and waggled his eyebrows.

It didn't take long for Arianna to get her revenge. Two days later she was at the fire station bright and early, helping wrap the toys and put together the Christmas baskets for local families in need of some holiday cheer. Several of the firefighters, as well as Hazel and the council members, were wondering what had happened to Connor.

Arianna smiled as she packed another basket, saying to Hazel, who was working beside her, "You know Connor. He stretches himself too thin. Always double booking meetings. Forgetting whom he's meeting with next. I'm sure it slipped his mind that he volunteered to help today. It's such an important community event that I marked it in red, just to be sure I didn't forget." Right after she'd wiped it off Maura's and Connor's planners and calendars.

Connor's cousin Liam, looking handsome in his uniform, came to stand in front of her. Fighting a grin, he offered her his cell phone. "Someone wants to talk to you."

"I'm a little busy right now," she said, knowing full well who it was.

Liam shared that with his cousin and then laughed. "He says, 'Game on.'"

Chapter Twenty-Three

♥

Colleen stood beside her canopied bed in the tower room at the manor, watching as her grandson threw clothes into his suitcases with Jasper looking on. "I tell you, the room is haunted, and I'll not be staying here another night. I can't take it anymore. Everything was fine until the night of the parade, you know. Always slept soundly, and then all hell broke loose. Books falling off the shelf. The same ones, mind. Always with 'traitor' or 'snake' in the title. Same thing she whispers in my ear just as I'm falling asleep." He stopped stuffing clothes in his suitcase to look over his shoulder at Jasper. "I think it's Granny Colleen."

"Is that so? And would she have reason to believe you're a snake and a traitor, Daniel?"

"Holy Mary Mother of God, you think it's her. Right here in this bloody room with me." He looked down. "I might have just shite my drawers."

Jasper stared down his long, narrow nose at her grandson. "What have you been up to, Master Daniel?"

"What hasn't he been up to?" Colleen muttered. But

at least Jasper was now aware he needed to keep a closer eye on Daniel. That gave her some peace of mind.

"The haunting began the night of the parade," Daniel murmured, and then nodded. "I know what it was that set her off. I'll put a stop to it." He looked around the room. "Granny, do you hear me? I'll make it right. Now you just hie yourself back to the other side. Say hello to my da for me." He slowly sank onto the bed. "I've made a right hash of things, Jasper. I wish my da were here. He'd know what to do."

"Your mother is here for you."

He shook his head. "No. I won't burden her with this."

"You don't give her enough credit. You let her fragile air and delicate beauty deceive you. She's a strong woman."

Colleen smiled, and so did her grandson. "I always knew you loved her, you know. I'm glad she has you. Glad you have her."

"And you have all of us. Your mother, me, and your brothers. Whatever burden it is you carry, you can lighten it by sharing it with your family."

Colleen looked at the man who'd been her trusted confidante for decades. "I hope I told you how much you meant to me, Jasper my boy. I hope you know it now. In many ways, you were more son than friend. Somehow, some way, I will return the legacy that was stolen from you."

"I notice you didn't mention my wife and daughters."

Jasper clasped his hands behind his back and rocked on his heels. "You've been here five months and you haven't spoken of them."

"Made a hash of it with Tara, just like I did the others. Barely know my girls because of it."

"We all make mistakes, Daniel. It's what we do about them that matters. When you're ready to deal with yours, come to me. But for now I suggest you take care of whatever you promised Madam you'd take care of and then get yourself ready for the mayor's ball. There's a tux in the closet. Do you still wish to move to another room?"

"Aye. I love Granny, but she always was a bossy thing, and her ghost is the same."

"So I've noticed," Jasper said under his breath. "Leave your suitcases. I'll have them transferred to your new room before the night is out."

Daniel thanked Jasper, picking up his cell phone as soon as he closed the door behind him. "Wilson, it's Danny Gallagher. The job I asked you to do, I... You have the information I need? A load of dirt you say?" He picked at a loose thread on the red-and-gold bedspread.

From the expression on his face, Colleen could tell he was thinking about reneging on his promise to Jasper. She turned to the bookshelves, focused her mind and energy on one book in particular, and sent it flying to the floor.

Daniel jumped and then muttered, "All right, all right." Raising his voice, he said to Ryan Wilson, "I have no need of the information you collected on Arianna, but I'll pay you for your troubles. I know it's not what we agreed upon, but things have changed. That's not my problem now, is it? Don't threaten me. Do with it what you will. Just leave my name out of it. I'll have the money to you this week."

He disconnected and looked around the room. "I wonder how much Granny's sterling-silver mirror and brush will fetch me."

Colleen sent the mirror he referred to off her dresser and onto the floor. It shattered.

"Now, was that nice after I made good on my promise to you? Wilson is not a man to be trifled with, and I've put myself in his bad book thanks to you, Granny."

She leaned in and yelled in his ear, "You should have thought of that before you got in bed with the man."

Daniel shrieked, jumped from the bed, and ran from the room.

Scaring the bejaysus out of him didn't make Colleen feel any better. She was worried he'd set something in motion that couldn't be stopped, afraid what that would mean to the beautiful couple greeting guests at the entrance to the ballroom.

With help from her friends, Arianna had turned the space into a spectacular winter wonderland. Standing beside Connor by the open doors, she looked stunning in a red gown with her blond hair swept up in an elegant style, and Connor in his black tux couldn't have looked more handsome had he tried.

Colleen realized she was wrong. Connor looked even more handsome when he smiled at Arianna as he did just then, his love for her shining in his eyes. "She's breathtaking, isn't she?" he said to Dorothy DiRossi, who'd just complimented Arianna on how beautiful she looked. Dorothy's husband, Gino, was beside her in his wheelchair, looking ruggedly handsome.

Dorothy twinkled up at Connor. "She is. You both are. And so is your dress, Arianna."

"She designed it," Connor said proudly. "It's an Arianna Bell original. The first of many more to come. They'll be selling her new line at Merci Beaucoup."

"Connor," Arianna said, clearly exasperated with him. "Thanks, Dorothy. And despite what Connor thinks, I haven't made up my mind about starting a new line. Enough about me. You look amazing in that dress."

"You were right, dear. I had to have it as soon as I saw it. Thanks for thinking of me and for asking the girls at Merci Beaucoup to put it aside."

"My pleasure." Arianna smiled.

"It's my pleasure to look at her in the dress, but I could have done without the other two bags that came along with it," Gino quipped.

They all shared a laugh, and then the couple moved away, waving to their daughter Ava and her husband, Griffin, Colleen's great-grandson.

"Stop pimping my clothing line that I haven't even decided to design," Arianna said out of the side of her mouth to Connor, smiling as another couple approached.

"Come on. Every woman here, and far too many men for my liking, are going crazy over your dress. You'd make a fortune. And you love it. It's your passion," he whispered out of the side of his mouth before smiling and greeting the couple who now stood in front of them.

When they'd moved on, Arianna side-whispered, "It's not the same. I liked working with Marilyn, but it was hard. Much harder than I expected it to be."

He put his arm around her shoulders and kissed her temple. "I'm sorry. I shouldn't have pushed you. I just don't want you to give up on something you love."

"I know. And although I'm loath to admit it to you, it was nice working with Marilyn. I really like her, and I like what she plans to do with Merci Beaucoup, but I can't make any decisions until after the twenty-fourth." She gave him a smug grin. "A little bird told me we're neck and neck again."

"So I've heard." He lowered his arm from her shoulder as another group of people approached. "I should have thought of bribing the town council with a special lunch catered by Rosa DiRossi."

"It was Glamma's idea," she whispered just before the couples reached them. "She said to tell you she'll take you out for a loser's lunch on the twenty-seventh."

Connor laughed and then greeted their guests. As the couples walked away, he asked Arianna if Helen was coming home for Christmas. She nodded, her face lighting up. Colleen was happy for her.

"What about Serena?"

"I don't think so, and I'm getting a bit worried about her. She's taking forever to respond. She says she's in Europe, but I don't believe her."

"You want me to have Shay look into it for you?"

"Yes, please. That would—" She shot a panicked look at Connor. "Why is Gary here?"

Colleen frowned at the two men walking through the great room toward Arianna and Connor. One was tall with brown hair, light eyes, and broad shoulders. Like Connor, he was a handsome man. But his features were softer and more refined, whereas her great-grandson's were chiseled and masculine. The other man appeared to be in his eighties, with white hair, a distinguished air, and a paunch.

"I have no idea why Summers and his grandfather are here, but I'll take care of it," Connor said, his voice hard. He glanced to where his mother and father stood at the mirrored bar, shooting Maura a pointed stare. His mother frowned and then looked past him. Her eyes went wide. She said something to Sean before rushing to Connor and Arianna's side.

"I'm so sorry. I don't know why Gary's here. I invited his grandfather and grandmother, not him." Maura wrung her hands. No doubt because she noticed the paleness of Arianna's face and the angry pulse of the muscle in her son's jaw. "You can't become governor without their support, darling. I wanted them to see you here. See you in a different light. Now that you're no longer with the Three Bs—"

"Mom, I'm representing his grandson's ex in their divorce. I'm going after Gary and—"

Arianna's gasp cut Connor off. She stared at him. "What do you mean you're representing his ex? He cheated on me with her. She knew he was married, and—"

Sean intervened. "Your mother and I will stand in for you." He nudged his head to an empty table in the far corner of the ballroom.

Colleen followed Arianna and Connor. He held out a chair at the table in the dark and quiet corner, then took the seat beside her, angling it toward her. Taking her hand in his, he said, "I'm sorry. I honestly don't believe my mother meant to hurt you. She probably doesn't even know or remember you were married to Gary."

"Or that you represented him in our divorce?" She withdrew her hand from his. "What does Danica have that I don't? Gary cheated on me with her, and now you're representing her when you wouldn't represent me."

"Don't even go there." He reclaimed her hand. "I told you why I represented him. Back then I didn't feel like I had a choice. But when he came to me to represent him this time, I refused. It was days after the fire, after I'd seen you at the hospital, and I was furious at him. I pretty much blamed him for everything that had gone wrong between us. For all the years I had to watch you with him when I wanted you with me."

She briefly closed her eyes, gave her head a small shake, then whispered, "I'm sorry. You don't know how much I wish I could turn back time."

"Not any more than I do."

She gave him a small smile before looking over her shoulder. "Do you think they'll leave?"

"I doubt it, not until he's had a chance to talk to me. The court date has been set for the second week in January. He didn't have a prenup. Danica is taking him to the cleaners."

"With some major help from you, no doubt. I can't imagine that made...You quit the Three Bs because of this, didn't you?"

"Actually, I got fired because of it, babe, and then Summers et al., got me blackballed from nearly every reputable law firm in Boston. So you can bet I'm going to make him pay. But mostly I'm doing it to make it up to you."

"Don't do it for me. You have nothing to make up to me for. Just do what you believe is right."

"What I believe is it's time Gary and the Summers family got what's coming to them." He stood up and held out his hand, helping Arianna to her feet. "What do you say we go back to greeting our guests together? We wouldn't want Summers Junior and Senior to think they chased us away, now, would we?"

"No. No, we wouldn't." She reached up to kiss his cheek. "Thank you."

"So, does that mean I'm out of the friend zone?"

"It's just four more days. I think you can wait." She laughed at the face Connor made.

Colleen smiled at Simon, who'd just deigned to join her. "What did I tell you? They've always been the perfect match."

She sighed when he gave her one of his *you're tempting fate* meows. But she didn't get a chance to do more than that because just then she caught sight of Daniel, and he had a shifty look about him. "What are you up to now?" she murmured when he glanced over his shoulder.

She followed his gaze and caught sight of Ryan Wilson peeking into the ballroom. While she debated who she should go after, they both disappeared from view. She searched the ballroom for them and caught the back of Daniel's head as he snuck out a side door. Moments later she left the ballroom to spy Ryan Wilson lurking at the bar in the great room. His eyes were pinned to the ballroom. If Ryan was after his money from Daniel, he'd have a long wait ahead of him. She just wished he'd do it elsewhere.

She looked at the anchor clock near the bar and wondered if it falling a foot from where he stood would send Ryan on his way. She was just about to give it a try, though she despaired of damaging the clock—it was a part of their heritage—when Ryan went on alert, his gaze following someone out of the ballroom. Colleen turned. It was Connor. She shouldn't be surprised, she supposed. Who better to blackmail than the man who loved Arianna? Ryan glanced from left to right, then followed Connor down the hall to the men's room.

"Gallagher." Ryan hailed her grandson before he reached the door. "I have something I think you'll be interested in."

"Nothing you have could interest me, Wilson. Now leave the manor before I throw you out." Connor turned to push open the door.

Wilson sneered as Connor entered the men's room and the door closed behind him. "You'll pay for that, Gallagher."

"Sounds like you're as fond of Connor Gallagher as I am," Gary Summers said, looking at the closed men's-room door. "Lucky you, you don't have to make a deal with the devil."

"Obviously you do. If you need some leverage, let me know. It'll cost you though."

"I'd pay a small fortune to have leverage against him. If I don't get him to agree to settle my ex's case against me out of court, I'll lose much more than that."

"Then this is your lucky day. I have exactly what you need and the perfect person to shut him down. I've got dirt on Arianna Bell, and no one has more influence over him than her."

"You have dirt on Arianna? Let me see," Summers demanded.

"Like they say, show me the money."

Summers got out his wallet. "Now show me what you have, and we'll agree to a price." He looked to either of end of the hall. "Not here."

"Follow me."

Colleen followed them into the library, shocked when Ryan opened the secret door to the tunnels. She tried to scare them off by sending books off the shelves, but nothing happened. Either her shock had rendered her ghostly abilities impotent or she'd wasted too much energy earlier on Daniel. She needed to find her grandson. He'd started this; he had to put a stop to it.

She hurried from the library to see Connor coming out of the men's room with his phone pressed to his ear, unaware of the two men conspiring against him mere yards away. Colleen followed him to the ballroom and to Arianna's side.

His cousins waved to him from the stage. Michael held up his sax. Connor held up a finger and said something in Arianna's ear. She laughed and shook her head, but he took her by the hand and led her onto the dance floor.

Colleen searched the crowd for Daniel.

"Play mine and Arianna's song, and then I'll join you," he told his brother and his cousins. Colleen's great-grandsons conferred and then nodded, taking their places onstage. Griffin and Finn on guitar, Aidan on the harmonica, and Michael on the piano. Liam picked up the mic. "This is for my cousin and the woman he's loved since he's sixteen, Ed Sheeran's 'Perfect.'"

"I thought we needed a new song," Connor said, taking Arianna into his arms. "The lyrics of this one do a much better job of saying how I feel about you."

She tilted her head to listen to the lads now singing onstage and smiled. "I think they do a pretty good job of capturing how I feel about you."

"Does that mean you'll put me out of my misery and take me out of the friend zone tonight?"

"You are persistent. I'll give you that." She smiled. "Sing to me, and I'll think about it."

The couple shared a romantic dance to the delight of the crowd, and then Connor delighted them further by taking center stage and stealing the show with "Rockin' Around the Christmas Tree."

She panicked when Arianna excused herself to use the ladies' room. Colleen had yet to find Daniel, and Jasper was nowhere in sight. Simon would have to do. She called to him. He must have sensed trouble was afoot and appeared almost immediately at her side.

"Come. We must protect Arianna. Pray Ryan and Summers have left the premises, Simon." And that

Colleen's abilities had returned, she thought, as they followed Arianna out of the ballroom. Sadly, Colleen wasn't holding out much hope for either. Arianna crossed the great room and walked down the back hall to the ladies' room. Colleen was just about to release a relieved breath when Summers appeared.

"Simon, get Connor. Get him now," Colleen said, looking for something she could use against the man if it proved necessary.

"Arianna, just the woman I wanted to see. It seems you and I have a lot to talk about."

She gave him a tight smile. "I don't think we do. Have a good evening, Gary."

He grabbed Arianna by her injured arm. "Get your hand off me," she said, her voice tight and her face pinched.

"You unhand her now, or I'll clock you," Colleen said, staring at the family's coat of arms on the wall. He didn't release her, and Colleen focused with all her might on the coat of arms, intent on knocking him out. It rattled on the wall but didn't fall. Which ended up being a blessing when Gary looked down at Arianna's arm with distaste and pushed her away from him, putting her directly into harm's way.

"You will talk to me, and you will talk to me now. Because of you, Connor Gallagher is trying to ruin me. In doing so, he will also ruin my family. But you're going to stop him, Arianna."

"Even if I wanted to, I couldn't."

"If you don't want him to find out you gave his son away, a little boy who is now dead because you did, I think you'd better figure out a way—"

Behind her Colleen heard a shocked gasp. She turned at the same time as Arianna to see Connor standing there. The girl's eyes went wide, her face stricken. She pushed past Summers to reach Connor. "You have to listen to me, please. It wasn't like that, I swear to you it wasn't. My mother told me he died. I was barely conscious, and she had me sign papers that I thought were for cremation but were actually adoption papers."

She clutched at Connor's arm. "You have to believe me. I wanted him, Connor. I wanted him with all my heart, but my mother thought I was too young and gave him away. I didn't even know about any of it until nine years ago. His grandmother, his adoptive grandmother, contacted me. She thought I knew about him, about our son. She wanted me to know he'd died in a car accident with his adoptive parents. It was an accident." She tugged on his arm. "Please, please say something."

"He was eleven. For eleven years he was alive, and I never knew him. He never knew me."

"I didn't know. I swear to you, I didn't know."

"You knew when you got pregnant. You knew then that he was mine."

"Yes, but we hadn't been together for two months, and...You don't know what it was like in my house then, Connor." She fisted her good hand in his sleeve. "Please don't leave me. Please let me try to explain. I'm sorry I didn't tell you. You have no idea how sorry I am. For all of us."

Connor looked like he'd taken a punch to the heart.

"Don't do it, my boy. Don't walk away from her. Rage at her, put your fist through a wall, but don't turn away from her. She's not like you and me. Everyone she's ever loved has walked away from her, left her on her own. Even her grandmother and your wee son, though through no fault of their own. Stay with her. Grieve together. Otherwise I fear it is a blow she'll not survive."

Colleen bowed her head when Connor did exactly as she had feared. He turned and walked away.

Chapter Twenty-Four

♥

Arianna sat beside the pink Christmas tree with Comet curled in her lap and the phone cradled to her ear. Instead of sniffing back tears, she rubbed her nose on her shoulder. She wouldn't let her grandmother hear her cry.

Gary had gotten his revenge on both her and Connor. He must have started pimping their story minutes after Connor had left Arianna devastated and sobbing her heart out in the back hall at the manor. The story appeared in a Boston online newspaper first thing this morning. Because of the Gallagher name, the story had gone viral.

But the only reason it had reached L.A. was because several of her mother's friends in Harmony Harbor had shared the news with her this morning, which resulted in her mother canceling their trip home for Christmas.

"It's all right, Glamma. Don't feel bad. I won't be alone. Comet and Connor will be here," she lied.

"Good. I was worried he might blame you for losing out on knowing his son. I should have had more faith in him. It's your mother who's the unreasonable one. Though I shouldn't be surprised. She's always been difficult. But she knew how much I wanted to be at the town hall for the announcement and to spend the holidays with you."

"Maybe she'll change her mind. If you have the tickets already—"

"She won't change her mind, darling. I'll be lucky if she lets me come this summer."

"Don't even joke about that. She can't keep you away, Glamma."

"She holds the purse strings and the deed to the house. I won't have her throwing you out on the street."

"She's threatening to throw me out of the house?"

"I'll not allow it, so don't worry about it. It's just one more thing for her to threaten me with."

"Glamma, you'd tell me if she was hurting you in any way, wouldn't you?" She hated to think it could be true.

"Unless you count her keeping me away from you, set your mind at ease. She's not hurting me in any other way. I'm glad you have Connor. It makes this a little easier."

"I didn't think you knew he was the baby's father, Glamma. You never mentioned it to me."

"Of course I knew. He was the only boy you ever loved. And I'll be proud to introduce him as my grandson-in-law. But don't tell him I've been singing his praises until after Hazel and the town council render their decision. I wouldn't want him to think I've gone soft."

"Glamma, I've decided to withdraw my name from the contest. I'm going to let Hazel know today."

"Why? You seemed so happy lately. You had so many plans, good plans, darling. And not just for Main Street. Irene told me about all you're doing for the seniors and the programs at the community center."

"Just because I won't be mayor doesn't mean I won't be involved. My friend Evie, the woman I've been telling you about, the one who owns Holiday House, she's done more good for this town in the past two months than the majority of elected officials have done in years."

"But that's not why you're withdrawing your name, is it?"

"No. It's because Connor has done so much for me, and I want to do this for him. I know it can never make up for not telling him about the baby, but I have to try. Besides that, he deserves the job, Glamma. You should see him. The man works practically twenty-four-seven, and he's amazing with people. He truly cares about them and this town. He's the best person for the job."

"What about the office building? What about changing the face of Main Street?"

"I presented a request to the council this past Monday and asked if they would put the project on hold to allow the business community more input. They agreed."

"It sounds like you've thought this through. I just worry about how you'll earn a living. Have you given more thought to designing a line of evening wear for Merci Beaucoup?"

"I've had another idea, and I wanted to run it by you. I'd like to design clothing for women with disabilities, seniors too. Clothing that's fashionable but easy to get into and comfortable to wear. I thought maybe you and I could do it together, Glamma. Our tastes and vision are so much alike, it would be easy to work together."

"Do you think we could get your mother to agree?" Glamma asked, sounding as excited as she'd been at the thought of coming home.

"If we come up with a way to sell it to her, I think maybe," she said, her heart twisting when she heard her mother's voice in the background telling her grandmother to get off the phone. They said a whispered and hurried goodbye.

Now that she no longer had to put on an act for Glamma, tears rolled down Arianna's cheeks. She didn't know what she'd do without Connor in her life. All along she'd thought it was the campaign, the idea of being mayor that had brought her back to life, but it wasn't. It was Connor. It had been him all along.

There was something else she'd been wrong about. She hadn't thought her heart could take one more loss. She'd been sure it would shatter into a million pieces, leaving her empty and numb. But even now, without a single word from Connor, with it looking like they were done for good, her heart was still beating. And as big a loss as Tie the Knot and her injuries had been, losing Connor beat that times infinity and beyond.

Yet here she was, dressed and out of bed, makeup and tree lights on. She was stronger now, more resilient, and as devastating as it was for the truth to come out, it had allowed her to release the pain she'd been holding inside since the day she'd learned she'd had an eleven-year-old son who'd died.

And now she had to call Hazel with her decision. She wanted them to keep it quiet. She didn't want anyone to know she'd withdrawn her name. She'd work up until the twenty-fourth and be there for the decision to be read.

As she reached for the phone to call Hazel, it rang. It was the Harmony Harbor clinic, reminding her of today's appointment to check her arm. Arianna considered canceling, but she was a little concerned her arm might somehow be behind the overwhelming tiredness and queasiness she'd been feeling of late.

* * *

Arianna arrived at the clinic ten minutes before her appointment. The waiting room was packed. With Christmas only three days away, she imagined people wanted to get checked out before the clinic was closed for the holidays. She felt everyone's eyes upon her, and she lifted her chin. She had nothing to be ashamed about. From the expressions on people's faces, they didn't think she did either. Though she imagined Connor and his family might disagree. Her stomach did a little wobble at the thought that Connor's cousin and cousin-in-law worked here.

She smiled at a teenager with a baby in her arms and took the seat beside her. "What a beautiful baby," she said. "How old is he?"

"A week," the girl said. She glanced at the other patients nearby, then dipped her head.

"Just a checkup, I hope," Arianna said, noting the disapproving looks being sent the teenager's way. She wondered what it must be like for her. To be so young and to have the responsibility of a baby while also having to put up with people looking down on her. "Is your mom or partner here? I can take another seat if they are."

"No. It's just me," she said, and then chewed on her bottom lip, looking so young and vulnerable that Arianna wanted to cry.

She offered her hand. "I'm Arianna Bell."

The girl gave her a small smile, shifting the baby to shake her hand. "Dawn, and I know who you are." She glanced around the room again, lowering her voice. "I read the story about you and Mr. Gallagher online. I'm really sorry about your little boy."

Arianna stiffened, then forced her shoulders to relax. She'd have to get used to this. "Thank you."

"My parents wanted me to give him up." She nodded at her son, wrapped in the blue blanket. "But I couldn't do it."

"At least they gave you a choice."

"I guess. Only I didn't make the one they liked, and they kicked me out."

"I'm so sorry, Dawn. What about the baby's father? Is he helping?"

"He let me move in with him." She shrugged. "We're...It's pretty hard."

Her heart broke for the teenager. Arianna's sister and

most of her friends were so much better at this kind of thing than her, but she was desperate to say something to make Dawn feel better, or at the very least give her some hope. "In the new year, we're starting several programs at the community center to help single mothers and families who are having a hard time. If you have any ideas what we, the town, can do to help make things easier for you and your baby, we'd love to hear them. Here." She reached in her bag. "Here's my card. I really would love your input. Or if you just need to talk to someone. Evie, the woman who owns Holiday House, she'd probably be better than me to talk to. Just drop into her store and tell her I sent you."

"I'd rather talk to you, if that's okay." The baby started to cry, and Dawn bounced him lightly on her knee, crooning to him, her face softening as she looked down at her son.

"It's more than okay." Arianna smiled. "Look at that. You got him to stop fussing right away. You're really good with him." She lightly stroked the baby's cheek with her fingertips. "His skin is so soft."

"Do you want to hold him?"

"I don't know. I'm not very good with babies."

"I bet you are."

"I guess you didn't see the video of me that went viral."

"No. I didn't," Dawn said with a half smile, and then lifted the baby, nudging her head for Arianna to put out her arms. Arianna looked down at the small blue bundle the young girl placed in her arms, and tears welled in her eyes. Throughout the years, she'd held the babies of her friends and members of Gary's family, but never before had she felt this overwhelming rush of emotion. She gently rocked the baby and willed the tears away, but when he opened his blue eyes and looked up at her, she lost the battle. "I'm sorry. I don't know what's gotten into me." She sniffed.

An older woman Arianna didn't recognize handed her tissues. "It's the stupid reporters' fault, reminding you and the Gallagher boy of all you lost. It'll be okay, love. You'll have more of your own one day."

"Thank you," Arianna said.

The older woman offered Dawn a tentative smile. "You have a beautiful baby, dear."

Dawn returned the woman's smile with one of her own. "Thank you."

"Arianna." Dorothy called her name and waved her over.

"I better go." She shifted to give the baby back to his mother. "I forgot to ask, what's his name?"

"David."

"A beautiful name for a beautiful baby. Merry Christmas to you both," she said as she stood and then reached into her bag. "Please don't be offended, but all the angels from the angel tree were gone by the time I remembered, and I like to give a gift at Christmas to someone in town that I don't know." She removed two hundred-dollar bills from her wallet and tucked them into the fold of the baby's blanket. "Buy something special for you and David from me." She leaned in and gave the girl a hug, then kissed the baby's forehead. "Thank you for letting me hold him."

"Well, it looks like you managed to make half the waiting room cry, lovey. I think that's a record," Dorothy said when Arianna reached her. She gave her a hug. "How are you holding up?"

"Better than I expected."

"How's Connor?"

"I don't know. He's not speaking to me," she confided because she'd felt comfortable with Dorothy from the first time she'd met her.

The older woman patted Arianna's arm as she held open the door to the examination room. "As I understand it, you've had years to live with the loss while he's had less than twenty-four hours. Give him time, lovey. He'll come around. It's obvious to everyone how much that man loves you."

"I'm afraid he might not know how much I love him."

"Then you'll tell him, and you'll show him. Over and over again until he knows it right down to his soul." She patted the examination table, giving a little cheer when Arianna hopped up on her own. "I guess I don't have to ask how the arm is doing."

"Actually, that's why I came. I think I might have an infection. Lately I've been tired and queasy."

Dorothy frowned. "You should have come in right away. Here. Let's get this off of you and have a look." She helped Arianna out of the sweater and removed the compression bandage.

"I haven't noticed any extra redness, but I, um, don't really like to look," Arianna admitted.

"Well, we're going to change that today. Oh, no.

Don't think you're going to argue or wheedle your way out of this. I might look sweet, but I'm a tyrant when I need to be. Just ask my husband." She gave Arianna's hand a gentle squeeze. "This is important, lovey, and not just so you're aware of any changes that might indicate infection, but because you need to accept it for you to truly heal."

She let go of her hand. "So while I take some bloodwork and your temperature, you're going to cream your arm, and instead of turning away while you do, you're going to look at every inch of your arm and hand and fingers. And as you do, you're going to thank God that you have an arm that works and fingers that are healing. Even if they never work like they once did, they do work."

Arianna nodded, knowing that Dorothy was right. And while she smoothed the cream over her skin, she thanked God not only for her arm and hand but for Dorothy and the young teenage mother and her beautiful son.

Chapter Twenty-Five

♥

Connor sat on the well-worn love seat in his great-grandmother's suite of rooms in the manor's tower. Rumor had it his uncle had vacated the suite because it was haunted. Connor wished it was. He could use his great-grandmother's wisdom and advice.

He placed his elbows on his knees, holding his head in his hands. He was hungover. He'd spent the rest of last night drowning his sorrows in a bottle of his grandpa Ronan's finest whiskey. His cousins and brother had joined him.

His cousin Liam knew something of what Connor was going through, but the one person who knew exactly how he felt, he hadn't been ready to talk to. Angry, feeling betrayed, he'd been afraid of what he'd say. Afraid he'd say things that would remain between them, things he couldn't take back. Because despite everything, he loved Arianna and always would.

The door creaked open, and he groaned. "Unless you have aspirin and coffee, go away."

"How about a cold cloth and my special morning-after drink?" his mother said. She smiled when he raised his eyes but not his head. "You look awful, darling."

"Thank you, Mother."

She draped the cloth over the back of his neck and picked up his hand to close it around the cool glass. "Drink up." Holding the cloth, he leaned back against the love seat and lifted the glass to his lips.

His mother walked to the French doors that looked out onto the harbor. "I knew I'd find you here. Whenever you were hurting or needed advice, you'd come to the tower looking for Colleen." She cast him a slight smile over her shoulder. "I was jealous of her, you know. I wanted to be like her, her and Kitty. I tried so hard to make them like me."

"You and Grams get along great now."

"We do, don't we? It's been a nice change. I shouldn't have tried so hard in the beginning, and then I should have tried much harder over the past several years. I don't think any of you realized how difficult it was for me when your father left politics. That's all we'd ever had."

He frowned, not sure what was going on, but he had the feeling his mother needed to get this off her chest. She certainly must have been deep in thought or back in her past because she didn't hear the door open or notice his father come into the room. Connor placed a finger to his lips. His father nodded and leaned against the bureau, arms crossed, looking at his wife standing with her back to them.

"You must have had more than that, Mom. How did you and Dad meet?"

"I was dating your uncle at the time. Daniel was fun, ruggedly handsome, always up for a good time. I know you're probably wondering what he saw in me. But once, a long time ago, I was fun too. Then my mother got sick, and we were having a hard time making ends meet. Daniel said he'd talk to his brother. He said if anyone knew what programs were available to us, it would be Sean. He was right. And the minute your father walked into our living room, all confident and take-charge, I was a goner."

"Poor Uncle Daniel," Connor said, glancing at his father, who waggled his eyebrows at him.

"Don't feel too sorry for your uncle. I think he was dating my best friend the very next day."

"So, when did you fall out of love with Dad?"

She glanced over her shoulder at him with a frown. "It's your father who fell out of love with me."

"Are you mad, woman? Where did you get an idea like that?"

His mother whirled around. "Sean. How long have you been here?" She glared at Connor.

He shrugged, wondering how he'd gotten caught up in his parents' drama. Did they not think he had enough drama and heartache to deal with on his own?

"Long enough to hear you spouting your nonsense." His father walked over to his mother and took her in his arms. "I've always loved you, even when you weren't the easiest woman to love."

She pulled away from him to wrap her arms around her waist. "I know I wasn't easy. I was actually pretty awful. And it's probably not a good excuse, but I was scared. I didn't come from your world, Sean. I worked hard to fit in because I wanted to make you proud. I never wanted you to be embarrassed of me. But then the world I worked so hard to fit into didn't want me after you left politics. All the friends I made, they weren't really friends. And when you went back to practicing law, you didn't need or want me to throw dinner parties or lunches, so I put all my hopes and dreams on poor Michael, and when he chose a different path than the one I'd charted for him, I lost any connection to the only world I knew. No one wanted me around, and then you retired, Sean, and you didn't want me either. If you weren't golfing, you were playing racquetball or poker."

His dad looked shocked, and Connor knew how he felt. "I had no idea, Maura. I wish you had told me."

"I tried."

"I'm sorry, Mom. Mike, Logan, and I should have picked up on it too."

"No. Don't apologize." She came to sit with him on the couch. "I honestly didn't come up here to talk about myself. I wanted to talk to you about Arianna and your baby. I'm so sorry, darling."

His father sat on the other side of him and rubbed Connor's back. "We both are, son. I wish I had the words to take the pain away, for both of you. Have you spoken to Arianna since last night?"

"No. I'm not sure what to say. I know she was young—we both were—and I understand she was having a tough time at home, but I deserved to know she was carrying my child."

"You did, but you have to remember this was not Arianna's decision alone," his mother said. "I imagine Beverly was very much involved. And she wasn't particularly fond of men at the time, having just been left by her husband for another woman. I'm sure the last thing she could think about was dealing with a pregnant teenager, and she certainly wouldn't have wanted you and your father and me standing in the way of what she saw as the solution to her problem."

"Your mother's right. You need to talk to Arianna, son. You need to grieve together. Don't let this come between you."

"And, darling, don't let the race for mayor come between you either. I was watching you with Arianna last night, and as much as I think you would be as wonderful a governor as your father, I don't want you to end up like us. I don't want politics to become your life."

"So you don't want me to run for governor?"

"Of course we do, if that's what you want. We'll be there supporting you all the way if you decide to run. I just don't want it to define who you and Arianna are as a couple. And I don't want you to feel that the only way to get our time and attention is running for mayor or governor or anything else."

"And you didn't have to take one for the Gallagher team to get your mother and me back together. Although it probably did help speed things up," his father said, reaching across Connor to take his mother's hand.

"Which of my brothers have you been talking to?" Connor asked his parents.

"Both." His mother smiled. "They're also worried

that the mayoral race will come between you and Arianna."

Connor leaned his head against the back of the couch and thought about everything his parents had just said. He thought about Arianna, the child who had been stolen as much from her as from him. And he thought about his future, one with Arianna in it and one without her.

He sat up. "I want you to know that while I may have entered the mayoral race for the wrong reasons, I wanted it too. I always have. Politics is in my blood, thanks to you two. I want to make a difference, and I think I can. And one day I will, just not now. I'm going to call Hazel and ask her to withdraw my name from the race. I'll ask her to keep it quiet, so you guys need to do the same. I don't want Arianna to think she won by default. She deserves it as much as I do, and she also needs it more than me. The people of Harmony Harbor will be lucky to have her. She'll make an amazing mayor."

"All right. Good. Now, get going. Your mother and I have lots to talk about. We have to figure out what to do with all our free time until you need us to run your next political campaign."

As he walked to the door, Connor heard his mother giggle and then the sound of kissing. "You do know that Uncle Daniel says GG is haunting this room, which means she's watching you make out on her couch?"

A book fell from the shelf, and Conner could have sworn he heard his grandmother chuckle.

* * *

Arianna walked along the sidewalk toward the redbrick church, her boots crunching on the packed snow. It was a beautiful winter night. The air was crisp with a slight tang of salt from the ocean, which you could hear if you listened close, and the smell of woodsmoke from the chimneys of the houses along the street. The stars and the sliver of moon above the church's white spire competed with the street's brightly colored Christmas lights.

She wondered if she was late and had missed the carolers who'd asked her to join them tonight. She took out her phone to check the time, listening for voices raised in song, but all she heard was footsteps behind her. She turned to see a tall man in a black coat, an incredibly handsome man, a man she hadn't spoken to since he'd looked in her tear-filled eyes and asked her why. She didn't think she'd ever forget the look of devastation and betrayal on Connor's face.

She didn't know what to say or do. Did she throw herself at his feet and beg forgiveness? Did she pretend the secret she'd kept for so many years hadn't destroyed their happily-ever-after? She glanced at the church, thinking God had been unbelievably cruel, giving her hope for a second chance only to steal it away.

She needn't have worried about saying anything. Like he always did, Connor took complete and utter control, holding her gaze as he walked the last few feet toward her and the individual clouds of their breath became one. "I'm sorry I walked away. I just needed some time," he said, folding her in his arms.

She nodded against the soft wool of his coat as all the scenarios that had played in her mind for the past twenty-four hours finally quieted. A sense of deep contentment and peace enveloped her. It was the best Christmas present she could have asked for or hoped for.

Lifting her head from his chest, she said, "I'm sorry I walked away from you that night at Kismet Cove. It was one of the worst mistakes I ever made. The others were not telling you about the baby—both times, in the beginning and in the end. *Sorry* just doesn't seem to be—" The doors to the church opened, capturing them in a beam of light.

Connor walked her backward along the sidewalk until they stood in front of the nativity scene, its life-size figurines housed in a stable. "I love you. I always have, and I always will, and I know you feel the same way about me. For now that's enough. We'll talk later," he said, smiling down at her as laughter and chatter filtered out from the doors.

"You're coming caroling too?" she asked, stepping out of his arms.

"Yeah. I—" He frowned, looking around. "Did you hear that?"

"Hear what?" she asked, and then she heard what sounded like a baby whimpering. She turned to look at the cradle in the nativity scene and saw the movement of a tiny hand. "Connor, it's a baby. Someone's left a real baby in the manger." She rushed inside the stable to the cradle. "Did you hear me, Connor? There's a—"

"I know, babe. I'm trying to see where they're watching from. They're here somewhere."

She reached inside the cradle for the baby and gasped. "I know him. Connor, I know this baby. It's David. I met his mother. Dawn—"

Connor rushed inside. "Put the baby back in the cradle and then push Mary out of the way and put her shawl over your head." He shrugged out of his coat. Placing it in the cradle, he motioned for her to put the baby down. "Come on. The carolers are on their way. We have to convince them the mother let us borrow him to play Baby Jesus."

"I don't understand," she said, even as she did what he asked and lay the baby in the cradle.

"If we can't convince them we're playing out the nativity scene and they discover the mother left the baby here, she'll be charged with child abandonment and endangerment," he said, pushing Joseph out of the way to take his place. He grabbed a blue shawl off the life-size figurine and put it around his own shoulders.

"We can't let that happen. I saw her with him, Connor," Arianna said as she nudged Mary out of the way, placing the shawl over her own head and shoulders. "She loves him. She's good with him. She just needs help. Her parents kicked her out of the house, and she's living with her boyfriend. They're young, so very young."

"Like we would have been," he said quietly, stroking the baby's cheek.

"Yes, like we would have been." They didn't say anything, both lost, she imagined, in thoughts of what their lives might have been like if Arianna's mother hadn't done what she had. She didn't agree with how her mother had handled things, but she'd gained some insight into what might have motivated her.

"Showtime," Connor whispered as they heard the crunch of footsteps drawing near.

Arianna held Connor's gaze as several people came to stand in front of the nativity scene. He gave her a confident smile and winked.

"Hazel, did Father O'Malley...? Oh my. Look, they're real. The baby is real, and so are Mary and Joseph."

"It's our mayors!"

"Look, it's Arianna Bell and Connor Gallagher!" someone else shouted to the sounds of more feet running their way.

Arianna kept her gaze on the baby and Connor, swallowing a groan when cameras on phones started clicking, the flashes blinding. And then the carolers began to sing "The Little Drummer Boy." She widened her eyes at Connor when, instead of ending with that, they launched into "O Little Town of Bethlehem." Connor touched the baby's cheek and nodded, indicating he was okay.

One of the carolers must have picked up on their concern for the baby and ushered the other singers along. Several people called out their thanks before walking away.

"I thought they'd never leave," Arianna said, reaching into the cradle to lift the baby into her arms. "You're safe, David. They won't take you away from your mommy."

"Unless she wants them to," Connor said.

"You're right, and maybe she will, but she needs to know what support is available to her before she makes her decision."

"That's what you've been working on with Evie, isn't it?" Connor said as he removed the blue shawl from his shoulders and put Joseph back in his rightful place.

She nodded. Connor came over, drawing the shawl from her head before wrapping both her and the baby in his coat. "I'm parked about a block away. Do you have any idea where we can find Dawn?" he asked as he returned the shawl to Mary.

"No, but I know someone who might. Dorothy DiRossi."

"Okay. I'll get her number from Ava, but first let me take another look around. When I left Comet on your porch, I didn't leave until I knew he was okay and you'd taken him inside. If Dawn is the kind of mother you're making her out to be, I can't help but think she's out there close by, waiting to see what we're going to do with the baby."

"You would have been a wonderful father."

"I'd like to think I would have, but we were young."

"Will wanted to meet us, you know. Our son, they named him William, but he was mostly called Will. Just months before the accident, he'd told his parents he wanted to find us. His grandmother said her daughter and son-in-law were apprehensive, but they doted on Will and wouldn't deny him anything. They promised to help him find us. They had no idea of the circumstances of his adoption. His grandmother was devastated when I told her. Furious at my mother's friend, the one I stayed with in L.A, who'd arranged the adoption. It was private, and they were old family friends."

She bowed her head, her stomach turning at what she was about to tell him.

"What is it?" He gently clasped her chin to force her gaze to his. "Tell me."

"Will had begun preparing to meet us. He'd written a letter telling us about himself, his likes and dislikes, his hobbies, his friends, his mom and dad. He'd put together a photo album with the help of his parents. Photos of all the important moments of his…of…"

"Take your time." He wiped away her tears.

"He was a beautiful baby, a beautiful boy. He looked like you. From his letter, you could tell he was sweet, kind, funny, and thoughtful. He wasn't angry we gave him away. He loved his life, his mom and dad. He was happy."

She could feel Connor's eyes upon her and looked up through her tears.

"The grandmother sent you the letter and photos, didn't she? That's why you went back to your office that night, isn't it?"

"They were in a locked drawer in my office. And now they're gone and he's gone, and I have nothing to remember him by. I couldn't save him, and I couldn't save the pieces of him that I had left, the only part of him I could have shared with you. I'm sorry. I'm so, so…"

"It's okay. We're going to be okay." He took her in his arms and rocked her. She felt his tears in her hair.

"I saw him. The night I died, I saw him. He was at

the end of the light. He was with my dad. I wanted to go to him, to them."

"But I called you back."

She nodded.

"I'm glad you came back to me."

"I am too."

He let her go and wiped the tears from his face and then hers. He smiled, lowering the coat to check on the baby. "I'll do a quick search for Dawn, and then I'll get my car."

"I'm going to bring him into the church. Father O'Malley will be sympathetic. He'll want to help Dawn. He won't call the police. He's been working with Evie and me on the family initiatives at the community center."

"All right. I'll meet you there within the next thirty minutes. Hopefully with Dawn."

Fifteen minutes later, Connor walked into the church with a shivering and tearful Dawn at his side. Once they'd reunited mother and child, Father O'Malley brought her to the rectory for hot chocolate, leaving Arianna and Connor to talk.

"I'm going to stay with them for a few hours to see if we can come up with a solution tonight. Evie's on her way over," Arianna said.

Connor nodded. "There's something I need to take care of. I'll be gone for a couple of days. I'm not leaving you," he said firmly, as though sensing the panic that welled up inside her. "Trust me. I'll be back in time for Christmas. I'll meet you at the town hall at three o'clock for Hazel's announcement."

Chapter Twenty-Six

♥

It was three o'clock on Christmas Eve, and Connor wasn't there. Arianna glanced around the packed town hall. She smiled at Evie, Dawn, who held her son in her arms, and Father O'Malley. Dawn had decided to keep her baby. Arianna, Evie, and Father O'Malley had signed on as Dawn's surrogate parents or, as Father O'Malley liked to tease, David's grandparents. It was then that Evie and Arianna changed their designation to surrogate big sisters.

Arianna glanced to her left. Connor's family took up nearly the entire front row. His mother leaned across his father. "He'll be here. My son always keeps his promises," Maura told her with a reassuring smile.

"Thank you." She appreciated her support. Arianna had been nervous when she'd first arrived at the town hall. Connor had been wonderful, but she hadn't known what to expect from his family, especially Maura, who wasn't exactly an easy woman. They'd all been lovely.

"Sorry. Excuse me." Arianna heard a woman's voice coming from the back of the hall. She glanced over her shoulder to see Dorothy DiRossi clear the crowd, rushing down the aisle to the front row. "Oh good. I'm not too late." She handed Arianna a card-size Christmas box. "This is from you to Connor."

"I don't understand," Arianna said, lifting the lid. At the sight of two chocolate cigars, one with a pink wrapper and one with a blue one, she dropped the box.

Maura squealed and dove for the cigars, which had fallen onto the floor. "Look, look. She's having twins!" She waved them in the air.

"She's not having twins. We don't know what she's having. Now, put them in the box before you ruin Connor's surprise," Dorothy said.

Arianna stared at the woman. "I'm having a baby?"

"Yes. You're definitely having a baby."

The crowd broke into cheers.

"How?" Arianna asked.

Several people started to laugh, and Dorothy shushed them. "When you told me you'd been more tired than usual and nauseated and your arm was fine, I decided to do a pregnancy test. And"—she waved the chocolate cigars in the air—"I was right. Congratulations, lovey."

The crowd started shouting congratulations too and asking when the baby was due.

Arianna sighed. "You might as well tell them."

"You're a nosy bunch. Arianna and Connor's baby is due next summer."

When the hall got so quiet you could hear a pin drop, Arianna shifted in her seat to see what was wrong. At the back of the hall, Connor stared at her.

"What's the holdup? Come on. Get going!"

"Glamma?" Arianna said, as stunned as Connor still appeared to be.

"Yes. Yes, it's me, and if Connor would stop blocking the way..."

Connor grimaced and then moved aside to reveal her grandmother and her two sisters. "Jenna? Serena? What are you all doing here?"

"We're your secret admirer's best and biggest surprises," her grandmother announced as Arianna ran up the aisle.

"You are. You definitely are," she said, half-laughing, half-crying, hugging the three of them.

"Your mother's back at the house with the dog," Glamma announced. "So we should probably get this show on the road. Hazel, are you ready with the announcement?"

"If you don't mind, I need a minute," Connor said, gesturing for her grandmother and sisters to sit down. As they released her and made their way to the front row, Connor took Arianna in his arms. "I wouldn't have minded a bit of privacy for this, but it looks like the whole town is in on it anyway, so they might as well know I'm going to make an honest woman out of you," he said as he went down on one knee. "Arianna Bell, mother of my son, mother of my baby-to-be, and the only woman I have ever loved, will you please put me out of my misery and marry me?"

"There's nothing I want more than to marry—"

"Wait!" a voice in the crowd shouted out. "Don't you want to know which one of you the town council and Hazel picked to be mayor?"

"When I figure out who belongs to that voice—" Connor began, rising to his feet with a gorgeous diamond ring in his hand.

"It doesn't matter," Hazel said. "They both withdrew their names. Since Connor was running in his uncle's place, we've asked Daniel Gallagher—"

Glamma shot to her feet. "Hold it right there. What about me? Arianna was running in my place."

"No. If anyone is going to be mayor, it's going to be either me or Arianna. We won based on our own merits. Now, just give us a minute." Connor looked at her. "I can't believe you withdrew your name. I wanted you to be mayor."

"I can't believe you withdrew yours. I wanted you to be mayor."

He grinned. "I can't believe we're having this discussion."

She laughed. "I can't believe we're getting married."

"So you were going to say yes?"

"How could it be anything other than yes? I love you. So, in case there's any doubt, yes, yes, yes, yes!" She put her arms around his neck and kissed him.

"I think that was a yes for me," Daniel Gallagher said.

"I'm her grandmother. Why would she vote for you?"

Connor sighed and then broke the kiss to look into Arianna's eyes. "Hazel, what do you say? Two for the price of one. Arianna and I will share the job."

Hazel and the entire town council nodded their agreement. "If you hadn't both withdrawn your names, we were going to ask if you'd consider it. We didn't know how else to break the tie."

"I can't believe we were tied again," Connor said.

"You really did think you were going to win, didn't you?" Arianna said.

"Of course I did." He grinned.

"Merry Christmas, everyone!" Hazel and the town council called out before leaving the stage.

"Bah humbug," Daniel said.

* * *

Early the next morning, Arianna sat in front of the twinkling pink tree with Connor while Comet nosed his way through the reams of Christmas wrap. Carols played softly in the living room as a light snow fell outside.

"How long do you think we have before they get out of bed?" Connor asked, glancing toward her grandmother's bedroom.

Her mother had shared the bed with Glamma, while Arianna had shared hers with Connor and Comet. Serena had stayed with Jenna. They were coming here for brunch, and then they were all going to the manor for Christmas dinner. Her mother included.

Arianna hadn't seen Beverly last night. She'd already been in bed when they'd arrived home from the manor, where they'd all gone to celebrate. Arianna couldn't remember a happier Christmas Eve. "It'll probably be another hour before they get up. Why?"

"Because I have something else for you, and I

wanted to give it to you in private." He drew a beautifully wrapped blue box from under the tree. She had an idea what it was as soon as she saw the box. Mostly because she knew the man who was giving it to her so well.

She lovingly stroked the box. "I bet Will's grandmother knew you as soon as she opened her door."

"She did." He smiled. "She's a sweet lady. Our son had a good family. He was well loved."

"I know." She took his hand and pressed it to her stomach to remind him that life offered as many blessings as it did heartache. "This baby will be too."

He bent down, replacing his hand with his lips, straightening at the sounds coming from behind her grandmother's closed bedroom door.

"Oh, stop it," they heard Glamma say. "It's Christmas Day. Now that you promised I can come home for good, Arianna will forgive you anything."

"Is she right?" Connor asked. Surprisingly, he'd been much more forgiving of her mother's actions than Arianna had expected. Spending time with Dawn and David had helped.

Arianna nodded. "I need to let it go, as much for my own sake as for my family's. Holding on to the anger and pain didn't bring our son back. It just made me bitter. I don't want to be that woman anymore." She didn't think she could be, not with Connor in her life and a baby on the way.

"I'm glad, because rumor has it your mother's moving in with your grandmother for good. Serena was talking about it too."

"I guess I'm getting kicked out of my house after all. Are you interested in a roommate?" she teased.

"How fast can you pack?" He smiled, reaching into the pocket of his sleep pants. "We forgot a part last night," he said, taking her left hand in his. "Arianna Bell, the love of my life, will you do me the honor of being my wife?"

"Yes, if you'll do me the honor of being my forever love," she said as he slid the gorgeous diamond onto her finger. Comet barked and jumped onto her lap just as she leaned in to kiss Connor. They both ended up kissing Comet instead, who rewarded them with chin-to-cheek licks.

Want more holiday stories from Debbie Mason?

Visit Christmas, Colorado, where a second chance at love is the best Christmas present of all.

Out of money and out of options, Skylar Davis returns to Christmas, Colorado, seeking the comfort of her best friends. With the small mountain town all decked out for the holidays, there's no place Skylar would rather be...until she comes face-to-face with one of her biggest mistakes: the town's gorgeous mayor. With snow in the air and the magic of the season all around them, will a Christmas miracle bring them back together at last?

Please turn the page for an excerpt from

It Happened at Christmas.

The next morning, Skye sat on the edge of the bed numbly staring at the expiration date on the condom box in her hand. *If* she was pregnant, it was her own darn fault. Flopping onto the fuchsia satin comforter in the guest bedroom at Maddie's, she stared at the pink chandelier overhead. It would have taken all of one second to check the box that night, but she didn't. And she knew why she didn't. Ethan O'Connor's mind-numbing, toe-curling kisses had sucked the common sense right out of her head.

She supposed the three glasses of champagne she'd had at Maddie and Gage's rehearsal party might have had something to do with it, too. As soon as Skye had seen Ethan standing by the bar in an expensive black suit that fit him to perfection, she'd been drawn to him like a bee to a daisy…or maybe a rose. Ethan was too sophisticated to be a daisy.

And the morning after, he'd looked even better. Which proved that champagne goggles weren't to blame. Lying in bed with a muscular arm tucked behind his head, he had a lazy, satisfied grin on his sinfully gorgeous face. The tangled sheets rode low on his waist and bared an impressive six-pack and a sculpted chest. She'd barely resisted the urge to crawl back into the king-sized bed and run her fingers through his sleep-tousled hair. She released a resentful sigh at the memory.

Physically, Ethan O'Connor was her dream man. Her every erotic fantasy come to life. He sent her hormones and pheromones into overdrive. And when he opened his mouth, he sent her temper there, too. The man stood for everything she stood against. There was not a single thing they agreed upon. If she said the grass was green, he'd say it was brown in that smooth, lawyerly voice of his.

And she might be having his baby.

Hot and cold shivers raced up and down her spine, her stomach rolling on a nauseous wave. *You're not pregnant*, she told herself firmly and sat up. Sliding a hand under the waistband of her black yoga pants, she brushed her fingers over her stomach. Firm and concave. No changes there. She brought both hands to her black, pink-trimmed sports bra and cupped her boobs. Definitely a change there. It hadn't been the Cake Fairy costume after all. And not only were her boobs bigger, they were more sensitive, too. Cupcakes—it had to be all the sugar-laden cupcakes she'd eaten. Sugar was poison, and she'd been poisoning herself on a daily basis.

Dear universe, please let it be the sugar, Skye thought as she picked up her iPhone. The one extravagance from her old life that she couldn't afford to let go. Even if she kind of couldn't afford to keep it. Because no matter what Maddie said, Skye's financial future rested on her blog. But before she checked for responses from the bloggers she'd e-mailed last night, she Googled pregnancy symptoms.

Missed period. She mentally checked off the box. *Morning sickness.* She gave it a half-check. Hers was an all-day sickness, or at least it had been up until a few days ago. *Tender breasts.* Another check.

She gave a guilty start as the bedroom door opened. Quickly closing the site, Skye tossed her iPhone and pulled up her legs to sit cross-legged on the bed, wrapping her right elbow over her left in a seated eagle pose.

Maddie stuck her head in. "Hi . . . What are you doing?"

"Yoga."

"Oh, okay. How are you feeling this morning?" she asked, a touch of Southern in her voice.

Pregnant. "Fabulous."

"You look better than you did yesterday. Your face is all glowy."

Darn it. Skye mentally checked another box.

"Did you sleep well last night?"

"Like a log." *Dammit.* Her stomach did a panicked dance as she checked off that last box. At any other time, with any other man, she would've blurted her fears to her best friend. But she couldn't. *If* Skye was pregnant, as soon as she started showing, she'd leave Christmas. She wouldn't tell Ethan.

There's no way she'd subject her child to the same harsh censure she'd endured growing up. And she knew only too well that as conservative as Ethan was, he'd insist she marry him. She didn't believe in marriage. Especially to a man who didn't like her, let alone love her. What kind of environment would that be for a child to grow up in? She knew exactly what kind, since it was the one she'd grown up in.

"That's good, because I just got off the phone with Grace," Maddie said as she walked into the room. "She needs you to help out today."

Skye had been mortified yesterday. Devastated that she'd made the little girls cry. She didn't know what had come over her. Okay, so she did. Ethan had driven her to it. Ethan and her worries over their maybe baby. Seeing Claudia take a picture of her, a picture that made Skye look like a fool, only made it worse. Ethan already thought she was a joke. One more reason for her not to tell him if she was pregnant.

"I can't work today. I have plans." She was picking up a pregnancy test. And she'd have to drive halfway across the state to ensure no one saw her do so. "Grace told me yesterday that she didn't need me." She hadn't said so in so many words, but after Skye had killed Ethan... the prince... she figured Grace didn't trust her to help out at the fund-raising event Liz O'Connor was hosting for her son. The Sugar Plum Bakery was catering the Strawberry Social at the O'Connors' ranch today.

"You have to. Desiree called in sick."

"Liz O'Connor hates me. She won't want me there." And that was one more reason to add to the why-not-to-tell-Ethan list. "And I don't want to see Claudia again."

Especially since Skye would be working the type of event she'd usually attend as a guest.

"Since when do you care what people think? You've always marched to the beat of your own drum, so keep marching. Grace needs you, and you need the money."

Skye's stomach dropped to somewhere in the vicinity of her toes at the reminder. She hadn't moved past the initial shock and horror of thinking she *might* be pregnant to think about all that entailed. Supporting herself on minimum wage was one thing, but supporting a baby, too...? She'd need health insurance. She'd need...Tears prickled at the backs of her eyes as the weight of her worries came crashing down upon her.

Maddie frowned and sat beside her on the bed, taking her hand. "What's wrong?"

Skye wanted to tell her, but she couldn't ask Maddie to keep a secret from her husband. Gage and Ethan were best friends. And she wouldn't put her best friend in the middle of the mess. Resting her head on Maddie's shoulder, Skye swiped at the tear burning a trail down her cheek. "I feel like a failure. I'm twenty-eight, and I have no money, no home, no career. I don't have anything."

"You have me, and you have Vivi. And you're not a failure. Come on." Maddie squeezed her hand. "What happened to the woman who always told me, 'When one door closes another one opens'? Or what about 'It always looks darkest before the dawn'?"

Skye snorted and rubbed her nose. "She had her rose-colored glasses ripped off her face."

"Maybe that's not a bad thing. I bet one day you'll

look back on this and say it's the best thing that ever happened to you. Everything for a reason, remember?"

"Are you going to quote every platitude I ever spouted?"

"Yeah, it's kind of fun. How about this one: 'Breathe and find your happy place'?"

Skye half-laughed, half-cried, and put her arms around Maddie. "I really do love you, you know."

"I know you do, and I love you, too." Maddie rubbed Skye's back. "We're going to figure this out. I checked out your blog last night. You weren't kidding. It really is popular. I made up a list of potential advertisers that would fit your target audience."

Wiping her cheeks with the back of her hands, Skye eased out of Maddie's arms. "Really?"

"Yeah, really. We'll talk about it tonight. You'll be back on your feet in no time."

With Maddie putting her stamp of approval on the plan, Skye felt more hopeful and positive. It made it easier for her to push her fears away. "You're right. I will."

"That's more like it. But until you are, you're staying with us," Maddie said as she came to her feet.

Skye shook her head. "You know how much I love camping. I'll be fine. Besides, I don't want to wear out my welcome."

"Don't be silly. Lily and Annie love having you around. Their Auntie Skye is way cool in their eyes."

"I am pretty cool, aren't I? But you and Gage are newlyweds. You don't need a third wheel."

"We have two kids and another one on the way. What's one more?"

Skye narrowed her eyes at her best friend.

Maddie laughed. "Come on. Grace wants you to wear black pants and a white blouse. I've seen your closet, so we'll have to raid mine. Let's see what I have that'll fit you." She gave Skye a quick once-over and frowned. "Have your boobs gotten bigger?"

* * *

The colorful glass beads holding up Skye's messy topknot clinked as the delivery van bounced along the one-lane dirt road. "Geez, I thought the O'Connors were rich. You think they could pave the road." She sounded a tad cranky, and Skye was rarely cranky. Her mood was probably due to the motion causing a return of her nausea. Either that or her inability to convince Grace that her working the event was a bad idea.

"You're not feeling well, are you?" Grace said, shooting her a concerned glance.

"No, I'm good. Just a little carsick," Skye lied. She wished it was the truth. Because she really didn't want to think about the other explanation. After she'd changed into Maddie's short-sleeved white blouse and black Capri pants, Skye had locked the bathroom door and filled one of the expired condoms with water. She repeated the experiment three times. They were all fine…no leakage. So she'd convinced herself she had nothing to worry about.

"I really wish I didn't have to ask you to do this, Skye. But it's my first big catering event, and I need your help. There's a lot of influential people attending, and it'll be great publicity for the bakery. I don't want to mess it up."

One more reason she shouldn't be there, Skye thought. Half the people attending the social were on her hit list. But after hearing how important today was for Grace, she decided she had to get over herself and suck it up. She'd do whatever she had to to make the event a success. "You won't. Once they taste your strawberry shortcake and strawberry tart, you'll be booked through to next year." And thinking of the theme for the social, her voice grew more enthusiastic. At least the Sugar Plum Cake Fairy wouldn't be expected to make an appearance.

"I'm so glad you moved to Christmas. You're good for my confidence. I hope you don't plan on leaving anytime soon." Grace's smile faded when Skye inadvertently grimaced. "You're not leaving, are you?"

"You know me, footloose and fancy-free," Skye said, forcing a lighthearted tone to her voice. "Never know when the mood will strike me. But don't worry, I'll give you plenty of notice."

New York had been Skye's home base for the last ten years, but she spent so much time traveling to remote corners of the world with her environmental causes that she was rarely there. Over the last year, even before she'd lost her money, her bohemian lifestyle had started to lose its appeal. She'd been thinking of settling down and starting a foundation of her own. But her financial problems had effectively ended that idea.

"Oh, I thought you were happy here." Grace wrinkled her nose. "Is it Madison? Did you guys have a fight when you told her you lost your trust fund? You seemed to be getting along okay."

"No, we're good. I, uh, I don't want to overstay my welcome." Skye stared out the passenger-side window at the aspens nestled against the rocky cliffs that encircled the private valley. As the landscape blurred into a verdant blob, she blinked back tears. She didn't know why the idea of leaving the small town—Maddie and her girls, the friends she'd made—left her feeling so darn emotional. She cleared her throat. "I'll probably camp out for a while, see how it goes."

"You're not living in a tent, Skye," Grace said firmly, tapping her finger on the steering wheel. "Promise me you won't do anything for now. I have an idea, but I have to talk it over with Jack first."

"I don't plan…" Skye began, then groaned as they drove through the open wrought-iron gates and up the long, paved circular drive. And it wasn't because the last time she'd driven through those gates she had been with Ethan. No, it was because she recognized the man standing on the cobblestone walkway in front of the O'Connors' stunning home talking to Liz O'Connor. Ethan's mother looked youthfully pretty with a black headband holding back her toffee-colored, shoulder-length hair. She made even a white denim skirt and black-and-white T-shirt look coolly elegant.

"What's wrong? Are you going to be sick?"

Skye sank down in her seat. "The man in the black Stetson is Richard Stevens, Claudia's father. You have to do me a big favor, Grace. No one can find out I'm broke. If anyone asks, tell them I'm just helping you out," she said desperately. All she'd need was for her father to hear she'd lost her trust fund. He'd never let her live it down, and neither would Claudia.

"Of course. Madison is the only one who knows you're on the payroll." Grace made a face. "And Jack."

"You don't think he'd tell Gage or Ethan, do you?" Skye asked, bending down to dig her cell phone from her purse.

"I don't think so, but I'll call him just to make sure."

"Thanks. I'd better call Maddie." Skye already had her phone to her ear. When the call went to voice mail, she left a message. They were heading to Lily's baseball game, so hopefully Maddie would get it before coming to the social.

Liz and Richard turned when Grace pulled the white van in front of the house. Catching sight of Skye, Ethan's mother's lips set in a disapproving line. *Let the fun begin*, Skye thought. She forced a smile for Richard, who offered her a surprised one in return. He opened her door. "Kendall Davis," he said in a booming voice as he hauled her into his arms. Richard was a loud, gregarious man in his midsixties who looked like Robert Redford. "Claudia told me you were here. I was going to look you up before I left. You haven't changed a bit. Still pretty as a picture. How long has it been?"

"It's been a while." Skye smiled. She'd always liked Claudia's dad. "You look great, Richard. You're doing well?"

"Can't complain, darlin'. Now, tell me what you're doing here. Last I heard from your father you'd been arrested for chaining yourself to a tree in Brazil."

Her cheeks heated. "Um, that was about six years ago."

"Oh, right, it was a forklift up in Montana."

"No, that was—"

He snapped his fingers. "Gotcha. Canadian embassy in Washington to protest the tar sands." Grinning, he hooked an arm around her neck. "This little gal's a pistol, Lizzie. Never knew what she'd get up to next. When she was ten, she snuck out of the house one night and set the neighbor's horses free." He chuckled. "Surprised your father still has a hair left on his head. Have you—"

"Richard, we probably should let Ms. Davis get to work," Liz interrupted him in an unamused voice. "The guests will be arriving shortly."

He frowned, looking from Skye to Grace, who'd started to unload the van. "You're working at a bakery?"

"Just lending my friend a hand." She patted his arm. "It was great to see you, Richard."

"You too, darlin'. We'll talk later."

"Grace, the boys are in the back setting up the tables. Get them to give you a hand. You can go through the house to the backyard," Liz said. She looped her arm through Richard's. "Come and see that horse I was telling you about."

"You should let Skye have a look at him. She's a regular horse whisperer." He chuckled and winked at Skye. "On second thought, you better not. She's liable to set him free."

Ethan's mother, whose lips were once again pressed in a disapproving line, gave a disdainful "Hmm."

Grace, standing with two containers in her arms,

stared after Liz and Richard. "Okay," she said. "I thought you were exaggerating, but you're not. Mrs. O'Connor is definitely not a fan of yours."

"Yeah. And hopefully Richard cans the reminiscing or you'll be on your own. If he tells her about my run-in with the NRA last year, she'll have me tossed from the premises."

Pulling a tray from the back of the van, Grace cast Skye a nervous glance. "I think there's a man from the NRA on the guest list. You won't—"

"Don't worry, Grace. I won't do anything to embarrass you or the bakery. I promise." She grabbed two trays from the van and turned to head up the stairs.

Ethan stood on the porch in a white dress shirt with the sleeves rolled up to bare his tanned forearms. A pair of navy dress pants showed off his narrow waist and long, muscular legs. "Glad to hear that, cupcake," he said, taking the trays from her.

She sighed. "Can you please give the 'cupcake' thing a rest?"

His hazel eyes warmed and his lips tipped up at the corners. "You prefer Cake Fairy?"

"Maybe you didn't notice, but I'm not wearing my costume. I'm not the Sugar Plum Cake Fairy today." *Thank the universe.*

"Oh, I noticed," he said as his eyes took a lazy head-to-toe tour of her body. "And you still look good enough to eat."

About the Author

Debbie Mason is the *USA Today* and *Publishers Weekly* bestselling author of the Christmas, Colorado, and the Harmony Harbor series. Her books have been praised for their "likable characters, clever dialogue, and juicy plots" (RTBookReviews.com). When she isn't writing or reading, Debbie enjoys spending time with her very own real-life hero, their three wonderful children and son-in-law, and their two adorable grand-babies in Ottawa, Canada.

You can learn more at:
AuthorDebbieMason.com
Twitter @AuthorDebMason
Facebook.com/DebbieMasonBooks/